ROSA MARÍA PASCUAL

Where are
you going, Iryna?

Muñoz Moya Editores

Sarrión

Title: Where are you going, Iryna?
© Rosa María Pascual
© of the English Edition: Muñoz Moya Editores SL
44460 Sarrión, Spain
e.mail: editorial@mmoya.eu
website: www.mmoya.eu
© of the English translation: Simon Berrill
Cover image: photograph of the child Eva Dushenchuk
and of Yulia Kachmar made by Iryna Vyzhanova
Layout and design: Javier Labrador Moya

EAN: 9788480103305
D.L: TE-148-2020

Contents

Please forgive me, but in honour of the great dignity you still possess, I need to turn your lives into a novel. Everything you have told me; everything we have lived through, felt, interpreted and loved must not be lost... like Ukrainian, which is being displaced by Russian and English. Only farmers speak Ukrainian. You farmers have to eat what you harvest. They say that what you harvest thanks to God is poisoned, and no-one wants it. Because you can't sell the surplus, you eat it yourselves. You start speaking Russian and learn English or other languages as soon as you can. Thanks to the Devil, this is the only way you can earn money. Ukrainian complains. It howls, its musical sound shrieking its way down the Dnieper like a sinking moon that's pretty to look at but unregarded. For a long time now, all the new moons have turned their kind face away from you. They show you the face of an old moon with a scythe – the ship of death. Poor Ukraine! The breadbasket of Russia, crossed backwards and forwards by all wars, for centuries providing slaves for the rich. Millions of people dying of hunger, until very recently, because their food had been stolen to feed the Russian monster. And now? Now you have achieved your freedom you are like birds who have been caged and don't know how to fly. Now, since the Chernobyl explosion, they have given you back your country, contaminated forever and ever. Now you are independent, you are poor as church mice...

Esperança

January 2013

5

Part One

Chapter 1

In the middle of a fertile plain among the steppes, with the uplands in the distance, stands a little house crowned by brightly coloured daisies that have come in from the woods and damp meadows. Now, with their thousand and one petals, they are poking up from the garden towards the kitchen window. A wagtail swings on one of the stems and looks inside: perhaps it wants to go in. Little Iryna climbs on to a chair and up into the sink, offering it a crumb. The bird takes it from her hand and flies off.

"You'll be back!" she says aloud.

Today they are celebrating the little girl's birthday. She is four. At home, everyone thinks she is pretty, strong-willed and clever – but time will show them she is much more than they now think.

They knock rainbow-sheened glasses together, shouting *"Na zdorov'ya!"* "Good health!" They sing, drink and dance. Suddenly they stand up and drink, singing the national anthem: "The glory of Ukraine can never die...". Vasyl, who is a year older than his little sister, wants to pick her up but he can't. She is taller and stronger, though, and she can get him off the ground and carry him to the doorway. Her new shoes are squeezing her feet. Without undoing them, she takes them off. Vasyl takes his off too and they rush out into the yard. The trees have small green fruits that are not yet ready for eating when the children take the first bite. They like them like this: nice and green.

"Hey! Iryna! Vasyl! Come here, there's cake!" shouts their mother.

"Come on! I've got to blow out the candles!"

Iryna has already picked up a few cherries, just in case...

They all make wishes. Olena, their mother, has her eyes full of tears. The salt mixes with the honey on her lips.

"Mummy, are you thinking about that day again? That day when everything filled with smoke? Why does it make you so scared if you and Dad didn't even see it? Why? You were living a long way away, with Granny and Grandad."

Olena can't answer. She was so scared when she was pregnant; so many friends had deformed children; so many had to abandon them in the home at Dobrokiv. She looks into the eyes of Vasyl, their father, sees the understanding in them and hugs their children. Happiness rolls down her cheeks, loosening her throat and she exclaims:

"Blow hard, Ira!"

"Blow hard!" everyone shouts.

As if Iryna were the wind. As if this spell could keep her safe from all the dangers brought by that terrible explosion.

Iryna blows out all the candles except for one: the candle of destiny.

The little girl takes the knife, plunges it into the middle of the cake and prepares to cut it. She looks into all their faces and counts them, starting on her fingers. But even with her toes she hasn't got enough.

"No, you're too little and you might cut yourself," says Granny.

"I'm not little, I'm big now. I'm four."

"Look, Ira, who's bigger, Ira or Grandad?" asks an uncle.

And she answers:

"Ira."

And she's quite convinced. From now on, she's the one who'll share out the cake.

There's plenty of music at the party and, towards the end, they move the chairs back against the wall to leave a space in the middle for dancing. They hear the well-known strains of Lara's Theme from the film Doctor Zhivago. All of them begin to nod and rock along to the tune. Grandad moves towards his granddaughter with an offer:

"Would you like to dance with me, young lady?"

Iryna climbs up on the chair and hangs on to Grandad's neck, holding him tight with her legs around his waist. They begin to move around, following the violins and the balalaika: a big nose pressed against a little nose, one hand on his neck and the other held like a treasure in Grandad's strong hand.

"Turn round, turn round more until we get giddy!"

The two of them alone, there in the middle, make the whole family's eyes shine.

Turning, turning, the day passes; that spring; new summers; the seasons... and the years turn.

***

AT THE END OF OCTOBER, the weather has begun to turn colder as the wind breaks free from the north-east. The leaves on the trees fly off and within a few days they will be left bare. Only a few sparrows and the occasional magpie will be left on the great branches. Impervious to the rigours of winter, they will wait among the snowflakes for another ray of sunshine. But today is Saturday and the two friends have got up early, all ready to go shopping in a big Kiev supermarket. Wrapping Lyuba, Iryna's daughter, in a shawl, they set off.

"Come in the front with me!" says Nadiya. "We'll be able to talk better. If not, I'm like your chauffeur."

Iryna tells her that in Catalonia no child travels in a car without a special seat held in by the seat belt and, as this car hasn't got seatbelts, it's better for her to go with Lyuba in the back. It's less dangerous.

"Don't worry about it! Remember, you're in Ukraine, not Catalonia."

It's still dark, but the little girl is wide awake and her eyes shine like tiny stars in the lights of every oncoming car. As dawn breaks, her eyelids droop and she falls asleep.

The images racing past the windows show that winter is coming and many people need potatoes and other supplies to store. The trees, shaken by the wind, rattle like skeletons dancing with their arms linked to pick up yellow leaves and dress themselves again. Just like zombies. The two friends chat away as they drive on, hardened to all the hands asking for charity or thumbing a lift. The only thought that bothers them is that those hands could so easily be theirs. The line that separates them from such a situation is too fine to accept easily. But they fight back any bitter feelings, singing and showing off the Metro supermarket card one of Nadiya's neighbours has lent them in exchange for bringing her ten kilos of flour. Yesterday, Olena was given two months' wages – the current month and one she was owed – and she has given them 600 *hryvnias* plus 50 more for emergencies. She told Iryna not to waste it but Granny Rus added that she shouldn't follow her example the time she went to the big city and came back without anything because she thought everything was expensive and she could do without it. Her words reminded her of the old myth: don't fly too low or your wings will get wet, or too high because the sun will melt the wax that holds them together. They will split the cost of petrol between them. And, if the little girl cries, Iryna will put some honey on her thumb or feed her at her breast. She now eats soup and mashed potato and drinks cow's milk, but breast milk doesn't need preparing, it's easier to carry and it's much better for soothing the child.

It doesn't matter that the car belonged to Nadiya's grandfather 50 years ago, and then to her uncle, before she bought it when her cousin swapped it for a less clapped-out Seat. The same one that still has brakes thanks to Esperança. Nadiya's feeling relaxed today because she's bought a driving licence with some money she saved from her Avon sales, bribing a civil servant, as most people do when they've got a bit of spare cash. Today's the first time she's used it and every time they pass a police checkpoint they feel bold enough to make rude signs at the officers. They hate the police because they know there are girls who use sex as the currency to pay their fines.

Iryna has spent the last part of the journey feeding Lyuba. She's been winded and now she's gone back to sleep. The wind whistles around the car, trying to get in where it can. Iryna leans against the window so her

13

back can stop the air coming in and making the little girl cold. As they drive through Kiev, the trees try to shake loose the plastic and paper bags that get caught up in their branches as they fly through the air. They're in the supermarket car park now and Nadiya turns to look at mother and baby:

"What a little angel!" she says, touched. "Let me hold her, Ira! That way you can rest your arms and I'll have a snooze too. I feel tired from driving."

"You want me to buy everything on my own?"

"Of course! Take a trolley instead of a basket."

Iryna puts Nadiya's list with her own, takes the money her friend holds out for her and goes off. At the entrance, the automatic doors open for her, but Iryna doesn't go in. She turns to look at her daughter, waving her thanks to her friend. On the other side of the road, the mist seethes and a faint sun makes the water of the Dnieper shine. The rays bounce off the river, blending with the gold of the city's domes. "It could be a good day, thanks be to God," as her Granny often says. But, be careful! The ground, carpeted with damp leaves, is slippery and smells of autumn.

Iryna makes up her mind, walks into the huge store and heads for the food section. She picks up packets of frozen meat, cereals and everything they can't get from the fields or the vegetable garden or the cow or the poultry they keep. She just needs basic essentials – they even make their own soap from fat. Her brain becomes a calculator. All the products have prices in dollars and *hryvnias*. She counts in dollars because the numbers are smaller. She has 300 dollars for all the shopping. She has already spent her part. She goes through the other people's lists and gets the items. Once she's sure she has everything, it occurs to her that Lyuba must have wet her nappy and that the cloths she put to dry in front of the fire last night were still damp this morning, so she hasn't got a clean one. So she decides to have a look round the children's clothes and accessories section. She's still got that other money – the money she's carrying just in case... Her eyes fill with nostalgia for Catalonia. Everything she sees reminds her of how people dress their babies there. Here, too, there are those brightly coloured velour pyjamas with joyful pictures on them that cover children from head to toe in material as soft as cotton wool or rabbit skin. Oh, and it's all man-made and easy to wash and dry... Clothes her little girl will never be able to wear. Iryna touches the clothes, stroking them. She would take them if she could. But she says to herself that with the hand-me-downs she's been given and what Vasyl brought with him she has enough. Her little girl is growing very quickly. It's not worth it – she would grow out of them straightaway. She takes her time and resigns herself to the idea. In the end she finds the nappies. She will have to buy a packet of just two. She hasn't got enough for the big packs that work out cheaper. Anyway, there's no need to waste money. That's where the spotlessly clean cloths made from cut-up t-shirts and sheets come in. Well washed with soap and disinfected with bleach, of course. Ah! And well rinsed too. As Granny Rus says, no child she has ever cared has ever had a sore red bottom. As she pulls out the bag with the two nappies, Iryna notices a set of grooming equipment for children: as well as some combs, there are small nail clippers and scissors, not too big or too small, that would be very useful for cutting Lyuba's hair and nails.

The little girl always wriggles when she cuts her fringe. The point of those rusty, blunt scissors they've got at home could take her eye out. When Lyuba was born it seemed as if she would have wavy hair, but now it's completely straight and she blows her fringe by turning her lips upwards and going buff!!! because it gets in her eyes. Once Iryna scratched her daughter's forehead. Since then, she always flinches when she sees those old scissors. That's why she does her daughter's hair with two clips that are always falling off because her hair is so fine! And it always looked so cute cut short. How useful those scissors would be! She looks left and right. No-one is watching her. She unhooks them, takes them out of the pack and hides it behind the packets of nappies. Then, with a distracted gesture, she pops them into the pocket of her blouse, as if she were a hairdresser or a barber. She feels the blood rushing up her neck to her face. She takes a deep breath and pushes the trolley determinedly towards the checkout. If they spot her, she'll say she got distracted. She puts everything on the counter: the packets of meat, the bags of sugar and flour, the pots of jam... and she also puts the card down so they can check.it. She opens her purse. But, just as she's going to pay, she hears:

"*Idit' syudy!* Come here! What about the scissors?"

"Oh!" she exclaims and makes a carefree gesture as if to return them.

"No, no! I've seen everything. Follow me."

He's wearing uniform. His red lips are parted by a tongue that wraps thickly around every letter. His eyes are a confused, sightless blue, like the colour of the wet patch in the vegetable garden that never dries out. And the smell of sweat when he lifts his arm also reminds her of that stagnant pond. The food is put to one side at the checkout. The guard makes her follow him to the manager's office. There he tells the manager that this little shit with her innocent face has stolen the scissors.

He shows them to him, taking from his pocket the plastic Iryna had hidden away. Everything is laid out on the office table to accuse her. The manager speaks Russian with an English accent. He asks her why the scissors caught her eye. He doesn't look a bad man. He seems to want to play down the matter. Iryna tells him simply that she had to watch what she spent on the shopping and that her little girl is overdue a haircut. They can see the car park through the window. She shows him where her friend is entertaining Lyuba, taking her for a walk in her pushchair like a queen.

"Papers?"

The manager smiles, glances at the identity card and gives it straight back to her. He asks her to wait. He insinuates that he will do everything he can so they don't cancel the card, but that needs time because when something like this happens it goes on the customer's record and they can't take away what they've bought or come back for who knows how long. He leaves the office, saying he's going to the checkout to pick up the card from the assistant. But, as he wants to frighten her a little so that she doesn't try stealing again, he goes to have a coffee in the Metro bar for a while. In these cases, he always does the same, and the security guard, still keeping Iryna in the office, knows it. They are alone and he moves closer.

"If only you knew the number of girls who are in prison for doing what you've just done..."

"I'm really sorry!" she mumbles. "Maybe you could help me? Please!"

"That depends on you." he answers, gripping the tab on the zip tight as he begins to undo his fly. "Perhaps you can help me undo my belt."

On the wall, a carelessly hung picture of her favourite poet – her Shevchenko – is looking at her, not quite straight. She closes her eyes and crawls forward in the tunnel.

Chapter 2

Winters in Ukraine are long and very cold. There are many days when children can't go to school because of bad weather.

Last night some of the snowflakes falling were so big that when Vasyl picked them up a single one filled his hand.

When this happens, their parents know they won't be able to do anything useful that day. Snuggled in their blankets, they go back to sleep and shorten the morning, saying they're tired. But Vasyl has reasons not to be sleepy. He's got up and, as he imagined, there is so much snow that, when he opens the door, he can't see even a chink of light. He picks up a spade and starts scraping, making a tunnel running from the front door to the middle of the field so he and the dog can slip out. Iryna has a terrible cold. She has taken wax out of her ears with a little stick and, as she has seen her parents do, she is applying it to soothe her lips, which are swollen from a cold sore. It heals them and doesn't cost *hryvnias*... She's finding it hard to breathe. Despite all the honey and onion home remedies they've tried on her nose, it's still blocked. The cool air coming from outside relieves it and she escapes with Vasyl. Where are they trying to get to? Perhaps to the neighbours' house to play for a while. Perhaps a lot further... to find out where Ukraine ends, now everything is white and seemingly infinite!

At school, the teacher told them that one summer's day when he was six – exactly the same age as Vasyl – their national hero, the poet Taras Shevchenko, left home without a word to anyone and went looking for the horizon, the place where the sky and the land are supposed to meet: the place where the world ends.

The two children remember that Taras so loved this huge, flat landscape that, although he was a just child, he felt as big as Ukraine and believed he could do anything. They recall the tale:

The first day he tried to reach the horizon, night fell and he had to return home unsuccessfully in silence. The little poet blamed the fact he had got up too late. "You need more time to cover all that distance," he thought. So, the next day, he left at dawn to give him time to get back before it got dark. The morning light shone on the little rainbow pearls rolling across the velvet grass. At about midday, he was surprised to see, in the distance, another village on the Earth. Perhaps he had walked in circles. When he got there, he met other people he had never seen before. The world was bigger than he thought! What if he went further on and there were thousands of villages instead of just one? He had to find out. So, when night fell, he was exhausted, but happy, as he believed everything he had seen had made the journey worthwhile: steppe birds flying off, frightened, as he approached; forests allowing him into the lairs of fantastic creatures that showed him the way forward, and fish in the river parting the waters for him so he could cross. Every branch had been a link with the infinite. Exhausted and smiling, he met some carters. They were *Chumaks* who hauled salt around the country, bringing news as they went. These good men took him home. He had no parents, but his big sister had been waiting and searching for him until it was pitch dark. When she found him, she hugged him, dragged him in to supper and told him "Go to sleep, wanderer!". The *Chumaks* continued on their way, telling of Taras's adventure all over Ukraine.

That's why if one day a foreigner says they have never heard of Shevchenko, the Ukrainians are surprised.

"Oh, no! Don't you know who Shevchenko is?" they will say and immediately start to recite a poem by their national idol.

Beneath the snow lies black, fertile earth: Ukraine is the world's biggest producer of beetroot and sunflowers. During the Second World War, many Germans took away trainload after trainload of this earth as fertiliser to improve their harvests. As soon as the snow has gone, Vasyl's and Iryna's parents begin working a plot of land miles from anywhere given to them by the State. They have to walk more than an hour to get there and they do it without machines. Behind the house, though, they have a yard with poultry and a cow. But potatoes and the cow don't provide enough to live on. The little girl often has sore throats that need medicine and both the children need to eat meat and a bit of fruit to help them grow. In Dobrokiv, anything that doesn't come from the land costs many *hryvnias* so their mother and father take on any paid work they can. Lately, their mother has been earning 300 *hryvnias* (50 euros) a month cleaning at the hospital. That's about the same as it costs to pay the gas and electricity bills to keep the house warm. A *kopiyok*, which is one hundredth of a *hryvnia*, takes so long to earn, for them it is worth almost the same as a euro in Catalonia.

The bad weather slowly recedes, as it does every year, and, in about April, the snow that begins to melt, leaving a pond in the corner of the yard. If the sky is clear, its colour is somewhere between blue and green. The bottom of the pond is as unknown and black as the future – very dangerous if children get too close and a bog in the very place they intend to plant vegetables. The swamp needs to be drained so the vegetables don't rot, as it clogs everything with mud. Bringing in a machine also costs them *hryvnias*, or many litres of milk.

The little girl says that, if she were a bird and had wings like them, she would fly a long, long way away, like her Taras.

***

IRYNA MOVES closer to the guard and kneels. In this position he looks even taller and stronger. Bit by bit, she undoes the belt. She wishes she were blind, like poor Perebendia in Shevchenko's poem. But she looks up: seeing pondwater eyes focused, for once, with twisted desire. His trousers slide half way down his legs. Below his blue uniform shirt, a pair of underpants appears, just like the ones she has seen hanging up in the clothing section. Their bright design attracts her attention. The girl's left hand begins by appreciating the silky feel of the material, which stretches, showing off a bulge. Then the hand works its way inside the boxers and weighs up his hardened testicles. His penis rises, standing up like the truncheon in his belt. She looks at it. The man's eyes move upwards. He is almost crying with pleasure. The left hand is cunning, touching everything so delicately...

"What wonderful hands you have!" he admits.

When the left hand has everything securely together, the dextrous right hand moves like lightning to grab the scissors on the table, where the man of order is resting his arse. In a single movement, it sticks the scissors into his balls.

"Aaahhhhh!"

The scream dissipates into a roar of pain. His body doubles up and he puts his hands in the place where blood is pouring out. The pent-up tension has gone.

His testicles have suddenly deflated and his voice is strangled in his guts.

Iryna runs with the scissors in her fist. Clearing her way with the point of her weapon, she reaches the car park and screams:

"Get in the car! Run! Run Nadiya! Ruuun!"

She scoops Lyuba up in her arms and pushes a trolley backwards, towards the door to block the way, although for the moment no-one is following her. Quite the contrary, the people watching are frozen. Some think she's mad, others wonder if someone has stolen her purse. Where is that security guard?

Nadiya immediately puts her foot on the accelerator and the engine starts spiritedly. Now they are in the car and the scissors fly out of the window, landing in the guts of a rabbit on a small table belonging to one of the many women selling farmyard meat alongside the avenue, a block away from the supermarket. Today is rabbit day. There are times when they breed too many and, if there's a surplus, the women sell them illegally in the street. The trees wave them off, allowing playful leaves to fall, while the burrowing flies are stuck to the raw meat and the shit, which makes everything stink.

"Quickly, Nadiya! I haven't got the card, we haven't got the food and I can't pay for petrol!"

"There's still a bit left. What on earth have you done? Tell me!"

She looks haunted.

"Don't ask! Let the Dnieper take it all down to the sea!"

And the willows suddenly bow down, asking the water for forgiveness.

***

SPRING 1997

The flowers return, the birds are singing and, well wrapped up in three jumpers each, good coats hats and scarves, they go back to school. Iryna has been one of the first in the class to learn to write her name and she's interested in anything with letters on. She even cuts up magazines, asking:

"Mummy! What does it say here? Will you tell me?"

Today, the teacher has given out a very interesting letter. Iryna can't read it, but she's listened to the teacher carefully. She puts it in her bag and carries it home like a treasure.

> **"1,000 Ukrainian children hosted:** The Ukraine-86 Twinning Association has organised temporary stays in Catalonia for Ukrainian children affected by the radiation from the Chernobyl nuclear power station since 1995. We are looking for children aged between five and 12 who have never left Ukraine and who belong to ordinary families without the resources to pay for their air tickets..."

While they have lunch, Olena reads the letter aloud to her husband. The children listen carefully, although Iryna keeps interrupting them: "Like us. We haven't got money to go by plane, have we?"

"During the stay, the children have medical and dental checks and an eye test. All the children have health cover from the International Cooperation Office of the Government of Catalonia. The most important thing about these stays is that they can live in a non-radioactive environment with plenty of varied food, so their defences can recover. It is said that every summer they come can extend their lives by seven or eight years. The Association already has next summer's project under way. You need to put your children's names down as soon as possible."

From the intonation, Iryna knows her mother has finished reading and she reacts immediately, like a little bird:

"You will let me go, won't you, Mummy? The teacher says it's very important... they give you very good food and take you to all the attractions. Haven't they given you a letter, Vasyl?"

Vasyl says nothing and wonders whether it was perhaps that sheet of paper he turned into an aeroplane which is now hanging from a tree at school. As he can't see radioactivity, he's not afraid of it, but if there's some kind of trip involved he wouldn't want to miss it.

Their father nods his head, convinced that when it comes to the children it's their mother who has the last word. His is the hardest job, doing everything he can to make sure there's always food on the table, but he leaves all the responsibility for their upbringing to his wife.

"I want to go! What about you, Vasyl?"

"If you go... I'm coming too!"

Chapter 3

"I STABBED HIM IN the balls with the scissors. If they'd been bigger, I'd have sliced them up," she says, regretfully.

Lyuba is crying, frightened to hear her mother's voice in a tone she doesn't recognise. Iryna consoles her, rocking her in an exaggerated way from one side of the car to the other until she falls silent. As she leans back on the seat, an uncomfortable feeling tells her she hasn't lost her bag. She was carrying it there on her back all the time. She opens it and can't believe her eyes: inside is all the money and the documents. She suddenly remembers that she hadn't yet paid when the guard called her and that the manager gave her back her card.

"Look! Look! We've got all the dollars!"

As if she understands, the baby celebrates by putting her hand into Iryna's cleavage, pulling her bra away, squeezing her nipple and sucking with an anguished calm. Iryna would never have thought that this action would bring her such peace. She gradually finds the words to tell her friend everything that has happened and everything that has been done to her. The landscape is foggy as the car heads homewards, its fuel gauge stuck on "full" as it has been for many years. At the moment, the last thing either of them is thinking about is that the engine can't keep running without fuel. A sad cry from Lyuba, followed by stomach ache convulsions after her hurried feed, concentrate their minds on what they are doing. They rock the cot. Looking into her little girl's watery eyes, Iryna comes to a firm decision. They can't go home.

"Where can we go, Nadiya? The first thing they'll look at will be the owner of the card."

"Where shall we go? I told you what those guards do with the girls they catch. They set them up as little tarts for themselves or they get them hooked promising them work and a passport to Europe in exchange for sex."

Suddenly, the mobile phone rings. It's Olena, who asks them how everything is going and where they are. As soon as she hears "Fine, but…" she tells them that the police have been to see their neighbour who lent them the card and that Vasyl, who was round there with the woman's son, managed to hear the questions they were asking. He came home straightaway on his scooter and is bringing them money and a few other things. He had time because the police went to Nadiya's house afterwards and they must have been talking to her parents. He says he'll meet them at the petrol station where they usually fill up, at the crossroads on the E40 leading to Rivno. They're not far away, but when they start off the car engine starts spluttering. They get out and Nadiya puts a dipstick into the tank. There's not a drop of juice left. They decide to hitch-hike, praying that someone will stop. Luckily for them, a tractor doing some kind of manoeuvre passes close by. They call to it.

"Kudy vy idete!"

The farmer, who should have been heading for his fields, lets them get on in exchange for a tip. He loads them into the trailer with the straw and takes them to the meeting place. There, Nadiya accepts 30 dollars from her friend to buy a can of petrol and says goodbye to Iryna and Lyuba. They kiss. They hug tight. They know it will probably be a long time before they see one another again. She leaves them sitting on the stone base of a sign shaped like a cross. Once the petrol can is full, she looks across at them out of the corner of her eye: they have their backs to the road. A last wave and she starts to walk back to the car with the petrol can, thinking of the story she's going to tell:

"I wasn't there. And when they ask about my friend, I'll say I don't know anything about it. When she came out of the supermarket, Iryna snatched the little girl and went off with her in a lorry. Perhaps the child's father was driving. Who knows? Well, if I don't need to I won't say anything about the child... He knows he can't come and pick Iryna up because he'd make things more difficult. The most sensible thing is for me to go straight home."

The half hour Iryna spends waiting for her brother seems endless. As well as her fear, she has physical needs. She's desperate for the toilet and she's thirsty. If she doesn't drink, she'll have no milk for the little girl. What can she do? She can't go to the petrol station – there are too many people going in and out. Nor does she want to go into the garage behind it. She moves towards the door and takes in the whole building with a glance. She can't see anyone in there. She sits behind some cans and notices there is a bottle of lemonade in a corner a little further on. She waits for the right moment to pick it up and, as she moves forward, she hears the engine of the Vespa.

"Vasyl! Darling Vasyl!"

In the space between the seat and the handlebars, he's carrying a big rucksack with bars to keep it rigid and lots of pockets. It's the one she'd used in Catalonia those other summers for going away on trips. In the middle section, there's half a blanket. Around that, food and drink. He's also stuffed in all the money he's got left from his summer job.

"Thank you so much! I'll phone you as soon as I can," she says, without putting down the little girl, who is stretching out her arms and saying "Tatata!" to her uncle because she wants to go on the scooter.

"Your mummy will take you on it now."

Vasyl lifts Iryna up in the air and the little girl hangs on to her mother's neck, chortling with laughter.

"Hey! Wait a minute, I'll fill the tank for you. If not, you'll run out straightaway. You know you'll only have enough for about 150 kilometres!"

"What about you?" she asks, making as if to give him some of what she's got in her purse.

Near their feet a puddle is painting the scene with colour.

"We'll manage. You know no-one ever starves in our house.

Fidgeting with worry, he finds a flat pebble in his pocket. He throws it skilfully towards the water. It slides off and bounces several times. The landscape trembles. Thousands of memories bubble up as he dives into the past, making him feel the present.

"Come on, don't waste any more time! Give me the little girl and get out of here."

***

1998, 99, 00, 01, 02, 03

Every year, Olena has filled in those papers with Iryna, who always wants to make sure she does it properly. They still chuckle as they remember the early years when little Iryna repeated over and over:

"Mummy, write clearly! Rounder letters, Mummy!"

As if being accepted depended on her handwriting.

But that was more than four years ago... it's now March 2003 and her children still haven't been lucky enough to get a place to go to Catalonia. "God willing!" thinks Olena. "It'll soon be May and my daughter will be 11 and my son 12." Thank God they look healthy are growing well. But their childhood is coming to an end and she would so much like them to have a good medical check-up and blood tests. That's impossible in Ukraine, even though she works in the hospital and she'd get a discount.

The truth is that she's sick of hearing Iryna talking like an old woman:

"It's for my health. I want to go!"

She's asked them to check the applications and, she admits, she's even taken presents on the day she's been asked to attend: some large eggs, a chicken, cheese, potatoes... which they've accepted as if it were the most normal thing in the world. But they still tell her the same thing every time:

"The Association can't answer all requests, it's short of resources. You'll have to wait, your turn will come. We select by difficulties. They are not the most in need."

Olena knows this is not true and she's noticed that the children who fly to Catalonia are often the children of well-off families from the town: those who continue to risk their health working at Chernobyl in exchange for a good salary; those who have found work in the capital with foreign companies; or the children of bankers. Because, under the table, the Ukrainian organisers charge a fee for paperwork equivalent to 50 euros per child. Parents who are really in need either don't have the cash or have to make a tremendous effort so they can enclose it with their application.

Olena works at Dobrokiv Hospital, next to the charity's offices and she finds out lots of other things... She doesn't just clean there. She has a healthcare qualification which she got in Moscow the year before she got married. So, when a nurse gets fed up with her pittance of a salary and leaves, Olena takes her place, even working in the operating theatre. And her colleagues have given her ideas. She's poor, but she's highly thought of. She's well aware of her own qualities – she's not just anyone... More than anything, though, she feels what they're doing to her children is unfair, and, as she can't fight it by fair means, she has decided to use cunning instead. She will target the director of the organisation with a quiet but firm threat.

After several drafts, she is carrying two letters in her hand. One is written in Russian and the other has been translated into Spanish by Natasha, a girl who has been to Catalonia and has learned the language quite well. Natasha has made Olena swear she won't tell anyone about the favour. God willing, or rather, if the people from the charity don't find out, next summer her host parents will ask her back to Les Franqueses, to their lovely flat which even has a lift. In gratitude, Olena has given her a few *kopioks*. That way she'll be able to buy a notebook for Kiev University, where she is studying foreign languages.

The letter pulls no punches:

"Dear Mr Fortunato,

> I am writing to you because I know you are a good, fair man. I have two children, Iryna and Vasyl, who know that your organisation is a humane one. My

children have been waiting for a place for more than five years. They go to the post office every day to see if there is a letter from you but the letter never arrives because we don't want to bribe anyone and anyway, we don't have the resources to do it. You rely on Mrs Moskova to set the priorities, but the places are not 'for the children of families that cannot afford to travel or spend time in an uncontaminated country', they are for people who have given money that is not accounted for anywhere. You should know, sir, that her family is building a nice house on the banks of the river at your expense, in the rich part of town – not exactly in the middle of nowhere.

My children are good and hardworking. They're tall and strong, although the little girl gets colds very easily and has a big mark on her stomach that needs looking at.

I look forward to hearing from you and I hope that your God, who is the same as mine, gives you many years of life to do good. I look forward to meeting you one day, when I can give you in person the embrace I am now obliged to send you from a distance.

Olena Piskun

Over the years, Olena has choked back floods of tears and has learned to control her indignation when confronted with the lie that children are "selected according to needs". She has never made a scene and always behaved correctly, greeting Mrs Moskova with a *dobroho ranku,* good morning, and a *na dobranich,* good night. Now she has everything ready, she has asked Mrs Moskova for an appointment. She has had to wait a month for it.

The director shakes hands with her and asks her to sit down. She remains standing and, holding her head high, asks her to please read the letter. The director reads it and her face changes colour, from reddish to almost blue. Allowing her adversary no respite, as if she were launching a new attack in a chess game, Olena shows her she also has the letter written in Spanish. The director makes as if to get up and accompany Olena to the door to send her away, but she quickly thinks the better of it and flops into the cushioned chair. She would like to threaten Olena, telling her that perhaps from now on her bosses will find dirt under the beds where she has swept... but instead she tears up the letter in a rage and throws it in the bin. Olena immediately sits down and rips up the sheet of paper she is holding too, handing it over to the director, as if to say "I'll forget this if you treat me differently from now on."

Which of the two women has forced checkmate? They stand up. Mrs Moskova comes out from behind the desk and moves close to Olena but when Olena holds out her hand to shake hers, the director transforms the gesture into a pat on the back. As Olena leaves by the same door through which she came in five minutes earlier, both of them believe they have earned a draw.

At least she knows that from now on she won't be ignored. She's made several copies of the Spanish letter just in case. Copies well hidden in the attic at home. Copies Mrs Moskova imagines she has. Copies that will do their work without ever being sent.

The children are becoming increasingly aware of the problem of radioactivity. This winter, a boy in Vasyl's class has died from an ordinary cold. Some said he lacked defences, others that he had been suffering from the "white sickness" for some time, as he was very pale. At school, they are seen by psychologists from different countries – French and Italian doctors – who help them get over the effects while at the same time studying the effects of radioactivity on children's spirits.

The children make fun of them and pinch their own cheeks to make them nice and red. They play at making calculations. Look, if you go to Catalonia for four years in a normal family you get back 7 × 4 = 28 years and, if you go to a good family it can be 8 × 4 = 32.

Instead of dying at 80 we'll go on living until we're over 100.

Their parents are obsessed with the figures and would give anything for their children to be able to go to Catalonia. The worst thing is knowing and not being able to do anything about it. Since the explosion, many friends of theirs have died of leukaemia and other forms of cancer. In the town many orphaned children are being looked after by grandparents or neighbours or living alone. The newspapers in other countries talk about them from time to time.

> 16 years ago now, on 26 April 1986, the failure of the fourth reactor at the Chernobyl nuclear power station sent radioactivity into the atmosphere equivalent to 200 of the bombs dropped at Hiroshima and Nagasaki counted together. It was the biggest nuclear power accident in history, with dramatic consequences. Unofficial sources speak of deaths numbering between 350,000 and 400,000. They claim that more than seven million people were affected and two million live in highly contaminated areas.

"Now they tell us," thinks Olena, thinking back to 1986 as she looks out of the window. She is enjoying the warmth of the spring, with the trees in flower and the green of the new grass. No-one knew anything about what had happened. It wasn't in any newspaper either on the 26th or the 27th or the days that followed. Only at the beginning of May did some newspapers talk about temporary problems and a situation that was entirely under control. Why did they take so long to tell the truth? And the question and the answer echo around her head together with the key words:

"On 26 April 1986, an unprecedented disaster happened..." Many people could not be evacuated because they didn't have the money to do it. In general, the evacuation was slow and inefficient. The people living nearest the power station (within a 30-kilometre radius) were not fully evacuated until 21 May that year. And the danger is still not over, with more than 100 tonnes of nuclear fuel and more than 400 kilos of plutonium still inside the reactor.

The reason they didn't tell us anything was that they were panicking that people would run away. Of course, hundreds of thousands did when they found out – those who knew what a nuclear explosion meant and were rich enough and rebellious enough and free enough of family ties that they weren't going to leave anyone to face the strange danger alone. But the State gave land and resources to encourage people from other, even poorer, regions to move there, promising them they would get free gas in exchange. When you're dying of cold, you don't care that what is warming you is also contaminating you. If you don't know it's contaminating you, you care even less. And if you do know, you try to forget it.

Olena and Vasyl were newlyweds who, like any loving young couple with a nesting urge, wanted a home of their own. There in the little hamlet where they lived – like many in northern Ukraine not big enough to have its own local council – they had to continue their parents' lives, and live, with them, in the house rebuilt by Olena's grandparents after the Second World War. Iryna liked to hear Granny Rus tell her about it:

"The men weren't here! They were in the Russian army which had taken them away to defend Moscow with the same idea they always used – killing the Germans with hunger and cold. But the bastards kept getting nearer. They were almost in the village."

"How did you escape?"

"My mother – your great-grandmother – who was called Katya, got the cow and put us children on it. She took us into the middle of the forest and there we lived in a cave for more than a year."

"More than a year, Granny? And what did you do so they didn't see you?"

"Yes, more than a year! When we went out, we all held leaves to camouflage ourselves. In those days we played among the silver birch like animals and we didn't go back to the village until my daddy – your great-grandfather – came to look for us."

"Your daddy beat the Germans and entered Berlin on the winning side, didn't he, Granny?"

"Yes, your great-grandfather had to rebuild the house. When we arrived, we found it all burned. All the old people, women and children had died except for us," she tells them, showing them a photograph of her father resplendent with rows of medals.

Katya's husband knew where they were because she had managed to give a partisan a letter for him before they ran away to the mountains. It is a pretty, cosy house. Every summer, when Olena has her holidays from work, she takes Iryna to her grandparents' house. It takes a whole day to get there. They set off early in the morning getting a lift into Kiev and then catching the train towards Belarus. They then have to catch a bus before walking the last few miles to the hamlet by the light of Grandad's torch. He always waits for them, sometimes for more than two hours, under the same silver birch.

"How you've grown, Ira! And how pretty you are! You look like Granny. Is Vasyl OK?"

"Yes. You won't recognise him when you see him. He's almost a man now, always helping his father. He's very hardworking," says an emotional Olena.

They go there for fun activities: they paint walls, clean carpets, sew and hang curtains in colourful flower prints that bring a little life into the white winter... But they also go there prepared to help their grandparents working in the fields, bending their backs:

"Back here again to pick potatoes!" whines Iryna.

Granny must be about 60, but she's very fat and can't bend down. It isn't that she eats too much, it's because her thyroid gland doesn't work. The same has happened to many women since the explosion. They wouldn't have absorbed the radiation if they'd just been given ordinary iodine – a really cheap preventive treatment the government could easily have provided. Iryna has known since she was very young that if the turnips and potatoes aren't picked before the rain comes, her grandparents won't have stores for the winter. When she sees her grandmother with her legs red and swollen, walking along with a rocking gait she notices the effort she is making and curses a country that doesn't give her treatment; a country that has damaged those eyes that were once as pretty as her own. "Poor old Granny!" she says to herself, as she recognises her.

She goes to hug her, hears that heart beating nineteen to the dozen, and wants to tell her that she adores her and that her kisses are the best in the world. Tenderly, she covers the mirror that robs her of hope, and dreams that when she's grown up she will be pretty and slim.

These lands they were given to prevent depopulation – the lands near Chernobyl – have been even more catastrophic for her mind than for her body. Since the great explosion, the wind is no longer wind. What does it bring them? They can't drink the water any more. Instead of nourishing them, the milk from the cows can kill. A silent death approaches. It wears no mourning clothes and carries no scythe, but that just makes them mistrust the remaining flowers and butterflies. To subsist, they need to hold tight to any positive idea that comes along. They say that, fortunately, the contaminated cloud didn't stay still for long, so maybe where they live there's less radiation than in lands further away. They do not need to look for new information: the most important thing is that they have somewhere to live and land to work.

They don't need to read any more about the subject. In 1986, Olena was 14 and Vasyl, who'd been her boyfriend since they were little, was 16. The two children grew up quickly. She studied everything she could in the local school and, as she got good marks, the Communist government paid for her to do her healthcare degree in Moscow. Before he was 20, he did his military service in Hungary.

On 29 May 1991, in a new house Olena and Vasyl had built more than 1,000 kilometres from the hamlet, they became parents of a boy. He was, and is, Vasyl's spitting image. There was no-one to help Olena and, three days after giving birth, she was back milking the cow and looking to see if the hens had laid eggs. Five months later, the boy's uncle, Olena's brother, an Orthodox priest, baptised him in Dobrokiv with seven or eight names, including his uncle's and his father's. That was the one that stuck and he became young Vasyl. Olena was 19, her husband was 21.

After many centuries of foreign domination, on 25 August 1991 – shortly after the failed *coup d'état* in the USSR, which everyone remembers – the Ukrainian parliament declared independence, a decision ratified on 1 December by a popular referendum. Some weeks later it joined the CIS, a rather ineffective federation intended to maintain its economic links with Russia. Ukraine was initially considered a republic with more favourable economic conditions than the other regions of the former USSR. However, the country suffered a deeper recession than the others.

Iryna was born in the same house, but by then it was a little bigger than the previous year. They had been able to add another bedroom on foundations specially laid for the purpose at the time the original house was built. But they hadn't been able to finish the house to their original plans because the measures promised by the Russian government lasted only two years. Since independence, things had been getting more difficult.

Like her brother, Iryna is also a child of Dobrokiv. The children's grandmother couldn't help her daughter at the birth. She was too far away, it cost too many *hryvnias* and her body was so heavy she couldn't manage to walk to catch the bus and then the train. They were near Chernobyl! Too far away! Olena's parents have only visited Dobrokiv once, in the spring of 1996, the time they had the party for Iryna's birthday. Another of Olena's brothers brought them. He'd managed to fatten three calves and sell them to buy a car, but in the end he couldn't afford to run it. Now he's a drunk with three children and a prostitute for a wife.

The cousins Iryna has from this uncle are lucky that Granny Rus makes their food and sews their clothes; they are lucky Grandad still has the strength to mow grass so that the only cow they've got left doesn't starve to death in the winter. Meanwhile, the other cousins they have in the hamlet, on their father's side, are miscreants and drug dealers. No-one looks after them. Their father's always drunk on vodka and their mother's a disreputable barfly. As if that were not enough, Iryna and Vasyl's father's mother is widowed and doesn't want complications, so she's never given presents or cared for any of her grandchildren. When Iryna and Vasyl were small and used to go and see her, she never even asked if they were thirsty, so they feel no love for her at all. Now they never go to her house and they say they won't take flowers to her grave when she dies.

In 1994, President Kravchuk agreed to bring forward the presidential elections but that didn't stop him losing office to the country's former prime minister, Leonid Kuchma. So far, though, he has been able to achieve little. The Ukrainian people are losing faith in independence: nothing is being sorted out as they'd hoped. At the end of the century, Ukraine is suffering inflation rates of more than 1,000 per cent. Dissatisfied with the economic situation, crime and corruption, the Ukrainians protest and organise strikes.

As they watch their children change, the years fly by so fast Olena and Vasyl don't have time to tear the pages off the calendar. They get up at cock-crow and go to sleep exhausted. Work in the fields is hard when there are fewer machines than hands and the fields are un-forgiving when what they produce is poisoned. If they only had money, they could buy the food the country imports for those who can pay for it. They need to find paid work, and there isn't much of that. Even so, they are still happy because their son and daughter love each other like crazy. They have the same friends and their laughter turns their parents' sorrow to resignation. Anyway, today is different: a letter has arrived. It's from the Ukraine-86 Twinning Association. There is a family interested in hosting Iryna.

"What about Vasyl?"

"They don't say anything about Vasyl."

"If Vasyl doesn't come, I don't want to go," says Iryna.

Her mother and father go to the Ukraine-86 Twinning Association's office to talk about it. They have to fill in a complaint form and they are warned there is an endless list of people who want to go to Catalonia. They should think about that because it's better for one to go than neither of them. In any case, the report will be passed on to Mrs Moskova to see if she can do anything.

This time, they don't have to insist. The next day, the director calls them in:

"There's nothing we can do. The family who are interested only want a girl. The boy is older, it would be difficult for him to accept the rules. No-one's interested in a boy that age."

"Anyway, lads are usually naughtier," adds the secretary, showing off a little because she was in Catalonia the year before.

42

"The people who've seen him on the list must think 'Ooh, he's from Ukraine, and he's from the country where they run wild like animals... who knows what he's like?',", adds the director.

Finally, both mother and father accept Vasyl's fate.

"You have to understand," says his father, "you're the older one!"

"But last year I was 11, the same as Iryna now. Why didn't they want me last year?"

"You know, your sister gets colds so easily, Vasyl. You're stronger. Let her go!"

"Vasyl, I swear to you I'll be good and say such nice things about you that they'll be dying to see you. Take a photo of him in his best clothes, Mummy, and I'll show it to everyone in Catalonia."

They're his sister's last words on the matter, and their mother will take the photo as soon as she can.

When they get home, they turn on the radio so they don't have to talk about it anymore. They hear Kuchma speaking to his people:

"During my time in office, the Ukrainian economy has been improving and, since 2000, we have been enjoying constant economic growth. The new Constitution has established a stable political system.

Despite this, Kuchma is criticised for having too much power, corruption, transfer of public property into the hands of oligarchs close to him, attacks on freedom of expression and electoral fraud.

"What a nerve! That pig!

Whatever's going on in politics, June arrives as innocent and joyful as the children who will travel by plane to seek good health in foreign lands. The cure is more than three hours away by plane. Iryna is a child who hardly ever travels by car but today she will fly away to an uncontaminated paradise. Her parents can't go with her to the airport – they have no way of getting there – so they say goodbye in Dobrokiv.

"Be good, Ira! Phone us as soon as you can!"

"You need to make sure you don't annoy the host families too much," advises the supervisor as she gets the children to sit in the van and gives the parents a letter. As soon as the children arrive, they will let the charity know and it will pass on the information.

Her parents keep the paper as if it were a guarantee that they will return their daughter safe and sound. It's all creased from their nervous fiddling. Now they try to flatten it out and make sense of it:

> "Between 1995 and 2003, the Ukraine-86 Twinning Association has managed the hosting of a thousand Ukrainian children. The Association has already begun the campaign for next summer and is looking for new families who want to host children..."

Olena and her husband read it several times. It isn't what they'd been expecting, but they understand that it talks about the continuity of the project. Their Iryna will be hosted this year and perhaps next. They expect she will learn the language and will be able to make herself understood when she explains that she's got a brother who has been wanting to go to Catalonia for a long time.

It is mid-afternoon when the *marshrutka* disappears into the green of the silver birches at the end of the long, long road. Iryna's parents look up – up to the west. They want to know how it can be that they, who have never had a holiday and have never been to the airport, could have a daughter who's flying to Catalonia. From now on, they will lift their heads whenever they see a white trail painted by a plane in the Ukrainian sky. "How high they fly!" they will say. "Too high, too far and too many days!" they will think.

Iryna is first in line and as she gets on the plane she feels her chest swell and her heart beat at every step. When she gets to the door she turns and raises her hand to say goodbye to her own country. The other children are in a hurry to get in, but she wants to record this moment forever.

"Come on, sweetheart, come in! When the plane takes off, you'll see it even better."

The stewardess accompanies the girl and finds her a window seat. She notices the child is wearing a dress as blue as her eyes, like the light of the sky in Kiev on a fine summer's day. The dress is a little short, perhaps from last year. It's probably a hand-me-down, but it's simple, clean dress which must be the best one she has, the stewardess judges, and she's right. Iryna's mother has put her hair in two plaits and has fixed them around her head. She doesn't want her hair to be a mess. Two ears of Ukrainian wheat are flying to Catalonia for the first time. But flour must be worked if you want the bread to rise and be soft... She's beautiful and she knows it, but she is so worried about messing up her hair or creasing her dress that she spends three hours on the plane sitting on the edge of her seat, without leaning back for a second.

She just wants to get there so she can give her host family – Pietat and Pau – the presents she is carrying in her suitcase. They are typical Ukrainian products they have had to make sacrifices to be able to buy: special chocolates, ceramic pots like mushroom-shaped houses for the woman; drink and tobacco for the man. Also, at the last minute and without permission, she has taken the box full of newspaper cuttings and postcards that explain what happened that day at Chernobyl. She has it stuffed into her handbag. She doesn't want Mummy to worry about the accident while she's away. But, during the journey, she opens the box from time to time and is horrified. She's thinking of showing it to the people in Rouralba. If she can't explain it or they don't believe her, she is sure they'll understand when they see the fire and imagine the burning people crying. When they see how many children are deformed or have incurable diseases.

Chapter 4

PRIPYAT, 26 APRIL 1986, 01.23 H (LOCAL TIME)

What was that? Where's that noise coming from? But, it's midnight. I get up, look out the window and see Vasya downstairs, talking on the phone in the court-yard.

"Hey, Vasya, what's going on?"

"There's been a fire at the power station. Go back to bed. I'll come soon."

A fire! I see him take the truck and drive off fast. A smile flashes from his lips, while his eyes urge me to sleep peacefully.

But I can't. I can't get away from the window. I blow a kiss into the distance. Pripyat is mirrored in the Pripyat. The moon shines a beam of light towards Chernobyl. A silver path. The great flooded valley stretches out towards the Dnieper. A pink cloud floats across the water and the river shudders. I see the reflection of a young daredevil who's afraid of nothing. Suddenly the whole sky is lit up by enormous flames and a rain of soot turns everything black. What can my husband do against that? Where can they go to put it out? Don't let him be burned! Don't let him be burned! My hands sweat and I shudder. It must be nerves. I ought to calm down... A small, strangled voice comes out of me: "Don't worry. You know they've got good facilities. They always have everything under control and well prepared."

The clock moves forward slowly: two, three, four, five o'clock... it's six in the morning and he's still not home. He's going to be really tired. And today we were supposed to be going to see his parents to help them plant potatoes...

It's seven and he's still not home. I hear the telephone and my heart leaps.

"How's it going, Vasya?"

"Sorry, I'm not Vasya. I'm phoning to tell you that Vasya's in hospital. Look, he's not hurt, but he's got to have some tests."

"How come they're doing tests on him if he's not hurt? Tests for what anyway?"

I leave the telephone hanging off the hook. There's a knot in my chest and I can't breathe properly. I run and run and run... it gets harder and harder. I'm afraid I won't make it... I nearly fall. The hospital is cordoned off by the militia. They won't let me through anywhere. Only ambulances are going in. The soldiers shout:

"Don't go near the cars! There's radiation all them!"

A group of women is trying to get in. I join them. I know some of them. They're married to my husband's workmates.

"Hey, have you been able to see them?"

"No, they're not letting any women in. No-one. They must be burned."

"But if it was just burns we'd be able to go in."

I'm finding it more difficult to breathe. My head starts spinning. I feel dizzy and lie down on the

48

ground. A car stops near me. The door opens and my face is brushed by a skirt half covered by a white coat. I recognise the wearer. She's a doctor at the hospital. I grab the edge of her coat. I'm kneeling in front of her. I plead with her:

"Let me in! If I don't see Vasya I'm going to die."

"I can't. He's in a bad way. They're all in a bad way."

She gives me her hand and I get up.

"You'll have to wait."

I block her path, pulling her so strongly that I tear her pocket.

"I'm begging you, please. I just want to see him!"

I repeat that I just want to see him. She takes my arm and, holding on to me, takes me into the building:

"Go on! Hurry! You've got 15 minutes, that's all."

"Where is he?"

She goes with me to the room. His face is swollen. This isn't him. It can't be him. He's all swollen. I can't see his eyes. Where are his eyes?

"What can I do?"

"He needs to drink milk! Lots of milk! Fresh milk. He needs to drink at least three litres."

"But he never drinks milk. He doesn't like it."

"Well now he's got to drink some..."

She brings me a glass.

"For our sake, Vasya, drink some. That's it. Good. One drop at a time."

***

"NO, NO, SHE'S MINE and she's coming with me."

"How?"

"Like this," she says, putting Lyuba, wrapped up tight in the blanket, in the middle of the rucksack and placing it between the handlebars and the seat in the footrest part of the Vespa. Only the baby's arms and head are sticking out.

It's not the first time Iryna has sat her there, sheltering her between her legs to take her for a ride. While the little girl waits for the noise as the scooter roars into life, Iryna ruffles her brother's hair and murmurs:

"I love you, Vasyl! Take care!"

He knows her words are true, just as he knows she's going to take the little girl however much he insists. He had an idea that she would in the end. That's why he put all those baby clothes in. Now she's confirmed what he'd imagined: she wouldn't leave Lyuba behind for anything.

The shawl Lyuba was wrapped in on the way to Kiev is half hanging down Iryna's back. Vasyl wraps it twice round her neck. He takes a breath.

"Be careful!"

***

During the summer, the whole town of Dobrokiv will speak of Collença as if it were one of the most important places in the world. For them it is: it's where their children are going to be staying in Catalonia. All the towns in the Vallès region are suddenly a topic of conversation. For Olena and the two Vasyls, the most important place is Rouralba. That's where their Ira has flown to. Every time her brother hears a plane flying he picks up a stone and throws it in the air, trying to hit the aircraft.

"Hey, Ira, come home now!"

But Iryna has arrived in Catalonia. Pietat and Pau have gone to wait at Barcelona Airport. The monitor shows the girl from a distance as she picks up her luggage.

"Look how she's dressed! How sad!" sobs Pietat.

Huge tears fall when they tell her she still can't take Iryna because she's going with all the new ones in the coach waiting to take them to Collença. Pau asks the Association the same favour but is also refused permission.

"When they come for the first time, both the host parents and the children are new. We have lots of things to tell you before we give you the papers and the permission slip. The airport's too crowded and busy. We might even lose one or two of them."

The hosts are a childless couple in their fifties. The wife has been telling all the neighbours that they'll probably adopt Iryna. She feels so sorry for these children and her heart is full of such compassion that she's been telling everyone about it all year. By word of mouth she's managed to get lots of people to help with her good work, and she's persuaded her husband to do the same.

When they mention their intentions, people usually look at them with approval and respect. Lots of Catalans say the same thing:

"Those Ukrainian children are so good-looking!"

It makes the couple feel proud: it's not like adopting a little black boy or a Chinese girl...

On the way back to Collença, Pau shows her a cheque for 600 euros which his company has collected for their guest.

"Look, Pietat, we can pay the air fare with that!" he says, pleased with himself.

"Oh yes! I like that. They need to realise we wouldn't be able to keep her on what you earn!"

Pietat hasn't told him that, because it's the first year, the Association is paying the air fare. He doesn't need to know. She's the one who takes care of the money and keeps it safe. Perhaps they can use it to pay for all the phone calls. Phoning Ukraine is very expensive, even if they do it from a phone shop with a special card.

It takes half an hour to get to Collença, where everyone is getting ready for the great arrival. There is an empty space in the middle of some large car parks: on one side, the new Ukrainian children; on the other, the host parents with their ears pricked for the strange-sounding name of the child they are hosting. There is a flurry of suitcases and hugs and kisses and no-one has enough hands. Iryna finds it very difficult to understand what they say to her. At home they have warned her again and again: you need to pay attention and do as you're told. She has promised them she would. Now she is silent, observing.

"This is the only bag you've got?" The girl indicates that they're giving something out near where the local television crew is filming. "Pau, go and ask. She must have forgotten a suitcase."

Iryna and Pietat wait. The Ukrainian girl doesn't know why. Pietat is showing everyone around her that she's got one of the poorest girls. When Pau returns with a pile of bags, hats, t-shirts, soaps, tickets for attractions and a health cards, someone takes a photo of them: Iryna smiling between Pietat and Pau – her Catalan family.

It seems as if it's all going so well at first, but when the people from the Association and her family told her to be good, she didn't know that meant: "Don't open the fridge without my permission; don't go poking your nose into any cupboards in the kitchen or dining room; you mustn't go into any bedroom that isn't yours; you can only go out in the street with us; and you have to smile at everyone and say: 'I'm from Ukraine...'." She hadn't imagined it would be so difficult not to touch anything in a house where you don't know how to ask for things! And when she feels ridiculed and belittled, her smile is so forced. When they introduce her, everyone looks as though they are thinking "Poor unfortunate plague child!" Some barely manage to hide their disgust when they are supposed to kiss her, for fear of contagion. "Perhaps she's got radiation!" they whisper. The only thing she enjoys is writing her diary because, as they don't know Ukrainian or the Cyrillic alphabet, she can leave it anywhere and they can't snoop on her. Or if they do they won't understand a thing.

She misses her mother, father and brother Vasyl a lot. She often remembers them saying goodbye with tears in their eyes. At the end of August she will return to Ukraine. She's counting the days and crossing them off on a calendar she's made on the last page of her notebook. Every day she crosses off the next day as if it has already passed because she's already wishing she was at home. Even so, she wants to remember some good times. They say there are lots of nice things to see and fun things to do. When she gets back to Ukraine she needs to be able to tell them that Catalonia is a paradise: the zoo, theme parks, cinemas and everything. She wants to make friends and the days are flying by. She wants to learn Catalan. There are some words Pietat really likes to hear: "*Sí, d'acord!* Yes, OK!"

She has to make an effort to eat everything, especially fruit. If she eats healthy food, next winter she won't get so many colds. If she doesn't eat everything or say a thousand times that it's all good and better than in Ukraine, they won't want her back next year. Here in Catalonia it's very hot. She can't get to sleep until the early hours and by 8am her host parents are calling her to get up. She's very tired. Her legs have never swollen up before but now the straps on her sandals leave marks on her, just like her Granny Rus. They make her shower: quickly, quickly, to wash away the sleep. No dreaming. She likes the bath better, full of soapy bubbles. She could spend all day in there, but they say it uses too much water. Only on the first day, when she arrived at midnight, was she allowed to lie in the bath for a while. In the end Pietat scrubbed her hard with a sponge. They couldn't have her dirtying the sheets. When she doesn't do as she's told straightaway, Pietat starts crying, calls Pau and says this little brat will be the death of her. And Pau, who is running short of patience and goodwill, only manages to get her to do what Pietat wants by promising her a present if she behaves. Iryna, who is thinking of asking him for some of those winter boots the snow can't get through, does as she's told. Once the row has died down, Pietat comes to her and strokes her hair, saying:

54

"*Ai, la meva filla petita!* My little daughter!"

They have bought her a Catalan-Ukrainian dictionary and Iryna has looked up the meaning of the word
filla. She doesn't want to be called that again. She
doesn't need a Catalan mum if she's going to be like
Pietat. When she hears her tell the neighbours she is
preparing the papers to adopt the Ukrainian girl, Iryna
wants to protest, saying it's a lie and that Pietat isn't
even sure she can stand her for the whole summer. If
she could, and if she knew how to, she'd tell them: "It's
all lies!"

What she does understand is that Pietat doesn't love
her. She invents things and she tells people Iryna's
really stubborn. She's always phoning the people at
the Association and getting them to come and tell Iryna off. As well as the supervisor, Mr Fortunato has
even been, and he's fed up with being woken up at
midnight... Pietat tells them Iryna only likes expensive
things; she doesn't want to eat vegetables; she wants
to go and see other Ukrainian children from her town
of Dobrokiv who are also being hosted in Rouralba.
She tells them that she doesn't want to learn the language, that she repeats everything in Russian and that
she hasn't yet unpacked her suitcase. "That way I'll
have it ready," thinks Iryna. "And I won't leave anything behind." Pietat might also make an effort to learn
her language! Saying "Good morning" in Ukraine, for
example, sounds so good...! *Dobroho ranku.*

If she were her mother, she'd want to see her happy. Her own mother hides her defects. Pietat only uses
her so she can look good or complain. For the first few
days she was homesick and she wanted to ask Pietat if
she would let her sleep with her, but she didn't know
how. Now she wouldn't ask her for the world. Perhaps
it would make her sick, she thinks.

"Poor little thing, if you could see how she was dressed the day she arrived! I had such a job to clean her up and sort out her hair with conditioner – it was like a pan scrubber! At least the TB tests have come back negative. But I'm sure she's got sinusitis – her snot is really green."

Her new mother is desperate because although she managed to get the local council to let Iryna attend the children's summer club free, she only wanted to go one day. Can't Pietat see that all the others were wearing tracksuits and trainers and she was dressed in a skirt and flip-flops? Pietat is tired of the girl "running up and down the street" instead of sitting still in a corner of the garden while she does the housework. Because Iryna doesn't help her – she doesn't know how to do anything. They probably haven't even got windows in her house! Who knows? How would she know how to clean them? Her new father gets really furious if, when he sits down for a meal, the girl is still playing with Maragda, the next-door neighbour, who has such lovely dolls... Children know plenty about language. They make themselves understood with exclamations, gestures, looks and laughter, and the first things they learn are swear words.

"*Os pedrer!* Damn!"

"*Os pedrer?*" repeats Iryna. "What does that mean?"

"It means if you're late again they won't let you see that film, Titanic!"

She has already seen the film time and again, but as it doesn't have much dialogue she understands it and imagines she's the heroine. She likes it so much that she'll promise anything: she'll go in straightaway and she'll eat up that mouldy cured ham with the soggy bread soaked in tomato... In the end they'll leave her alone. She has a great time watching the film again, stretched out on the sofa, when Pau, who always takes up all the space, goes to bed and Pietat follows him. But it's not so great really. Her mother's not there, nor is her father or Vasyl.

To the vocabulary she learns from Pau is added the litany of "Bad girl, little witch, selfish cow!" rammed into her head by Pietat. "For her own good", she has started to say:

"This girl mustn't get used to luxuries! She's a little tyrant. Am I going to spend on her what I've never spent on me?"

That was the idea in her head when she didn't want to buy Iryna that tracksuit she asked for or let her look in the cake shop window, or buy her ice creams or anything she'd dreamed of. And at home they'd told her all Catalans were rich and they'd give you whatever you asked for!

Iryna doesn't need them to tell her they don't love her, she just knows. She doesn't know the language, the cat's got her tongue and she can't answer. Blushing silence instead of words. Choked-back tears run down her throat and drown in her stomach.

She has to put up with Pietat's boasting and moaning all day:

"Did those trousers I sent fit your father?"

Trousers Pau had already worn...

"Here we eat fresh fish!"

And how hard it is to swallow! Because fish from the sea tastes quite different from the river fish she knows.

"Oh, come on! Drink some milk. This stuff isn't contaminated."

But the taste is horrible compared to the milk from her cow.

Pietat doesn't even want to buy bottled water and the girl is used to water from her family's well, which doesn't have chlorine – although it must have all sorts of other much worse contamination after the explosion.

"No chlorine," she manages, because the Ukrainian and Catalan words are very similar.

And the thing Pietat complains about most is that, according to her, Iryna isn't making progress with her Catalan. Every morning, when they go to the allotment, they pass a house with a garden protected by a large, intelligent dog. The girl stays to talk to it – the dog understands her. He barks and out comes Esperança, a young woman who works as a teacher and has two daughters about Iryna's age. Now, of course, as it's summer, she's on holiday.

"Look, Iryna, if you're not learning anything you'll have to go to classes!"

"What a pretty girl! Would you like to come in?"

"What called dog?" she asks in broken Catalan, while she hugs him and looks at his owner.

"He's called Rovelló," she answers, pointing to a kind of fungus that's sprung up among the moss in the courtyard. The dog is named after a type of wild mushroom.

The girl understands straightaway and continues:

"In Ukraine many mushroom!"

"If you want to come, I'd like to help you learn the language."

"If you do want to, when we come back from the allotment you can stay for a while."

Pietat has explained to Esperança that the allotment where they go isn't hers. They've been lent it so the girl doesn't get too bored. They don't know what to do with her and, for the moment, she's only learned the things that interest her. There they make her pick potatoes and other vegetables. They're amazed when they see how quick she is at weeding. But they don't tell people about that. Only the sacrifices they're making and how much the clothes and the air fares cost.

Thank goodness Pietat now has somewhere to leave Iryna every morning. Iryna arrives at about 11, gets the mud off her fingers and then starts work. She's often still there at lunchtime. The hugs she gives Rovelló the dog have stolen Esperança's heart. Her love for their dog has won over Esperança's daughters Laia and Naiara too. They think it's wonderful to be able to learn her alphabet and, all together, they are making really good progress. She smiles and is always saying:

"*Molt bé! Gràcies!* Very good! Thank you!"

"How do you say that in Ukrainian?"

"*Chudovo! Dyakuyu!*"

The sisters make an effort:

"*Chudovo! Dyakuyu!?*"

"*Tak.* That's it!"

Esperança's husband is called Miquel. He likes cars and he's a mechanic. At his garage, there's a Ukrainian lad who teaches him a few words in that language. Every lunchtime, Miquel amazes his daughters by repeating them. It's a shame most of them are only the names of garage tools. Iryna thinks: "How well he'd get on with Dad and Vasyl! I bet he's fed up in a house with so many women!" They don't see Miquel much, as he's working all through July.

In a week of games and swimming in the pool, the girls have learned lots of expressions in Ukrainian. And Iryna in Catalan. They make cakes in the kitchen and she already knows the names of all the ingredients. She sometimes manages to get Pietat and Pau to let them take her to the beach, but they are always repeating:

"Make sure you don't hurt yourself. What would the people at the Association say?"

She's got a lovely exercise book where she's worked on all the letters and sounds, and she's made a special drawing for each new letter. For R she's drawn a reactor and a big explosion. She expresses her feelings in those drawings in full colour. And the words that come from her mouth are written down with the help of the dictionary and a passion straight from her heart.

Pietat has scheduled a series of appointments at the Rouralba doctor's surgery. They give Iryna blood tests and vaccines. The tests have shown that her cholesterol levels are high for such a young girl and her thyroid gland doesn't work. So Doctor Trini has had to make more appointments at Collença Hospital.

After a few days, they visit the specialist, who, plays down its importance.

"There are a lot of children here with deficiencies," he says.

Iryna snaps:

"In Catalonia they treat sick children and in Ukraine they don't treat them. They can't. They haven't got euros."

"That's all nonsense. The radioactive cloud also reached Catalonia!"

"What are you saying?" asks Pietat.

"That the radioactivity came here too."

"Buuuut... it's not the same. We're 30 kilometres from Chernobyl, you're three hours in a plane. And haven't you seen the mark I've got on my tummy?" replied Iryna, lifting up her t-shirt and showing the black bit around her belly button.

Hearing her and seeing her so vehement, the doctor's fallen silent.

And he's also silent because he's just discovered a heart murmur on her electrocardiogram. For this reason, he has finally sent her to the Vall d'Hebron Hospital, where they've got more equipment and can do more detailed investigation. All paid for by Social Security. All free. "But, of course, there are all the journeys," thinks Pau. "And the petrol and the wasted time. Who's going to pay us back for all that? If Pietat had imagined the girl would cause them so many problems, she'd probably just have sponsored her and kept her conscience clean that way. But if it has to be done, it has to be done. What can we do about it?"

And a fortnight later they were in another consulting room, this time at Vall d'Hebron.

After a whole morning waiting in a grey room full of people with her tummy rumbling because she hadn't had breakfast in preparation for the tests they needed to do, they ask a nurse. She tells them they're not doing blood tests and there are still four people in front of them. The girl's hungry and they can't buy sandwiches there. There are just machines – very nice ones – selling packaged biscuits and cakes, but Pau says they're a rip-off and Pietat says it's junk food anyway.

At about four in the afternoon they call her in. After looking at her with various pieces of sophisticated equipment, some of which hurts because it squashes her chest, they reach their conclusions and tell the couple the verdict, which they will also give them in writing:

"Iryna's got a malformed heart valve. Next year, when she's older, she'll have to have an operation."

"Operation?"

"Yes. It will probably be a simple matter, using a catheter," he says, to calm them. And, as the girl has shown us that mark on her stomach, we are accompanying this letter with an appointment we've made for her to visit the dermatologist Anna Fontclara on 20 August at 9am."

That's all they need. Pietat can't leave this child to the mercy of God, but heaven and earth will have to hear her on the subject.

"Now you know, Iryna, not too much strain, no running and certainly no more swimming pool. You're a sick girl and we've got to look after you. And no asking for sweets or croissants. People with high cholesterol have to eat vegetables."

"What are vegetables?"

"They're green things like chard and runner beans. This girl's got no idea about being on a diet. This is going to make things really difficult for us!"

"Why us? We need to take the letter to the Association and they'll see to her. We've done enough. Fancy giving us a sick child!" says Pau. "How dare they!"

The Association agree to see them that evening. They speak to Mr Fortunato, who praises the work of host parents in difficult cases. When he finishes, he speaks to Iryna:

"There, see how lucky you are! Thanks to Pietat and Pau, next year they'll sort out this problem for you.

"Will Mum be able to come? Will you pay for her air fare and food? I don't want an operation if I haven't got Mum with me."

In Barcelona they said it would only be a few days and then a week of recuperation at home.

"Afterwards – until our flight back to Ukraine – Mummy can help Pietat or go and do some cleaning. Rouralba's got some very big houses!"

"We'll do what we can, Iryna," says Mr Fortunato. "Our responsibility is for your health and yours is to behave well with the family you've been lucky enough to be placed with."

Iryna says nothing. She is thinking though. She is thinking that unfortunately those two are almost as bad as the explosion that happened in Ukraine.

In the end, July has been a profitable month. In Esperança's house, Iryna is learning Catalan so quickly it seems as if a fairy godmother is making her wish to communicate come true. Often, with Esperança's children, she gets things off her chest about the strange couple who are hosting her.

"Last night, Pietat sick. She was very upset, shouting, crying. 'Go Pau!' she said. 'Go back to your mother if she's the one who makes you a better escudella. I'd boiled mine for so long!'."

"How silly! Can you hear what she's saying?" shout Laia and Naiara.

"Don't you think Pau is a bit old to be asking for *escudella* like his mother makes it? He won't be able to come to Ukraine. The way we make soup is very different!"

Esperança has smiled conspiratorially but she doesn't want to continue in this mocking vein.

"Weren't you going to the dermatologist tomorrow? If she's not well, who's going with you?"

"I'd like you to come, Esperança. I want to ask doctor how to get mark off," says Iryna, who is fed up with hiding the mark when they go to the beach.

"OK then, I'll phone Pietat and tell her that I've got to go to Barcelona and, if she wants, I can take you."

"Brilliant, Mum! Whoopee!" says Naiara.

"Can you take us to Tibidabo? I want to go to the amusement park," says Laia.

"Good idea!" her mother answered. "As the appointment's at nine in the morning, if everything goes well we can go to the park when we come out."

"Go on, phone Pietat!" they all urge her.

She phones straightaway. Pau answers, telling her that Pietat has had a bad attack of neuralgia and when that happens she has to rest a lot. He thinks it is a good idea for Esperança to take care of Iryna:

"Yes, if you can do us that favour it'll be great. We're tired of going from pillar to post."

"OK then, if you like, she can sleep here tonight too. We'll have to get up at seven tomorrow to get to the appointment on time. That way, Pietat can rest."

The girls, who were listening, start to dance, hopping from foot to foot, and running to their bedroom. "Look, we'll put the two beds together. What do you think, Iryna?"

"Lovely! Will you let me sleep in the middle?"

"Yes, but we'll put the beds crossways. If we don't, you'll have a bad back tomorrow!"

"I'll bring a box with postcards and photographs of Ukraine..."

Esperança calms them down:

"Let Iryna go now."

Talking to her, she adds:

"You'll have to go home now. Be good and help Pau make the lunch. We'll come and pick you up this evening."

"In the afternoon, Mummy, please!" demands Laia.

"OK, in the afternoon." Esperança lets them decide.

"Don't forget the photos," Naiara reminds her.

"Yes, but don't go thinking... Some are very sad ones..."

Chapter 5

PRIPYAT, 26 APRIL 1986, 09.23 H (LOCAL TIME)

I ask him:

"Vasya, what do you need?"

"Get out of here! Get out! You're expecting a baby!"

"But how can I leave you?"

"Save the child!"

"First I'll bring you some milk, then we'll see."

As I go out to buy milk, I meet my friend Tanya, who had come in the car with her father. I tell her what's happened. We get in the car and go to look for milk in the nearest village. We buy six three-litre containers of milk so there's enough for everyone. The guard at the entrance only lets me in.

"This is doctor's orders."

A nurse helps me bring the milk in. The doctors say they've been poisoned by gases and the milk will do them good. But the milk makes them terribly sick. They lose consciousness and it has to be injected in drop by drop. But the doctors still ask them to make an effort and drink milk. Milk has always been good against poisons. Not all of poisons, but... don't they say milk is good for you? Well, I'll buy more milk... I'll bathe him in milk.

It's getting dark. Mustn't spill the milk! If I can't buy milk, may heaven curse me and poison my blood! I'd like to stay with him. I don't want to leave his hands.

I can't leave them. Mustn't spill the milk! Mustn't spill the milk! Mustn't spill the milk!

"Vasya, I've got to go out for a minute."

"Blow me a kiss and... don't come back! Take care!"

I go out to buy more milk. The crowd is still at the door. I escape, pressing myself against the wall. The city is filling up with military vehicles. All the main roads are being closed. They say the coaches and trains aren't working any more. Not even skeleton services. They're cleaning the streets everywhere. The soldiers are wearing masks. Outside the hospital everyone is sheltering.

My stomach is rumbling. I ought to eat something. If I don't eat, I won't be able to help him. They're pulling the shutter down at the shop where I sometimes buy things.

"Hey! Don't close! Have you got any milk?"

"Everyone wants milk today. Is your husband in hospital too?"

They've only got a little bit left in the bottom of a bucket. They pour it through a funnel into a bottle for me. I buy a piece of bread and an apple.

I've been out for less than an hour. The same guard isn't on watch anymore and the new one blocks my path.

"Hey, let me in, I've got permission from Dr Alexandra!"

A sea of people surround me and want to sneak in with me. They all shout:

"We've got permission from Dr Alexandra!"

The patients come to the window. They shout. They make signs. I recognise Vasya. They're telling us something important. They're shouting as loud as they can. Finally, I understand.

"They're taking us to Moscow!"

"Oh! I'm coming with you!"

The soldiers push us and we scratch and bite them...

"Let us be with our husbands!"

They start coming down the stairs. From outside I see that he's only half dressed, with his gown tied in only one place. His whole back is bare.

"Why are you taking him like that?"

"We haven't got enough gowns for so many people. Go home and find clothes. His have been burned."

There isn't a single car in the streets. Back home again. I run and run and run. I get pyjamas, underwear, a couple of pairs of socks and some shoes and I run and run and run.

I'm the first to arrive. A plane is taking off from the meadow in front of the hospital. I must have got it wrong! I go into the hospital. Not a single doctor or patient. They've fooled us. It's completely empty. Cleaners are starting to come in. I go outside. My friend arrives.

"They've taken them... They don't want to hear us screaming. They don't want to hear us crying."

I think I'll scream until I lose my voice. I think I'll cry my eyes out. I need to hold him. I need to hold him. He needs milk. I have to give him some. Apathetically, I start walking to his parents' house. I want to tell them. They live in a little village more than 20 kilometres away. They haven't got a phone. I can't find anyone to give me a lift. I take a shortcut, walking with a torch. By the time I get there, they've gone.

***

THE VESPA starts off, heading west, towards Rivno, according to the road sign. Meanwhile, Vasyl heads north. The boy returns to Dobrokiv the quick way, taking quiet paths.

The muted light of a weak sun shows him the way. Iryna rides carefully, as close to the kerb as she can. She doesn't like the E40, full of lorries camouflaged in the mist. Every time they overtake her it feels as if the air is sucking the scooter in. She imagines they'll end up under the great wheels and she shudders. It's now midday. She must have covered more than 100 kilometres and she's had to stop a couple of times because Lyuba was complaining. She's let her chew buttons, zips and laces... In her daughter's face, she's discovered some of Vasyl's features and, in her hands, the ability to open pockets. She looks for something with sounds and lights to entertain the little girl and, as she isn't thinking of using the mobile phone for fear of being caught, she gives it to her. Lyuba loves having it. Until now, she has never let been allowed to, however much she stretched out her little arms. She's snuggled down at the bottom of the rucksack and gone to sleep. By the time they get to a very small village where it says Zitomir 50 kilometres, the needle is dropping into the red. She goes into the village and asks for a petrol station. Luckily they've got a pump and, as Lyuba is still hidden, she can fill up without difficulties. And now they're back on the road. She doesn't know this area and can't risk the forest trails.

If she wants to get to Poland, it's best if she doesn't hang about. Come on! On we go! The little girl wakes up, sticking her head out like a puppet, befuddled and bleary eyed. Iryna stops again to change her. Poor thing, she needs it. She unwraps the blanket and stretches Lyuba out on a bank near the road. She opens the bag... it's the last nappy she's got. Oh no! What's she going to do? But look what her brother's put in the rucksack pockets! Wow! She might have known he would: baby clothes and some cotton nappies. She thinks that with that and a plastic bag she'll make leg holes in to turn into a pair of pants, Lyuba's clothes won't get wet. She also takes out a thick sleepsuit – the one Vasyl brought her from Catalonia – with feet and a little hat. She'll be fine in that! Once she's changed Lyuba, she looks for a snack to eat. In another pocket she finds food – bread, cheese, apples and a sealed lemonade bottle full of milk from their cow. She takes an apple. She allows Lyuba let off steam crawling in a dry patch. Meanwhile, she looks for some wormwood, the bitter herb with a smell that will instantly calm the little girl.

***

SUMMER 2003

Iryna, Laia and Naiara are happy. It's all been as wonderful as they'd planned: they've had dinner, they've played cards, they've gone to bed at 11 and they've chatted into the small hours when it cooled down enough so they could rest.

At about seven in the morning, Esperança finds the three girls asleep with their feet curled together and arms linked. "How peaceful!" she says, leaving them in bed until a quarter to eight. Then she gets them up and ready to go in just 15 minutes. At the hospital, they see the dermatologist come out to say goodbye to a patient.

They weren't expecting a black, male doctor.

"What about Anna Fontclara? Isn't she seeing patients today?" Esperança asks the nurse.

"She's on holiday. Doctor Alassane Ahdjo is a very good specialist and he's standing in for her."

As soon as the nurse turns round to go off for the next appointment, Iryna jumps up, looking sceptical:

"A black man! What can he possibly know about diseases from Chernobyl?"

Esperança tells her that people from abroad have had to pass the same exams as the doctors here and that she mustn't judge him by his origins.

"Don't you think he's handsome?" says Naiara.

"Yes, he looks tall and friendly," says Iryna.

Once they are inside, the doctor looks straight at Iryna and asks her:

"Will you let me see that mark?"

"How does he know she's the one with the mark?" Laia whispers softly in her mother's ear.

The doctor has heard her.

"Because I've got an appointment with a girl called Iryna and you don't look like an Iryna or like a Ukrainian girl... Would you like to show it to me?"

Iryna lifts up her t-shirt and shows her the brown area in the middle of her stomach. The doctor looks at the mark and tells her it's not a disease. They can't believe it.

"Are you sure?" Naiara asks him, looking at Laia and her mother.

"Before I came to Catalonia I worked in a hospital in Cuba specialising in malformations following the Chernobyl accident, many of which could not be treated... But you can rest assured, changes in the colour of the skin are rarely a serious medical problem. It's a case of hyper-pigmentation with melanin."

"What does that mean?" asks Iryna.

"Nothing important. You just have to keep an eye on it and put high-factor sun cream in that area. A normal FPS one is OK for the rest of your body."

"What do you recommend?" asks Esperança.

"The FPS is an index that indicates the time we can be exposed to the sun without the risk of burns. The higher the FPS, the higher the protection from the sun's rays. If a person can be in the sun for 20 minutes without getting burned, choosing a number 8 photoprotector will give eight times more protection.

"And what can have caused this mark?"

"It must be a craving your mother had when she was pregnant. Perhaps she wanted to eat a dish of strawberries. It's quite round, you see, like a circle full of hearts."

"Yes, that's what Mum says. She says they're *polunyci* she saw on a market stall. They smelled lovely but she didn't have *hryvnias* to buy them.

"It's a sign of distinction. There must be thousands of Irynas in the world, but you're the only one with *polunyci* on her tummy."

"What's good about that, though? Can't you take it away? I don't like that mark... When I go to the beach, if I wear a bikini everyone looks at me. I always have to wear a one-piece swimsuit."

"They look at you because you're very pretty. The boy who falls in love with you will want you just as you are. And he'll remember you with this little picture. It's as if you'd been tattooed. OK?"

Iryna still looks doubtful, imagining how nice it would be if someone loved you so much they didn't mind you having a defect.

"Thank you very much," says the teacher. "No-one could have looked after her any better."

As they leave the hospital, they can see the church of the Sacred Heart on top of Tibidabo and the park near to it, but as Esperança has to leave some papers at the Department of Education in Carrer Casp and they'll be closed in the afternoon, they go and park in Plaça Catalunya. While she runs her errand, she lets the girls wander off, provided they promise to be in the middle of the square by the fountains in an hour's time. Let's go! What a good time they have, looking at stalls, imitating the living statues and having fun with the clowns and juggling shows. When Esperança comes back, she finds them absolutely still, imitating a replica of some storybook characters.

"What shall we do now? Do you want to go to the cinema?" she asks them.

"No, Mum, we said we'd go to Tibidabo!" says Laia.

"We could go to Montjuïc instead. It's nearer!"

"No Mum, we said we'd go to Tibidabo!" repeats Naiara.

They get their way and now they're heading back up to Tibidabo. Esperança manages to get them to sit down for a minute to eat some salads, but they take their burgers away, biting into them as they decide what they're going to go on first. Iryna wants to go on all the attractions: in the haunted house she squeals and laughs more than anyone, and on the big wheel she spreads her arms wide, as if to enfold the entire city and take it away with her.

"What's that? And that?"

Seeing her enthusiasm, they promise her that one day they'll go to see the Sagrada Família, the Columbus statue and everything.

They walk through the doll and toy museum. In the hall of distorting mirrors, for a few seconds she thought she saw her brother Vasyl beside her. How he would love all this! What fun he would have! After that, she can't get him out of her head. On the trampolines, lots of people stop and watch her for a while. She jumps so high it's as if she wants to touch the sky. She imagines holding Vasyl's hand going round and round in space, like trapeze artists. She sees him happy and squeals excitedly. She does forward and backward somersaults. Her skirt and blouse go up in the air and she doesn't care if people can see her mark. Then they go to a shooting stall and she hits a cuddly toy giraffe in the neck.

"You're good at this! You could be a policewoman!" the sisters tell her, admiringly.

75

"Oh, it's very easy! You should see Vasyl. There wouldn't be anything left on the stall."

Ukrainians are very good shots – the best snipers in the world.

At the end of the afternoon they go back to the car park and anyone who could hear them would know it's been an unforgettable day. The sisters want to know if there are attractions like Tibidabo in Ukraine, but Iryna is now distracted. Her head is filled with an irresistible desire, so she asks Esperança:

"How old do you think that doctor is?"

"Barely 30, I'd say."

"Not much older than me, then!"

***

PRIPYAT, 27 APRIL 1986, 07.30 H (LOCAL TIME)

Loudspeakers boom through the town:

"Everyone out of their houses! To the country! We're taking you to the countryside!"

Hundreds of buses have come from all over the place to evacuate the town. On the radio they say it will be for three days, maybe six, and that we should take winter clothes because we'll be living in tents in the forest. The people, unaware of what's been going on, are happy:

"The countryside! How lovely! We'll celebrate Mayday! It'll be different. We'll get meat ready to have a barbecue."

No-one can imagine what has really happened. They're so innocent and ignorant. I look at them and just see stupid fools.

The only ones against it are the ones like me: the women whose husbands have been taken away. Someone forces me on to the coach. I feel a stabbing pain in my head – a very strong pain. And another one. I don't remember the journey to the country. Music is playing on guitars and radio-cassettes. People get together sitting around on blankets with the food in the middle. I notice I'm protecting my stomach. I look for Vasya's parents. Everything looks blurred and unreal, like in a film. Finally I see them. I touch them. Yes, it's them. I have to tell them. I have to tell them everything. I tell them.

"Vasya's in a very bad way. They've got him in Moscow."

They answer:

"No-one's told us anything. We've just sown the allotment! How could we have known?"

***

SUMMER 2003

Driving along the Barcelona ring road, Esperança sees in the mirror that the three girls have fallen asleep with their mouths open. It's very hot. They've got the windows down and their t-shirts have ridden up. Iryna is sitting in the middle with one of her hands resting on her dark mark. When they reach Rouralba they are all soaked with sweat. They park in front of Esperança's house to pick up the things Iryna had brought to spend the night. While Iryna waits for the two sisters to get out on either side, she notices she's left the seat red and wet. Her mother had warned her:

"If that happens one day, don't be scared. You should be very happy. It means your body's healthy and ready for you to have children."

So, since she was ten, she's been looking forward to having her period and "practising" with her mother's sanitary towels. But now her mother's not here and she's sure Pietat won't be at all pleased... As soon as she gets to the room where they'd slept, she tells her friends. Laia congratulates her:

"That's cool, Iryna, you're a woman now!"

Naiara agrees that Pietat doesn't need to know, and nor does their mother. They divide up what needs to be done. She will go and wash the blood off the seat before it dries and her sister will look for sanitary towels in the bathroom drawer. Iryna asks:

"But shouldn't I wash myself first?"

"Of course," says Laia. "Hygiene's important with these things."

"We should start heading across to Pietat's house," she hears Esperança say from the other end of the lounge.

"Wait a minute, Mum. Iryna would like to have a bath. She's very sweaty and you know Pietat doesn't want her to use too much water."

"OK, I'll get on with the dinner then," she answers.

Laia and Iryna bolt the bathroom door straightaway. Iryna takes off her clothes and starts pouring water in with the shower head. She soaps herself. The whole bath is pink. Suddenly, there's a soft knock on the door:

"It's me! Open up..."

When Naiara sees the colour of the water she can't help herself:

"Don't bleed to death! You'll have to lie down. That way it won't come out so much."

"Perhaps it would be best if you used a tampon!"

"How do I do that?" asks Iryna.

"It explains it all here. It should be easy," answers Laia, looking at the drawings on the box.

Iryna does everything they tell her:

"Relax."

"Are you relaxed? OK. Now lie down like that and breathe."

"Lift your leg up and put it on the edge of the bath. The other one too. Take this little mirror and look for the hole where the cotton thing has to go in."

Laia removes the protective plastic:

"Take it between your index finger and thumb. Like that, with the string hanging down."

"Put it in as deep as you can."

"Where?"

"In your vagina."

"No, it won't go in."

"That's because you're not relaxed. Let me try. I'll rub a bit of moisturiser on it. Keep still."

As if they were playing doctors and nurses, they end up getting the tampon inside her. They give her clean clothes, along with the whole box of tampons and leave the "surgery".

"Does it hurt?"

"It feels a bit uncomfortable, but that's all."

"Don't worry. You'll get used to it... They say it's the best invention ever for women."

Once she's cleaned up, they accompany her to Pietat's house. Pietat must be feeling better because she's already waiting for them on the balcony. When they ring the bell, Pau comes out. Without asking them in, he gets to the point:

"What did the doctor tell you about the mark?"

"That it's a craving for a dish of strawberries."

"So you're not going to need laser sessions?"

"No. Strawberries disappear when you eat them up..."

"The dermatologist Anna Fontclara told you that?" asks Pietat from the balcony.

"No, there was a black doctor – he was very hand-some and nice – standing in for her. Wasn't there, Iryna?" says Naiara, and Iryna nods her head.

"Good grief!" says Pau, trying not to swear in front of educated people.

"Ah! That must be why he thought it was normal."

Faced with such ignorance, Esperança withdraws towards the car, without asking Pietat whether her headache has gone. Her daughters follow her, giggling:

"Who wants a polunyci?"

Iryna, between Pietat and Pau, lifts her t-shirt and continues with her joke:

"Here they are! Nice and cheap!"

Iryna, who not so long ago couldn't say anything more than "Yes, OK", now knows how to make fun of people. And she writes too! She makes mistakes, of course, but everything she puts down on paper is quite understandable. When she doesn't know how to say something, she asks Laia or Naiara. Esperança also corrects her so she can make progress. In two months, she has learned the most important constructions and knows how to use the dictionary whenever she needs it.

So, at the end of August 2003, she writes the following letter:

Dear friends of Esperança and Miquel,

My name is Iryna and I've come from Ukraine. I haven't come on holiday, I've come for my health. My town is very near Chernobyl and still has a lot of radioactivity from the explosion that happened there.

81

I'm very pleased to have got to know all these people from Catalonia who have opened the doors of their homes to me, taken me to the doctor and look after me. Also because I've met this lovely teacher who's taught me Catalan and can explain to me. I'll be leaving soon and my blood tests now are better than when I arrived. They say this might help me have a longer life. Every time they say that it breaks my heart because my brother, who's a year older than me, has never been able to come. No family has ever wanted him. He's a normal, good boy, like me, but the Association only pays for one trip per family and I've been the lucky one. If, between all of you, you could collect money for his air fare, perhaps a family would want him. My family are very good people, but they've got no money. Dad earns about 50 euros a month. That's very little. We've only got enough for a few things we can't get from the allotment or the cow. Dad works as a forest guard and he brings us wood, because winter is very cold. Mum earns a bit more. She works as an operating theatre assistant at the hospital [Iryna doesn't like to say that she only does this when they are short staffed and that she's really a cleaner]. All the hospital does for poor people is help them in emergencies. My brother and I have never been to a doctor. Now, thanks to the appointment I had here, we know that I've got a heart malformation and that I'm going to need a heart operation. I mustn't overdo things. Next year, God willing, I'll have an operation here in Catalonia. I want my mum with me to hold my hand in the operating theatre. But what I most want in the world is for Vasyl to come. This winter, I'll start teaching him Catalan and I'll pray so that next time he'll be lucky and someone will take him into their home.

Iryna

Esperança has prepared tea and has invited her friends: couples from a book discussion club who she belongs to who know about her new young Ukrainian fan. On the table there is a special crispy cake called coca de vidre, nuts and chocolate. Naiara, Laia and Iryna come in and out, licking their fingers.

When everyone has drunk their tea or milky coffee, Esperança shows them the letter and reads it.

As they listen, their eyes are filled with tenderness. Iryna smiles sweetly at them from a corner. Then, Esperança's friends react, each according to their experience, each according to their possibilities.

"What a well-written letter! Did you dictate it to her? I can't believe she's learned so much in one summer!

"She asked for help so as not to make mistakes, but the words are straight from her heart," says Esperança.

"We usually have lots of visitors – we've got grandchildren now and they come with their friends – but we'd like to help so her brother can come here one summer," say Andreu and Àngels.

"I've also got a bit put by for special cases," adds Montserrat.

"You have to be careful with these people. They often come with the idea that we're really rich and we can sort out their lives for them," says Tomàs.

Carme adds:

"We've had some bad experiences and we know of one girl from Ukraine who gave the family from Can Garrigó a horrible summer."

"Maria Rosa and Manel told us that their Karina only wanted money and demanded they buy her designer clothes. She didn't want to go to any of the places they were looking forward to taking her. The day they were getting ready to take her to the Port Aventura theme park she said it was crap and she wanted to go to Euro Disney. Her language was dreadful and she was sitting on the husband's lap all the time. When they got in the car, she wanted to sit next to him in the front and she followed him all round the house. Poor Maria Rosa had to put up with a shameless Lolita and, as if that wasn't enough, she was a thief too."

"They found out the day Collença Council was preparing a welcome party for them, just a fortnight after they arrived."

"How did they find out?" everyone was asking.

"One girl suddenly saw that another was showing off a gold bracelet that looked like hers. 'Hey, where did you get that?' she asked the one who was wearing it and she said: 'It's a present Karina gave me because she's got three bracelets,'"

"It seems Karina had been invited to the house where the girl who'd lost the bracelet was staying. What a coincidence! It must have been her who stole it and she gave it away so Maria Rosa and Manel didn't find it."

"She put them in a very difficult situation. She was spoilt, from a well-off family. Her parents spent the summer in the Crimea in a luxury hotel, while Maria Rosa and Manel had to put up with her..."

"What a nerve! If something like that happened to me, I'd give her a clip round the ear first and then ask her why she'd done it," says Miquel, who's just arrived from the garage and hasn't missed a single detail of what Carme and Tomàs have been saying.

Esperança passes Iryna the cake and says:

"Don't take any notice. He always says he'll sort children out with a good hiding, but he wouldn't hurt a fly. Mind you, sometimes his shouting can rattle the windows. I think in a case like that we should hold the Association responsible. They're the ones who choose the children. And, with so much poverty, it's a scandal that we end up with rich spoilt brats whose families could send them to spend the summer wherever they like."

"Look, we've got coats and anoraks our children used to wear which are still as good as new. If Iryna wants to take them, that will be a sign that her family aren't rolling in money. I've got storybooks and novels, too, from when I was at secondary school. If she really wants to read and learn they'll be good for her," says Jaume.

"In the attic at home there are some new suitcases I was given free by the automobile club. They've all got wheels, they roll really well. I've also got the leather ones from when we got married. They're really good, but they're heavier and haven't got wheels. I can go home and get a couple whenever you like," offers Maria Mercè.

Chapter 6

August comes to an end in the blink of an eye. The last week has been spent packing. Iryna wanted to take everything the two families and their friends had given her. She's got presents for everyone at home, even her grandparents and cousins. She opens a case, checks what's packed into it, adds things, tries to close it and, if she can't, sits on it and tries again. The night before she has to leave, she barely sleeps half an hour. At three in the morning she's showering and drying her hair. Pietat hears her and lets her get on with it. The sound of the shower doesn't bother her. She can't sleep either. Thoughts are running through her head: "Maybe when she's gone I'll miss her..." She thinks how her marriage has changed since Iryna arrived. Pau can now boast at work of having a pretty girl at home. She remembers the day she had a migraine and the two of them managed on their own, even bringing her meals in bed. She imagines that if Iryna's there all the time he might not be such a typical pampered husband.

It's still three hours before they have to load up the luggage and say goodbye. She sees hosting Iryna as a chance to get back the much more exciting life she'd lost years ago. She thinks back, looking for reasons. "Pau was so proud of his virility and so disappointed when the tests they did showed how weak his semen was... no good even for test-tube fertilisation. Yes, no wonder Pau is so proud of a girl who should have been born in our home when it was the right time for both of us.

"Maybe next year, when Iryna's mother comes, we'll suggest that she lets her study in Catalonia. Then we'll gradually make her ours..."

She falls asleep and forgets all these thoughts.

Finally, at seven, the alarm goes off and Iryna knocks on the door of the couple's room, all ready. She has even put on some eye make-up. "Where did she get that? Probably from my make-up bag. Look how bold she's become, nosing through my things. All these girls are little Lolitas." She wants to have it out with her, but holds back. "Shhhh! Contain yourself. Not now." But Pau can't believe his eyes and bursts out:

"Iryna, how pretty you look! You remind me of Pietat when she was younger."

"Yes, everyone says so. Both blonde, with turned-up noses and the same eyes. Aren't we, Iryna?" Pietat wants confirmation.

Iryna smiles for a minute, remembering that in Dobrokiv they say she looks like Granny Rus, so far away near the Belarus border. When she was young, she was as pretty and strong-willed as Iryna is now. But a sudden giggle betrays her, as she thinks how sorry she would be look in the mirror and every day and see that dopey face of Pietat's... She turns round to conceal her laughter and starts moving her luggage downstairs.

At the airport, the people from the Association tell her she's carrying too much luggage and that she'll have to leave the least useful things behind. She replies:

"Everything's useful in Ukraine!" Then she has the idea of distributing packages among children who've only got a rucksack. There's no danger any of them will get lost. She'll remember to pick them up when she arrives in Kiev.

Not all the children are as forward-thinking as Iryna, who has kitted herself out for the whole winter. Some are just carrying cuddly toys, video games and the countless trinkets their Catalan parents have bought them during the summer. Some of them would give everything they're carrying to stay in Catalonia another day, like the group of orphans and children from broken homes. You can see it because they cling tightly to their host families. They hope the time to board the plane will never come. Others are nervous, looking for other Ukrainians so they can boast of what they've been doing all summer. Forgetting that they have to go, these children are smiling at every compatriot they see. But, when they get on the plane, most of them begin desperately seeking familiar faces: host parents, the parents' children, friends they have made. When they don't find them, or see them getting smaller and smaller, the windows of the airport waiting room reflect their desolation. Farewells are bound to be hard for those who have only the loneliness of an orphanage to look forward to. Iryna is happy and sad at the same time. She is happy to have made new friends and happy because she's finally going to see her family and tell them that maybe Vasyl will be able to go next year. And sad because for ten months she'll have no more home comforts or good food. As if that were not enough, she won't see Esperança, Miquel, Laia and Naiara, who have treated her so well.

"Whatever you do, take care of yourself and wrap up warm. Don't catch cold," were the last words of Pietat and Pau, relieved to be rid of her and already building up their strength for next year.

"We'll miss you so much. Write. Copy sentences you like from the books we've recommended and look through the notebook you've written," is Esperança's advice. "That way, you won't forget what you've learned.

If everything goes well, next year your brother Vasyl can come and stay with us. In January, we'll ask Twinning Ukraine-86 for him by name."

–*Duzhe dyakuyu, zavzhdy!* I'll always be thankful to you!" She can't contain a solitary sob. And she leaves them the box of tears and sighs she brought from Ukraine.

During the flight, some children cry. Others run about and shout. A whole plane full of children! The supervisor is a young girl who barely knows all the children from her own village. On the outward journey, she called a register at Kiev Airport, but by the time they got on the plane two children were missing, and she had to get off and look for them. She found them wandering round the shops. She only recognised them because they were standing there with their mouths open. During the summer she's met children from families who've had problems, but all that many. Iryna behaves well, but the boy behind her won't stop annoying her. He keeps shaking her seat, pulling her hair and saying disgusting things. She's had her hand up for two hours to tell someone, but no-one comes to help her. In the end, the hair-pulling hurts so much that she jumps up, turns to the culprit and kicks him in the leg. Grateful for the soles of her new shoes, she goes back to her seat with her nose in the air, turning to look at him as she sits down. She knows she looks pretty and she's pleased with herself, ready to enjoy what's left of the journey. She slides her fingers inside her bag and pulls out the photograph taken of the three friends on the Tibidabo tower: Laia, Naiara and Iryna in the middle. She brings it to her lips and kisses them. See you next year, dear friends!

***

MOSCOW, 28 APRIL 1986, 05.00 H (LOCAL TIME)

During the night, I throw up. I'm in my sixth month of pregnancy. I feel so terrible... I can't take any more. In my dreams, I hear Vasya calling me:

"Lyusya, Lyusya!"

Early in the morning I get up and tell my in-laws I'm going to Moscow.

"Where do you think you're going, child, in your condition?"

"Vasya needs me."

Vasya's father goes to the bank. He takes out all his savings and comes with me. During the journey, I have a waking dream: I see Vasya following me on foot. He takes the hand of a young girl, who smiles at him. She's in love. It's me! We're so young...! We have our whole lives ahead of us and we love each other. We really do love each other. We've only just married. We haven't even had time to realise we're happy... I don't know which towns we pass through, the names slide out of my head as soon as I read them: landscape, people, smells... There's nothing left in my head. I touch it.

It's already night-time when we arrive in Moscow. I'm trembling. I'm afraid that they won't want to tell us where they're keeping them. Vasya's father goes ahead of me and asks the first soldier we find. We're surprised when he answers us straightaway:

"Clinic number six. At Schukinskaya."

It's a special radiology clinic and they don't let you in without a pass. I beg. Vasya's father pulls me aside and presses some notes into the security guard's hand. That's how I get into the office of the head of the radiology section: Angelina Vasilievna Guskova. She asks me straight out:

"Have you got children?"

I can't tell her the truth! If she knows I'm pregnant she won't let me see him. I look at my stomach. Fortunately, I'm thin and I'm not showing at all.

"Yes, I have. Two: a boy and a girl."

"Well, if you've got two I don't think you're going to want any more. Now, listen: his nervous system is completely destroyed..."

She looks me in the eye. I don't answer. I think: "What can we do about that? He'll get a bit more nervous, that's all..."

"I'll let you see him, but if he starts crying, I'll throw you out straightaway. You mustn't hug or kiss. And it's better if you don't go too close to him. I'll give you half an hour," she says, leaving the room.

Is this woman completely heartless? One minute's probably gone already. I need to get organised. You can do a lot in half an hour. I'm not leaving without my Vasya. That's the vow I've made.

I go in and find my husband's workmates sitting on the bed playing cards. When they see me, they burst out laughing and call him:

"Vasya!"

"I don't believe it! You've even found me here. There's no hope for me!"

He says it as if the hospital were a bar and I were a jealous woman clipping his wings by stopping him going there with his friends.

"You don't fool me! Lots of us would like to have our wives with us," says one of his workmates.

Vasya looks so funny. They've given him pyjamas that are three sizes too small for him: the sleeves and the trousers are really short. But his face isn't swollen any more. What must they have injected him with?

We want to hug, but the male nurse separates us.

"You can't do that! You've got to keep a distance away."

The Pripyat firemen make jokes to hide their fear. They ask me:

"How are things at home?"

I tell them the town's been evacuated for a maximum of five days. With that, the nurse leaves. I want to be alone with Vasya. His workmates notice and each of them invents an excuse to go into the corridor. I throw my arms round his neck to hug and kiss him. He moves away.

"Don't come too close. Get a chair."

"But you're feeling OK, aren't you? It must all be non-sense!"

"Do you know where the explosion was? What do the papers say?"

"That it's all under control."

"I think someone did it on purpose. All the firemen think the same."

I open the suitcase and show him the change of clothes: the immaculately ironed shirt, the trousers...

"Your father's here. He's drawn money out. He wants to take you to another hospital. Get dressed."

A team of nurses comes in, supervising the men who had gone out. They take the things that were on the bedside table and separate them.

"Everyone should have their own room. You shouldn't be in the corridor. You mustn't go there. If you need something, just ask."

"Why?" I ask them.

"People mustn't be exposed. Radiation is passed on. You catch it. Each body reacts differently depending on the dose of radiation, so what one person can stand another might not."

"What about you?"

"It's our job and we're expecting some protection for our lungs... We've taken all the patients not exposed to radiation out of the hospital."

"What happened? Tell me."

"The roof of the power station, which was made of asphalt, was burning. We had to put it out."

"We did it without special protection."

"No-one warned us."

The room is left empty. I imagine my husband and the other firemen walking on the roof, putting out the flames with their feet. Vasya puts away the clothes laid out on the bed. I put them back into the case, get out some pyjamas and he puts them on. We start hearing banging on the wall. They're telling us something in Morse code: dot, dot, dash...

"Hey! Vasya, have you got a spare toothbrush?"

"Have you got a handkerchief?"

More than an hour's gone by and no-one is throwing me out. A nurse informs me very pleasantly that an elderly man wants to talk to me. It's Vasya's father.

"I've been to see some people I know in Moscow and they want you to stay at their house. Do you remember, Lyusya? Vasya liked working on the farm so much that we built him a house so he could stay with us. All this wouldn't have happened if he'd been a farmer. Damn power station! They could have built it in Moscow instead of Ukraine."

"But the army took him away. He did his national service in the Moscow fire brigade. And when he came back all he wanted to do was be a fireman... He wanted to earn money."

"And marry you. I told him: 'If you want to marry Lyusya, then marry her, but love her always,'."

"And he loves me a lot... He's a big softy. He loves you and he's so happy you're going to be grandparents."

I don't know if he's heard me. He gives me almost all the money he has left and he goes back home.

"No-one will take better care of him than you."

***

HIDDEN UNDER THE LEAVES is a muddy puddle, several inches deep. By the time Iryna notices, her little girl's face is all muddy and she's wet from head to foot. She puts her finger in her daughter's mouth and makes her spit out the mud. Lyuba is making horrible noises and crying pitifully.

"You could have drowned, child! Shhh, sweetheart, mummy's not going to leave you alone again for a second. Do you hear me?" She consoles Lyuba while cleaning her with a piece of gauze moistened on the surface of the puddle. Now the baby's safe, she has other concerns.

"Look at you! Just what we needed! You're going to catch pneumonia on me. I'll have to put you back in the clothes you were wearing before. Hey, Lyuba! Keep still and I'll change you."

It's a cold day and the air's freezing. She wouldn't be surprised if it snowed – it's happened before at this time of year. She thinks that if her father Vasyl was there he'd give her a good hiding for what she's done and for travelling with her daughter in these conditions.

"How pleased Grandad was with you, Lyuba! Do you remember how he used to lift you up in the air? He'd come in, tired of working in Kiev, ready for the weekend... and his face would change as soon as he saw you, little one!"

But it isn't her father behind the bushes. There's a pair of pointed ears and a long nose sniffing the rucksack. Camouflaged, it stealthily awaits its moment.

"Oh! "You're frozen and shivering. I can't undress you in this cold. I'll have to make a fire."

She's pink all around her eyes and there are tears on her purple cheeks.

She looks for the cigarette lighter in her bag, reminding her of when she used to smoke with Willy. She fumbles inside with one hand while holding the little girl tightly under the other arm. She's not going to let Lyuba escape again. She can only crawl, but she's very quick. She searches through everything but she can't find it. She pulls the blanket and turns it upside down. The nearest thing that comes out is a cigarette packet. She opens it and there's something inside: a couple of cigarettes and the lighter.

With the little girl still under her arm, she starts collecting dry leaves, piling them up with some twigs and a bigger branch. She takes the cigarettes out of the packet and tears it up, placing the pieces under the leaves. She flicks the lighter. Yes, a flame comes out. It hasn't taken long to make a bonfire that's really warm. Facing the fire, she sits Lyuba in her lap. She takes the baby's clothes off, making sure there are no leeches attached to her. When she was little one got on her arm once. She was lucky her father smoked then and could use his cigarette to get it off. She remembers how he half closed his hand to blow smoke on to the creature until it released its sucker. She can still feel the disgust, the pain and the anguish. But there's nothing there, Lyuba's skin is perfectly clear. And thanks to the improvised plastic pants the water hasn't got into the cloth nappy, which is dry. She wraps the little girl in the blanket. With a couple of sticks, she improvises a drying rack for the sleepsuit. It starts giving off steam straightaway. It's made of material that doesn't absorb much water and dries easily.

The fire does its work. And, leaning back on the stump of an oak near the fire, Iryna lifts her jumper and allows the little girl to feed, sucking from her. She puts the bottle of milk to her own lips and, as the little girl drains her, she tops up her courage.

By the time the baby lifts her head, the sleepsuit is quite dry and one sleeve is scorched.

"Oh! Uncle Vasyl's sleepsuit!" says Iryna, regretfully. "But that doesn't matter. You'll be dry!"

Once Lyuba's dressed, Iryna tries to strap her in again, but she won't have it. The baby complains, bending her body into an awkward shape.

"Please, Lyuba, you'll drive me mad!"

The two cigarettes are still in front of her, tempting her, but she's in such a state her hands are shaking. She takes one and lights it from the remaining embers. The image of her uncle struggling to hold one between his lips makes her less sure. Lyuba wants to take the cigarette from her and, as she moves her away, it falls on to a bush.

"There's already enough poison in Ukraine!" she shouts, throwing the plant and the cigarette on to the fire. It is consumed by perfumed flames.

Lyuba moans again and Iryna tells her off:

"Hey! Not again! You've done quite enough crawling!"

She throws the other cigarette on the fire, breathes in the smell of the plant and distracts the baby, asking her softly:

"Who's the prettiest little girl in the world?" Lyuba is. Lyyuuuubbbaaa! Ah! I know what you want to do. You want to walk. Come on then, we'll walk. But first we'll put the fire out."

She throws a few handfuls of earth on to the embers and spreads them around with a stick. Lyuba imitates her but she wants to suck her fingers to see what that black earth tastes like. Her mother brushes off the mud and distracts her by marching her round to the sound of a train whistling in the distance. Except that it isn't a train, and it's not whistling, it's howling. It is the sound of wolves just waiting for another voice to guide them. She senses something, turns and sees two sharp bright points behind the branches of the undergrowth.

"Bastard!" The abuse is heartfelt.

She raises the stick, challenging the animal, and runs towards it, shouting. The surprised wolf runs off with its tail between its legs. This time it will have nothing to get its teeth into.

Iryna snatches everything up, starts the scooter and leaves the forest behind. Pairs of green circles begin to shine out from behind the darkened trees around the harvested fields, and the fluting "too-it" of the scops owl echoes rhythmically along the route. They reach Novohrad at seven in the evening. It's getting dark and she's exhausted. The freezing air smells of woodsmoke – meat and garlic roasting on the barbecue. There's a shop open beside the road. She chains the Vespa to a tree and goes in with the little girl in her arms and her rucksack on her back. There's an elderly couple behind the counter. The shelves are rather chaotic. There are no nappies, but there are large sanitary towels. She buys a couple of bags of them for the little girl and some paper handkerchiefs. When she's paid, she asks.

"Do you know somewhere we could spend the night?" Iryna's eyes are struggling to stay open. Her voice sounds like a prayer. She feels as if she's sleepwalking.

***

AUTUMN 2003, WINTER AND SPRING 2004

Iryna's arrival in Ukraine stirs up all kinds of contradictory emotions: joy and sadness, anger and tenderness. She's back with her family and friends. She swears to her brother that next year he'll be going with her. She gives out presents and notices that some people envy everything she's experienced and everything she shows off to them. She goes shopping at the market and can't help comparing it with the one in Rouralba. In Dobrokiv there are shortages of everything except flies, beetles and rubbish... She knows there are big supermarkets in the capital, but why go to Kiev if you haven't got hryvnias. From now on, she'll be a foreigner in her own country: a heroine frantically waiting for another life where she can fly high instead of dragging herself along.

In November, first Pietat and then Esperança receive news of what's going on in Ukraine. Although the letters are full of mistakes and strange constructions, they're quite understandable. On Esperança's envelope, in a good hand in thick felt tip, she reads:

"There's no better teacher than Esperança
Josep Ma de Sagarra 123
Rouralba – Catalonia".

8 November 2003

Hi Esperança and Miquel, Laia and Naiara: How are you, how things in Catlonya?

I very good as usual, but now not so much because don't see you and Rovelló (I like a lot) every day.

My family said very, very thanks to you and the people who help me. And they said people like you needed in world. Lots of kisses for you and your husband and girls.

Now a little study book you showed me to read and start teach brother who very happy because I tell him lots of good things for him of you.

My Ykpaiha (Ukraine) is very bad and very little things because of thief of whole country.

Everything I know, I know thanks to you, Esperança. In Russian, Esperança spell Hagie and pronounce Nadiya. Next letter, I'll put Hagie on envelope because you are hope for my brother and everyone at home.

Many, many, many kisses, wishes and hugs,

Iryna

The next page is a series of cartoon drawings of Esperança, Iryna, Naiara and Laia working and studying. There are hearts drawn all around them.

Esperança writes back straightaway. She tells Iryna her letter has made them very happy and that they've read it to all their friends. She explains that there are thieves in all governments and that the most important thing is to be healthy, to get on with things and not to be subject to Russia. She recommends Iryna should study and should also look at the dictionary when she has to write again because she was writing Catalan better in the summer. She says goodbye with hugs for all the family because, even though she hasn't met them, she is already beginning to love them. Miquel also signs the letter. The two sisters add another page talking about friends. They decorate it.

Today, Pietat and Esperança have met at the market, rummaging through a pile of anoraks. Both of them are looking for medium size and a bright colour.

"Hey, Pietat, have you heard anything from Ukraine?"

"Yes, last month. And I could understand it all."

"We did too. Did you know Miquel and the girls and I have decided to take the boy next year? When you hear from the Association, you'll tell us when's the right time, won't you?"

Pietat says she will and that now Esperança will see how difficult the first days are. As they seem to be on good terms, she jokes:

"Good thing she had a good teacher. I hope you'll still want to teach her next year."

"Of course I will!" says Esperança. "I'll do lessons in the morning for brother and sister together."

Suddenly, they see an anorak they like. One holds it by one sleeve and the other pulls it by the other.

"Do you want it for Laia or Naiara?"

"No, they've got coats. I was thinking it could be for Iryna."

"What are you talking about? I buy Iryna's clothes. You'll have the boy."

"Yes, I thought I'd find a tracksuit or some warm clothes for him, but as I saw this bargain. It'll soon be Christmas and I wanted to send them a parcel."

"I'll tell you what to do so it doesn't cost so much. There are coaches that go from Barcelona that accept parcels. You need to know when they're going. I'll tell you."

"If you don't mind, I'll bring what I buy to your place and you can put them together. You can let me know what it costs. I've got so much work with marking that wrapping it all up and taking it to Barcelona would be a lot of trouble."

"Yes. You need to know what's going on. If you become a friend of the Association and sell lots of Christmas raffle tickets you might not have to pay so much for the flight. The Association pays for a single air ticket per family and that's only the first year. So next year I'll have to buy the tickets for the mother and the girl and you'll have to take care of the boy's flight."

"There's no choice, really! But perhaps if you bring me books of tickets, the children at school will help me to sell them. The pupils ought to know about the tragedy that's happening in that country. They need to learn to show solidarity."

Pietat complains about the organisation because they still haven't found a job for the mother, but she's completely forgotten all the problems she had with Iryna. "Perhaps she's putting herself in the girl's shoes," thinks

Esperança but she says nothing, and reminds Pietat that it's still seven months before they come and if no-one finds work for the mother she could help her and...

"Perhaps she could also do some hours at my friends' houses so she could earn a bit. That would be really good for her!" Esperança chatters on, sounding concerned.

Since they got to know Iryna, both families find what's going on in Ukraine is now relevant to them. They phone each other asking if there's been news. Even Miquel, who never looks at the weather forecast, looks out for any bad weather there. So many degrees below zero! Down to 30 or even more! It seems that the hanging branches of the Ukrainian silver birch trees have brought sweetness into their hearts, melting ice only thawed by loving Iryna and her family.

The children in Esperança's class have made a mural of everything their teacher has told them. They begin to relate the world of wellbeing in which they live with another of danger and contamination. They've explained so well to their parents and neighbours who is going to benefit from the Association's raffle tickets, that they've sold them by the bookful. They'll be looking forward to meeting their new friends in June.

The older ones at the school have found a game that gives them an idea: it's called S.T.A.L.K.E.R.: Shadow of Chernobyl and many of the pictures that appear in it show real places. According to the school headteacher, who set up the computer room and knows a lot about these things, it's made in Ukraine.

"What? In Ukraine? They're all so poor there! Do you really think they've got that technology? Can't you see it's in English?" someone contradicts him, trying to be clever.

"What do you mean by that? We've got all the programs in English here too. In case you don't know, the first computer in the world was created by a certain Sergey Lebedev."

In the spring, for Iryna's and Vasyl's birthdays – because they're now 12 and 13 – the excited, motivated, generous children send them a nice card: a drawing with each of them in it, as if it were a group photo and, behind them, a collection of sentences each of them has written, putting all their feeling and imagination into it.

The day Rouralba school receives the first letter from Ukraine there is a big fuss and half the town knows about it. It's the end of April and the letter's postmarked mid-March.

When the children in Esperança's class notice the date, they say:

"Letters from Ukraine take a long time to get here, don't they?"

In the envelope, Iryna has put a cutting from a newspaper in Spanish talking about the terrorist attack in Madrid on 11 March.

> "The terrorist attacks were carried out on 11 March 2004 on four local trains in Madrid by a local Islamist cell trying to emulate the actions of Al-Qaeda. 191 people have died and more than 1,700 were hurt [...]"

First of all, Iryna asks if anyone from Rouralba has been hurt. Then she asks what emulate and other words she has underlined mean. She explains that she got the newspaper cutting from the charity in Dobrokiv and that Natasha, the supervisor who knows Spanish, couldn't explain it very well.

She urges the pupils to protest – to do the same as they plan to do at her school in the autumn: take part in an orange march to call for things to change...

The children in Esperança's class answer that the orange march seems like a good idea and they explain that many of them went to a demonstration in Barcelona not long after the attack and they made a lot of noise because they banged pots with kitchen tools as if they were drums. Many of them bring in cuttings of the latest news items and they select a few of them to send:

> "Spanish soldiers leave the Al-Andalus base heading for Iraq [...]. As was announced recently, all the political parties are in favour of withdrawal except for the Popular Party..."

All the letters and cuttings are kept in an envelope and sent to Ukraine, together with the teacher's letter:

Rouralba, 29 May 2004.

Dear Iryna's family,

Sorry for taking so long to answer you. As you can see, things are difficult here too. Don't worry. Thankfully nothing happened to us, although some pupils in Laia's year were on a trip to Madrid to go to the Prado Museum and they'd caught the train early in the morning.

*Emulate is a word journalists use a lot. In this context, it means to imitate the evil behaviour of the well-known Al-Qaeda group when they attacked the Twin Towers. The whole country is very worried and hoping the new prime minister will be more sensible. We'll see how all this ends, but we're sending you cuttings from the newspapers in Catalonia.

Meanwhile, we continue to work for justice and peace in the world and we're really looking forward to your arrival.

Many good wishes for the whole country of Ukraine, and for you, your brother and your family a very big kiss.

See you soon! Less than a month to go now!

Esperança

In a corner of the classroom is the box Iryna brought. The papers written in Cyrillic script take on the voices of the characters in the photographs, and this litany spreads through the streets of Rouralba.

Chapter 7

MOSCOW, 29 APRIL 1986, 08.00 H (LOCAL TIME)

They let me cook with their kitchen things. I take food for Vasya and the five other firemen who were on duty with him on the day of the explosion: Vaschuk, Kibenok, Titenok, Pravik and Tischura. There's nothing at the hospital. I go to buy them toothpaste, soap, flannels...

Every day when I come in, the people in the house where I'm staying ask me:

"How is he? How are they all? Will they live? And what about you? Are you feeling OK?"

It's obvious it's not me they're worried about. I get up one morning and find they're throwing me out, three days after doing me the favour of taking me in. Wilder and wilder rumours are circulating. They know they're at risk.

I go back to the hospital, just as I've done every day. When I go in, they give me a medical overall, as if I were Vasya's personal nurse. But every night at about nine they tell me:

"Come on! It's time to go and rest."

If they let me stay, I wouldn't move from there.

***

JUNE 2004

Just as they had promised, Esperança and Miquel signed the agreement with the Ukraine-86 Twinning Association to take Vasyl. They put their names down and paid his air fare back in January.

Pietat and Pau have asked for Iryna again, as well as her mother, Olena, provided the Association finds her something to do. Pietat repeats that this way she'll earn some money...

"They need it so much! If not, the best thing would be for her to go back to her own country as soon as Iryna has recovered from the operation," she insists.

"That's impossible. You know the tickets come with an arrival and departure date and she's entered on the documents as accompanying her daughter as a tourist. She can't go back early or work legally. If you find her a job, we don't want to know about it. It will put us in an awkward position. She can't have a contract. Of course, she'd make a bit of money and it would be good for her, but you mustn't tell the Association."

People who know them are surprised that, after complaining so much the previous year, they have now promised to host two people. Pau explains that her relationship with Iryna improved a lot after she had Catalan lessons and could hold a conversation. They are also sure Iryna's operation will be an easy one:

"If all goes well, they'll operate on the second of July and she'll be at home by the fourth."

There's something that bothers them, though.

"What's Iryna's mother going to do for two months without working, here in Rouralba? Because we're going to have to entertain this woman!"

110

"She can clean and sew... She'd better not start thinking we're going to take her to the attractions and the cinema! And we're not going out for a pizza on Sundays... it costs a lot more for four than two!"

***

Today, as she thinks back to how long the year has seemed and how much she's been wishing she was here, Iryna can't believe she's back in Catalonia, and that she's come in the same plane with Mum and Vasyl.

Pietat and Pau pick up Iryna and her mother in their car from Barcelona Airport. But because it's the first time he's been, and the rules have to be followed, the Association takes Vasyl by coach to Collença, where his new hosts will be waiting for him.

Iryna wants to relive her own first arrival and in the car she keeps begging:

"Come on, Pau, why can't we go to Collença? He must be feeling so nervous...!"

"For goodness' sake! You've been together all the way here, haven't you?

"Yes, but he's not... You don't know how shy Vasyl is... The faces he makes!"

"Poor thing, what kind of face do you want him to make? Like you, filleta!" says Pietat.

As she insists, Pau begins to feel a twinge of curiosity. He conceals it, asking:

"Do we really need to?"

"Go on, Pau! It'll be easy. Instead of going straight to Rouralba, we can go there first. OK?"

"All right," says Pau.

In half an hour they're in Collença. Just like last year, in the same car parks, the new Ukrainian children are on one side and the host parents on the other, with their ears pricked to hear the name of the child they are hosting over the public address system. There is a flurry of suitcases and hugs. When the name "Vasyl Piskun" is shouted, they realise that only Esperança has come to pick him up.

"Where's that woman's a husband?" Pietat is surprised. "How come she's come on her own? It's a good thing we're here..."

It's impossible to miss the teacher, who's holding a poster with a heart painted entirely in glitter. Inside it is Vasyl's name, correctly written, embraced by the names of Laia, Naiara, Miquel and Esperança.

"How lovely, Esperança! What great ideas you have!" they congratulate her.

"The girls painted it before they went to England," says Esperança. Iryna is taken aback: "That wasn't the welcome I got!"

"What about Miquel? Why hasn't he come?"

"Miquel won't be back for a few days. He's working in Madrid, at the international motor show, and the girls have gone to do an English course in London. They'll be back at the end of July."

Several people take pictures of the poster. The people from the Association give them all the paperwork. Vasyl and his bag move forwards. He looks lost in the middle of the asphalt, with his head bowed and his cheeks red. Esperança leaves the poster in Iryna's hands and runs up to give him a hug. The boy lets her do it, as if he were some kind of doll she had just bought. Iryna keeps taking pictures of them with Pietat's mobile, while she looks on fearfully, in case she breaks it, forgetting that last year it was Iryna who taught her to put phone numbers in and pick a ringtone for incoming calls.

"Hey, Vasyl, this lady is Esperança, who's your host. Introduce yourself in Catalan."

And his sister reminds him of the phrases they've been practising for months.

"Hello. Pleased to meet you. My name is Vasyl. *Duzhe pryyemno, mene zvaty Vasyl*" he repeats in Ukrainian in case they haven't understood, as if Catalan were a strange language to all of them.

"You pronounce your Catalan very well, Vasyl. *Duzhe pryyemno, mene zvaty* Esperança." How am I doing?

"Very well!" Iryna can't help laughing at Esperança's Catalan accent.

Finally, people start to drift away, each of them with the boy or girl they are hosting; each with their own story. Pietat, Pau, Iryna and Olena kiss Vasyl goodbye and disappear.

It's gone midnight by the time Vasyl and Esperança are alone beside the car. Esperança begins with a joke: she gives him the car keys and asks him to drive, in sign language, as in Catalan the only thing he seems to know how to say is "What's your name?". He looks very serious, moves towards the driver's door and opens it but does not dare to sit down. He looks at her as if to say: "I'm only 13. How am I supposed to have a licence?" And, struck by his innocence, she stops teasing him and begins clowning instead:

"Ah, I had no idea! Vasyl can't drive?"

He gets the joke and laughs, walks round the car and gets into the front passenger seat.

On the way to Rouralba, Esperança keeps looking at him and telling him things. Even though the boy doesn't understand her, she thinks he needs to get used to the sound of Catalan. Esperança is used to dealing with girls, but she suddenly realises she has a very different kind of character alongside her. She sees a boy with attractive features: a broad forehead, a straight nose, fleshy lips and greeny-blue eyes so deep and so sweet that they make an immediate impression. He is very similar to Iryna but he already has a masculinity that promises to make him easy for girls to fall in love with. It is the same beauty and grace that will very soon make his sister a lovely young woman.

Rovelló welcomes them with howls that sound as if he's trying to talk. He sniffs the newcomer and jumps up, perhaps in a playful attempt to show him who's strongest. The kitchen clock is showing one in the morning when Vasyl sits down to a large pizza. He finishes it in four bites and looks as if he wants more. The dog is lying under the table, waiting for some crumbs to fall as some kind of compensation for having spent half the day in the sun. Suddenly, he lifts his head and can't believe his eyes: the plate is sparkling clean – not even a piece of crust. It's as empty as his bowl. He turns his head left and right, cocks his ears and, expressing his disappointment with a long bark, treads on Esperança's toes. She feels she has to answer both of them:

"There's no more! I'll make more tomorrow. Would you like some milk?"

Vasyl sniffs the milk carton and says Ni, turning his nose up and twisting his head away. Of course, fresh milk at his home must be very different from the sterilised stuff we drink!

"Would you like some fruit?" Esperança offers, giving him a basket of bananas, peaches and apples.

"*Tak! Yabluko.* Yes, an apple," he answers, taking a green one and biting into it.

It's a big house. Vasyl is going to sleep on the top floor and Esperança in the double bed in the bottom bedroom. Esperança takes the suitcase intending to carry it upstairs, but he takes it from her, looking as if he doesn't want her to carry too much weight. In front of them runs Rovelló, who stops every two steps to see if they are following. She shows him the bed, the lights, the toilet and the remote control in case he wants to switch on the portable television. His eyes widen in surprise: a shower, bath and toilet just for him! And television! Esperança moves towards him and kisses him goodnight. He gives her half a hug. Rovelló watches them and waits.

"Good night, Vasyl!"

"*Na dobranich,* Speransa."

Alone now in the large, well-lit room, he opens the wardrobe to put away his only jacket, which hangs there ridiculously. The two changes of clothes he has brought rattle around in the bottom of a large drawer in the dressing table. He goes to the bathroom and the toilet things he leaves there look like rubble forgotten by a builder. He looks in the mirror and his faded clothes contrast with the red bathrobe Esperança has left ready for him. When he sits on the bed, he is filled with a strange feeling of shame. He feels as stiff as a piece of furniture in that room and he can't manage to lie down to sleep. He's been looking forward so much to arriving and now he regrets having come. He wants to phone his father and tell him: "I should have stayed to help you mow the grass for the cow to eat in the winter. I'll never leave Ukraine again! Never again!" He also misses his dogs, smaller than this Pyrenean mountain dog, who said goodnight to him with a long bark. But now Rovelló comes back to see him, sniffing and rubbing round him, grumbling, with his eyes cast down and eyebrows raised. The dog looks so sad Vasyl can't help passing his hand over his muzzle. He remembers his sister's words: "Don't worry, they're good people."

The dog lies down on the rug at the foot of Vasyl's bed and, when he's sure the boy can be trusted, he turns over on his back with his paws in the air. He doesn't go down to see his mistress until the morning.

It's already midday when Esperança comes to wake him up. She sees Vasyl has slept on top of the bedspread and has pulled it one side to cover himself, as if she hadn't put any sheets on. "Perhaps they don't know how we get into bed here," thinks Esperança.

"Like this, Vasyl!"

She shows him how to get into bed in Catalonia. The boy hangs his head, as if to say "I'm sorry. I didn't know. What I wanted was to wake up alone and leave it the way I found it." He looks shyly at her and finds her eyes looking back at him, warm and trusting. Esperança smiles and he smiles back. Feeling more relaxed and keen to obey her request to get up quickly, he goes down to the kitchen in his underpants... Once he's dressed, he watches for a while as Esperança makes a good sofregit by lightly frying onion, tomato and sausage. Then he wanders round the living room and now he's walking into the garage with a remote control, trying to work out what it's for. They haven't got one at home, although he knows they turn on televisions and videos. But the one he's holding is no use for any of those things. He's concerned: it doesn't turn on the washing machine or the tumble dryer or the vacuum cleaner. What on earth is it for? He wants to ask Esperança, when she finds him with a Phillips screwdriver trying to look and see if its batteries have gone.

"*Shho ce?* What's this?"

"Thank you. You wanted to fix it, did you? Thank you!" she tells him frankly and naturally.

Esperança is realising what it must be like to be in another world. She takes his hand and pulls him towards the window. She makes him press the bottom button of the control and... look at that! The shutter, which she had left up yesterday, comes down, leaving the room dark.

They have brunch: macaroni and chicken. What full plates! And for dessert a couple of chocolate and vanilla ice-creams. Once they're full, he starts repeating:

"*Ira, mam, kudy?*"

"They're at Pietat's house. We'll go and see them later. We'll wait a bit, they'll be having lunch now."

And she makes signs to set his mind at rest, showing that, in the garage, there's a bicycle for him and one for her. They ride through the nearby streets and she points out where his sister and mother are living from a distance. At that moment, Iryna comes out on to the balcony, notices them and shouts:

"Vasyl! Vasyl!"

Behind her comes Pietat, shooing her in. They must be having lunch. In the middle of the afternoon, Iryna phones and asks if Vasyl can come so they can talk and he can get to know her host family a bit. Esperança accompanies Vasyl to Pietat and Pau's door.

"Here he is!"

Esperança doesn't want to get in the way and, with the excuse that she has work to do, she leaves. But within half an hour, Vasyl is back in Esperança's house.

"Are you here already? That was a quick visit!" she says out loud, trusting that if she keeps talking to him, he'll learn the language.

The next day, at ten in the morning, as they'd arranged, Iryna arrives for her lesson and, more than anything, to talk to her brother. From time to time she has to remind them: "Come on you two! In Catalan!" The teacher sees Iryna has a good memory and notices that Vasyl doesn't find things so easy. Instead of making an effort to understand Esperança, he relies on Iryna saying things to him in Ukrainian. At about midday, Pietat and Pau appear with Olena to pick Iryna up. The boy wants to show his mother his room and the whole house. Every time Olena goes into a room she admires it, saying:

"*Krasyva!*" And, finally: "*Dyakuyu, Dyakuyu, duzhe Dyakuyu...!*

"Mum says thank you very much!" And she says you have a very nice house," Iryna translates.

"Stay for lunch!" insists Esperança.

Between all of them they set the table. Meanwhile, Esperança, who has bought fresh fish, makes a large paella. As neither Olena nor Vasyl have ever seen whole langoustine, complete with claws and tail, on a plate, they push them to one side until Pau says:

"If you don't want those, I'll have them!"

But, Esperança takes Vasyl's plate, breaks the animal's shell and shows him the flesh.

"Try it, Vasyl!"

The boy breathes deeply and swallows it. Iryna helps her mother, who also wants to try hers.

"Do you like it?"

"*Tak*," they nod, without any great conviction.

First, they turn up their noses, as if the fishy smell offends them, but then, when they see everyone is chewing the claws, they join in. At about four they say goodbye, because tomorrow is the day when the tests on Iryna's heart are to be repeated at the hospital, and they've got things to do. Vasyl accompanies them on his bike, showing off his skills. He jumps up pavements and does wheelies in the middle of the road. These things horrify Pietat, who phones Esperança as soon as she gets in:

"He's a street child! I'd never let the girl have a bike. Rouralba isn't Dobrokiv, where there's no traffic."

Esperança says she's already shown Vasyl the right way to ride along a one-way street and told him he has to look out for cars. She thanks her for telling her about the tricks he was doing and adds:

"I'll make it quite clear to him that he can only do that in the park, away from people."

"Please yourself. I wouldn't want those responsibilities. If something dreadful happens it's be you who has to sort it out!"

As if Esperança was irresponsible! Pietat just wants to stop him riding the bike so his sister won't ask for one. She's got a new bike and these kids don't take care of anything, she'll be thinking. As Esperança realises what Pietat is up to, she manages to end the conversation without sounding offended:

"I hope everything goes well at the hospital! We'll phone you tomorrow!"

***

MOSCOW, 30 APRIL 1986, 0.25 H (LOCAL TIME)

I don't know where I'll be able to spend the night. I go down the stairs into the metro station. In a corner, a poor woman is beginning to cover himself with cardboard. I approach her. She's a good woman and she makes room for me. I drink from her bottle of vodka and cover myself. I thank her from the bottom of my heart. The nights are still cold and we sleep huddled together. She has a trolley with a bit of food and the essential kitchen items: a plate, a cup and even a little stove. She makes me a cup of tea and it's good. I warm myself, we get by with a couple of words and we sleep for a few hours. Meanwhile, the ingredients of the soup boil. As soon as I can, I wake myself with water from a drinking fountain, but I've got no soap and nowhere to get changed.

It's mid-morning by the time I arrive, with the soup in a bottle wrapped in newspaper. Vasya smells me and wrinkles his nose:

"Ugh! Were you out on the town last night?"

"Yes, I met an old friend."

"I like to see you having fun. You should listen to music... they say it's good for pregnant women."

"Yes, yes," I agree.

I calm him and his voice weakens. He drops off to sleep with his mouth open, his breath whistling like a far-off train coming towards us.

One of the carers, quite an old lady, prepares me:

"Some diseases have no cure... You should sit close to him and stroke his hand."

Every day they're becoming more aware that I can't get by without him.

I sleep with the rubbish collector for two more nights, keeping my money well hidden. I only buy two pieces of underwear because, although I could do some washing, I don't know where I can hang it to dry. I can't spend any more... we need it to get home when they let Vasya out of hospital.

Today it seems the doctors have found out that I haven't got anywhere to sleep and they've invited me to stay at the hotel where the health staff are living. I'm happy. But what am I going to do? There's no kitchen. How am I going to make them the soup and the apple juice? I'll have to manage with a little alcohol stove. Perhaps I can use the washbasin as a sink to wash the dishes and the clothes...

I bring a glass to his lips. Oh God! He can't swallow a drop of water. How stupid I am! There's no point in cooking any more. His stomach has stopped digesting food.

***

JUNE 2004

Today, Iryna won't come to her class as she's at the hospital. Esperança has plans to entertain Vasyl. She wants to take him to the beach. They have breakfast late, while she tells him what they're going to do. He listens and seems to understand. But suddenly he gets up and goes to the garage to get the bicycle.

"No! Not today. Not the bicycle. Go upstairs and get your swimming trunks," she shouts, pointing at the stairs and showing him her bikini. Vasyl thinks that perhaps he's being punished. He goes upstairs and stands on the landing.

"Go on, get your swimming trunks!"

But the boy must think the bikini is her underwear and he looks at her as if to say "Hey, I haven't touched anything of yours."

"*Kudy, kudy?*" he repeats several times, holding on to the railing at the top of the stairs. He doesn't look as if he's going to move.

"Kudy, kudy?" repeats Esperança, trying to understand what he wants to tell her and continuing to get ready to go to the beach until it occurs to her to turn the computer on and look for the word in a bilingual dictionary. When he hears the music the computer makes, Vasyl comes down and helps her write it properly. That's it! It means "where".

"Ah, you want to know where we're going. Well, we're going swimming," she tells him, miming strokes and showing him the bikini, which she's now put on. Then, Vasyl looks in his bag and takes out some shorts. "Well, perhaps they swim in those," thinks Esperança.

"Go on, put them on, then!"

In the car, they say the important words as they pass the things they refer to: roundabout, motorway, tunnel, which is the same in Ukrainian... When they reach the coast at Mataró, he turns his head and watches the sea all the way to El Masnou, which is where Esperança's sister and their mother Griselda live.

"Dnieper?"

"It's not a river, it's the sea!"

"*Voda!* Look at all that water!"

First they go to Esperança's sister's house. She's there with her son Arnau and she invites them to lunch. Arnau is interested in showing him computer games and explaining how to play. Every time Vasyl doesn't understand in Catalan, Arnau tells him again in Spanish.

"This boy doesn't understand Spanish, he's Ukrainian! You know what, Arnau? We Catalans are so used to everyone here understanding Spanish that we use it to speak to all foreigners."

"Of course, you should teach him Spanish. It'll be more useful for him."

Esperança cuts her sister off. "If he wants something useful, English will be better!"

After a good lunch they play a car racing game on the console and, once their food has gone down, they head for the beach. Vasyl, who has never seen so much blue, spreads his arms. There's plenty of sand and he runs across it in search of the water. A wave briefly stops him but Arnau dives straight in and Vasyl eventually does the same. A temporary madness takes hold of him: he dives in, swims four strokes, comes out again and dives back into the water. He's content and having fun, but always looking to see if Esperança is watching him. He doesn't need a towel and seems tireless – until his exhausted body flops on to the sand.

On the way back to Rouralba, once they're through Parpers tunnel, the sun is setting over Collença and, away in the distance, misty and grey, they see the protruding silhouette of Montserrat.

"Montserrat is a very beautiful mountain, but the one nearest to us is called Montseny."

"Montseny?"

"Good. You've got a good ear. You're getting there, bit by bit..."

"You're getting there bit by bit," repeats Vasyl. Just then, they are shaken into full alertness by an oncoming car.

There are traffic jams on the main road and they take a shortcut. At the exit, awaiting clients, is an attractive blonde girl in a very short skirt. Basil looks at her disapprovingly. He thinks of Nadiya, a neighbour from Dobrokiv, who had a very bad time... Esperança mutters sorrowfully as she sees a car in the reeds of the dried-up river bed they have just passed. There's another girl, who must be at the same game.

"My goodness, what a shame!" she repeats, continuing to drive along the stony track. It ends in a sharp left turn but she's distracted and the car goes into a skid.

"*Corba a l'esquerra!* Left-hand bend!" she shouts. "This is a *corba.*"

Vasyl looks hard at her and adds.

"*Kurva. V Ukrayini bahato kurv.*"

Esperança thinks that *bahato* means bend. It's several days before she realises that *bahato* means "many". She will have to say the word "*corba*" several more times when she goes round a bend, with Vasyl saying "*ni*" and making faces, before she realises that, in Ukraine, the similar sounding word *kurva* is a word often used to mean prostitute.

When they get home, the boy drags her to the telephone:

"Yes, now I'll phone Pietat. Let's see how Iryna is getting on."

He's impatient to see how his sister is.

"How did it go?"

"Well, we were back by lunchtime. Iryna phoned you, but you weren't there. It seems that the heart murmur they found last year has got a lot better and now they think there's no need to operate."

"That's great! It's sorted itself out!"

"*Vse dobre?*" Vasyl asks.

"Yes, very well!" Esperança tells him.

He takes an instant liking to these two words and from now on he'll say them at every opportunity.

"Yes, all that fuss for nothing. And now I've got the mother here with her feet under the table. I don't know what I'm going to do with her. She's clinging to Iryna all day speaking Ukrainian."

"But Iryna must tell you what they're saying, surely."

"Iryna's tired of translating. Often, I think she just summarises or invents things, because they're laughing all the time. It's as if Iryna's a baby again, with her mother here. When they watch television, she even rests her head on her lap..."

"Can I speak to them?"

"No, they're in the courtyard, watering the plants. From the squealing I can hear, they must be splashing each other. They'll be coming in soaked and leaving footmarks all over the tiles."

"Tomorrow we're going to Montseny and we're going to have a swim in the pools in the River Tordera. If you like, we'll take Iryna and that way you'll be able to have a walk round Rouralba with her mother. Maybe she could stand in for someone who's on holiday..."

"Yes, maybe. She can go with you and we'll ask the cleaning companies, the bars and so on... we'll see if we have any luck."

When Pietat tells Iryna what she has planned with Esperança, the girl happily translates it all for her mother, and tells her:

"I'll look carefully to see which way we go and, if Pietat wants to, on Sunday, we can go back there with you, Mum and Pau."

Because what she most wants is for her mother to have a holiday too, even if it's the only time in her life she gets one.

In the end, Pietat has found work for Olena on a cattle farm. She has to leave early in the morning walking along paths leading out behind the town. It must be ten kilometres away, but she's used to walking. There she works all day and has lunch, not coming home until the evening.

In the morning the lessons continue: today it's the letter b. Brother and sister have drawn a bathtub and Iryna reads what she's written:

"Mum is very happy and, with the euros she earns, we'll put in running water at home. Now the water we drink is from the well and it isn't safe enough. We'll have a tap in the kitchen and perhaps a shower and a bath."

"When you come to Ukraine, Esperança, you'll be able to have a bath. I'll put it in for you," adds Vasyl, who is now beginning to make himself understood. His sister assures her he knows how to connect pipes and fit taps.

"That's great! I'd really like to meet your father and your grandparents. Perhaps in a few years I'll come."

Before they leave, Iryna talks to Vasyl alone for quite a time. As soon as she's gone, he asks Esperança if he can phone Ukraine, managing to make her understand that, at Pietat's house, neither his mother nor his sister has been allowed to talk to him.

"Of course you can phone, Vasyl! Tell your father you're both well and send him my best wishes."

As they haven't got any kind of phone at home, he phones the neighbours, who tell him his father's not at home and that he's gone to see the grandparents in the north, near Belarus, and he'll be away almost a week, but not to worry because while he's away they're looking after the animals and watering the allotment. What no-one knows is that one side of his face has been bothering him for some days, or that yesterday he could hardly open his mouth or that, when he forced it so he could eat a little, so much blood came out that it frightened him. Or that he only managed to stop the bleeding with alcohol. Or that, hiding the pain, he went to ask the neighbours for a favour and then hitch-hiked along the main road to Kiev to go to hospital.

Today is Monday and Iryna should have come for her lesson half an hour ago. Esperança phones Pietat. The girl answers and says she can't come out because Pietat's gone to the market and has left her shut in. "How strange!" thinks Esperança. Well, perhaps she got delayed and didn't have time to send Iryna over. She knows Pietat likes to rummage through all the clothes on the stalls and, if she goes alone, she can perhaps surprise Iryna with some bargain she finds.

Vasyl, who has picked up on the conversation, goes out for a bike ride and, saying nothing to Esperança, calls in to see his sister. He rings the bell and Iryna goes out on to the balcony to see who it is.

"Hi, Ira! What's the matter?" he asks her straight out.

"What's the matter? Can't you see? I'm shut in."

"What about Mum?"

"Working. Any news of Dad?"

"Yesterday Esperança let me phone the neighbours and they told me he was helping Granny and Grandad. Did you ring too?"

"No chance! Even though I asked her again in front of Mum. But you know what? Pietat left her mobile on the bedside table while she was at the market so I've been phoning too. They told me the same thing. Now I was thinking of phoning our uncle who lives in the village near Granny and Grandad so they can give me a phone number and we can warn them and speak to him."

Passing the phone down from the window and then back up again, they try different ways of tracking down their father. It's gone two. Vasyl is fiddling with the phone when Iryna notices that Pietat is about to come round the corner pushing a bulging shopping trolley.

"Vasyl, she's coming! Throw it to me!"

He just has time to get the phone back to her and escape. Iryna wipes the calls they've made and leaves the phone on the bedside table.

After lunch, Vasyl innocently asks Esperança's permission to go and see Iryna and their mother.

Before long the phone rings:

"I can't stand this Vasyl anymore. He's so rude. He opens cupboards and sticks his nose in everything. Do me a favour and please control him. I've got enough to cope with the mother and the daughter. If you can't keep your eye on him, why did you want to have him here? Ah, and Iryna says she doesn't want to come to classes anymore. She says they're very boring and she knows enough now."

"Don't worry, Vasyl won't bother you anymore," replies Esperança. "But I'd like to talk to Iryna to see if I can convince her to carry on. It's very strange that she wouldn't want to come to lessons. She's always seemed very happy to come."

"You know how stubborn and ungrateful she is. She doesn't want to come any more now. What can we do about it?"

Esperança feels a chill in her heart. From now on she has no idea how things are going to go next. How can she make Vasyl understand that he can't go and see his sister and that Pietat has no patience?

"Pietat is stupid. She's very bad!" complains Vasyl, who was thrown out just because he wanted to have a closer look at a videotape.

"I want to talk to Mum."

But what does his mother know about this anyway? They take the car and head for the farm. It's five in the afternoon and the part of the farm that's used as a shop has just opened after lunch. Esperança introduces herself tactfully, introduces Vasyl and asks:

"How's Olena getting on?"

"Oh, she's very hardworking! It's just a shame we only need her in the morning to feed the cows and in mid-afternoon, when it's time to clean out the yard."

"And what does she do for the rest of the day?"

"Look, you see that tree over there? She sits under it, reading a strange newspaper she brought from home. I don't know, it must be in Russian. She must know it off by heart now! I told Pietat to come and pick her up at lunchtime, but she told me they usually went to see her parents then and that it was better for her to be here with us in case we needed her to give us a hand. And the truth is that she does everything she can."

"And where is she now?"

"She must be in the yard."

They walk round the farm and find Olena in rubber boots, with a hose, cleaning up the cow dung, which is almost up to her knees. The ammonia smell makes Esperança hold her nose.

"Ugh! It stinks!"

Vasyl has never seen so much filth in one place and it disgusts him. He goes and kisses his mother and takes the rubber hose from her fingers. Olena's eyes are crying and she wraps her arms round her son. In Ukraine, the cows graze freely and never make this awful smell. Once the work is done, they all go to the

131

house, and then they drop Olena at Pietat and Pau's door. They hug her goodbye. Vasyl repeats what is now his final judgement:

"Pietat is stupid, she's very bad!"

It's a good thing she can't have heard him. Olena waits for Vasyl and Esperança to go away before she rings the bell. She probably won't tell them anything about the visit she's had. Perhaps she won't even tell Iryna.

Iryna doesn't come for her lesson the next day and Esperança thinks it won't be good for her brother to be on his own, so she takes him with her to the Sports Centre to talk to a colleague who teaches Esperança's class PE during the school year. He takes the boy with a great deal of interest and asks him what he can do. Vasyl shows him he has no trouble shinning up the wall bars or doing acrobatics climbing ropes. Some boys come up to them. Marc and Jordi, who used to be in Esperança's class, ask, open-mouthed:

"Is this your Ukrainian boy?"

"Yes, that's right. Will you tell him what to do?"

"Yes, Esperança," they say. "We'll help him to understand."

In the evening, Esperança's doorbell rings. Vasyl opens the door. In the street are Pietat, Pau, Olena and Iryna. He makes signs inviting them in and waves them in again with his hand, but there they stay, glum faced, in the street.

Vasyl goes to look for Esperança and drags her to the front door by her arm.

"Listen! Listen! Want talk!"

"Tomorrow will be Olena's birthday. She'll be 33. We've come to ask you if you'll please let Vasyl come to dinner with us," begs Pietat.

As if it were Esperança who had cut relations between them! So, indignantly, she tries to find out what they are trying to achieve now:

"Well! Didn't you say you didn't want him in your house ever again? Weren't you telling me how badly he behaved? Yes, we'll say happy birthday to Olena, but this boy is not coming to dinner with you. Not unless you let me talk to Iryna for a while anyway."

Iryna makes as if to enter Esperança's house and Pietat holds her back.

"What you want is to turn this girl against me. Why are you saying I don't want the boy?"

"Because that's what you told me. Look, Iryna, why don't you want to come to lessons? What have we done to you?" She speaks directly to Iryna in an effort to find out the truth.

"I want to come, it's her who says you're very busy with my brother and that I know enough Catalan, and that if I speak Russian to him I won't learn anything anyway."

Her mother's eyes don't understand all this nonsense. She's just praying her son will be allowed to come on her birthday. Esperança gives in. She says she'll let him go, but as soon as he's had his dinner she wants him home. No later than ten. Pau questions his wife.

"Is it true you won't let Iryna go to lessons? Why?"

Pietat can't answer for so many of her incoherencies in front of so many people – even though half of them don't understand the language properly they're not stupid – and she finds another way out of the problem:

"Goodnight! We'll come and pick him up at eight tomorrow."

Pietat's group has hardly got to the neighbour's house before Vasyl is repeating:

"Pietat's stup....!"

Neither of them is in any doubt of it. But the boy wants to go to the celebration, Esperança knows it and she prepares everything so that it all goes well.

And it does. Today, when Esperança's doorbell rings out comes Vasyl, looking his best behind a bunch of four roses they've chosen at the florist's: one represents Mum, one Dad, one his sister and the other himself. Outside in the street his mother and Iryna are waiting for him. It has taken him all afternoon to make the card with "Happy birthday, Mum" on it. Although drawing isn't his favourite thing, he's taken care with it and made it with all his love. Olena sees him, so smart, with his new white tracksuit done up to the neck, even though it's hot. She's feels full of emotion and very proud of her Vasyl. She takes his arm, brings the roses close to her and shows off her son. The smell is something she will take back to Ukraine with her, even though it's not the same as the smell of the roses in her own garden – the ones her husband brings her. The ones here are more sophisticated, as if they've been polished and perfumed with a spray of Calvin Klein fragrance. From now on, every time a piece of clothing smells like that, she will feel a tremendous surge of joy.

At ten on the dot, Vasyl comes back to Esperança's house. He wants to tell her about it. "Pizza and *Na zdorov'ya!*" he says, raising his hand as if making a toast. "I told Mum Dad's helping Granny and Grandad and she was very happy because he'll eat well there. I asked if tomorrow come Iryna and Pietat say 'In the mornings she's tired and wants to sleep'. Is lie, is very bad!"

"Well, as long as they've had a good time."

But she thinks: "You're absolutely right. It's really sad that they've fooled you all and the worst of it for me is that Iryna can't come to lessons. She was learning so much! Oh, and if only that was all! It wouldn't surprise me if that woman did something really stupid..." Esperança doesn't understand how she could behave like that with children who are so keen to be liked, who are scared of not being asked back next year, and who don't have enough words to make themselves understood.

***

"HERE, IN THE VILLAGE, they're all private houses. Where on earth are you going with this child?"

"I'm going to Rivno. My daughter's got a hernia and she needs an operation in hospital."

"And where did you say you're from?"

The name of the village that comes into her head is the place where Granny Rus lives – the tiny hamlet near Belarus.

"Wouldn't you be better off in Kiev?"

"I've heard very good things about this hospital..."

The more they talk, the more complicated it gets. But she gets away with it. In fact, the little girl has got a little lump on her tummy button. She undoes Lyuba's pyjamas and shows him. With the couple's permission, she changes the baby on an upside-down fruit crate and fleshes out her story:

"There's a friend of my mother's who lives at Rivno and who used to work as a nurse at Dobrokiv."

She almost chokes as she gives the name because there was no need to have said it. She knows that the fewer details she gives, the less they can ask or check. Anyway, even if they noticed how much it disturbed her, they don't seem bothered by it.

"Well, if it's just for one night," the woman shrugs her shoulders, looking at her husband. "We can let them sleep in the children's room."

The couple invite them to have dinner.

Mmmm, hot soup! And lots of things to nibble. Little Lyuba likes tasting a bit of everything... The shopkeepers entertain the newcomers as if it was one of their own children visiting. They love watching Lyuba crawl across the rug towards the chairs so she can pull herself up, bending one leg and using the other as a lever. She is so tubby that her bottom sticks out as if she were an old woman with backache, but she's good at it and every time she manages it she happily shows off the only two teeth she has. How clever she is! She's still very young to be doing this. The couple tell her they have four children who all work abroad except the youngest, who's 30 and is the only one who hasn't given them grandchildren. The man picks up Lyuba as if he were her grandfather and kisses her on the cheek. Irina's eyes shine with tears:

"*Didus'!* Grandad!"

It's the memory of what she's lost. It's the suffering her *babusya* must be going through. It's the prayers of the whole family that nothing bad happens to their girls. She offers her hands to Lyuba, who throws herself into her arms. Iryna kisses the little girl all over and she imitates her mother, patting her on the back to console her.

CHAPTER 8

MOSCOW, 2 APRIL 1986, 05.00 H (LOCAL TIME)

He's starting to change. Every day, it seems as if I'm meeting a different person. His skin is falling off. His burns are coming out... They appear in his mouth, on his tongue, on his cheeks... At first they are small ulcers, but they grow. His face has turned from red to blue and now grey.

"I love him. I didn't think I loved him so much. I've got to help him to the very end. And I mustn't cry. I haven't got time for drying tears. He's got to see me always smiling. If everything's gone wrong, the one thing that can't fail is love. I still don't know how much I love him, I only know that it's more and more every day and no-one can stop that. Are you listening to me, my little son? My daughter? My love is radioactive too. That must be why I can bear what your father has to bear. We've only been married such a short time... We used to walk around holding hands in the street. Your father, who's such a clown, used to surprise me with daft jokes. He'd suddenly lift me up and spin me round. And we irradiated the people we passed our happiness. I can still feel his kisses. You need to be brave and wait... You understand I've got to look after him, don't you? Your father loves you a lot and he's made you a beautiful bed. When you're born you'll rule the roost in our house. Now you're moving. What are you telling me? Yes, yes, you're right. I'll shut up."

Voices come to me condemning him – curses from the mouths of doctors:

"The course of a radioactive illness lasts a fortnight. After that, the patient dies."

***

SUMMER 2004

The peace is an illusion. It lasts less than half a day. At four the next afternoon, Iryna turns up at Esperança's house sobbing.

"Pietat's shut me out of the house. She says if I love Esperança so much I should come and live with her."

It's all Iryna's fault. It seems she's been insisting on going to her lesson all morning but they haven't let her. Then, at lunchtime, they've given her a plate of greens and she didn't want to eat them because she said she wasn't ill or on a diet. When Pietat loses her pity she has nothing left to give, and now she's thrown Iryna out. Her mother's out at work and doesn't know anything about what's happened. When she does come home, at seven in the evening, she's surprised Iryna's not waiting for her in the garden, as usual, and that the gate is locked. When she rings the bell, they shout at her from the balcony:

"Ungrateful pair! Thieves! Look at the mobile phone bill I've just got: €400. All calls to Ukraine! We wouldn't spend that in ten months! I don't want you here anymore. Go to Esperança's house!" Along with the unkind words, she receives a wetting as the bunch of roses Vasyl gave her for her birthday is thrown at her head.

Crying desperately, she comes to Esperança's house:

"Why? What have you done?" asks her daughter.

"Me? Nothing. Mat!"

Iryna calms her. She tells her Esperança's already phoned the Association and they say they're coming.

Pietat has also phoned them and told them she's thrown Iryna and Olena out because they're dirty thieves. She's also demanded a document from the Association saying she is no longer responsible for either mother or daughter.

Fortunato and Jesús come to Esperança's house and, sensibly, take Iryna and her mother to a nearby park to speak to them alone. Iryna's mother just imitates her daughter's gestures to confirm the story she's telling. The girl swears in God's name that she's taken nothing from her host family and that she's always cleaned everything they've told her to clean. She says she and her mother are not bad and the only old witch is Pietat, who makes her mother wash all the clothes by hand when she comes in tired from the farm, who fusses about all kinds of things and who doesn't want to turn the washing machine on so she can save electricity...

They decide that this situation can't go on any longer and all four go to Pietat's and Pau's house. Jesús rings the bell. Pau soon opens the door and lets them into the living room.

"Here are the suitcases with their things. We don't want to see them again. Ah! And give us the document certifying we are no longer responsible for this scum."

"Just a minute," says Fortunato. "People aren't vases that you can just move around whenever you want to. Anyway, I don't know if you remember, but at Christmas we gave you ten books of raffle tickets to sell and you still haven't paid us for them. Where's the money?"

"The money! The money? Anyone would think you were squeaky clean with your finances. Go and get your money from whoever's decided to take this pair in. I'd like to know what you do with the contributions people pay you."

"Hey! We don't make any profit from this. All we do is help people. We're going to report what you're doing to the Catalan government's social services department. You're the hosts and you signed up for it."

"This year we haven't signed anything, so you haven't got things so well organised."

"Where are they supposed to go now? They can't sleep in the street! People aren't vases," Jesús repeats.

"People aren't vases. They're not vases!" repeats Pietat, over-excited and mocking their poor attempts to defend their corner. "I'll throw the vase at your head if you carry on like that here!" she says, showing them the one that had contained the bunch of roses.

Seeing that the couple are beside themselves with anger and that they are clearly not going to get any money for the raffle tickets they never should have entrusted to them without payment in advance, they give Pietat and Pau their certificate:

"... From today's date, the Association is solely responsible for the control of the child and the accompanying adult..."

After Pietat reads it, Pau reads it and then both of them read it at the same time.

"Is that OK? Well, let Olena have a last look round to see if they've left anything."

"The certificate's fine, but I'm not letting these thieves rummage through the house. Get out!" Pietat shouts.

"Then we're not signing or sealing the certificate for you," say the two men from the Association.

When she hears this, Pietat, who has the paper in her hands but hadn't noticed the uncompleted detail, takes the key and locks them all in before dialling the number of the local police station. The switchboard passes the call to a patrol car which by coincidence is in the area and, when they hear "Thieves! Thieves!" over the radio and through the wide-open balcony doors, they turn on their siren.

All the neighbours come towards Pietat's house. So do Esperança and Vasyl, who want to know what's going on and aren't too far away.

The police do what they can, which consists of making Pietat and Pau open the door so the "thieves" can get out with the two suitcases.

Once in the street, the police accompany Olena and Iryna to Esperança's house to talk for a bit. Both mother and daughter have red eyes and their mouths show disgust and despair. They're exhausted and when the two men from the Association suggest that they should each take one of them home to give them somewhere to go, Esperança says:

"Maybe it would be better for them to be together tonight... I'm sure if they can talk they'll comfort one other a little. If they want to, they can stay with me... There are two beds in Vasyl's room and another one in the room next door."

Iryna and Vasyl nod. They know Esperança will do everything she can to make them feel at home.

"It's a good thing it's the first time we've had a case like this," complains Fortunato.

"I wouldn't still be with the Association if this had happened before," adds Jesús.

"You don't know how many times this silly woman has phoned the Association. I'm sorry we ever let her be a host..."

"Goodnight! We'll decide what to do tomorrow."

The next day, at lunchtime, the Association phone asking how everyone is and saying that, for the moment, they haven't found a house for Iryna and Olena to go to and that, if Esperança doesn't mind, they'll phone again in the evening. She reassures them:

"Give them a bit of time to recover! Both of them can stay here with Vasyl while you look for another house. I hope you'll help me if I have any problems."

"Of course! You can rely on us and, if you want both of them next year, we'll give you a discount when it comes to paying for their air tickets. Can you tell Iryna to come to the phone?"

"Look, Iryna, if you're a bright girl and you know how to get on with people, we'll give you one last chance. Pietat is a difficult woman, you're right, but perhaps if you'd made more of an effort..."

Vasyl guesses what the conversation is about and he keeps inventing silly things to say. Iryna makes faces, laughs and sobs. Fortunato continues his sermon, finally asking:

"One day you'll have to tell us what Pietat did for you to say she made a fuss about everything, do you understand?"

Iryna can't take any more and she gives the phone to Esperança.

"You'll have to forgive her, she's just a child."

Fortunato asks her to get Iryna to talk because he wants to know everything about Pietat and Pau. They're planning to write a full report on what's happened. It's best to get your retaliation in first. They don't want Pietat publishing lies in the local newspapers. That would give their work a bad reputation. Until now, everyone has been full of praise for the Association.

Esperança wants them to forget it all and doesn't talk to them about it. Every time Pietat's name comes up, she steers the conversation away and follows Vasyl's system of saying something silly:

"It's a wrap!"

As everyone is helping each other, Esperança also wants to do things properly and take care of them as best she can. She asks Iryna for her medical report and also wants to know if they gave her any explanation about the diet she has to follow. Iryna goes through her things and can't find them:

"I bet Pietat's kept them!"

Their new host feels she should phone. But as no-one answers either in the morning, at lunchtime or in the evening, she thinks of another way of getting the information.

"Perhaps Dr Trini at the Rouralba surgery has a copy. Did you know we were at school together? I'll ask her for an appointment at the end of the afternoon. That way she'll be able to have a look at your mother and she can also see if Vasyl's OK."

With these ideas in her head, they go down to the surgery. The doctor opens the door and can't resist commenting:

"Look at you! Where are you going with these three?"

While they hug and she asks them into her consulting room, she asks:

"Hi, Iryna! Why's Esperança with you today? Isn't Pietat well?"

The girl goes closer and kisses her, looks at her and, between sobs, the doctor can make out:

"She's thrown me out. She says we're... dirty... and thieves!"

"Come on, Ira! Eh!" her brother wants to make her laugh.

"Oh! I'm afraid there's no cure for that Pietat! Don't take any notice of her..." She lowers her voice and can't contain herself: "She's completely hysterical."

She remembers the day when Pau came to fetch her to tell her that his wife was paralysed and couldn't get up. It was summer, she was on duty and she went round straightaway, even though she had other urgent appointments at the surgery. She found her sitting on the end of the bed. She can still see her, hair messed up and eyes half rolled up into her head. She went close and stroked Pietat's head. She made her lie down to examine her. Pietat squealed with pain when she touched her legs. She allowed herself to be massaged but complained constantly. It was the day of the town's annual festival and suddenly the music that announced the traditional giant figures that paraded through the streets every year could be heard. As soon as she heard it, Pietat got up and went to the balcony so she could see them, shouting:

"You might stay at home instead of going out for a walk!"

Trini has to keep patient confidentiality and she won't tell them about it. But "hysterical" is very similar to the equivalent Ukrainian word and Iryna has picked it up. To let off steam she turns to Esperança and says:

"Do you know what Pietat did the day we went to the river with Mum?"

***

MOSCOW, 9 MAY 1986, 09.00 H (LOCAL TIME)

What day is it? How many days is it since the accident happened? There's a calendar hanging on the wall. I look at it. He thinks it's for something else... It's the ninth of May. He always used to tell me: "You can't imagine what Moscow's like on VE Day. I must take you to see the fireworks one day." He opens his eyes.

"Is it day or night?" he asks me.

"It's nine in the evening," I answer.

"Open the window. The fireworks are going to start now. I promised you I'd take you to Moscow and to all the festivals and that I'd give you flowers."

Then he takes three carnations from between the pillow and the wall. He gave the nurse some money to buy the most beautiful ones and she's done it for him.

I hug him and he protests:

"What have the doctors told you? You can't kiss me! You can't hug me!"

147

They don't let me hug him, but I get him up, I sit him down, I change his sheets, I put the thermometer in and take it out... I spend the day beside him and that helps them a lot.

We remember the first day we saw one another.

At night, I cry, face-down on the pillow, but I don't wet it. The tears well up hot inside me, then suddenly I feel a chill down my spine – the fear of losing him. The terror of having to live in the past forever – of never again having a future. What kind of monster has swallowed all our plans?

***

SUMMER 2004

When she's finished with mother and son, Doctor Trini looks for Iryna's report and can't find it. It seems that Pietat should have brought her a copy but with all the fuss she can't have had time. As she wants to spare herself hearing Pietat's version of events, she says she'll ask for one from Barcelona and they can fax it over. She says goodbye, wishing them a good summer. She'll give the results of the blood tests they'll do on Olena and Vasyl by telephone but, from what she's seen examining them, she expects them to be good.

In the street, Iryna's feels the need to let off steam and repeats again:

"Do you know what Pietat did the day we went to the river with Mum?"

"What?"

And her anger comes out, as if this was her great opportunity to show how stupid the woman was:

"She hadn't wanted to bring her swimsuit and, as she wanted to cool down and didn't want to get her knickers wet, she took them off and stood there just in a t-shirt. Pau was going bright red... he could hardly breathe because every time she bent down to get past a rock you could see her whole bare bottom: 'Please, Pietat, behave!' Pau asked her and she said: 'There are nudist beaches aren't there? Well this is like that!'."

From the tone and gestures, her mother guesses what she's talking about and adds, in Ukrainian:

"In Ukraine women sometimes swim in their bra and knickers if they haven't got swimsuits, but they only take their clothes off when they're sure no-one can see."

"I was ashamed. There were people there the other day, weren't there? Well, imagine it on Sunday. When we went it was so hot and everyone wanted to cool down. I'm sure more than one person noticed."

"And did you remember to take them to that place on the Tordera where we'd been with your brother?"

"Yes. It was very easy. We took the road from Santa Maria to Sant Esteve de Palautordera and carried on and on. And when we got to that sharp bend where it starts going up the mountain I made them take the track on the left. It was just as pretty, but without you, Esperança, I didn't see those blue flowers on the bank and without Vasyl no-one dared to jump into the pool from that rock. I missed you a lot. I also wished Rovelló was there so I could throw him a stick and he could bring it back like our dog does. I'd have thrown it right into the middle of the pool."

"Yes, like Vasyl did, and he got all wet."

"It was so different without you! I was so ashamed!"

A week later the doctor phones one morning to say both Olena's and Vasyl's blood tests have come back normal. Their white blood cell count is a bit high, but that must be due to constant exposure to a radioactive environment and it's bound to settle down to something more normal during the summer. She's also received the electrocardiograms and all the tests from Vall d'Hebron Hospital that they did on Iryna and perhaps her cholesterol is a bit high, but that's normal because they eat a lot of butter in her country.

"What else can they eat? What they've got: butter and potatoes! With that terrible cold weather!"

"And if we've got no food, vodka!" says Iryna, chuckling bitterly and running up and down the hall with Vasyl until their mother stops them. Iryna says:

"In my country everyone's drunk!"

Suddenly she turns serious. She wants to show the photos of a party where most of them ended up smashed and even the women put alcohol in the tea.

"Would you like to see them? We've got one of an uncle with a big moustache telling jokes while smoking a cigar. He was Dad's big brother. He's dead now, poor thing. He had...you know, that bad disease, what's it called?"

"Cancer?"

"Yes, the doctors said he smoked too much, but it was because he liked going to pick wild mushrooms and berries. They're the most contaminated thing. He didn't take any notice. Because they're so good and don't cost any *hryvnias,* he ate a lot of them. He went into the woods near the power station which are bigger."

"Was he much older than your father?"

"No, not much. A year ago this winter he died and that day we set the table in front of his tomb with a casserole full of stewed mushrooms Dad had gone to pick for him, with some of the tobacco he liked and some of Mum's home-made vodka."

"We take flowers for the dead, but never food."

"Of course, the dead person doesn't eat! The food is for those having the party to remember them. It's the living who eat, although as soon as we leave, the poor people take away what's left, or the drunken gravedigger drinks it.

"Perhaps it's like the *Castanyada* which we have instead of Hallowe'en in Catalonia. Although we have it at home. By tradition, on the night before All Saints' Day, which is the first of November, while we eat chestnuts and sweet potatoes, we remember those who have left us. The next day the cemeteries are full of people taking flowers to the tombs of their loved ones."

As she listens, she looks for the photographs of her uncle, but then she remembers...

"Oh no! The photos! They're at Pietat's house. Pau kept them with the ones of the river that we had developed..."

"We'll phone them again and I'll ask for them. What does she want them for anyway?" wonders Esperança.

"I'll tell her. I remember where Pau put them," says Iryna.

Esperança listens and lets her get on with it.

Pietat sees the caller number, takes the phone off the hook and waits to recognise the voice. Iryna explains... she hears anguished breathing, followed by a few moments of silence and then:

"So you want the photos? Well, you can pay me 50 euros and 25 cents, which is what they cost me.

"You can keep the ones from the river! We only want the albums we brought from Ukraine. They're photos we've got of before my parents were married... of when we were little... They're the only ones we have!"

"If you want them back, bring the money," she demands, in a voice that makes Iryna think that in passing she might shout rude things at her or pull her hair, like she did that day when she didn't want to eat her spinach.

Esperança won't let her go:

"Don't worry, we'll think of something. Miquel comes home tonight and we'll tell him about it. Yesterday I rang him. He knows everything and he's very happy that we've taken you in. He says that, if we're careful, seven can eat as cheaply as four.

Miquel's there by mid-afternoon. He's brought a whole ham, some cured sausage and a box of peaches. He's always full of surprises. After kissing Esperança, he greets the new family affectionately and lets Iryna and Vasyl explain what's happened in their own way.

"So you're Vasyl? What a pair you are! And tomorrow Laia and Naiara arrive from England. Well, well, well! Let me have a shower and we'll go down there. These things need sorting out quickly."

"She says we've got to pay her 50 euros and 25 cents."

"You'll find it in my pocket," he says, taking his clothes off to cool down. "I've got a lot of change in there to pay the motorway tolls." Esperança gets it out all in change, which will be good for paying the exact amount. She doesn't want anyone having to give change.

"Come on, let's go!"

Miquel, Vasyl and Iryna are on their way to Pietat's house. They are almost there when Iryna tells them she's had second thoughts about going, asking Miquel to carry on with her brother. She doesn't want to see that *Jozhka* ever again. They give her nightmares. Then she pretends to go back, but in fact she goes a different way... The two men react, telling her not to worry, it's their business, and they continue on their way to Pietat's house. "The wicked stepmother should be alone at the moment," thinks Vasyl. "Pau won't be back from work yet."

"Where's Iryna? She's not scared of me, is she? I said I'd give her the photos. You'll regret taking her in, you know. She'll suck you dry like she did us."

Miquel replies:

"Fantastic! There you are, count it!"

Vasyl, who has the money, checks that there's neither too little nor too much.

From the other side of the road, Iryna is preparing one of her surprises. Mentally, she ticks off a list of everything that was left at Pietat's house: a watch with an imitation diamond face, which Maragda's mother, who sells Avon products and sometimes gets prizes with the points they give her for the things she sells, gave her and she still hasn't worn. Also the earrings Pietat made her take out to go in the river and which were still in her room. Oh yes, and the suitcase Maria Mercè had given her, which was empty in case they needed to fill it with things people might give her. That was in the garage.

So, while they are coaxing Pietat to give up the photos, Iryna climbs in the back window which is usually open during the day to air the garage. The window is small and rather high. She takes a piece of tree trunk to climb up on. She pushes herself into the garage with her palms. From there, she goes up to her bedroom and takes everything that's hers. The kitchen smells of soup – the kind that made her feel sick. She turns off the heat so it stops steaming. On one of the worktops there's a cloth made of cut up knickers, which makes her giggle. Out of spite, she spits in the soup and throws the cloth in too. Suddenly she hears footsteps – Pietat is coming up. She hides behind the kitchen door with the brooms. Through the little gap between the hinges, she can see the hallway and the master bedroom. Pietat goes in: from among the sheets in the cupboard she takes the albums and the bag with the photos of the river and spreads them out on the bed. She separates out any compromising pictures and... she turns suddenly, as if she feels she's being watched. Iryna's heart leaps and the door creaks. Her eye is reflected in the little mirror in the hallway, but Pietat's in a hurry and she doesn't notice. She hurries downstairs to get her money, holding the albums any old how. Vasyl and Miquel are still at the door.

"Here you are! Do whatever you like with them!"

"Here, count it with that wretched husband of yours: ten, twenty, thirty, forty, fifty and twenty-five."

Pietat has just gone up a couple of steps to go back into the house when she hears a bang from the garage.

"Is that you, Pau?"

As no-one answers, instead of going up into the flat, she goes down to the garage. Animals are not welcome in that house, and she knows all the noises. This noise comes from Iryna, who's just thrown the suitcase out the window. She doesn't have time to try to climb out, so she hides behind the car and goes round in the same direction as Pietat, who, when she sees nothing strange, remembers the pan and goes upstairs. She doesn't want to be left without soup just because she got confused about the direction of the sound. But no, the pan is uncovered and there's something strange floating in it.

"Oh no! Good thing I turned it off. But what's that? I don't know whether I'm coming or going with those dreadful people! Thank God I threw them out – they'd have driven me made."

As Pau is about to arrive, she doesn't have time to repeat the soup. She adds water and waits for it to boil. She smells it and thinks it's substantial enough.

In her haste to find out where the noise is coming from, Pietat has left the front door open, and Iryna sees the light from the garage. With her booty in her hand, she walks out of the front door, like the lady of the house. She walks through the garden and picks up the suitcase. Now at the gate, she meets Pietat's neighbour, Maragda, who thinks she's seeing things.

"What are you doing here?"

"I've come to pick up the watch your mother gave me. Do you want to come with me? I live at Esperança's house now."

Maragda runs off to tell her family:

"Iryna's come to take the things she'd left behind."

"Really?"

They can catch her if they can! Pietat takes a while to find out what's happened. She knows nothing until Maragda's mother tells her from the garden:

"So Iryna's been round then. Have you made things up with her?"

"Iryna? She wouldn't dare come anywhere near here!"

"But Maragda saw her with all sorts of things... weren't they hers?"

Now she reacts. Playing the frightened martyr, she protects her home with an alarm and has iron bars welded on to the garage window to make it difficult for thieves to get in. She explains sadly that she's still recovering from all the distress Iryna's stay has caused her. She never specifies exactly what the distress is, of course, but her outpourings spread through the town like low-lying mist, and they have their effect. From now on, Maragda, Iryna's best friend in Catalonia, doesn't want to know her and, when she phones, she tells her she is ungrateful and that if she ever does what she's done again no-one in Rouralba will want to know her and she'll never be able to come back for the summer.

"If I meet her in the street, I'll turn my back on her and pretend I haven't seen her," Maragda assures Pietat and her mother.

And, if that were not enough, when Esperança looks for the telephone number of some girls from Dobrokiv who seemed such good friends of Iryna's so they can go to the swimming pool together, they make excuses too.

Nor do they want to know anything about what's happened, as Pietat has been kind enough to phone them and put them in the picture. They avoid Iryna. They wouldn't want people to see them with her and tar them with the same brush so they weren't allowed to come back.

Poor thing, being treated as a thief. What could she have taken from that house anyway? A ten-cent coin...? And to think that it was Pietat who kept the Christmas raffle money... The Association hasn't been able to prove it, but now they don't give any books of raffle tickets to anyone who hasn't paid in advance. If they have any left they keep them for themselves.

Every morning, Vasyl goes to the Sports Centre. Iryna, who hadn't signed up when it was time, can't go, but she doesn't mind at all because Naiara and Laia have arrived from London and they ride round on their bikes or go to the swimming pool. In the afternoons they watch TV for a while, listen to music, water the garden and cut the grass if it needs it. Later they do homework, with Catalan classes for Iryna and Vasyl. When Miquel arrives in the evening, they take Rovelló for a walk while Esperança and Olena make the dinner. The four children do the washing up and clean the kitchen following a rota drawn up by Miquel. The first time it's Vasyl's turn to do the washing up, Olena goes to save him having to do it.

"Hey! That's not fair!" complain Naiara and Laia.

"Boys never do the washing up in Ukraine. It's women's work! If people there saw them, they'd say they were gay," says Iryna, taking her brother's and mother's side.

"Really?" says Miquel, taking the apron from Olena. He turns to Vasyl and tells him: "I'll wash and you dry!"

"OK!" says the boy.

Meanwhile the two women look after the clothes and the house. Because Olena is so hardworking, Esperança has less work than when she does it on her own. All of them have to tell her:

"Olena! Stop working!

You already do enough on the farm."

The summer's ending, like all summers, but this one feels even more melancholy. For the last few days of August they go together to a house they have near Tamariu, in a small development in the middle of the woods ten minutes from a cove. Olena, who has never been on holiday, enjoys her first, and probably her last, summer in Catalonia like a little girl. From her bedroom she can see the sea. Every morning she looks at it as if it were a blue silk bedspread for her to slide and stretch all the way to her own River Dnieper – the pillow. Every night she looks up at the stars. It's the last night tonight and the full moon is rising over the sea. "Good night!" she tells it, but it carries on telling her all kinds of things until morning. As the moon fades, the jealous sun winks at her to wish her good day.

In the bigger bedroom next door, the three girls are lying in a double bed, with Vasyl alone in a single one. With a knot of joy squeezing her heart so tight she can feel the pulse in her wrists, Olena pulls the shutter up just a little – they're still asleep next door. Fascinated, she puts her eyes between the window slats as the cloud moving across turns pink and stops time. Pines and holm oaks twist and salute His Majesty the Sun. Their roots follow the cracks in the rock: grains of quartz and mica slide down like constant offerings to the god Neptune. Far away are the brush strokes of a sleepy prince, mixing seaweed with emerald green: the islands with their sand and a freshwater stream seeking out the brine. The water has come from far away to seek her out. The Dnieper is calling her. It draws her like a giant seashell put to her ear, whispering the mysteries of the deep seas: "You can't see it, dawn has just broken. The sea is calm. Come to me! Remember, it's the last day!"

She rushes to put on her swimsuit and a t-shirt. She is the first one up and about in the house. She prepares juice and breakfast for everyone and... come on! Esperança, who hears her, gives the orders:

"Let's get down to the beach! It's the last *den*. Come on, when we come back you'll have to pack."

Last year, Iryna had already had everything packed for days. This time they were clearly in no hurry to leave.

"Miquel will take you to the airport at midnight. The girls and I won't fit in the car."

The women fold the things and Miquel and Vasyl get the boat ready: they fix it to the car and put in the engine and the fuel. Once at the cove, they hold the boat to make it easier for the others to get aboard: the three girls step in lightly. From above they hold out their arms to Olena and Esperança, who always slip and find it more difficult. Off they go again to the reefs and islets! They reach empty coves as if they were the first people in the world to set foot in these landscapes. But today they are too sad to pick up sea snails or starfish. All they take are small shells and pieces of sea-smoothed glass. Without water to wet them they will be the dead colours of memories.

Esperança looks into Olena's eyes: a watercolour of dissolved blues and greens, like a wave. She understands that Olena wants to record everything she likes in her eyes. That's why she's always taking and showing photos. Why couldn't this summer last for ever? Why couldn't her husband, the older Vasyl, ever see this?

When they reach the Formigues Islands they take their chance to do a bit of diving. That really is something else! Colours, light and life everywhere. They would all like to enjoy more time at the bottom of the sea, but it's already two o'clock and they need to head back. They start the engine, the boat speeds up and... in a few minutes the trip's over. Now back at home, showered and dressed again, Miquel says that, as it's the last day, he wants them all to be able to rest so they'll go to the restaurant for lunch. There, eating, chatting and laughing, they discuss how the summer has gone. There is praise for Olena's desire to work and learn. Without any lessons, she can now read the Western alphabet and she knows lots of expressions. They also celebrate everything Vasyl has done and they laugh, recalling the day he turned up at home with a television set he'd found next to a rubbish container. He was quite sure it would work and he wanted to take it back to Ukraine. Or the other time he brought home a plastic sunbed... Then Iryna tells them about the scares she had at Pietat's house when she went to get the things they'd left there, and how she took her revenge by throwing the knickers in the pot. They laugh and laugh and, in the end, Miquel gives Olena some money so she can buy the children bicycles to rid to school when they get to Ukraine. Esperança is clear, though, that this is on one condition:

"You must let your parents have the bikes when they need them." The children agree with all the advice and promise to be good.

On the way back home, the two men clean the boat and fishing gear and put it away because Miquel says they won't be needed until next year. Seeing the way Vasyl looks at the tools, Miquel gives him some. For the women, getting the suitcases ready, the afternoon has flown by.

Suddenly, Iryna and Vasyl realise it's nearly time to leave their friends and they shout:

"We want Esperança to come to the airport in her car! We want Laia and Naiara to see us when we get on the plane!"

"Yes," say the sisters. "We want to be with them right till the end too!"

"There's no need for such a fuss. You know this year the flight's at three in the morning. You'd be leaving here at midnight. We'll stay here for a few more days. We love you a lot!" adds Esperança, delighted that they are all so fond of one another.

With the work done, sitting on the sofa, they watch a Bruce Willis video all fighting time together, but letting it pass quickly. The film's in Spanish and, from time to time, Vasyl, who's seen it countless times, gets ahead with the dialogue:

"¿Qué te pasa, negrito?" "Ibas a llamarme negro" They all giggle because his accent in Spanish sounds as if it's straight from rural Catalonia.

At the agreed time, the suitcases are brought down the stairs of the house in Tamariu. Everything is packed inside them: warm clothes, like the fleeces of all colours; nice new bras, socks and knickers; tools; a video to be mended and also a medicine kit with antibiotics and anti-inflammatories to get them through the long, hard winter. Between them all, they work out the best way of fitting the cases in the boot. They take them out, put them in again before finally cracking the puzzle and putting the pieces in the right order. The three big cases go in the back and Iryna and Vasyl hold the three small ones on their laps. Like royalty, in the front, ride Olena and Miquel, who's driving.

Now they're at the airport and a while ago Fortunato took their passports and social security cards. Without calling attention to herself, Iryna, who's done this before, manages to find someone who hasn't got much luggage who will take their small cases, as with just the big ones they already had excess baggage. Miquel kisses mother and daughter goodbye and pats Vasyl on the back to give him strength, helping him prevent his feelings getting the better of him. They follow the path taking them up the escalator, through Customs, always facing backwards so they can keep looking at Miquel, who can't accompany them here.

Love is capricious. Despite the two men's efforts everyone's cheeks are wet – and it must be making them see visions. First, they begin to lose the calm, sad figure of Miquel, alone on the tiled floor. Then, after a few seconds, they see Esperança, Laia and Naiara.

It can't be them! But it is! They've come to say goodbye. When they see them, Iryna and Vasyl push down the escalator, faster than the movement taking them the other way. Olena has got to the top but starts rushing down the ordinary staircase. Vasyl, emboldened by contained emotion, takes Esperança by the waist as if she were a spinning top, lifts her up and whirls her round. Then he does the same with Naiara and Laia. There are hugs and kisses they will always remember, although more will be given every year they come back, because this is the instant they realise exactly how much they will miss each other.

They will fly towards the sun that comes up an hour earlier – towards their Ukraine. As they fly over Kiev, they will be able to read the capital's propaganda boards: *Ukrayina lyubyt'* – "Ukraine loves you", in case anyone's forgotten...

Chapter 9

I'm very tired. I'm at the hospital day and night. I feel faint, my head is spinning... I go out into the corridor and collapse. With my fingers I can feel a window sill but I haven't got the strength to get up. A doctor comes past and helps me. Thank goodness for that! If he hadn't come past, no-one would have seen me. I feel sick and vomit. The doctor suddenly realises what's going on...

"Are you pregnant?"

"No, no," I answer quietly, fearing someone will hear us.

"Don't try to fool me!"

He's found out my secret and he takes me to the head of the radiology section, Angelina Vasilievna Guskova:

"Why did you lie to me?" she asks.

"I had no choice. If I'd told the truth at the start you'd have sent me home. Let me stay, Angelina. I'll be grateful to you my whole life..."

I go back to the room. He's looking at me with fixed, glassy eyes. Someone's told him.

"Hey, Vasya! What have they told you? I felt a bit faint... It was nothing."

He remains still, expectant. I soak some cotton wool in water and moisten his lips. A choking wheeze boils up in his chest. He's hardly getting any air. I shout:

"Girls, let me phone Ivano-Frankivs'k! My husband's dying!"

They give me a line straightaway.

"Help me! Vasya's dying."

My whole family comes to Moscow. They bring me some things and some money.

Dr Gale, an American doctor who's just arrived, comforts me:

"There isn't much hope, but there's still a chance. He's such a strong young man with such a powerful body! We must try to save him. I can give him a bone marrow transplant."

"Can you use mine?"

"No, it has to be from someone in his family, the closer the better."

I phone all his relatives.

"You must come. The doctor says so. Only people with his blood can save him."

***

AUTUMN 2004

In the middle of the night a stormy gust of wind must have blown open the attic window and knocked over one of the tools kept up there. The older Vasyl has been sleeping fitfully, like anyone who's waiting for something. Now he's woken up and gone up to shut it. He takes his time to get back to bed but he still can't sleep.

He's wondering whether to tell her what's happening to him. That's why he didn't feel like phoning from the neighbours' house or writing a letter during the summer. Even lying down, he is choked by anxiety. He's got up, opened the wardrobe, got out his Sunday clothes, worked out how he looked in front of the mirror and thought that if he dressed up a bit it wouldn't be so noticeable. The chemotherapy session they gave him at Kiev Hospital has made him quite a bit better. No. For the moment he's not planning to say anything. Yesterday he cleaned everything and now, in the morning, he has cut flowers for the table, as Olena usually did, and hung a garland of pink gladioli on the front door. Everything's ready. Bossi the cat, the cow and the chickens seem just as nervous as he is. They've not been sleeping either and when the family arrive, the animals welcome them with a cacophony of noise.

"How handsome you look, Dad! Very nice!" they say, all three of them hugging him.

"And you, you're all tanned! It's been such a long time!"

"Yes! The summer's seemed so long because I haven't been able to speak to you on the phone," says his wife. The only news she's had from him all summer has been a couple of comments from the neighbours.

"Yes, but they told you, didn't they? That I was in Belarus helping your parents."

And she nods and looks at him surprised.

"How come you've had your hair cut so short?"

"Well, you always cut it for me, don't you? I thought it would be easier just setting the clippers to number one. That way I look smarter than letting it grow for two months."

"I think you look a bit thinner. Have you been eating properly?"

"Yes! The thing is, I've missed you..." he says again, tenderly.

It's more than a year since that first sore appeared under his tongue. As it seemed as if it was going away, and as it didn't hurt him, he ignored it. He's never liked going to the doctor. And he touched his whole neck and he didn't have those bumps that came up in his brother. And his ear and his jaw didn't hurt either, like his brother's did.

The presents they've brought are gradually handed out and the clothes and medicines are put away for when they're needed. Elena shows him the euros she's earned and they decide they'll spend the money on the house. Everything they've done this summer will give them plenty to talk about for the whole year.

They can't believe it when their father tells them that when they left he promised himself he'd give up smoking.

"How come?" asks Iryna. "You even used to talk with a cigarette in your mouth!"

"I said to myself: 'If you can go for two months without your wife and children, you can do without cigarettes too.' Two months without you! I've missed you so much!"

"So now I can't light your cigarettes for you anymore?"

"No, Ira, I've made a promise and a promise is a promise."

"Not even a crafty one in secret, Dad?" she asks him with a conspiratorial look. He falls silent.

When they told him in July he had cancer of the tongue, he couldn't believe it. Who would have thought it possible? The blood that had poured out of his mouth in the summer was precisely because the disease was going inwards, through the veins. They assured him that, if he looked after himself and if they injected him with those really strong chemical products, he would avoid metastasis. As he had no money to stay in hospital, he lived at the house of a friend who lent him money to buy the drugs they had to inject. His friend and his wife managed to arrange things so one of them could go with him to each chemotherapy session. Vasyl came back feeling so sick, vomiting and in such terrible pain, that he lost a lot of weight, so they made him eat purées and soups which were easier to swallow. Thanks to them and the treatment, he recovered, and now the last thing he wants is the kind of compassion Olena reserves for the sick. Two months are a long time. As soon as he returned from hospital Vasyl went to Olena's parents' house to help them. For the moment, Olena doesn't suspect anything about what he did in July. Her husband has faith. He'll probably be cured... and he so wants to hold her and sleep with her again...

Autumn returns. In every corner, dry leaves swing in freshly-spun spiders' webs. In Catalonia, they soon receive a letter telling them that everything is white. That at night, the moon tiptoes across the mirror of the fields so as not to freeze its feet... Who protects Iryna's and Vasyl's family from the bad weather? Laia and Naiara are surprised when they read that it's snowed in Ukraine.

"How come it's so cold in Ukraine if it's almost on the same latitude as Barcelona?"

169

They can see on their globe that Germany, Poland, Sweden, Norway and Finland really are a long way to the north. And they ask themselves strange questions:

"How can they love Ukraine if it snows there so much?"

"Do they get the cold from Siberia or from poverty? Because it's unbearable when there's no heating."

Warmth comes from letters and phone calls. Never a month goes by without one, and, when the Catalan family can, they send a parcel and some money. They trust their friends and they know the things they send will be welcomed and well used. Esperança wonders whether it is legal to steal the souls of children with a sick future in exchange for a holiday. The photographs Iryna brought are Lyusya's tears. They have penetrated her own soul.

Every day Esperança's girls look in their mailbox to see if there's a letter from Ukraine. When there is one, they literally jump for joy and feel the need to tell all their neighbours. When they see Iryna's distinctive handwriting, they feel her tenderness. Of course, there are mistakes, but she makes herself understood.

> My Ykpaiha is very badly and goes very slow because of the thief in all the country. I'm making orange scarf for me and my brother to go to Kiev and shout we want Viktor Yushchenko and Yulia Tymoshenko. The whole school go and we are ready and if police want to get us, we escape.

The news broadcasts on radio and television in Catalonia don't often talk about Ukraine. There are still lots of people who don't know the details of what happened there and how the explosion at the Chernobyl nuclear power station is still affecting them.

But over the last few days it has been talked about because Prime Minister Viktor Yanukovych has been declared winner of the presidential elections and people are sure the votes have been manipulated. The international observers who were there say as much. As Iryna explains, the scrutiny of the elections has led to popular uproar in support of the opposition candidate, Viktor Yushenko, who has led the peaceful Orange Revolution against the results.

In mid-December the Ukrainian family are also waiting for the post, as Christmas is coming and every year they get a card from Rouralba.

Iryna has had to stay at home on her own for a couple of days because she has a bad cold. Her parents are working and Vasyl has gone out to play in the streets, as there's a teachers' strike. When she's least expecting it, their neighbour, Olga, comes looking for her to tell her she's got a phone call from abroad. The air is freezing, so she puts a blanket round her head and rushes out as quickly as she can. She knows phone calls are expensive and anyway, she's eager to find out how her Catalan friends are.

"Is that you, Iryna? You know, we saw you on television last night. My pupils wanted me to phone you before the Christmas holidays and it's break time so we're doing it now. They're all around me right now."

"Where did you see me?"

"You were in Independence Square in Kiev, with your orange scarf."

For a minute, Iryna believes her.

"Really? What, did you record a video of us?"

"No, I'm joking! On the news they said there were more than a million of you. And in the end you're going to get the president you wanted, aren't you?"

"Yes, we've all got *nadiya*... Do you remember what that means, Esperança?"

"You told me you had a friend called Nadiya and that it meant 'hope', just like Esperança. So trust your feelings!"

After asking after everyone and chatting about this and that for a while, Esperança realises she's been on for a long time. So she gets to the point: she tells Iryna she has been able to save 300 euros and that she's sent the money by Western Union. She asks her to take a pen and note down the transfer number, adding:

"It's in the name of your mother, Olena Piskun."

"OK, thank you very much, Esperança!" She's touched and it shows in her voice.

"My friends helped as well. Have a good Christmas! Lots of love."

"Love to you too!"

Meanwhile, Vasyl has managed to unlock a mobile phone Miquel gave him in the summer. It was a broken one, lying around in garage. Vasyl saw the opportunity and asked him if he could have it. Back in Ukraine, he and his friends have been trading spare parts and they've now managed to mend it. They have a card for phoning abroad which might have been stolen. There are 20 minutes left and they've saved them for today – New Year's Day. The idea Iryna and Vasyl had was to get their parents to practise a few words in Catalan so they can give their friends a surprise.

"For Happy New Years always!" "Pozdravljaju!" they toast, singing to their hearts' content as they pass the telephone around, drinking green tea and little glasses of vodka and eating little cheesecakes.

When they say *"Na zdorov'ya!* Good health to everyone!" Olena notices that her husband is just taking little sips. When he feels he is being watched he frantically pours the rest down his throat. "This could be the last Christmas I'll be with you..." is on the point of escaping his lips. It's now a month since he should have begun localised radiotherapy. The sore under his tongue is extending down his throat and looks whitish, like meat that's gone off. He suddenly rasps and coughs. He gets up and goes to the cupboard where he hides the cigarettes.

"What about your promise? Do you think I don't know you're smoking again?" Olena scolds him.

"Come on, let me smoke a cigarette," he insists. "You know it's the only thing that calms my nerves."

"Here you are, Dad!" Iryna lights him a cigarette, drawing in a good lungful herself.

The Catalans hear all the noise mixed with the New Year toast *Vitayu z Novym Rokom!* This time in Ukrainian, as they add their own version of Happy New Year:

"Bon any nou! Feliç 2005! Vitayu z Novym Rokom! We know you've got a new president, Viktor Yushenko, and that woman with the plait, Yulia Tymoshenko. Let's see if they keep their promises. So, how are you celebrating?"

"With good food! To start with, *holubci.*"

"What's that?"

"Mum makes it with minced meat mixed with fried onion, carrot and spices, all nicely wrapped up in blanched cabbage leaves. She puts the rolls in the bottom of a pan and adds vegetable stock while they cook. Once she's cooked them, she serves them with butter sauce, which is like the white sauce you put on cannelloni in Catalonia. When we're short of hryvnias, she uses mushrooms instead of the meat. We really like the *chantarelle* mushrooms Dad picks all through the summer, until the first snow comes."

"*Salut! Salut! Nasdorobi!*" shout Laia and Naiara, clinking together the rainbow-sheened glasses Iryna and Vasyl brought as presents to Catalonia.

In the background, the last minute of the call is marked with the tune of the song *Shchedryk,* which began in Ukraine and became famous around the world as the Carol of the Bells. But neither of the families knows this.

***

MOSCOW, 13 MAY 1986, 10.00 H (LOCAL TIME)

To carry out the transplant at the hospital they've asked his two sisters from Belarus to come, as well as his brother who is doing his military service in Leningrad and little Natasha, who can't stop crying. She's 14 and very scared. In the bone marrow tests, it turns out that she's the most suitable.

Vasya can sometimes still express himself coherently. He won't have them taking bone marrow from his little sister.

"I'd rather die! Don't touch her! She's the little one!"

The eldest – Lyuda – is 28. She's a strong, good-looking girl... And she's the one with fewest commitments.

She's never married, she's a nurse and, although she knows it's a risky operation, she offers to go through with it:

"Do whatever you need to me so he can live."

Finally, she's the one they choose. There's a big window in the operating theatre. They are lying alongside one another on two tables. The operation takes too long. When it's over, Lyuda feels worse than Vasya. She has struggled to come out of the anaesthetic. I run from one ward to another, to see him and visit her. He is in a hyperbaric chamber behind a transparent curtain and no-one can go in. There are special instruments for giving him injections and putting catheters in without touching him. They do it with a special grip with suckers on... I learn to use it. Next to the curtain there is a little chair.

I look at it. He's resting there like an angel on a slab. The folds of the sheet cover his ravaged body. Be strong, Vasya! My brave husband! My man! The father of the child inside me!

I close my eyes and rest a little while he sleeps. Sleep comes against a background of unease. He's saying something. I move my ears closer and try to read his lips.

"Lyusya, Lyusya!"

"What do you want my love?"

"Lyusya, Lyusya, where are you?"

"I'm here with you, my love. I'm not going to leave you on your own. I'm never going to leave you..."

***

WINTER 2005

Christmas is over, but some lovely cards have just been delivered. They must have cost lots of hryvnias. Esperança realises that correcting their Catalan writing at a distance is very difficult and, as they can now make themselves understood, they haven't made much progress lately. She thinks it would be a good idea to phone the Association to see if they have any contacts in Ukraine who could carry on giving them lessons until they come back to Catalonia. Fortunato gives her Natasha's telephone number and Esperança calls her straightaway:

"Hello, I'm speaking from Rouralba. It's Esperança here. I had Iryna and Vasyl last summer. Do you know them?"

"Yes, I often see them at school."

"Are you a teacher?"

"No, I just give after-school Spanish lessons."

"And how are Iryna and Vasyl getting on at school?"

"Whenever I see her, she's studying. He's out in the playground all day with his friends listening to music."

"But, doesn't he go in for lessons?"

"Here in Ukraine, if a child doesn't want to study you just let him get on with it, as long as he doesn't cause trouble..."

Esperança has found out quite a lot in the course of the conversation, including the fact that Natasha finds Spanish easier to speak than Catalan. So she decides to ask her if she'll give the children Spanish lessons, because it's a language that will also be useful for the children to know if they keep coming to Catalonia. Natasha says she'll speak to the children and, if they're interested, she'll do the classes on Saturdays, which is the only day she has free for beginners. They come to an agreement about hryvnias and Esperança tells her that when she comes to Catalonia in the summer with the group of hosted children she will give her the money for all the classes. She's happy with 60 euros.

***

MOSCOW, 14 MAY 1986, 3.50 H (LOCAL TIME)

He starts feeling bad and won't stop calling me: "Lyusya, Lyusya!" And I soothe him, saying "I'm here, I'm here my love!"

Some soldiers have arrived. I don't know where they've come from. They've come to act as nurses because the health staff have refused to do it: they want isolation suits. The troops are very young, simple lads. I go closer to see how they do things. I ask them:

"Please! Go to the other hyperbaric chambers. I want to look after this one myself."

The soldiers get out the buckets, clean the floor, change the sheets... So do I. I take the gauze, I change his dressings, I clean him. Every day we find out that someone else has died:

"Tischura's dead."

"Titenok's dead."

Dead, dead... the word hammers in my head. 25 or 30 defecations a day, with blood and mucus. The skin on his hands is beginning to break up. He's covered all over in boils. When he moves his head, hanks of hair are left on the pillow. He tries to joke about it:

"Look, now you won't need the comb for me."

Soon the soldiers shave all their heads.

"Let me have the clippers. I'll do him myself."

I want to do everything myself. I want to stay there 24 hours a day. I feel bad about missing a minute. Must this be love? Or do I just want to die alongside him? They keep giving him injections to make him sleep. When he wakes up, his face asks me:

"What's going to become of me?"

I'm as evasive as I can be. I don't want him to think about death. I hate death because it wants to take him, and Vasya is mine and mine alone. Someone says to me:

"You mustn't forget that what you've got there is not your beloved husband. It's a highly contaminating radioactive element. Be sensible, not suicidal."

I don't answer. Crazy women can allow themselves the luxury of not answering. I'm crazy for Vasya: I love him! As he sleeps, I repeat to him, softly, over and over:

"I love you!"

I go into the hospital courtyard and pray: I love him! I bring him the bedpan and I can't contain it: "I love you."

And in dreams I take his hand all night, like before. And when we wake up our hands are clasped, like before... Let's make everything like before – as much as we can. But he knows that the future is running faster than dreams... and if he can't catch it, it will be too late.

"I really want to see our baby!"

"What shall we call it?" I ask him.

"Well, that's for you to decide," he answers.

"Why me on my own? It's something for both of us, isn't it?"

"Well, I thought that if it's a boy we could call him Vasya and if it's a girl, Natasha."

"I've already got a Vasya – you – and I don't want another one."

***

WINTER 2005

Once Esperança has spoken with Natasha she phones the children and it seems as if they will go to the classes, although Iryna says she has a lot of school work because Dobrokiv wants to bring its school up to European standards and they are suddenly asking about topics they've never been taught.

"Well perhaps Natasha will be able to give you a hand. You know, when you're grown up you'll be pleased you've learned Spanish. If one day, when you're old enough, you come to work in Catalonia... Is Vasyl listening to me? Please put your brother on."

"Hi, Esperança!"

"I know you like to be free, Vasyl. But I wouldn't like it if you were one of those lads who can only do hard, dangerous work – shifting bricks and stones and lugging cement and sand. Or one of those men stuck in boring jobs in factories or putting out roadworks cones or bending metal for railway bridges. Do you understand me?" she asks him. After hearing a faint "Yes" she continues. "Is Iryna still there?"

"Yes, I'm here."

"You're so pretty, Iryna, I don't want you to be one of those women who spend their time cleaning from morning to night. And I certainly don't want you to get disappointed with the world because it doesn't give you what you expected. You'd end up as one of those women who throw their beauty away to earn easy money. You're both so creative and clever. And you're good people, so I'm sure that won't happen. Certainly not if Miquel and I can help you. If you get the most from your lessons and revise the notebooks we made you'll know Catalan and Spanish and that, together with Russian and Ukrainian, will open doors for you. Do you hear me, Iryna?"

"Yes, I understand you. But we don't know what we want to do yet."

"I know you're only 12 and Vasyl's only 13. But you're so bright you're not going to want to leave your future to chance. Do you understand what I mean?"

"What do you think? Here most children know how we're going to end up... We need to earn money so we go to work long before Catalan children. I'm thinking about other things: I'd like to know if our country can sort itself out. Also, I don't know if I'd have the strength to be away from my family for a long time. If you only knew... how much I've missed my family and friends these two summers while I've been away! And remember, Esperança, you've got your own daughters. Are you going to be able to cope with all of us?"

"It's quite normal for you to think about your family, but you'll soon be 13! You're gradually going to want to fly the nest and you'll be even keener to go if you know it's going to mean you can help them too... Maybe we can set up a restaurant for you, or a motorbike repair garage, but to understand people you have to know the language. OK?"

"Don't worry, Esperança, I'll never forget my Catalan. When Vasyl doesn't want to practise with me, I speak it on my own. What I do is imagine I'm with you and that I'm telling you the things I've done during the day and that you're answering me."

"Poor Iryna! Be patient with Vasyl. He's got a good heart even if he's a little thoughtless. He'll end up studying, you'll see. Remember when I made him learn his multiplication tables? I did it so he would value his numbers and would know them by heart. Who would have thought he'd end up knowing them better in Catalan than in Ukrainian? What about your parents? How are they?"

"Mum's still cleaning at the hospital in town and she also helps out in the operating theatre. This month she's earned 200 extra hryvnias. Thank God for that, because Dad's working on a pig farm in Kiev and they don't pay him anything."

"How come they don't pay him?"

"Every month they tell him it'll be the month after and they end up never paying."

"What about the cow?"

"It's fine now, but you know the neighbour takes sometimes it out to graze and then we take hers out? Well, a few days ago while it was eating it fell into a very deep hole."

"Wasn't there a warning sign?"

"There used to be a big iron cover, but people took the metal to sell so they could make some money. Someone told us as soon as it happened. The cow was shouting just like a person. You should have heard Mum crying. It cost a lot of hryvnias to hire a car with a counter-weight to get it out. And you can't imagine the noise the poor cow made."

"And was it still alive?"

"Yes, but Mum was very worried about the calf it was carrying. She prayed that nothing would happen to it," Iryna explains very seriously, but she hears giggles from Esperança at the other end of the line. "Yes, it's funny now, but you should have seen her then. You don't know how much Mum loves that cow. And also we're lucky that with the money we make from the milk we can buy bread and other food. Without that, how would we manage?"

"I know you have to work a lot. But...will you go to classes with Natasha?"

"Of course I'll go. And I'll do everything I can to see that Vasyl comes too."

They have also mentioned that this week, in accordance with one of Kuchma's final orders, Ukraine is withdrawing the troops it was sending to Iraq.

"I've read that eight Ukrainian soldiers have died. Is that right?"

"It seems there are more but because we're independent we've got the right to have opinions and change a few things... How is your independence struggle going?"

They keep finding more parallels between the two countries: the Ukrainians' desire to be a nation has already been fulfilled but they hope that if Catalonia ever becomes independent it will not be because Spain has abandoned it as no longer being any use. And that Catalonia is never plagued by a curse similar to Chernobyl.

What the children would be telling Esperança, if they only knew it, is that the older Vasyl is, for the second time, using the hryvnias he gets paid at the pig farm to have his radiotherapy sessions. He's doing it because the doctors have told him that in many cases it makes the cancer cells stop multiplying, or at least slows them down.

Esperança has stretched out on the sofa remembering young Vasyl. She suddenly imagines him saying his tables again: $9 \times 0 = 0$, $9 \times 1 = 9$... sitting there, just 13 but looking more like 16. In the summer, Laia and Naiara teased him when he got it wrong and, irritated, he took the sheet with the times table he was studying and went off for a bike ride. As soon as he was out the door, he rode with no hands so he could read the piece of paper half stuck on to the handlebars. Then, when he knew them, he turned up at Miquel's garage and said them there. Later on, at dinner, Esperança's husband said he knew them all and Vasyl puffed up with pride as if to say: "Look, when I put my mind to something...".

***

MOSCOW, 15 MAY 1986, 23.00 H (LOCAL TIME)

Until now, I haven't thought about the little one – the treasure I have inside... How come it's not complaining? When I don't talk to it, I don't even feel its heart. It doesn't move. It's quiet, waiting. It knows it has to behave. That my belly will protect it. That its father needs me.

"My dear child, I don't even know if you're a boy or a girl, but listen to me. I love you. I chose you a young, tall, strong, generous father, but he's hurt and maybe you'll never meet him. I also used to be young and brave, but I'm tired now..." I find it hard to move with my swollen legs, blue to the knees. I'm going to lie down on the bed. I can't go on.

He says they've been to photograph him when I wasn't there. I wasn't even away an hour and they've already been taking advantage. They know I wouldn't have let them do it – I'd have beaten them away with my bare hands. He belongs to me, not to science! How dare they! They've taken photographs of him with no clothes on – naked. I find him covered with a light sheet, soaked with blood, like a statue of Christ. When I change him, the material sticks to him and pieces of skin fall off. He cries piteously:

"Let me die, Lyusya!"

I beg him:

"Help me, my love. I've got to put your bottom sheet straight."

Every wrinkle in the material means a bedsore. I pare down my nails, drawing blood, so I don't hurt him.

I go into the corridor. I bump into the wall and the chairs. I can't see the soldiers. In the end, I find the duty nurse.

"He's dying."

And she answers:

"Well, what did you expect? He's received 1,600 roentgens of radioactivity and 400 are enough to kill. You're sitting next to a reactor."

I've spent all day sitting in the chair beside him. I don't know where my legs or my body are. There are two forces inside me. One is asking me to rest and think of the life I'm carrying inside me... The other keeps me tied to my husband's bedside. From time to time, the second force allows the first a little relaxation:

"Vasya, I'm going out for a minute. I'm going to rest for a bit."

He opens and closes his eyes and lets me go.

***

WHO WOULD HAVE IMAGINED they'd have such a stroke of luck? The shopkeepers offer Iryna a big, soft, warm bed. In a corner is a chest of drawers covered with a cloth embroidered with coloured cross-stitch. On it are the photographs of the younger members of the family, framed in bright colours. The Virgin Mary, wrapped in another embroidered cloth, presides over them. They can't resist telling her who all the people are. And it must be a long time since they've seen them because in two of the photos the man has got the details wrong and his wife has had to remind him.

"No, that's Blada. This is Katyuska. Put your glasses on!" she chides him, passing him her reading glasses.

"But little children all look the same, don't they?" he apologises.

"Yes, they do. At home, when they look at the few photos they've got of when I was young, if it wasn't for the dress and the hair, they'd mix me up with Lyuba."

"Well, goodnight, you must be really tired. Tomorrow will be another day!"

"God willing! Goodnight!"

Tomorrow she's thinking of asking them where she can fill up with petrol. How silly of her to have imagined that they could have got as far as the border today! Once she's closed the door, she checks through the rucksack from top to bottom. She finds her brother's euros in a blue bag closed with a long piece of elastic. Esperança made it for him... she used to tie it to Vasyl's waist so he could carry the money people gave him. She wraps it round like he used to and fixes it with her knickers. She chuckles to herself, remembering her brother showing off the outfit. Then she takes the dollars from the purse and splits them into two bundles. She could hide them in a handkerchief in her bra, but she often leaks milk and they might get wet. As her brother has put some clean socks in for her, she puts on two pairs and hides the notes flat, like a sandwich between them. She is so tired that she drops off almost as soon as she puts the child to her breast. She sleeps uneasily. She dreams she has to go down the long staircase inside a dome. She's carrying her daughter on her shoulders, holding her with one hand and with the other gripping the buzzing metal rail... The more flights she goes down, the darker it gets... Suddenly, she finds one of the steps is broken. She looks up and sees the shopkeepers who have taken her in. Her foot is shaking... The woman asks her: "Where's the little girl?" Then she notices that she's not carrying her. She's coming down on her own. She crosses the empty space as best she can to look for Lyuba, but she's disappeared. When she gets to the bottom, she finds her stretched out on her back on the floor. Her eyes are looking at Iryna as if nothing had happened, but from the back of her head something pink is oozing. There is a little blood and, half stuck in there, a kind of transparent bag which Iryna, terrified, pushes back into her brain through a hole in her head. She wakes up with the sinister feeling of having sticky fingers. She's soaked with sweat. The little girl has stopped sucking, but she's still fixed on to Iryna's nipple with a tiny tooth. Now awake, Iryna hears voices of doom. She concentrates, but can't quite understand the conversation. On tiptoe, with the little girl in her arms, she moves towards the bedroom next door. He says he wants to phone. She says it's too late, they can do it tomorrow. Perhaps they've seen Iryna on the television. They must want to tell the police. They must be scared. She doesn't believe anyone will offer them a reward. Her bedroom window overlooks the road. She pulls back the curtain and is horrified: there's another transparent curtain out there with little white dots that keep on falling. The snowflakes are clinging to swollen branches of the trees, forming a white frieze. The snow shines with the moon and, against it, the line of fir trees guards the road like a row of black ghosts. In a couple of hours, the handlebars of the Vespa have become branches and the scooter's engine the trunk that supports them. The night is cold and dark. She can't just jump out the window with Lyuba and get back on the road. She hears the man head down to the shop, where she has seen they have the telephone. She runs out of the room and stands in front of him.

"Don't do it! For my daughter's sake! For God's sake help me!"

She takes two hundred dollars from her sock, presses the money into his hand and folds his fingers around the notes.

187

Chapter 10

Iryna and Vasyl have returned to Catalonia and July and August have flown by. They all laughed a lot when Iryna told the story of how the calf was born.

"It was Saturday, very early in the morning. Mum had to go to work at the hospital and, before she went, she told me: 'Feed the cow and phone me if you see she's not well.' I stayed at home, sleeping. I suddenly woke up to some horrible noises. 'Oh no! The cow!' I thought. 'I haven't given her anything to eat or drink!' I got up straightaway and when I got into the shed I found her lying down. The calf's nose and front legs were half out. I tried to help her and... you can't imagine how slippery it was. It seemed as if it had been oiled. I ran to look for cloths and gloves to pull it like Mum does... 'Thank God!' I said, when it came out. It was normal: it had four legs and wanted to suckle."

"Of course. You must have been really happy. I know how worried you were when the cow fell in the tank!"

"Yes! And it was worse because strange animals – monsters if you like – are often born in the contaminated area."

When the children arrived they were even taller and better looking than the year before, and, now they are leaving, they are more tanned and less sad. But, for some reason, while everyone else chatters away in the car to the airport to catch the plane back to Ukraine, Iryna is silently staring at her mobile phone.

"What are you looking for, Iryna?" they ask her.

As if relieved from pressure that had been tormenting her all summer, she explains that, in the winter, Pietat had kept sending her strange messages and that now another one has arrived. She's already read it several times.

"Really?"

"Look."

The girl shows the mobile and on the blue screen they can read: "How are you getting on with the whitewashed tombs?"

"Who gave her your number? You didn't have a mobile when you were with her, did you?"

"No, we didn't have it then... it's the one Miquel gave to Vasyl. She might have got the number by phoning one of the children who came the first year I did..."

"We didn't want to tell anyone in Ukraine what happened to us with Pietat," says Vasyl.

"You know, Esperança? I looked that expression up in the encyclopedia and it was the image of a dream I've often had..."

It's almost the last thing anyone says at the airport but afterwards Laia and Naiara have a barrage of questions for their mother and father:

"What does 'whitewashed tombs' mean?"

"You know what a tomb is – a place where it's completely quiet. You really don't want to know any more.

There's no need to stir it all up," Miquel answers them.

The next day their mobile phone bill arrives. Miquel opens it. Normally they pay 70 euros a month, this one is for 230. What on earth is going on? They look at the details and they are all calls to Ukraine made from Esperança's phone.

"Esperança. Did you give them the mobile to use?"

"No. Well, once to phone their parents. Oh! Lots of calls were made the same day and always to the same number."

They look in the contacts and it's the number of the children's neighbours in Ukraine.

"Why would she have had to phone so many times? Because it must be Iryna who's done it. Vasyl will do anything to avoid talking. He doesn't even want to phone his friends and when Iryna phones their parents he only says a few words to them at the end of the call."

Esperança is quite angry, but after thinking for a while she tries to calm Miquel.

"Do you remember, we had to do something about our two as well, or they would have ruined us? And their phone didn't have any prepaid balance. They only received messages. They can't have imagined it would be so expensive."

"What do you mean they didn't know? They've fooled you like they fooled Pietat! Read the letter that was in the envelope with the bill."

It's from Iryna:

191

Esperança, please forgive me. I know I've been very, very bad, but I'll never do it again, I'm very ashamed. I went to the mailbox to see if there were letters from Ukraine and I found the phone bill and I opened it. I couldn't believe how much. I couldn't sleep all night. I thought I'd hide the letter and not put it in the mailbox until the day we left. Forgive me, please, I love you a lot and I didn't want you to be angry. I'll never forgive myself because I shouldn't have done it... Forgive me for not admitting it to your face. I didn't want a bad end to the summer. I'm not telling you because I'm afraid you won't want to help me anymore. It's because I feel very bad about deceiving you and I have to tell you.

I don't know if I've told you other times, but we believe in dreams a lot. A month ago, I had a recurring one that worried me. My dead uncle got out of his tomb and came up the road towards home, followed by three more men who were buried during the winter. One was a friend who'd had a motorbike accident. The other two had suffered the horrible disease. Dad's brother was very well dressed. He was holding an Easter egg in his hand and he asked them to open it. I thought that the mother of Nadiya, our neighbour, could help me and that was why I phoned so many times. I had a premonition. Were the dead coming looking for someone at home? Who could it be? When she told me everyone was fine, I felt reassured.

I didn't know how to tell you. Please forgive me.

I love you a lot.

Iryna

Eyes full of tears, Esperança reads the letter from her Iryna again and, although she isn't happy about what she's been told, she forgives the girl. But Miquel is full of mistrust for Iryna's neighbour, Iryna herself and everyone:

"Perhaps it was that woman who gave Vasyl's mobile number to Pietat... And what about Iryna? The older she is the more shameless and brazen she gets! Just don't mention her name to me!"

Esperança is used to fighting her battles silently and she accepts that life always gives you less than you expect. But to carry on she needs to believe in Iryna and the Biblical quotation about the *whitewashed tomb* obsesses her: can it be true that she's painted outside while inside everything is rotten? The phrase continues to bother her as she tries to solve the mystery of why she took in Vasyl and Iryna. Why does she believe she has a right to form part of their destiny? Is the fact that she's got two spare beds and can easily feed two extra mouths enough? Would she make the same sacrifices for these children as she would for her own? Or perhaps they are like pets, providing entertainment and distraction?

Esperança does not want to be understood or applauded. There is no way she wants to become one of those pious ladies who visit the poor and take food to charitable organisations the way that farmers' wives get up early to throw corn to the chickens. Esperança doesn't want to give charity, she wants to put herself in the shoes of those who are suffering. She wants equal opportunities for those children and their family. That's why she always feels she isn't doing very much... and why she's always thinking of them.

When the children have been gone for a month, she sees an exhibition of projects carried out during the summer by the local council. She goes in and sees a display board explaining that Rouralba spends 0.7% of municipal tax revenues on this. In one of the photographs, she sees a group of children with the mayor and the councillors... They are the *Sahrawi* children from the Western Sahara hosted in the village. The board explains that this summer, as they are every year, the children were invited for tea in Riera Park and the host families were grateful to have their travel costs and outings paid for...

"Look, the *Sahrawis* get all that and the Ukrainians don't!" she says to Miquel when she gets home.

And, although she knows the official period for applying for reimbursement is over, she takes all her receipts for Iryna and Vasyl's municipal outings and their air fares to the town hall. The secretary of the Municipal Council for Cooperation and Solidarity tells her he will raise her case at the next meeting. She phones several times to find out what they have agreed. Finally, they call her in and the secretary gives her a cheque for 80 euros. He asks her for a signature and a photograph of the Ukrainian children to provide justification for their expenses.

"This won't even pay for one of the kids' outings with the sports club!" Esperança complains.

"In other words, the Council knows I've got Iryna and Vasyl – two children who are hosted because they are in a situation of extreme poverty, although in this case, they've also got problems resulting from radioactive pollution – and you've got the nerve to pay some families their air fares and others a pittance? What kind of justice is that?"

"We assume that families host children of their own free will because they can afford it. The Council agreed to help the Friends of the *Sahrawi* People Association but not Twinning Ukraine-86. Perhaps if you were on the Council they'd consider your case and you'd see that we do everything by consensus..."

"So many Awareness Days to show Rouralba's solidarity and now it turns out that hosted children from Ukraine have no right to tea in the park!"

It makes her feel misunderstood – an immigrant among her own people. She has doubts about the whole Council, let alone whether she wants to join it. "Who knows what I'll be getting myself involved in." Finally, just in case she's wrong and because she doesn't want Iryna and Vasyl to miss out, she asks the mayor if she can attend the Council's meetings. After a few days she receives confirmation that she will be allowed in.

***

MOSCOW, 16 MAY 1986, 02.00 H (LOCAL TIME)

I go to the hotel. I can't get on to the bed because I hurt all over. I stretch out on the floor. "Don't go to sleep," I say to myself. But I have to rest. I've promised Tanya Kibenok we'll go to the cemetery together. If I don't sleep a little, I won't be able to comfort her. I won't have the strength to go with her.

Today they're burying two friends: Vitya Kibenok and Volodya Pravik. The night before the explosion, we put the timer on the camera and took a picture of us – three couples together. We'd just had dinner and we made a toast. Who could have told us what was going to happen? I haven't got the photo here, but I see it as if I had it in my hands. I move my finger over Vasya and I can feel his warmth again.

"All mine! The thing I love most in this world!"

On the way back from the cemetery I pop into the hotel to pick up some things I've left scattered around and I talk to the nurse on the telephone:

"How is he?"

"He died 15 minutes ago."

"But...how? I was with him all night. I only went out for three hours..."

The bedroom window is open, I'm on the verge of shouting:

"Why? Why?"

The people from the hotel leave me alone. They're afraid to come near me. They think I'm mad. I don't know where I get the strength. No-one comes to the hospital with me. "If you don't make a real fuss you won't be able to see him," I say to myself. I have to see him one more time. The last time. They've still got him in the mortuary, they haven't taken him away... They tell me his last words were:

"Lyusya! Lyusya!"

They tried to calm him, telling him:

"She'll be back soon. She's popped out for a minute."

When he heard that, he sighed and went quiet.

"I'm here now, with you! I won't leave you now!"

I look at him: he's one giant sore! I embrace him tenderly. I can feel his bones move and, although he's dead, he spits pieces of lung and liver when I try to move him. In the early hours, I'd helped him clear his throat of gunk so he didn't choke. Now all I can do is pray for the little piece of his flesh I'm carrying inside.

They put him in his dress uniform cut down the back, with his helmet on his chest. He's not wearing shoes because his feet are so swollen they haven't found any to fit him!

"Oh God! In a plastic bag! No! As if he were rubbish. No, no, no!"

They tie it up and shut it in the coffin. Now they wrap the coffin in transparent cellophane as thick as cardboard. The image is blurry, but I'll always remember it.

"Stay with me, Vasya!" I say to him, as I hear them putting this coffin inside a zinc one. "You'll always be there in my heart!"

Only the helmet remains on top.

***

AUTUMN 2005

Esperança goes to some of the meetings of the Solidarity Council. Every time, they all sit down to a meal using napkins printed with sad-looking, dark-skinned, starving children. There are glossy, full-colour leaflets that charities quite happily publish with other people's money. Printed page after printed page with objectives, rights, obligations and powers, none of which anybody reads. How many publishers does hunger feed? Who are these people who travel the continents to see if their projects are being carried out? Mostly a bunch of social snobs. And, as if that were not enough, when the minutes are approved they drink a toast with *cava*. Maybe she could get the Council on the side of the Ukrainian guest children, but to do it she would have to sell herself much too cheap. She doesn't want to and she doesn't need to. "These are the whitewashed tombs!" she says to herself, holding tight to her chair as if it could protect her from outside influences. When they raise their glasses for the toast, her wish is quite clear:

"I hope to God I never need your help!"

How happy and self-satisfied they were before she came along to bother them! She can see their eyes telling her what they think of the weird woman who won't play their game. And she would like to be able to answer that everything she's learned with them has done her more harm than good. She would like to explain that she used to believe in solidarity and that now she's sure that the word was invented to soothe the consciences of "rich whites seeking poor blacks".

As she gets up to be the first to leave, the Council, by consensus, agrees to spend 50 per cent of its budget on this year's tsunami and the rest on Mauritania.

Every month, Esperança continues to receive notices of Council meetings, sealed and written neatly on one side only of pieces of nice, thick paper. She uses them for writing notes on the back, but she no longer bothers to answer them because she can't bring herself to agree with what goes on at these meetings. It's not worth making a fuss. She's decided to devote all the time she would have spent going to the meetings to answering the letters she receives from Ukraine, all of them written on sheets ripped from a spiral notebook with the little bits of paper cut off the top so they look neater. She refuses to have anything to do with the kind of politics that negotiates with feelings, and she no longer corrects Iryna's spelling mistakes. What matters is that she carries on writing and telling her what's happening in Ukraine:

Dear family,

My Ykpaiha is very bad and very slow because of the thieves all over the country. And they show silly news to hide problems: they say chickens give you flu. Dyou believe that? We won't even be able to eat eggs! President Viktor Yushenko has sent soldiers to houses to control virus...

Iryna

Esperança goes ahead with her life, but she keeps looking back, searching for the causes of the injustice. Her dreams are nostalgic. She thinks the Orange Coalition can win. Today on the news she has heard that more than 3,000 people have been in hospital because of the cold and that hundreds have died. She remembered the pictures she saw in the Sunday colour supplement last week, with Viktor Yushenko bravely having a lovely swim in the Dnieper. She wants to believe that things are getting better, but she doubts it. At the moment, her task is to carry on protecting those children. She's no longer hosting foreign children for the summer, she's concerned about four children all year round. And Miquel lets her get on with it, which in itself is a lot.

"So they're coming back next year, are they?"

"Yes, Miquel. In the end you'll see that we need them more than they need us."

***

MOSCOW, 17 MAY 1986, 10.00 H (LOCAL TIME)

They say we're all dead now. There's nothing left in the hospital. They've taken the plaster off the walls, pulled up the floor and ripped out all the wood and the doors.

The family have come: his parents; mine... We buy black handkerchiefs in Moscow. We want to talk to the hospital managers. We are received by an Extraordinary Committee. They all tell us the same thing:

"We can't give you back the bodies. We have to bury them in Moscow in a special way, under layers of concrete. You have to sign these documents for us."

If we do it for them, they say they'll go down in history as heroes.

"They're not yours any more: they belong to the State."

The relatives and the soldiers get on the coach. A colonel shouts over the radio:

"We're awaiting orders! Hang on!"

In the end they start off, but they kill time, going round and round the Moscow ring road. They don't let us into the cemetery, which is surrounded by foreign correspondents. I'm furious:

"Why can't we bury him? He's not a criminal!"

My mother calms me, stroking my head. I go on:

"Why do we have to hide him?"

The colonel reports over the radio:

"Keep an eye on this woman. She's having an attack of hysteria... Let her through."

The soldiers escort us as far as the coffin and then they take it away. We're the only ones who have managed to get there. Only we can see the way they cover him with earth. There is no ceremony. It's as if he were a decomposing dead dog.

"Come on, hurry up!" orders an officer.

We have to sneak back to the coach, hiding all the way. A man stays with us. He's in civilian clothes but his manners are military. He gives us our tickets to go home. We are watched all the time. They have us in a hotel and they don't let us out, not even to buy food for the journey back. We can't speak to anyone, let alone cry... We have to pay for the health service hotel ourselves. When we leave, a worker puts all the sheets in a polythene bag so they can be burned.

***

SUMMER 2006

Iryna and Vasyl spend the whole of July in a camp in the Pyrenees and make lots of friends. The mountain peaks, which until now have seemed inaccessible places, where they can never go, make them want to be far away with na-diya – the hope that life will give them what they dream of. In August, the whole family returns to the coast at Tamariu and, when they see the sea, it feels like they are discovering it for the first time. Iryna and her brother can't help saying:

"How blue it is! How big!"

Vasyl once again climbs the cliffs, but before diving head-first into the sea he shouts:

"Esperaaança!"

This year even the three girls dive in, but they scream:

"Miqueeel!" as if they were afraid he would be jealous.

When they talk, after meals or while sunbathing, they often compare the way summers are spent in Ukraine with Catalonia.

"Our street is full of children. We all know each other."

"Here, you only say 'Good morning' to the neighbours. At home, we make fires in the streets at night and we tell each other what's worrying us and what makes us happy."

"Now our parents will be talking about what we used to do when we were little. Maybe they're making plans for when we're grown up."

"And they have competitions dancing the *kozachok*, the traditional Cossack dance. Dad and his brother always used to get to the final. Didn't they, Ira?"

"But Dad's was much better!" says the girl. Thinking about it in Catalonia, she can't imagine her father sitting down while there's music playing.

But in fact the older Vasyl doesn't want to dance any more. His brother's death two years ago from a disease so similar to his own has put him off, and it also hurts him when people notice that his legs aren't as strong as they used to be.

Both Iryna and Vasyl would like to show them their country. They are in love with their Dnieper, their Kiev, their customs... They want them to meet their father so he can tell them his plans. Olena also wants to see them again. She has so many good memories of that summer in Catalonia that she even wants to introduce them to the cats, the dogs and the cow. That doesn't mean they're not aware of what they're lacking or of the desire that others help them.

"This winter Dad lost his job on the pig farm and Mum had to work a lot," says Iryna.

"A good thing too, Ira! In the end they weren't paying him anyway."

"What a nerve!"

"Yes, but in fact what he likes best is going into the forest every day. He always comes back with lots of stuff. He hires the neighbour's horse and brings back big tree trunks. He takes advantage of the horse being cheap in the summer, because it's really expensive at potato harvest time. He always has plans in his head: he says he's going to extend the house in case we get married one day and want to stay there to live with them."

"Our house is all made of wood with big windows and, at this time of year, it's full of flowers... Wouldn't you like to see it?"

The talk goes on and on and one day as they're coming up from the beach they decide that next summer it will be Esperança, Miquel and their daughters who go to visit Ukraine. That way, Vasyl can help his father cut up the tree trunks in the good weather and learn to build walls like he does.

Their preparations and dreams fill the months from September 2006 until they finally go to Ukraine in

August 2007. Esperança started telling her friends at the beginning of the year and they have brought her everything they can find with information about Ukraine: dictionaries, tourist guides, telephone numbers and so on. The whole thing has snowballed and they're so excited about it there's no going back now. But they do take their precautions.

Every summer, Laia and Naiara spend July in England, but this year they're not going until August – the same time their parents will be in Ukraine.

"It's not fair!" complain Laia and Naiara, but, as they also miss their English friends, who fit better with their lifestyle anyway, they don't make a fuss.

Why aren't Miquel and Esperança taking their daughters? The truth is that they are worried about different kinds of problems. Firstly, it is a way of lightening the load for the Ukrainian family, who won't hear of them staying in the village guest house. It will be easier for them to feed two than four.

"You've had us at your house lots of summers and one year there were three of us. Can't we have you for just a week at our house?"

Also, it will be a long journey to a mysterious country with an unknown language and strange customs. They are also concerned about hygiene and afraid of radioactivity. They don't say anything to anyone, but in fact they are really quite scared. If they could, they'd even take bottled water from home.

If it wasn't for Esperança's compulsive habit of making life difficult for herself and her desire to find out more about what happened at Chernobyl, they wouldn't be going at all. Miquel just goes along with her. He's very busy because their week away coincides with the few last days of an exhibition of cars they're putting on in Madrid. That means his wife will have to make all the preparations.

***

KIEV, 20 MAY 1986, 10.00 H (LOCAL TIME)

They've had to take me to hospital. They say I've slept for three days and nights. They thought I was dead. I have a terrible dream. My late great-grandmother comes to see me and I ask her: "How come you're decorating a Christmas tree in the living room when it's summer?" "It's for Vasya, who's coming to see me soon..." she tells me. Vasya is dressed in white and he shows himself to me thanks to our daughter Natasha, who hasn't been born yet but appears to me quite well grown. Her father takes her and throws her in the air... Both of them laugh happily. I walk on water with him and the little girl. We walk down the Dnieper looking for the sea... Suddenly a giant wave with the face of an evil spirit breaks over the two of them and swallows them up.

Part Two

Chapter 1

At five in the afternoon, Miquel and Esperança are in the airport queue to check in four suitcases, two with their clothes and two others full of things their friends have given them for the family in Ukraine. In the middle of the commotion, Miquel's mobile phone rings:

"Dad, can you hear me? Listen, they've moved Naiara to another hostel – she's been taken to another town."

"Isn't she with you in London?"

"No!"

"Why? What's happened? Can you put me on to the director?"

"He'll phone you now but you won't understand each other. He hardly speaks Spanish. And he's going to tell you a lot of lies anyway."

"Lies?"

"Yes. He'll tell you Naiara's a criminal and that she's been arrested for stealing. But the poor girl only picked up a packet of chewing gum from the stand at the shop entrance. She thought they were free. You need to come, Dad."

"I'll come, don't worry. I'll ring you straight back," he promises and hangs up.

Esperança, who doesn't suspect who he's talking to because their daughters only flew to England yesterday and she knows the journey went well, asks:

209

"Who is it?"

He has an idea. "The foreman's phoned and he says there's a Chinese company interested in the revolving platform we've got on display in Madrid."

"The one that looks like a puzzle you designed to show the new electric model?"

"Yes. They liked the fact that it could be dismantled into such small pieces and they want to place a big order."

"That sounds like it might be a good deal..."

"Yes, yes, but only I can sign the contract. I'll have to go."

"How?"

"Look, you go to Ukraine. Stay in the queue here and I'll go and try to sell my ticket or exchange it for a flight to Madrid. Give me my case. My clothes are in this one, aren't they?"

"Yes, but... how am I going to manage without you? We've always travelled together!"

"I'm sure you'll be OK on your own. And they're expecting you. I bet they've got everything ready. Go on, you go at least!" he says, kissing her so he doesn't have to listen to her objections or alternative solutions.

Esperança moves forward over the polished floor as if hypnotised by the letters of the word "Kiev", growing larger on the screen. Her feet slide on the tiles. Every one she passes brings her closer to the children she hasn't seen for ten months. Esperança is used to fighting her own battles and, to stop herself getting angry with her husband and the circumstances, she talks to the people around her in the queue. As all of them look like Ukrainians, she thinks this is a good way of starting to get to know the country. One of the passengers helps her, taking one of the three suitcases she has been left with. He tells her that he left Kiev for Buenos Aires at the age of 14 and has not had the chance to return until now, in his seventies, with a stopover in Barcelona.

He is sad that many of the people he left behind are dead, but pleased that a neighbour he still writes to is awaiting him. He tells her about his life: he and his friend are now widowed and he dreams of swimming in the river again with her and plaiting her a necklace with long water lily stems.

"So far away! And this is the first time you've been able to return to your own country!" says Esperança.

"Ukrainians are scattered everywhere, but most of us are in Canada, the United States and Argentina. Keep your ears open here in the queue and you'll find out for yourself."

It's a strange way for Esperança to kill the time but she has a knot in her stomach she can only undo by talking. The oppressive feeling grows because the journey isn't something she needs to do and she's not going for pleasure either. She wonders now if it wouldn't have been better to stay at home. She's looking for quick answers because the plane in front of her doesn't look very modern and mechanics are working underneath it. She should have boarded at 18.25 but they are not allowed on until 19.12. Meanwhile, Miquel has called saying that he managed to sell the ticket for Ukraine and buy one for Madrid and now he's getting on the plane. He'll take off before she does.

Once she's sitting down with her seatbelt done up, the great bird in the plumage of Ukraine International Airlines entertains itself by taxiing along the runway very slowly. By the time it takes off, creaking irritably, it's gone eight. The Port of Barcelona shrinks at the same speed as her chest tightens when she sees only water below her. After an hour or so she sees broken coastline and islands and feels more secure. Many people are sleeping; others are reading. Esperança's eyes are fixed on a sun that doesn't seem to want to set. The rays turn, only just perceptibly, from pink to purple and, in a breath, the great disc disappears from the sky. Suddenly she sees that millions of little lights have come on. They are flying over the continent. The intercom announces that it is now midnight in their destination country. The pilot lands smoothly and all the passengers applaud. She does too.

The prospect of passport control scares her little because she knows very little English and almost no Russian. In her hand she is carrying the address where she will be staying, carefully copied in Cyrillic script, from the sender's address Iryna wrote on one of her letters, on to a piece of card so it won't get creased or lost. When one of the Customs officers speaks to her and she understands nothing, she shows it to him. But despite this and the police wanting to handcuff some idiot who lies down on one of the luggage conveyor belts, she is allowed through with no further questions.

It only takes a minute to pick up the suitcases and she's heading for the exit. In the crowd, she immediately makes out Olena and Iryna with open arms and tears in their eyes.

"Where's Miquel?" is the first thing they ask her.

"He's had problems at work."

212

"Didn't he want to come?"

"Of course he did! Something came up at the last minute. A Chinese company is interested in the exhibition display platform for cars."

"Is that the one that looks like a puzzle which he was welding last year with Vasyl?"

"Yes. They liked how it could be easily stacked up... It seems they like it a lot!"

They hug and kiss joyfully. The need to see one another is so sincere that their hands remain clasped for the 100 kilometres from Kiev to Dobrokiv. The journey takes two hours in a Lada driven by the family's friend Nadiya, a very pretty young woman of 25 with long, straight dark hair and eyes green enough to light up the night. Seeing her reminds Esperança that the Ukrainian word nadiya means the same as her own Catalan name: hope! "Trust them and everything will turn out fine" she repeats to herself.

As they leave Kiev, the lights disappear and they begin to pass signs with the names of towns and villages written in Cyrillic. When she works out what some of them say, she feels a little less lost... With all the bumping around and the anxiety, the night seems longer and, when she reads Dobrokiv, she is ready to leap out of the car.

"Not yet!"

They pass through the middle of the town: the square, the market, some shops, banks and, after a few roundabouts, they come to an unlit district surrounded by fields, consisting of a single long street. All the houses look the same. They are all dark – well, not quite all of

them! One of them has a couple of people in a lit doorway – the two Vasyls, father and son.

"You have grown!"

"I'm 16 now! This is my last year at school and next
year I'll be off for my military service."

"Surely not! So young?"

"We don't want him to go either," says Iryna. "Mum's
paid a doctor to write a report saying he's got some sort
of problem, but they haven't given it to her yet. We've
got to wait, but we've only got until autumn."

"What problem am I going to have? I bet I end up
going!"

She's so tired from the whole journey that she flops
into a chair in the courtyard. In front of her, two cats
and two dogs are waiting to introduce themselves.

"Come in," Iryna invites her.

The entrance looks like a jungle, with green palm
fronds, and there are three doors: the kitchen, at the
end, has a corner bench, some flowery curtains and a
table full of food; on the right is the bathroom, which
manages to cram a bath, toilet, a washing machine and
boiler into four square metres; and on the left you go
into a lounge with two sofa beds and a television.

From here, she can enter what will be her room.
Everything smells new and freshly painted. So freshly
painted, in fact, that Esperança has got green stripes on
her back from the chair she's been sitting in.

"What a lovely, tidy house!"

"I did it," says young Vasyl, pointing all around him.

"Don't you believe it, Esperança! All he did was paper the walls and paint the floor. Dad had to sort out and alter the second-hand furniture we've bought this year. Mum and I have tidied everything up."

"And these sunflower curtains?"

"Do you like them, Esperança? I made them with Mum."

After having dinner and chatting, her eyes are closing. Anyone would think she would sleep like a log tonight. But she doesn't. She has to go to the toilet several times... She tries not to make a noise, as her bedroom leads into the one where Olena, her husband and Iryna are sleeping, and she also doesn't want to wake Vasyl, who's sleeping on the sofa in the hall. Once she gets back into bed, she realises that, more than sleep, she needs some sort of waking dream, so she can plan ahead and make the most of the days she will be here. She wants them to be useful, so she can tell everyone about things that many people have kept quiet. She prays a little for her daughters, sure she will be able to call them tomorrow, and thoughts immediately return to Ukraine. For Esperança, it's not enough to give her spare cash to charity, she needs to find out more about the wrong being done and discover solutions so something can be done about the outrage.

**

DOBROKIV, FRIDAY, 10 AUGUST 2007

The Earth turns and the sun in the east slides over the moss, making the dew shine on the flowers, drying the pathways and waking the cockerel, who does his best to wake them all. The children turn over in bed and their parents get up to feed the poultry and the cow before it starts mooing. Then, Olena milks it while her husband strokes its nose. It's the same as every day, but with one small difference: today the cow feels it's being watched and turns to look towards the window, where Esperança is taking a photo.

"Oh, no!" says Olena, smiling shyly, as she runs her hand through her hair to tidy it.

Esperança gets dressed and tries to phone her daughters, but can't get through. When she gets Iryna and Vasyl up, they work out it's some kind of misunderstanding between mobile phone companies, but they don't know what can be done about it.

She can't speak to Miquel either.

"What can we do?" she says. "Well, they'll phone me, I suppose. No news is good news! It'll only be a week."

For some time, she's been able to smell baking bread, which stirs her appetite. It tastes wonderful with home-made butter and a mug of fresh milk from the cow.

When they've finished, it occurs to Esperança to ask whether they have boiled the milk.

"No, we only boil it if we make fresh cheese," she's told.

"What if there are bugs in it? You could get tuberculosis!"

"There are no little creatures like that here. The radioactivity's killed them all."

And they start laughing because the water they're drinking comes from the well. They say that, if the cow doesn't die, nothing will happen to them either. The mains water tastes heavily of chlorine – they rinse their teeth with it and spit it out. Esperança feels paralysed but, seeing as everyone is watching her, she decides to take the bull by the horns... From now on she's going to follow the same logic and she intends to eat and drink everything they offer her.

They spend the rest of the morning together in the *bassejn*, a kind of pool near the fields where they plant potatoes and wheat. At one end is a long board where Vasyl runs and shows them his best jumps, going in feet first and head first with forward and backward somersaults. The older Vasyl gives Bossi the dog a bath and the animal stands like a statue while he rubs him. If he stops, he'll demand more fuss with deafening barks. Esperança rests quietly...

"It was Dad who taught Vasyl to do all that," says Iryna, looking at them proudly. "What about you, Dad? Aren't you going in?"

"Tomorrow, Ira... Today I'm tired," he says, winking at his daughter as if he were shy to stop her insisting.

Olena takes care of everything and, before leaving the house, she's left the cabbage leaves stuffed with rice and pepper to carry on boiling. When they get back, all she has to do is drain it and serve it on a tray. For dessert she kneads a dough of flour and egg, rolls it out, makes rectangles, wraps pieces of fresh cheese in it and throws it into boiling oil. Somehow, they seem to disappear as soon as they come out the pan, until Olena smacks Vasyl's hand away saying:

"That's enough! Do you think they're just for you? Greedy pig!" As she tells him off, she looks for support from Esperança, who bursts out laughing, because if it hadn't been for the intonation she'd have understood nothing.

They have made toasts with a home-made drink made from fruit and they're sitting around talking after the meal:

"Would you like to try a drop of vodka? It's home-made. We make it in this still."

Olena and Vasyl drink it straight down and Esperança pours hers gradually into her green tea. They tell her that this week a neighbour is standing in for Olena at the hospital and that young Vasyl has passed his hop-picking job on to a classmate.

"I'm happy to stop for a few days because this season it's been really hard work. The flowers are very light and the plants climb more than eight metres high. It takes a day to pick a kilo and they pay me one euro."

Iryna has had better luck: she works as a waitress in a restaurant which she says looks like one of Gaudí's buildings. She works there from 11 in the morning to 12 at night, or later:

"They pay me one and a half euros a day, as well as lunch and dinner. Marina, who's the same age as me, is standing in for me now."

"And now the harvest is over, Dad spends his time cutting up tree trunks," says Vasyl, looking at his fingers, which are also bruised.

"What terrible poverty!" she thinks. If they had a way of improving their position it wouldn't be so bad, but from what she has been able to see walking round the town, everything that doesn't come out of the ground or from animals is more expensive than in Catalonia. It must be impossible to save a single cent.

It's gone six when they decide to go to the place where Iryna works, outside the town centre.

"It takes me more than an hour to walk, so we've asked Nadiya, the neighbour who brought us back from the airport yesterday, to take us. We're lucky... She says this week she's available to take us anywhere we like."

They get into the car – the two Vasyls and Olena are in the back, with Iryna sitting on her lap. Nadiya is driving and Esperança is in the front passenger seat. As they're going through Dobrokiv, Nadiya puts her foot down and they take a wide road that crosses a long bridge over the Teteriv, a tributary of the Dnieper. When they see the river, the two Vasyls try to explain that they often go and fish there with a kind of cage, handmade from rushes and canes.

"And plastic thread from net bags we get in the market," says Iryna.

"Fish or shellfish are attracted by the bait inside, they go in the handle end and then they can't get out of the funnel."

Esperança is listening but, when she's least expecting it, the brakes squeal and the car pulls up sharply. Nadiya gets out and lifts up the bonnet.

"What's going on now?" Esperança asks.

"The thing is, look... Can you see them? The police are on the other side of the bridge. Nadiya hasn't got a licence and she's pretending the car's broken down."

"Could you drive, Esperança?"

"Yes," she says, in a very small voice.

Inside the car, Esperança slides into the driver's seat and Nadiya gets in the other side. She looks at the gear stick but there's no diagram on it of where all the gears are. Her front-seat passenger guides her hand while she puts her foot on the clutch. They drive all the way across the bridge in first gear. The police stop them and ask for the papers for the car. Then they also ask for the driver's documents.

"All in order."

The restaurant is three kilometres down the road. The walls, balconies and balustrades are covered in river pebbles. Walking through the arched doorway, the impression is of exploring a cave full of secrets. The separations between tables create what look like corners of forest, with dried trees and stuffed animals. Half hidden bears, wolves, foxes and rabbits stare at them with glassy eyes. Birds perch on their branches as if they were still alive. At the end of the room, a waterfall tumbles over stones, making a stream where goldfish swim. Beavers build their lodges along its flowery banks.

They do not sit down until Iryna has given her a tour of the whole building: the bedrooms are on the upper floor; downstairs there is a large room decorated with stalactites for parties and dances. The toilet also looks like a forest and, out the back, there is an old-style carriage lit up in the middle of the lawn. They all go in and take photos. In the garden, they choose a round table made from a silver birch trunk. It's easy to count the tree rings – there seem to be more than 100. Esperança runs her fingers over it thoughtfully and says quietly:

"These are the links of friendship that only become clear at times like this."

Then she asks:

"But how come Nadiya is driving without a licence?"

"She hasn't got a licence because they cost lots of hryvnias, but don't worry, she's a very good driver," answers Vasyl.

"Nadiya always has to be in the car because she's the owner; the police will always check that it's not stolen. As she rarely goes outside the town, where she uses it to get around when she sells Avon products, there isn't really much risk of her getting caught."

Esperança looks at Nadiya, very surprised. She had no idea that the Avon cosmetics company also operated here, and she still can't believe that she'll have to take over behind the wheel every time the police appear.

"Well, if I do have to drive, I suppose you'll explain the traffic signs and the driving habits... It seems so different to me..."

"Of course we will!" says Iryna, getting up and going to the counter to ask her friend Marina for the waitress's pad. With a napkin over her shoulder, she comes back to the table, smiling.

"And what would the ladies and gentlemen like?"

"What do you recommend?" says Esperança.

"The house specialities are the fruits of the forest ice creams." And she offers them the menu.

"Cherry morozyvo, poppy morozyvo, melon morozyvo, hazelnut morozyvo, strawberry morozyvo..."

"The sundaes are wonderful! And everything's natural. No spray cream!"

Vasyl proudly tells Esperança that, when it came to choosing the waitress, a lot of girls turned up at the restaurant and they picked Iryna because she was the quickest making coffees. And also because some Spanish people came in and she understood them straightaway. And also:

"Because she's really pretty. Isn't she?"

This is certainly true. Her attitude also charms everyone. Once they have been served, Iryna talks a little with her friend Marina, kisses her to thank her for allowing her to put on the performance, and goes back to sit down with the group. She says Marina's parents don't let her stay out late and that she'll have to replace her at nine. So they spend the rest of the evening in the restaurant.

At about eight, Olena tells them it's time to go because they're having dinner somewhere else.

"It's very expensive here. I've bought some meat and we'll go and have it at a barbecue place near the main road. A friend of mine who went through the nuclear accident works there."

Esperança likes the idea.

They all get up. Esperança opens her purse and moves towards the bar with the older Vasyl, but Olena bars her way and, taking out some notes her husband must have worked for many hours to earn, says:

"You pay in Rouralba! Here it's our turn."

They say goodbye to Iryna and arrange that they'll come back and pick her up in Nadiya's car once they've had dinner.

They fit in a little more easily without Iryna and, in the mirror, Esperança can see young Vasyl's face. He's sitting between his parents acting as guide: what a good lad he is and how handsome he looks!

At the barbecue they are welcomed by a tiny, slim woman with a smile twisted by sadness. For what Esperança can understand from Olena's whisper, her husband was a fireman at Chernobyl.

The owners of the bar have gone to a wedding and she had put the meat to marinate, as Olena asked her to do. The Vasyls add silver birch wood and the group sit around the fire, crowned by the moon and stars. Esperança would like to know what happened to the woman's husband and asks quietly.

"Her husband was a fireman," they repeat.

Lyusya, who guesses what they are whispering about, takes a deep breath. She doesn't want to forget... She may be alive but if she wasn't allowed to talk about her Vasya she wouldn't mind dying right now:

"Sit down, please. Where would you like me to start? I don't know what to talk about... Death or love? Or perhaps they're the same thing? What do you want me to tell you?" she asks, joining the circle.

Vasyl translates some of what she says. Nadiya, who spent some time in France and speaks French well enough for Esperança to understand, also helps. She

223

understands the rest from the plaintive tone and the gestures.

"We hadn't been married long. Vasya spent every moment he wasn't working with me. As he only had an hour for lunch, I used to prepare a packed lunch for both of us and we would meet somewhere near the river bank. We used to spread out the blanket, have a kiss and a cuddle and, if we had time for it after all the love, we'd then have our lunch. That year spring was early and all the flowers joined in our mad love-in. As soon as he finished work, he'd come home and we'd put music on. We danced and we didn't go to bed until we were exhausted. Those are the recollections my memory has chosen, anyway."

Lyusya looks young again as she enjoys a few moments remembering her happy past. Then, her lips narrow and her smile twists.

"We lived in Pripyat in one of the two flats above the firemen's hostel. I was woken up at midnight by the dreadful heat and noise. We had just one kitchen for everyone. There was lots of coming and going and I shouted to Vasya to bring me some cold water, but no-one answered. Then I heard the noise of the door to the fire engine garage. I poked my head out the window. Vasya and his colleagues were heading to their fire engine with sandwiches in their hands. I asked him where they were going and he said there was a fire simulation exercise and that I should go back to bed, he wouldn't be long... As they moved away towards Chernobyl, the sky began to light up as if the sun were coming out at midnight.

It was a huge, long sun reflected in the River Pripyat and it set everything on fire. At the same time, rain fell. It wasn't cool rain, though, it burned your skin and irritated your throat. It seemed like the end of the world... The silhouettes of the trees, the tall buildings and the amusement park attractions due to be opened on 1 May stood out black against the light burning at Chernobyl. Everything was like one of those big-screen films that make you feel queasy because you can't take it all in. It was like the Apocalypse when Saint John predicted that a blazing star would fall. I didn't know what was going on. They might have been cleaning the reactor chimneys and burning the soot, or maybe they'd turned on special lights. I was worried it was some kind of evil angel and I went inside to pray that it wouldn't take away my Vasya away. I spent the whole night wishing for it not to happen. I didn't know it already had."

Esperança relates the words with the story in Iryna's box. She lets Lyusya tell her story but tries to find out what actually went wrong.

"So the simulation became real, did it?"

Lyusya remains silent for a minute while she takes some big grilles and spreads the meat out on them. She throws a handful of salt on the flames – the lean meat will cook better if the fire is low. The crackle of the embers is like the voice of her lost love asking her to go on:

"That night, while we were having dinner, Vasya had told me they were carrying out a safety experiment at the power station. They were trying to make use of the rotating movement of the alternators. He knew full well this was dangerous because in the core of the power station there were bars of graphite and nuclear fuel. When they called him out, he lied to me, telling me it was an exercise and not to worry, but he already knew there was a fire."

"And the stuff that was falling, was it soot?"

225

"No, they were subatomic particles as vicious as a death ray..."

First the firemen went and, after a time, the Soviet government gathered together groups of men to put out the fire and deal with the radiation. They were protected only by lead aprons and pig-snout masks that caused ulcers on their faces. Some volunteered while others were recruited: all of them went to a certain death with no idea of what they were up against. They worked shifts of just a few minutes because the lead didn't protect them from the radiation and they suffered from convulsions. Their work consisted of flinging rubbish into the hole where the radiation was coming out. They went to help, but more than anything they went because the civilians were promised huge rewards and the soldiers were told their entire military service would be remitted.

All they achieved was the fulfilment of the Biblical prophecy: "a great star fell from heaven, blazing like a torch, and it fell on a third of the rivers and on the springs of water. The name of the star is Wormwood. A third of the waters became wormwood, and many died from the water, because it was made bitter". In Russian, the word *chernobyl'nik* means "wormwood" and in Ukrainian *chorna* means "black" or "evil" and *byl* means "omen". The only reward was bitter, black evil.

Lyusya stops her story again and asks them what they want to drink. The table is set. In the centre is a cabbage salad striped with melted cheese. Olena gets them to sit down and starts sharing out the pieces of meat.

"At seven they told me he was in the hospital at Pripyat. It was difficult to get them to let me in. I had to beg and grovel..." She relives the experience as she flicks through a magazine with the toxic cloud on the cover.

"Many doctors, nurses and especially auxiliaries at that hospital soon got sick and died. But no-one knew then," says Olena, picking up the French magazine Lyusya has passed them. She gives it to Esperança, who reads the open page aloud and immediately sees that the horror of those days was echoed around the world by Svetlana Alexievich's book, which in English was called Voices from Chernobyl.

"I know you suffered, but whose fault was it?"

"Now you're asking! There are more than 110 written and documented versions. But the firemen and soldiers who went through it at the time always told it the way it's appears in this magazine."

As Lyusya speaks, she takes the magazine from Esperança again, breathes deeply, and begins to read:

01.07 h In the control room, three workers see that a series of anomalies is beginning to happen. They hear loud knocking in the core. The new foreman tries to cover up his lack of training and they continue the experiment of making maximum use of the electrical power to cool the reactor.

01.22 h The situation worsens and they begin to make out a cloud of xenon which can act in nuclear fission. The workers do not know how to solve the problem. Pressing the button to cancel the test operation would be enough to achieve it, but they don't do it. The person who would have to authorise the manoeuvre is not there.

01.23 h The knocking intensifies. The technician arrives and orders the lowering of the graphite bars to reduce the energy building up. The operation is insufficient. When they finally press the stop button, it does not respond.

01.24 h The great explosion is heard and 300-kilo blocks fly through the air, lighting up the sky like fireworks which grow as they expand, filling the heavens.

Lyusya pushes the magazine to one side and continues:

"Then the power station went completely dark. Those who survived the explosion felt sickness and nausea when they came out, and they realised their skin had darkened. Some started to dissolve, as if their organs were made of burned plastic. Those who weren't inside and were putting out the fire with no special protection, like my Vasya, died after a long agony."

Their storyteller disappears during the dinner and does not return until it's time for dessert and coffee. But the conversation carries on as before. The older Vasyl takes advantage of the fact that the names of the chemical elements are very similar in all languages to give Esperança more details, illustrated with dramatic gestures:

"The colours of the clouds that formed were caused by iodine 131, which went round the world three times in eight days; caesium 137, which will remain in the soil and the water for 30 years; strontium 90, which will remain for 90 years; xenon 133, which we will have for six centuries, and plutonium 239, which could stay for 239 centuries. The amount of material released was 500 times greater than the atomic bomb at Hiroshima. The first country to sound the alarm was Sweden, when high levels of radioactivity were detected on a worker's boots in one of their power stations. They quickly located the origin, but the Soviet government denied everything, even though ten hours earlier they'd been putting out the fire. They did that because they didn't know how to protect the civil population from the atomic rain and had no idea of the kind of panic it could cause."

"And are the photos Iryna brought to Catalonia real pictures?" Esperança wanted to know.

"They were taken by Igor Kostin, a military pilot and photographer who got the news and went to Chernobyl by helicopter. He didn't know he was flying over a cloud of toxic gas. He was able to take 90 shots, but he soon felt sick and his camera jammed. When the images were developed, they were all fogged by the contamination except one, which is the one that appeared in the papers."

Suddenly, they notice Lyusya motionless, holding a tray of coffee and vodka. Olena helps her leave it on the table. Her vision is clouded by a transparent, glassy tear, which then makes its way slowly down her cheek. She dries it. She does not want to pity this shadow of the girl Lyusya once was. Despite her efforts to avoid it, the woman in front of her is rushing towards the well in which the past is reflected, and she throws herself in:

"I ask him 'Vasya, what shall I do?'. 'Get out of here! Go! You're pregnant!' 'But how can I leave you like this?' 'Save the baby!'."

"Lyusya, for goodness' sake! Let's talk about something else. It's hurting you and it's not good for you... Forget it now!" begs Olena, while her friend looks at her, her face saying "Just let me drown".

Night is falling and the stars are twinkling like living, listening souls. How Lyusya would love to enjoy the treacherous hope of that far-off past once again! Suddenly, she lifts her head, breathes in the smell of the silver birch and fills her lungs with a sweet breeze from afar that murmurs a sad song: "It's Vasya. Shall we go to bed?"

"In dreams I hold his hand all night, like we did before... and when we wake up our hands are together and his other hand's on my stomach, like before...

"With his lips brushing my ear, he whispers: 'I really want to see our child!' and I ask him: 'What shall we call it?'"

Esperança has already read everything that follows and the others have heard it goodness knows how many times, but it will never be enough. And there will never be enough love to provide forgiveness and bring justice.

"I met some lovely people, I don't remember all of them... I know there are still some left who want to help us, but there are also some who have taken advantage of our misfortune like vultures on corpses. The children always get the worst of it. They're so vulnerable and there are so many of them..."

She is quiet for a moment, drawing in a lungful of air. Meanwhile, Esperança takes notes in a book that will never be far from her side on this trip. She can't stop writing. She puts down what she understands herself, what they translate for her, and what she imagines from the movements and the tone of voice. Seeing that she is getting so involved in the story, Lyusya warns her:

"You can't tell this story, Esperança! You'll never be able to put across this pain. Even people who identify with it will never be able to bear it. The only thing that saved me was the fact that it all happened so quickly that it didn't leave me time to think or cry. I had to help him until his last breath. I loved him. I still didn't know how much I loved him. I still feel his kisses. I still have the last flowers he gave me." She gets up and, making as if to pick up a bunch of flowers, she looks at her fingers as if each one were a carnation as she once again receives the bunch. She places her hands on her belly, once full, and strokes it.

Lyusya whimpers, cries and dries her eyes. An extraordinary mask of pain covers her face, leaving her speechless. She is as pale as the moon in the sky. When she finally recovers, she sobs:

"Mine alone! The person I most loved in all the world! And I'll never have him again!"

"Poor thing! There was a time when all she wanted to do was sleep, and she even had waking dreams in which she saw Vasya walking through familiar places as if he still lived among us... Ukrainian culture places great importance on the interpretation of dreams, you know, Esperança," said Olena.

"There was a dream that repeated: we were together, but he was barefoot. I looked at his feet and asked him: 'Why do you always go barefoot?' He answered: 'Because I've got no shoes'. I went to church and told the priest about it. He told me: "You must buy him some shoes in his size and put them on the coffin of a dead friend with a note saying: 'These are for Vasya'. Your friend will get them to him. The dream means he needs our permission so he can leave home and follow the path of eternity. I bought the best, most comfortable pair of shoes I could find in the shops in Kiev. I thought the best thing I could do was to take them myself to the Mitinski cemetery in Moscow, which is where they buried him. I spent all my money on the shoes and there was nothing left for the journey. I didn't want to torment my parents or his. I just wanted to die. That way I could put them on him and we would walk together towards the paradise we lost. Never would a pair of dead people be so happy or so alive. More alive than any of the living who walk around dead..."

Lyusya remains quiet for a long time. It's almost midnight. Nadiya has to go to pick Iryna up, but she wants to go on.

"You have to know! We have to tell you. The whole world must be reminded before something worse happens."

They agree that the next day she will come with them to Kiev to see the Chernobyl Museum. It will be Saturday, so she won't have to go to work.

Chapter 2

Iryna and Nadiya have got home at four in the morning. The car broke down. Iryna's father is drying the spark plugs and young Vasyl is pumping up the tyres. When Esperança gets up, she's is very surprised to see what they're doing:

"What a good job you're making of it!"

They continue their work, an expression on their faces as if to say "What on earth are we going to do with this piece of scrap?"

It must be nine when, after breakfast, they all get back in the car. All except for the older Vasyl who isn't feeing too well. As they've got to go to pick up Lyusya, he thinks it's a good idea to stay at home working, with the excuse that this will give them more room in the car.

Lyusya is waiting for them. The owners of the barbecue place are busy when they arrive, but they greet them.

"Hello. How's it going?"

"Well, we're really happy because our friends from Catalonia have come to see us. Lyusya must have told you about it."

"Of course she did! And we're pleased about it and very grateful you're taking her out. She needs it."

Olena says to Esperança:

"They're lovely people and they love her so much. They took her under their wing after picking them up in their van one day... She was apparently hitch-hiking so close to the main road that cars had to swerve to avoid her. The noise of passing traffic was drawing her in to her death. More than one car was on the point of running her over, before the couple stopped and asked her: 'What do you think you're doing, girl?' as if she were one of their daughters."

"I was lucky that they took me to the railway station and bought me a return ticket to Moscow. They also told me they were from Dobrokiv and gave me their address and phone number in case I ever needed it."

Now the owners are talking. Their daughters are coming to work there at Christmas and they're complaining because it's the only time they're going to see them.

"They soon won't remember how to speak Ukrainian... We're lucky to have you, Lyusya!" they tell her, stroking her hair. Advising Esperança not to go too fast, they say goodbye to everyone.

As she drives, Esperança's attention is drawn to the large number of people hitch-hiking on both sides of the road. Where the road is wide enough to stop, there are also elderly people offering a few potatoes, pumpkins, peppers, pears, apples and other beautifully arranged fruit for sale.

"You don't see that in Catalonia, do you? Most of them come and go from Kiev, picking everything from their own allotment. It's spare food or stuff they have to sell to make a few hryvnias," they tell her. And on they go.

After a few kilometres the landscape starts becoming monotonous: beech woods alternate with huge meadows. They only notice they are getting near to a village because the number of roadside stalls increases. With the monotony, the descriptions cease, and Lyusya is left talking alone:

***

MOSCOW, 16 July 1986, 10.00 H (LOCAL TIME)

It's two months since Vasya died, but my love for him is very much alive and I hold it inside me. I will soon be able to hold it in my arms. I travel to Moscow by train to take him the shoes and, as I'm there, I decide to visit doctor Angelina. She tells me:

"When it's time to have the baby, come to me."

I walk from the station to the cemetery to see him! In one hand I'm carrying a bag with the shoes and, in the other, a parcel with a change of clothes for me and a basket with the baby clothes.

"Vasya, my love, you're going to be a father soon!"

The contractions begin in the cemetery. Someone calls an ambulance and they take me to hospital. With doctor Angelina's help, I have a baby girl. She shows her to me:

"Natasha. Your father wanted us to call you Natasha."

She seems a healthy baby. With her little arms, her hands with all the fingers, her legs... and a beautiful little face.

They check her and study her in the delivery room. They tell me: her pulse isn't right. Cirrhosis of the liver can clearly be seen. She has 28 roentgens... She's also suffering from a congenital heart defect.

Not long after being born, she dies.

"What did you do to her?"

"We couldn't do anything for her. Now we need to look after you. We need to clean you and sew you up."

"Me? You're not going to touch a hair of my head. Give me back my daughter! She's very much alive. I can hear her breathing!"

I get off the bed and drag myself towards the table where my little treasure is. Two nurses hold my arms and force me to lie down.

"It's dangerous to touch her. We can't give her to you!"

"What do you mean you won't give her to me? I won't give her to you! Do you want her for science, because I hate your science! I hate it! Your science took him away from me and now it wants her as well... I won't give her to you! I'll bury her myself, with her father."

I have her in my arms. Nobody is going to take her away!

Two men dressed in black approach me. The vultures are bringing me a little box and clothes to dress her in.

I put her tiny arms into the silk blouse. I cover her bottom with a nappy. I cover her with the lacy dress she was supposed to wear for her christening.

I wrap her in a pale cape her grandmother embroidered for her. I look at her for a few seconds: she's like a white daisy with a pink centre. When I take off my nightdress to get dressed, I collapse with her in my arms. A nurse lies us down in bed and loosens my grip on her.

"For God's sake, put her at my husband's feet and tell him it's our Natasha."

I collapse. All I can see is a diminishing light and, in the middle, my little doll is smiling at me as she runs towards her father with open arms, looking for his caress.

***

SATURDAY 11 AUGUST 2007

The advertising hoardings tell us we are reaching the capital. Lyusya is quiet for a while, but, when an old woman appears offering us gladioli near a gold-domed church, she starts up again:

"I always go to see them with two bunches of flowers: I leave one for him at the head of the tomb and then I crouch down to leave hers in the place where they buried her little coffin."

And she repeats her soliloquy:

"I killed her. It's my fault she's dead. But my little girl saved me. She took all the radioactive impact, she was the receiver for all that bad stuff... So little! Just a little scrap... Death, life, death – what a cruel miracle!"

***

When they read the first signs for Kiev, she points out an area of the city:

"They gave me a flat here. In a big block where the people affected by the power station accident live now. They're two-bedroom flats, like the one Vasya and I always dreamed of. But I couldn't stay there, it was driving me mad! I saw him everywhere. Wherever I looked,

Vasya was there. Two years went by... One day, they brought me my husband's medal. I couldn't admire it for long because tears came to my eyes. Finally, I left the district.

A neighbour, Tanya, accompanied me to the outskirts of Kiev. I was planning to hitch-hike to Dobrokiv and she didn't leave me until a lorry driver picked me up. Luckily, he knew where I wanted to go, and he dropped me right in front of the barbecue place. I've been with them ever since. They put up with everything from me. If I don't talk to them some days; if sometimes I look at them but don't see them, they know I can't help it and they understand.

"And does Tanya still live here?" asks Esperança.

"Yes. Her husband also died from radioactivity. Then she married again, secretly wanting a baby. Her new husband worked as a baker and he slept during the say. So, when I used to live there I often had her in my flat remembering old times. She was 25, like me, but she was more delicate. When we used to talk, I told her she should tell her husband about wanting a child. I said if people told her she wouldn't be able to stand it, she shouldn't believe them; that if a doctor told her the child would have a hand missing, she should answer that he could write with the other; that she should accept compassion from no-one because 'when we needed it, no-one gave us any and now we don't want it'. I kept telling her. Tanya wasn't afraid of radioactivity, she had had that under control for some time.

"And was she able to have a child?"

"Yes. He must be your age, Vasyl. Every time I come to Kiev I go and see them. If you like, we can go when we come back from the Chernobyl Museum."

"Can't we go now?" says Esperança. "First people and then museums."

The flats Lyusya points out are on the right of the avenue. And she suggests they take the first exit they find to get there.

What a coincidence! Just as they reach the street, she recognises her friend some distance away:

"There they are! Andriy and Tanya!"

Esperança sees two people coming straight towards them. Lyusya, with her head out the window, calls to them until the car pulls up alongside.

They hug.

"This is my son, Andriy!"

Tanya tells them they were going to the park beside the river.

"He likes to read under the silver birch trees. I stay with him and knit," she says, showing them the woolly jumper she is finishing.

She tells them she's in love with her son, who's a treasure. At school they say he's very hardworking and he gets excellent marks for everything. What he most likes doing is reading and he'd spend all day in the library...

"He manages all that even though in winter he only goes to school about every other week. He's a very sensitive boy and he's often ill. More than once both of them – mother and son – have had to go to hospital. It's a good thing that when the good weather arrives we recover and can make the most of the days when we're healthy. She's so scared of losing him that, when he was small, she always held him very tight," says Lyusya.

"That's true. One day in the street I even imagined that a lorry might run him over and I squeezed his wrist so tight that I left a bruise that lasted for weeks. Didn't I, Andriy?"

Reliving it, she strokes his hand:

"Don't worry, Mum, you know perfectly well I'll never leave you."

***

Now Esperança wants to know more about Tanya and her district.

"Who lives here?" "Only people who were affected by radioactivity live in the Chernobyl district," Tanya answers.

"Pripyat, the town that had been built for the workers families near the power station is deserted, but they still do guard duty there and carry out studies. No-one lives there, but there's a rumour that there's a reactor that still gives electricity to the Americans."

"The Americans? How can they send it to them? By sea?"

"Now you're asking!" exclaims Iryna. "The Americans know everything."

"Can't you see that's impossible?"

"Well everyone in Dobrokiv believes it."

"Come on, didn't all Europe want our energy? Now we have to rely on their charity. Why don't they invest money in helping us instead of manufacturing arms?"

"Our country has great wealth if we only had a government that knew how to exploit it!" laments Andriy.

"Our town is sick. It's zombie territory. Many people die suddenly, even just walking along the street. Someone's walking along and suddenly they fall down dead. They go to sleep and then don't wake up. You take flowers to a nurse and suddenly her heart stops. The doctors tell everyone we're all OK. We're fine until we die!" says Lyusya sarcastically.

Talking is cathartic, it purges them. Lyusya knows it, but the wind takes her words away. That's why she'd like everything she's told Esperança to be written down.

"Publish it, Esperança, even if it has to be a novel."

They all insist on the idea. Andriy and Tanya want to come to the museum, too.

"Can we go?"

"Great! Of course you can! Where there's room for six, there's room for eight."

"Open the windows to let some cool air in! It seems as if we've got the heating turned right up!"

"No Esperança, that grille is for the engine to breathe."

The air that comes out goes on to their feet and the sun is very hot, so they're sweltering. And she was so afraid of being cold!

On the way, Andriy tells them:

"The Orange Revolution has opened up new directions for our country and it will soon be truly European. All we need are the political alliances. If we go the Saint Andrew's way to the museum, you'll see there are shops and brands from all over the world."

Esperança opens her eyes as wide as she can: the buildings that appear in front of her are even more impressive than any of the photographs that encouraged her to come. The view of Kiev is unmistakable. The Lavra monastery with its shining domes stands out above Saint Sophia's cathedral and Saint Michael's monastery.

In the 11th century, Kiev was considered the biggest city in Europe and it was the centre of Slav culture. Ukraine had libraries and top-level diplomatic relations. In the time of King Yaroslav the Wise, the city was known all over the world.

"How lovely! It looks like a landscape from a story illustrated in gold... Each dome is like a sun greeting that beautiful blue sky."

"It seems impossible, almost some kind of destiny, that the city could have been reborn from the ashes so many times after it was destroyed by the Mongols, the Nazis and the Russian tyrants," says Tanya.

"Kiev is seeking its place in the world in a tremendous hurry. There is some savage capitalism going on. The Soviets can't tell us what to do any more. We don't take any notice of anyone, but Kiev is still beautiful. It's a shame that nowadays only the rich can afford to study: Ukraine is fourth in the list of countries researching and exploring space behind the United States, Russia and France, and it's fourth in the world in terms of the number of people with university education," says Olena. She's proud but at the same time sad, as she was able to study in Communist times, before the separation from Russia while now, after independence, it will be a miracle if her children can get the education she wants for them.

After driving round for a time, they manage to park. On the way they get distracted by the market stalls. The dizzying climb to the museum is territory reserved for old Communist iconography.

Here you can find Lenin's head, the most coveted collectors' item. But there are also Soviet pilots' helmets, flags, red stars, t-shirts, pins, books and photographs. Each stall holds a surprise and the air is full of nostalgia for a time that is never coming back. The *matryoshka* dolls are almost always smiling. They don't care that someone has put a tiny Lenin inside one of them.

The church of Saint Andrew acts as the entrance to the museum they want to visit. The museum is a like a scream against the great failure of the Soviet system: the tragedy of Chernobyl. In the museum's different galleries there are *phantasmagorical* figures hiding, ready to contradict the stubborn official cover-up. Portraits, photographs, posters and mementos to ensure the world does not forget what happened one day.

Around every corner is a new horror and Esperança is left speechless. There are so many unanswered questions in her head:

Why did the Soviet party bosses choose nuclear energy when the USSR had huge oil and natural gas reserves?

What exactly happened at the power station during the fateful night of 26 April 1986? Was it what Lyusya said or did the reactor have deficiencies? Where did the parts come from? Which country manufactured them?

How were the consequences of the Chernobyl accident managed?

What happened at the "battle of Chernobyl", in which about a million people took part? Where are those heroes?

How did the Chernobyl situation become a terrifying test for the policy of openness promoted by Mikhail Gorbachev?

What has happened to the animals and plants in the evacuated areas?

How do people live in the contaminated territories, which occupy an area five times greater than Catalonia? Do they have medicines to combat cancer and deformations? Do they suffer?

What are the health problems and long-term prospects for the affected population in Ukraine, Belarus and Russia, which is largely rural and very poor?

Is it true that many people did not get used to living in the accommodation they were given in Kiev and slipped back to the closed, prohibited zones, where they survive as monsters and thieves?

Or is it more likely that flats were promised to all those affected but only the ones they had seen were ever built, while money ended up in the pockets of the politicians?

What is clear in the exhibition is that plutonium-239, which contaminated the city of Pripyat, has a half-life of 24,110 years. This means that in 24 millennia in Pripyat there will still be half the current quantity of this highly toxic element, which nature cannot recycle.

After visiting the museum, the group walk through the street in low spirits. It's lunchtime but no-one has said anything yet. They cross a square presided over by an angel raised up high and no-one gets out a camera to take its picture. The square is full of colour. Three years ago here, it went orange.

Suddenly, Esperança realised the boys are missing. Andriy and Vasyl are nowhere to be seen.

"Where can they have gone?" asks Iryna.

"Don't worry!"

And in a few minutes they arrive triumphantly with a bunch of roses, which they hand out to the women: Esperança, Olena, Lyusya, Tanya, Nadiya and Iryna.

"Where did you get those from?"

The boys point to some staircases leading below the square.

"In Kiev and all over Ukraine we like flowers a lot and we give them on any excuse. Today we have to celebrate the fact that we've made new friends," says Lyusya.

And they hug all together in a ring, jumping as if they are doing a Catalan sardana dance. "Perhaps our national dance started like this," imagines Esperança.

When they reach the car, Nadiya takes a compressor out of the boot. "What does she want to do now?" she wonders, but she soon finds out: the two back tyres are down to the wheel rims and the front ones are very low too.

"Goodness me! What are we going to do now?"

"Don't worry! It's normal. We've been out a long time so of course they've gone down," says Vasyl, who's the one who blew them up in the morning.

"And you think that's normal? We can't drive around on those tyres! Don't you know a garage around here?"

"Yes, my husband takes the van to one in our street," says Tanya.

"Come on, then. Once we've put some air in them, let's see if we can get there."

Once they're blown up, the tyres last until the garage. It seems they don't lose so much air on the road. In any case, Esperança buys two new tyres for Nadiya, who puts them on the front of the car, moving the old ones to the back. They look at the two they'd taken off and choose one, which they leave as a spare, as Nadiya didn't have one.

Nadiya is so happy that she keeps on saying thank you. She says that, if ever she gets married, she'll invite Esperança, who'll have to bring her whole family to the wedding.

Tanya is in a hurry because her husband will be getting up soon and she'll have to get a meal for him before he goes to the bakery, but first she says goodbye to their guest:

"Stay and have something to eat. All I've got to do is boil the macaroni. The sauce is already made."

"No. Thanks a lot, but I've also got some food ready prepared at home, and my husband will worry," says Olena.

Once again, silver birch trees are going by to the left and right. The road towards Dobrokiv slides by smoothly under the new tyres. The stalls have disappeared. It's the hottest time of day and the produce sellers have probably gone for something to eat and a snooze. Sometimes a hitchhiker appears, keeping his thumb raised as the car passes. "Perhaps he can't see the people sitting on top of one another in the back," Esperança says to herself, looking in the mirror. Now Lyusya is sitting beside her.

Inside the car, she once again thinks about the tragedy at Chernobyl. In her mind is the picture on the cover of a novel about it that she read with her daughters for school. It is true, as the author says, that reality always goes further than fiction. No-one will ever know for sure how many people suffered cancer and other diseases related to the passing of that black radioactive cloud. As if she were reading Esperança's mind, Lyusya starts talking again:

"The great Ukrainian expert, Dmitry Grodzinsky, says that, without knowing it, we all took part in a 'negative lottery'."

The geographical extent of the areas directly contaminated is horrifying. The nuclear sarcophagus is surrounded by cursed areas that have taken on a blurry, irregular appearance. "Chernobyland" is a large region as big as one-third of Spain and inhabited by 9 million people, including 2 million children.

Suddenly, the car stops, just as they are passing behind a lorry that is slowing down. The brake pads have worn away and iron is rubbing against iron, with sparks coming out. Finally, the car stops dead. Everyone in the back is shaken forward and raise their heads.

"What's happened?"

"I braked... and now it won't move. It won't go at all." Vasyl and Nadiya get out and open the bonnet. The spark plugs have gone crazy – there isn't a spark in sight.

They dry them again and again, and use the cigarette lighter on them. Finally, it starts.

When they arrive, the two girls plan to spend the afternoon rummaging through the suitcases Esperança has brought them, and before the sun sets she wants to contemplate and photograph the gentle light that fell yesterday on the chickens and the cow alongside the flowers. They won't eat the cannelloni that Vasyl has prepared until the evening.

At about eight, Iryna comes into the kitchen in a low-cut red silk dress that Esperança's friend's eldest daughter once wore to a wedding. Her soft blonde hair falls on to her shoulders and back, tanned from picking potatoes at her grandmother's house. But she hasn't told Esperança how she got the tan, and to her Catalan friend she looks like a poppy in the middle of a wheat field.

"Why are you looking so smart?"

"I'm going to work and everyone's very well dressed in the restaurant on Saturdays."

Half standing up, she takes something from the kitchen table and goes to the bathroom, emerging with her face heavily made up and her eyes and lips professionally outlined.

"But you're just a child!" Esperança can't help blurting out. "Do you really need to look so flashy?"

"Here in Ukraine even young girls want to look good," says Nadiya, who's happily wearing some jeans whose origin Esperança forgets. They fit well, though and she's combined them with an openwork blouse through which her bra shows... It's exactly the same colour as her eyes.

"They've told them in the restaurant that a group of actors who are filming in the villages around the Dnieper and Kiev would be back today," says Vasyl.

"Well, everyone knew except me!"

"Yes, and there's a rumour that from now on they'll be staying in the rooms in the hotel where Ira works."

Caught out, the two models blush.

"Ah! That's it? You want to impress the director. Who knows, perhaps they'll have a part for you."

"Do you think we look good?" asks Nadiya.

"No doubt about it. I doubt you'll be coming home tonight..." says Esperança, joking now. "Be careful, you two look so good someone might not want to let you go!" She feels a little responsible for the girls' alarming change of clothing, but she can't help being pleased that they've managed to combine the things she's brought with such good taste.

The looks the girls exchange betray the fact that they didn't think her last comment was very amusing, but now is not the time – and they haven't got time anyway – to explain why, and they leave.

When the two of them have gone, young Vasyl pulls Esperança by the arm to the room where he sleeps. There he's got the laptop he brought from Catalonia last year plugged in. He also uses it as an mp3 player so he invites her to sit down on the bed and puts on some quiet Ukrainian music sung in English. With the sound of the strings of the *bandura* in the background, they catch up on one or two things:

"Don't those two get on well! And Nadiya must be at least ten years older than Iryna."

"Yes, we'll have to see what happens! She's always round here. When she came to Dobrokiv she didn't speak to anyone, but one day her aunt and uncle introduced her and since then she and Ira have been inseparable. She takes care of Ira like a big sister. Because, after all that happened to her..."

"What happened to her?"

"Hasn't Ira told you?"

"No, I only know she went to France for a few summers, which is why we can understand each other, because I also studied French, you know. It's really good to know languages. Next year you'll have to go back to Spanish classes."

The boy turns up his nose, but she insists:

"Won't you?"

"Look, they say all that stuff about her going to a host family there to cover up what really happened. I think she was hosted for just one summer when she was small. The truth is that she's had a really bad time."

"Has she?"

"Nadiya comes from a little village in the south. She studied law in Odessa. Living in the city is very expensive and, to make a little money, she used to work as a waitress when she finished at the university every day. One day, in the bar, she met a very well-dressed girl and they soon became friends. She told Nadiya she'd made a lot of money in Europe and she offered to advance her the cost of a flight to France in case she was interested in going to work there in the summer. She told Nadiya she was prepared to do it because she didn't like to see her working so hard for such little money. She said she could repay the debt when she came home. She showed her an advertisement to work as a waitress in a town on the coast of Provence. When she got to the airport, the company was waiting for her and they accompanied her to the place she was going to work. But it wasn't a hotel like she was expecting, it was a strip club.

"She looked so pretty they wanted to take advantage of her..."

"Yes, and not just dancing, if you know what I mean. They asked for her passport telling her they needed it to sign the contract and they'd give it back to her in a couple of days..."

"And did they keep it?"

"Yes, and as if that wasn't enough they also told her she owed them 10,000 euros for the trip."

"And how much did they pay her?"

"I don't know. More girls from Ukraine and Moldova arrived and the boss, who was Russian, told them how they could earn the money that, according to her, they owed them."

"No…"

"Yes! They had to have sex with the customers all day. Every time they refused to do it, they were fined 30 euros."

"And couldn't they escape?"

"They had them in a flat, her and five other girls who wouldn't stop crying. They only went out when a customer came and wanted a fuck. Then they went to a private suite where they could only get out by phoning the boss."

"And what were the customers like?"

"She says some of them were wearing all kinds of jewels, but they were all horrible."

"And…"

Esperança couldn't carry on asking questions. Her whole body was trembling and her throat was dry. She imagined the horror of this girl, whose name was the same as her own, and who perhaps even looked a little like her when she was young, when she was so keen to study, see the world and fight for good causes. When she would trust anyone.

"As she moved well, she soon became part of the club show. One day, while Nadiya was dancing on her podium, she noticed a boy who couldn't take his eyes off her. He gestured for her to come over. He had a trustworthy face, although he approached her with the excuse that he wanted to flirt with her. They ordered a gin and tonic from the bar. His French was Russian accented. They went to the special suite and, when they were alone, she told him what was happening to her."

"Wasn't he from the same gang?"

"She doesn't think so, because a few days later the police arrived. The boss of the club had to give her back her passport so she could show it. Once it had been checked, the boss accompanied her to the flat and asked for the passport back. Nadiya had an expired passport in her bag and gave the woman that one instead. Luckily, she didn't check it. The next morning, now with her travel document, she got ready to leave the show.

"She asked permission to go and powder her nose and in the toilet she put on a very lightweight, although not transparent, black dress that she had ready in her toilet bag with her passport. Camouflaged like a shadow, she waited for the right moment to jump into a taxi that had just dropped a customer at the door of the club. She asked it to take her to the city centre. As soon as she got out, she went to the police station and reported them. A charity paid for her to return to Odessa."

"And how long has she been living here?"

"Three or four years, perhaps. When Nadiya reached her village, she discovered that the gang had destroyed her parents' house. It was a good thing that some relatives in Dobrokiv took them in... that's why they live here now. They're scared to go home."

"Won't the gang come looking for them here?"

"I think they've changed their name. She was probably called Elisabet before because sometimes when her mother calls her she gets it wrong and calls her Lisa."

"You learn something every day!"

The music has stopped. Vasyl is resting his head on Esperança's lap. She tangles her fingers in his hair and he takes on the posture of a puppy jealous of its owner. He's scared of losing her. Ten months without seeing her is a long time. Meanwhile, in the kitchen, his father is flicking through an album of photographs of when he did his military service and waiting for the chance to show them to Esperança. As soon as she gets up, he calls her in and offers her a drink.

"Oooh! That burns! Is it vodka?"

"No, it's better than Russian vodka. It's *horilka*. Vodka means 'water' and *horilka* is 'hot water'. I distilled it myself and it's stronger than genuine Nemiroff," he says, his son translating for him.

"She'll sleep well tonight," thinks Olena, who carries on washing up. She has her back to them, but turns round to sneak an occasional look at the photos. Sometimes she comes over and smiles because there are also some pictures of when they were a young couple. Like when they went to Moscow with the fur hat and coat, all snowy, with that cold that froze their breath. Well, they're still young. They're 36, but they've had to work so hard that their faces are lined before their time. When she closes the album, Esperança runs her fingers over the arabesque decorations that the older Vasyl had made on the cover. Suddenly, thinking aloud, she breaks the silence:

"You know what we could do tomorrow? In the morning we'd have to change the brakes and the spark plugs. We could get some second hand."

"No, I'd like to get Nadiya's car properly fixed up. Or if not... if you know a place where they sell used cars we could go and look. They can't cost much here, can they?"

Hearing this, young Vasyl stands up to consult his father, who is paying attention, sensing good news even though he doesn't understand a word. He says that in Kiev there's a special market for used cars.

"Well, we'll go tomorrow if we can change the brakes and the spark plugs first."

***

"WE DON'T WANT TO HURT YOU. My youngest son can tell you how to get to the border, you know? That's where you're going, isn't it? Well, I'd like to call him so he can help you. It's so obvious you're escaping... I thought you'd hardly got any money and that you'd only got the bike. But with what you're carrying it will all be easier."

Iryna nods her head and looks outside. She's carrying sleepy Lyuba with her face resting on her shoulder. An empty, far-off feeling of poverty invades her. It isn't that the shopkeeper has discovered her, it's that she needs to tell him who she is and what's really happened to her. Slowly, she tells him everything, with the same calm as the spinning snowflakes; the special steadiness of the falling snow, capable of stopping time and transforming the landscape into an unreal dream beyond geographical limits and human borders; a film set that covers everything, wiping out all that has happened; an illusion that transports her to a happy place from a childhood memory. Will her little girl be able to run and make tunnels in the virgin snow, like she used to?

"Tell him I'm travelling with my daughter and I won't leave her for anything in the world."

"Let me call him!"

255

Iryna agrees. Gratitude replaced her mistrust some time ago. Without thinking, she approaches the man and kisses his forehead.

"Do you know what?" he says. "It would be best if you brought the bike into the storeroom. You can't leave it out there with this snow falling. Give me the little girl. Come here, lovely!"

The man makes a gesture and Lyuba throws himself into his arms.

"I'll phone while I'm holding her for you."

And he passes her a thick jumper so she doesn't get wet when she goes out.

"Just imagine I'm your father."

When Iryna comes in, Lyuba looks surprised. She's only been out for a moment, but she's covered in white. She has to shake herself. The shopkeeper lets the baby take a snowflake from her mother's shoulder and bring it, now turned to water, to her lips.

Chapter 3

SUNDAY 12 AUGUST 2007

By the time Esperança gets up, the whole family is already on the go. Even the two girls, who must have come in at one or two in the morning, are up and ready. It seems they've been told they might be going to the car market. They're all sitting round the table waiting to have breakfast together. Young Vasyl is getting ready to say something. He looks impatient, his eyes staring excitedly into the distance.

"You know what? I had a weird dream last night. I saw Ira flying on the back of a black swan."

"He did, yes. When we got in, we tried not to make a noise, but Vasyl sat bolt upright shouting: 'Iryna, I want to go with you!'."

"And did she let you get on?" Esperança asks Vasyl, as she hears Olena muttering. She also had a dream and she wants to know what Vasyl is saying.

"Mum saw Dad swimming in a pool full of people."

"The pool was as deep as a well I was stretched out on the ground and I stretched out my arm, hoping Dad would come through all the people, so I could take his arm."

"Vasyl's dream is clear, but we ought to ask your mother how to interpret this one," Iryna says to Nadiya. "She knows a lot. Sometimes these things are premonitions."

"Are they? And what did she foretell for you? That you'd marry a prince, maybe?"

"No, but you know that talking to her has often helped me sort myself out... and I apologised to you."

"What about you? Have you dreamed anything?" Vasyl asks Esperança. He hasn't understood Esperança's comment or his sister's reply and knows nothing of the calls Iryna made that summer – still less what they cost.

"Yes," says their guest, hesitant and seemingly downcast. To join in the conversation and lighten the mood, she invents a dream with a meaning. "I was with Miquel in a strange bedroom. Suddenly, twins appeared in the middle of the bed – a boy and a girl. We had them covered up with the sheets and blankets. Neither of us knew whether they were ours or not, but we could see they wanted us to look after them. Miquel brought them to me and I fed them: the girl drank from my left breast and the boy from my right."

"Good thing you've got two breasts, then!" Iryna burst out laughing, realising that it was more a fantasy than a dream.

"Be quiet, Ira. Let her go on," murmurs Nadiya, who is doing everything she can to follow the translations the pair of them are providing.

"They got grumpy and started moaning. I touched my breasts and they were so empty that I left the children and ran out to the chemist."

"The chemist? Better to put them under the cow's udder," says the older Vasyl, when they translate the shaggy dog story for him.

So, the significance of Olena's dream, which has left her husband thoughtful because he should have told her what's happening to him a long time ago, is dispelled.

Nadiya tells them she has daydreams. She wants to have money to get her driving licence and buy a new car: a four-wheel-drive that wouldn't have problems with the snow in winter or the puddles.

After breakfast, they get ready. Esperança gets out some notes and gives them to Nadiya so she can go to the village and change the brakes, the spark plugs and, if necessary, the battery.

"Come on! The sooner we get this sorted out, the sooner we can set off for Kiev. Today we're going to the car market!"

The market is on the outskirts of Kiev, in an industrialised area. It is very big, and to get there they go through a strange wasteland, full of filth, rubbish and abandoned industrial units. It's a long way from the Dnieper that served as a landmark for them yesterday. To Esperança, it all looks chaotic. On the motorways, the exits are on the left, while the traffic lights are camouflaged, popping up when you least expect them. Shining dimly or not at all, they try to control the anarchy of ancient cars with their squealing brakes. After the interruption, the river of scrap metal moves forward again. In short, it all seems highly dangerous.

Meanwhile, Nadiya, eyes fixed on an old map, is looking for the address she'd been given in Dobrokiv. She's never been to this part of the city. Everyone wants to help:

"Esperança, *napravo, napravo!*" says Nadiya.

"Right!" translates Iryna.

"Ni, ni, no, no, nalivo."

"Left! Left!"

"Straight on! Straight on!"

And just when it seems she's reached an easy section of the journey, they suddenly shout:

"Ryzykovanyj povorot"

"Dangerous bend!"

Another scare like that and her heart will leap straight into the ditch. They go on straight on for miles and miles and it seems as if they've left Kiev behind. She's sure it was all much easier yesterday. Nothing of what they see looks like yesterday's dream city. The day is humid, with the sun lighting the sky from behind clouds, and the vehicles drift through mirages shining on a road like a filthy sea in a foul dream. It's a good thing they got the car fixed up well beforehand. But then a clapped-out vehicle pulls alongside Esperança so close that it almost touches their car. There are even more people inside it, and they're making gestures. What has she done wrong now? Maybe it's the one she overtook earlier now trying to demonstrate its true power. How silly!

But it's not. The car is weaving from side to side but miraculously staying in its lane. It's a good thing it's on the right. It pulls close again. The front-seat passenger leans half out of the window to point out something happening under Nadiya's car. The passengers finally see what the crazy man is talking about:

"Oh, the back wheel's twisted and it looks as if it might fly off!" shouts Nadiya.

"*Ryzyk*, Esperança! Danger! Brake! Stop!"

Now everyone is on the tiny verge, looking to see what they can do. Just getting back in again would be a risk. The wheel is hanging on by one bolt and the rim is bent. Where are they going to find a mechanic? The two Vasyls walk in a line along the hard shoulder, father in front, son behind. They are followed by Esperança and then the others, like mourners at a funeral. They walk and walk and walk until they find a sign with a wheel and a hammer. It's lunchtime now and they're bringing down the metal shutter but, as it's an emergency, the boss makes an exception. Normally he only works in the mornings on Sundays. The inner tubes cost 530 hryvnias, but he assures them they're better than the ones they've got on the front. So he takes off the four tyres and puts the really good ones on the front and the not so bad ones on the back. As Esperança is paying again, Nadiya can't stop thanking her, with hugs and kisses.

Now the car glides along *bistro, bistro* – very quickly – at 85 kilometres an hour, the top speed for one of these models. Finally, at three in the afternoon, they reach the market. It's a huge car park where each vehicle has a cardboard notice in the windscreen with the price and the owner's address. In many of them the owner is snoozing, jumping up as soon as someone approaches.

Nadiya takes the lead, with her mobile phone calculator open to convert the car prices from hryvnias to dollars and then euros, but they are all expensive. Esperança is prepared to spend up to 1,000 euros. Someone who knows tells them the area where cars in this price range are, but when they get there they see they are old bangers even worse than Nadiya's car.

"In Catalonia you have to pay to get rid of a car like that," thinks Esperança. "If I buy something like that, it'll let them down for sure – and they've got no money to get it fixed!" Faced with all these difficulties, her attention is drawn by a line of motorbikes.

"What if I buy you a little moped?"

"Yes! Let's go and look at the bikes!" says Vasyl, pulling his father and the rest of the group along.

***

"THERE'S A CHANCE of getting out of here tomorrow afternoon. He told me you should stay here; a vehicle will come and pick you up. Off you go, woman, go and have a nice sleep!" he tells her.

His wife can be heard snoring at the back of the house. Tomorrow he'll tell her everything that happens while she's sleeping.

First thing in the morning, the cock crows in its run behind the house. It's time for another feed and Lyuba demands her milk. A beam of light filters through the curtains. Iryna opens them. It's not snowing any more.

"The sun's shining, sweetheart! It's sunny, Lyuba! Let's hope the wind sends the clouds back home to the north!"

A light breeze shakes the stiff branches of the fir trees and tries to break up the leaden sky. Through gaps it tears in the clouds, a yellowish light begins to melt the thin layer of snow until the asphalt shows through. The door of the room where mother and daughter are sleeping creaks as the *babusya* puts her head round. She's carrying a steaming glass, full to the brim with warm milk for Iryna. The woman watches for a few moments as Iryna puts the baby to her breast. When Iryna has thanked the woman, she withdraws and leaves them alone. But within ten minutes the telephone is ringing. Iryna hears voices... and she doesn't like the tone. The woman immediately appears again, with a contorted gesture:

"My son says a lorry that helps get Ukrainians to Western countries hasn't got through. They've caught them and made everyone get out. No-one knows who they were looking for but they're bound to take them to jail. The police are usually happy to take a few banknotes hidden inside a passport. They must be under pressure from someone," she says, as she gives Iryna warm clothes from the time when their grandchildren lived with them.

"Come into the kitchen and have breakfast with us and then you can go. They might come and search the house."

**

SUNDAY 12 AUGUST 2007

They have a good look round and fall in love with a shiny new scooter.

They ask the price and it matches the one Esperança gives them. The crafty seller thinks he knows how to get in with Catalans:

"*Vovk* love Barcelona!" he says, showing them a stack of photos of the Costa Brava. Nadiya, whose expression clearly shows that she doesn't trust him, asks:

"And when will you bring us the scooter?"

"Tomorrow. Today I've got no transport, it's Sunday."

"There's no need, I'll ride it away now," says Vasyl.

"You? Why you?" asks his sister.

"Can't you see there's a lot of traffic and it's a very long journey?" says Esperança, who realises what's going on from the gestures they're making.

"I've seen this scooter cheaper in Dobrokiv," says Nadiya.

"In Dobrokiv?" Everyone is surprised.

"Yes, my friend Nikolaj's got one in his garage. And you can try it as many times as you like before buying it."

Vasyl, who was keen on the idea of buying this one, turns up his nose. Iryna, who is as surprised as he is, agrees because she doesn't want anyone to say she's got no patience. But both of them would be stamping their feet and storming off in a huff if they didn't think it would make them look silly. Nadiya repeats the advantages of buying it in the village.

As it's already very late, and although they are hungry, they just buy a cola and a very light snack and go home. Nadiya once again gives the orders:

"Napravo!"

Meanwhile, Iryna translates:

"Turn right! *Bistro, bistro!* Quickly! Quickly!"

It's six in the afternoon and they're very near the restaurant where Iryna works. The girl keeps telling her father they should have something to eat there because they've got no food ready at home and they're all dying of hunger. Poor Vasyl doesn't say so, but he's got no money to pay for a meal. Esperança, who guesses what they're talking about, parks in front of the place anyway. Iryna gets out of the car and goes straight to see Marina, the friend who's standing in for her. When the others reach the bar they find the pair whispering secrets to one another.

Iryna blushes as she pulls her friend towards the group and shows off her work of art: Marina's got a nose piercing.

"Well, do you like it?" asks Iryna.

"Did you do that?" shrieks Esperança, who knows the kind of thing Iryna is capable of.

"*Tak,*" Marina moves her head up and down, showing her best profile, and waits.

"I did it last night. I threw on plenty of that vodka Mum makes. It disinfects everything. It didn't hurt a bit and it's perfect. In Kiev they charge a fortune to do it, but I didn't ask for anything. Marina's so happy that she'll be my walking advert: there are lots of girls who'll ask me to do it for them, and that'll make me a few hryvnias. I'll tell them I learned to do them in Catalonia and that there everyone has got them. I'll get one done next year, when I come over. You'll let me, won't you?"

"You're going to get yourself arrested as a con artist or sued for injuring someone," predicts Esperança.

"There are plenty of traditional young people in Rouralba too... Why would you want a bit of metal in your nose?"

"It's all right! Laia and Naiara will want one too. We've already decided we're going to do it for each other."

"That's all we need! Doesn't it get in the way when you blow your nose? If Miquel was here he'd tell you that a cathedral doesn't need decorations. Look at Nadiya, she hasn't got one!"

"Nadiya wants one too, but she hasn't done it because her Avon customers are really boring old ladies," she says, mocking them. "She's worried about losing them."

Olena and her husband are worried about day-to-day survival: where will we get the money to go shopping? What will we spend it on? Young people just want to forget this story of struggle and they're dazzled by the world offered by television. If there they see young people who are not poor with tattoos and earrings, why can't they have them?

Suddenly the restaurant manager comes and sends Marina to show them where they can sit: around a long table made from the trunk of a pine tree cut lengthways.

They could go on commenting on the modern habits of young people, but they have more important things to worry about – hunger and the motorbike. To start with, they order a tomato and cucumber salad accompanied by fresh cheese; to follow, chicken with onion, stuffed and grilled; and, to drink, some generous mugs of a drink made with fermented bread.

Just as they are about to order some cheesecake for dessert, Nadiya looks at her watch and warns them:

"Hurry up! My friend closes at eight!"

They all get up straightaway. But as no-one comes with the bill, the youngsters go ahead in the car to buy the scooter. Meanwhile, Esperança, Olena and the old-

266

er Vasyl wait to pay. Vasyl is nervous and Esperança knows it. She lets him pick up the piece of paper Marina gives them and, when the girl turns her head away, she passes him a big banknote so he can pay. She knows that's what he'd do if he had the money.

Then they set off to see if the young people have found the shop open.

"Let's see what Nadiya's friend has got..." says Esperança.

As they walk in line across the bridge over the River Teteriv, looking at the water purring along underneath, they notice a film is being made beneath their feet. Olena recognises one of the actors:

"Look! It's that guy who looks like the one in Titanic!"

Little do they know that this is the boy who is in love with their Iryna. When they reach the shop, which looks nothing like one, they see Iryna and Vasyl sitting on the steps at the front with their elbows on their knees and their heads in their hands.

"What's the matter? Where's Nadiya?"

"The owner's already closed up and she's gone off to find him at home."

The delay continues and they all end up on the steps, as if waiting for a show to start. Finally, when Nadiya and her friend arrive, they almost burst into applause.

The owner, a tall, slim young man, takes a large iron key out of his pocket and opens the store, which is just an empty house full of domestic appliances – a load of fridges, washing machines and cookers, all with televisions, videos and radio-cassettes on top. Dodging past these obstacles, they reach the covered courtyard at the back where the motorbikes are. They immediately see Nadiya's scooter. It's the same make and the same colour as the one in the market in Kiev.

"How much is it?"

Nadiya, calculator in hand because everything is marked in euros and dollars, shows them on the screen: 784 euros x 6.86 to get *hryvnias* = 5,378.24 *hryvnias*. In Kiev they were asking for 6,000. The price is better, just as she'd said it would be. If they'd known they could have saved themselves the trip, but...

"Will it work?"

Young Vasyl, cautious now, says that he wants to try it out before they pay. He'd be really angry if they were cheated by someone from their own town. As there's only one way out of the house, they have to get through the maze of domestic appliances before they can get it down the steps.

The salesman has given them a litre of fuel and now he shows them how to start the scooter up and how the brakes and the lights work.

Vasyl jumps on and Iryna gets on behind him. Like a bird in a familiar landscape, the scooter sets off around the square in front and then, waving goodbye, the pair set off for a spin round the town. Their eyes are shining with happiness. Olena and her husband hug Esperança. The children have never been given such a useful present. They have never been given a present they liked so much. And as it's just a small scooter, they won't need to get a licence.

"Thank you! Thank you!" the couple repeat again and again.

"Time to go home! It's already dark." Now only the couple are in the back, with Esperança and Nadiya in the front. They're in town now, and Nadiya is back behind the wheel. When they get home they see Iryna and her brother have already arrived.

"How did it go?"

"Great! Come on, get on!"

Then they all take it for a turn. The street is dark and the only light is from the scooter itself. They get on in all possible combinations: Olena taking Esperança is a real laugh! The dog follows them, barking all the way. Poor thing, when they try to put him on it, his heart starts racing and he shakes all over.

Iryna realises she's going to be late for work and she needs to go straightaway. In a flash she's changed and put on her make-up.

"I'll take you!" says Vasyl.

"But what will you do then? Will you wait until I finish?" She looks at Nadiya and tells her she can have a day off today.

"Are you sure? You're going on your own?"

"Yes, it's really easy."

"Won't you be afraid you might run into some nutcase on the way home? Call us when you come out and, if you take too long, we'll come and find you. Be careful, there might be drunks on the road! And don't take the shortcut because there are lots of hiding places along there."

Once Iryna has gone, Nadiya, who has been left on her own after being relieved of taxi-driving duties, starts telling them what's going on:

"The actor who's interested in Ira is from Ireland. He's called Willy Calors."

"And how do they understand each other?" asks Esperança.

"For the moment, with smiles, the couple of words of English Iryna has learned in school, and the little bit of Russian the boy knows.

The whole thing started a few days ago in the restaurant where Iryna works. The people making the film are staying there now. That night, Willy, who's about 20, was staying there with the director and the cameraman, who are quite a bit older, waiting for the dinner menu.

'Hey, Molly!' said the director.

"Iryna looked left and right. When she didn't see anyone else standing there, she assumed they were talking to her and she made a sign to tell them she'd be right back with the menu. She didn't dare say anything to introduce herself and she kept her head down while taking the order. But then they felt the spark between them. Ever since then, the whole team has called her Molly Malone. She's one of the legendary characters the film is trying to bring to life.

"They say there was a Molly who used to walk through the winding streets of the port of old Dublin calling out 'Fresh cockles and mussels!' while pushing a barrow.

One day, Molly died of a fever in the middle of the street. Her premature death began a legend that has been kept going in the form of a song. That was 300 years ago, but her ghost still walks through the world. The song James Yorkstone wrote in 1880 is going to be played in the background at one point in the film.

In Dublin's fair city,
Where the girls are so pretty,
I first set my eyes on sweet Molly Malone..."

Willy Calors, the director and the cameraman are finishing their dinner and, like that night back in June, the three of them are singing the chorus as a way of saying goodnight until the next day.

Iryna, who has served them tonight more gracefully than any other day, has a scooter for her family, and she feels more fortunate than a millionaire with a limousine.

She looks at Willy and answers sweetly: "Goodnight!" He has stayed to the last, smoking a cigarette.

"What about Nadiya? Isn't she coming to pick you up?"

"No, today I'm on my own with the scooter."

"The scooter?"

"Yes. Come and see!"

She has the scooter parked in the courtyard of the restaurant, near the old carriage, parked in the middle of the lawn. Willy has a look and asks Iryna:

"Is it new?"

Iryna's voice fails her and she just nods her head. The boy runs his hand over the scooter as if stroking a fur and she copies him. Their fingers accidentally-on-purpose find one another and entwine. Iryna looks down and is shocked by a kiss on her neck, as their feet move towards the carriage... Sitting in it, neither of them knows how to say "I like you" or "I love you". Outside the window, the night weaves dreams with threads of stardust. Everything that didn't develop in July, happens with a rush that August Sunday. There is no sweeter yearning that one satisfied right here and now. When they realise it's very late – gone midnight – Willy gets up and takes her to the seat of the scooter, following the line of her nose down to the tip and kissing her on the lips again. Running towards his car, he starts it up to act as her escort. It's a bright night and the moon is reflected in the river, marking a path to follow, away from the road. Who could resist? Iryna stops the scooter beside an oak tree and Willy parks too. The heat they feel seems stifling. Desperately, they throw off their clothes in the reeds on the bank: one piece here, another there. Birds, woken among the ferns, cry out. Completely naked, they move into the shining water, the moonlight calling them to follow. But where are they going? They both spot the same little island. Willy helps Iryna jump the little waves. They run madly in circles because they want to hold both hands and like that they can't move forwards. When the current is almost up to their chests, Iryna trips over Willy's feet and he takes advantage to lift her up. The girl's body slides over the boy's like a ballerina's until she reaches his waist. Iryna holds on to him with her legs, puts her arms around his neck and they kiss again, ever more deeply. They rub together with fascinated skin, feeling the vibrations of love. When the fire has died down a little, he reaches for the moon for her with both hands and she drinks it.

Chapter 4

MONDAY 13 AUGUST 2007

Midnight...One o'clock... When everyone at home has been worrying for some time and they are about to send out search parties, they recognise the roar of an engine.

"She's back!"

"Phew! About time! Thank goodness for that!"

They all go out to greet her. And they are all astonished to see that, as Iryna opens the gate, a tall young man with a freckled face and long, curly hair is parking the scooter.

"His name's Willy."

As soon as they see him and hear his name, they all know he's the star of the film that's being made.

"He's come home with me because we finished late and he was worried that... I'd fall off the scooter in the dark."

"Well, well, well!" someone says, and they all raise their eyebrows. He shakes hands with them. "A pleasure," he says, saying goodbye to everyone.

When he's gone, everyone starts questioning Iryna:

"He's an attentive lad, isn't he?"

"What's the film called?"

"What's it about?"

Iryna answers that she doesn't know yet, she'll ask, and...

"*Na dobranich!*"

"*Na dobranich!*" they all reply.

The truth is that she doesn't much care about the plot of the film. What she wants is to be a star in Willy's eyes... Lying on the sofa bed, tucked in and covered with the sheet, her mind wanders as she closes her eyes. Under her eyelids, the sparks of the fire flicker: on her hands is the smell of the boy she has been caressing; in her throat, the taste of wild strawberries. She breathes in, and the moon – still inside her – expands gently.

But in the next bed, Olena tosses and turns as she dreams of the pool over and over again. Now she's swimming in the pool, with her mouth paralysed by lots of sewing needles. One goes through it and chokes her. She is woken suddenly by a sharp pain. It makes her hair stand on end – she can still feel the discomfort in her throat. Her husband stirs with the movement.

"What's the matter?" he asks.

"I'm worried about Ira. She came home later than usual and you didn't say anything to her. That actor might just want to take advantage of her."

"What do you want me to say to her? To be careful? Or that I never want to see her with that boy again? You know I've never told Ira off. I've always given her everything she's asked me for. Anyway, look at her!"

A beam of light is streaming in through a crack in the curtain and they can see their daughter sleeping like an angel, with silky hair that invites you to sink your fingers into it.

"Who would want to harm such a pretty girl? She's just like you when you left the village to go to university in Moscow!" he whispers in her ear, as his hands caress the nape of her neck, and then her breasts, following the curve of her body as he starts making love to her, like he has other nights.

"All the boys used to fall in love with you. I went to Moscow with you because I was scared of losing you. Do you remember?"

Olena turns towards her husband to return his tenderness. She relives their attraction in her heart and holds him tightly against her. But however much she kisses him and looks for him, there is no satisfaction...

"Aren't you feeling well?"

"Not very..."

"What's the matter?"

"I'm nervous because I've got to go back to Kiev next week."

"Again?"

"Yes, to the pig farm."

"Those people who owe you so much money? You can't possibly believe they're going to pay all the arrears..."

"No, they don't owe me anything. I didn't tell you, but I spent the money on my brother's treatment. And they also gave me a loan. As I can't repay it, we agreed I'd work there for another week. I'm sorry I didn't tell you before..." he says, deceiving her again.

What he really meant to tell her was:

"No, they don't owe me anything. In fact I owe them my life. But I'll only tell you if you promise you won't tell anyone else. Swear you won't tell Iryna or Vasyl! I've got cancer. But I'm going to pull through. I've been fighting it for four years. Next week I've got to go back and it will probably be the last time. I want to get the better of life, but life is trying to get the better of me."

And she would have answered:

"I'll come with you, my love. I'll ask them to transfer me to Kiev Hospital, like when your father and then your brother were ill. I'll tell that friend of mine who's an oncologist. They'll have a proper look at you... your case must be different. You've always been stronger than them."

Her husband chokes back the anguish and it remains inside him, to the left of his stomach, like a needle in his heart which he might never have time to free himself from. When death finally comes for him, he'd like to tell his Ira not to cry, please, just pray and sing. He wants her only to remember her father for fun and laughter and, more than anything, for being the one who chose the heroine's name that has made her so brave, free and beautiful. If he has to talk to her, he will tell her that God has hidden many treasures in her path and that she must take every opportunity to look for them.

***

ESPERANÇA HAS GOT UP intending to go to the UNESCO centre where they have activities for children. She

276

has read that it was an initiative by the international community in Paris as part of a special programme to alleviate the effects of the tragedy, and that it has support, although more symbolic than effective, from the Ukrainian government. They say that at Pravdiriava people can get help to overcome the problems, fears and phobias resulting from the Chernobyl disaster. And also that they choose the children who are sent round the world every summer to improve their health.

She also wants to visit Dobrokiv Hospital, which she's been told is very nearby. The others all frown. Only Olena offers to go with her if they go on foot, as she does when she goes to work at the hospital. It's more than three-quarters of an hour's walk.

Esperança had hoped Olena would introduce her to the famous Mrs Moscova, who was in charge of choosing the children to be hosted, but she doesn't work there anymore. She'd have loved to have given her a piece of her mind... She'd have done it subtly, though. She wouldn't have wanted it to affect the hosted children or the host families. Now she'll have to keep it all to herself. But the unfriendly-looking woman who greets them – the new manager – is a worthy substitute.

When Esperança talks to her about Catalonia, Mr Fortunato and the Ukraine-86 Association, the unpleasant woman shows no sign of wanting to talk. She gives them an information leaflet in English as if they were ignorant tourists. It's hardly surprising that Esperança can't help letting out a:

"Very kind!" in a tone the woman can't have liked because she suddenly hurries them up.

"*Bistro, bistro!*" she says, pointing at her watch, which shows five minutes to two.

As they tour the building, Esperança opens the leaflet and tries to translate it:

> "Pravdiriava opened its doors for the first time on 24 October 1994 [...]. After the explosion in the fourth reactor, which happened at the same time as the break-up of the Soviet Union, the economy sank into a deep crisis, which still continues today [...]. All schools, hospitals, social centres and official bodies date from the Soviet era and the lack of resources makes it difficult to keep the centre maintained and operating normally [...].

"They opened it when Iryna was only two, and my son was three," recalls Olena.

The children have warned her that all the work they would see was done many years ago and that none of the computers works – or maybe just the one in the manager's office. One wall is covered by a huge mural with the year of the explosion outlined in black, running from one end to another. The whole painting is in orange and red, with people running and shouting with such desperation it burns into your heart. The ends of the mural have got folded and they're starting to hang down. There are also shelves with craft work in clay, wire and plasticine imitating the power station and its reactors, all of them with a layer of dark dust in the corners. All this backs up what Vasyl and Iryna have told Esperança, leading to a feeling of impotence of the kind found among many people living in the area.

When the two of them come out, they meet the others, who have come to pick them up. Some are in the car, while Vasyl and Iryna are riding around on the scooter. When they see their mother and Esperança they come up and ask:

"How did it go?"

Esperança's first words confirm what they had told her:

"It's a really good thing that the people from the Association come and check what this centre does and what it could do. What about you, why don't you ever go?"

"What for? There's no equipment and no-one teaches us to do anything. Didn't you see?" says Vasyl.

"Do you want me to go and see the psychologists?" asks Ira. "Why should they care about my life?"

Olena does not cut them off because they are translating for her and they are right, but she confirms what Esperança has said and thanks her for it.

"What a good thing we have Mr Fortunato and Jesús! I know on good authority that over the last few years they've worked on the list suggested by the Pravdiriava Centre and now, thank goodness, it's much fairer. This spring they went from village to village and house to house to find out the real situation of the new children to be hosted in Catalonia."

What Olena doesn't tell anyone is that she's already saving to pay (under the counter) for her children's enrolment at Pravdiriava next year: 40 euros for Iryna and 40 for Vasyl – so many hryvnias! She can't tell anyone because she's afraid that if the Association finds out there will be problems and her children will not be among the chosen ones.

"Come on! Let's go and have lunch!" says Vasyl to Esperança, with "that's enough visits" written all over his face.

"If you like we can go and see our grandparents to-morrow. They're always asking about you. They live in a small village. You'll see how nice their place is!" says Iryna, thinking about the curtains she recently helped Granny Rus to hang.

"No, we've got to go to the hospital now. If we don't go now we're here, I'll run out of time and I won't get there at all."

In the end, she doesn't really need to see beyond the dented ambulance at the entrance to imagine the rest.

"Oh, Esperança, what do you think you're going to find in there?" says Nadiya, recalling the Caesarean a friend of hers had in the hospital.

Olena confirms the story, lifting up her jumper and showing a foot-long scar across the middle of her stomach. This winter she had her appendix out, but the scar goes so far up it looks as though she's had her heart removed. That rough, twisted snake across Olena's skin reinforces Esperança's determination to go inside the building. She hasn't come to have fun, she wants any direct information she can get. Olena sees she is so determined to go in that she accompanies her once again, leaving the others in the street. The older Vasyl and Nadiya stay in the car, in the shade of an elm tree, while Iryna and her brother drive round on the scooter, feeling such freedom as the air streams past their faces and blows their hair.

As they go in, there is a little room on the left with two women knitting and silently moving their lips. The patterned jumpers moving down their needles might suggest that they are old ladies from the town, but in fact they are in charge of running the accident and emergency section:

"Where are you going?"

"She's from Catalonia and she'd like to see the hospital," answers Olena, with a gesture of bemusement.

"Didn't you say you were on holiday this week?" they tease her.

"Can we come in or not?" asks Esperança.

"*Xot?* What?"

"We're coming in!" says Olena determinedly.

"If you want."

They say thank you and carry on walking. On the ground floor, all in the same room, are some patients who were operated on a few days ago. Their beds are all different – some are higher than others, some of wood and others of iron. All the convalescents must have brought their own sheets and bedspreads from home because the colours, patterns and sizes are clearly all different. Some are dragging on the floor while others don't even cover the mattress. When they see Esperança, some of the patients approach her. They must think she's a new doctor. They grab her arm and point to the parts of their bodies that hurt. Olena calms them down, telling them Esperança isn't a doctor, but that they will tell the doctor on the top floor to come and see them.

Going up the neglected stairs made of disintegrating granite, they meet a man who has his entire leg in plaster and bandages. He is supporting himself with one hand on the rail and the other on a home-made walking stick. The gauze around his leg is suppurating blood and Esperança thinks she'd have been able to bandage him better than these people. They help him get down

"Well, they're all at home. You've got a permanent job! And you earned plenty of hryvnias in Catalonia! You must have paid off your mortgage by now..."

She sits down, humbled. How can he envy her for a job that mostly consists of cleaning up shit? And anyway this year they've gone back into debt so they could have everything ready for their Catalan visitors: they've done work on the house, had mains water put in, bought furniture, a fridge, a boiler and curtains, and they've decorated.

"A cripple in the car – that's all we need!" everyone thinks, but as they all know they've needed assistance themselves at one time or another, they help him lie down in the back. Iryna, Bossi and Vasyl, who are going round and round with the scooter, come closer to have a look. Ira is driving and the dog is sitting on the platform. He's sticking his muzzle through the handlebars and has his front paws on the girl's hands. It looks as if he's starting to enjoy going for a ride.

When they reach home, they bump into Nadiya's parents, who are carrying a couple of baskets packed full of food. Her father is slim and athletic. Her mother has Nadiya's face, but she is so enormous it's impossible to imagine she once had her daughter's body. She's almost completely round.

"What a lovely scooter! Whose is it?"

"It's ours. Esperança gave it to us."

"What a generous woman she is! Our Nadiya is very grateful for all the improvements to the car she's paid for. We'd like to invite her for something to eat in the meadow."

"Have you been waiting a long time?"

birch trees. The green light gets stronger and then paler as they get nearer to the river. Here they find a sprawling carpet of flowers and rushes framing the water. The car moves on without landmarks, like a boat at sea. Above them is the blue sky and beneath their feet a mirror of wet grass. The wetlands are full of water lilies. They suddenly stop and someone asks:

"Here or over there?"

"Here!" says the older Vasyl.

They park the car right next to the bulrushes surrounding the entire lake, with a small gap for some steps leading into the water, welcoming them to this land of crystal and watercolour. The men take off their trousers. The women are in pants and bra. All of them have their ordinary underwear on except for Nadiya, who is showing off a lovely flower-pattern bikini. She discreetly places a towel around the shoulders of her mother. The woman blushes with the shame her body causes her daughter.

When Esperança enters the water, the older Vasyl, who was the first one in, offers her a bunch of water lilies with stems so long she can make a chain out of them and turn them into a pretty necklace. She looks like a South Sea islander. Suddenly, they all shout:

"Hey! Hey!"

The scooter ridden by Vasyl and Iryna is approaching. The two youngsters wave as they're carried along by the marvellous machine.

"Where have you been? Didn't you set off before us?"

"We were at home looking for the swimming things Esperança bought us last year."

"Look at them showing off!" think their parents. What they don't realise is their swimsuits are already wet. They've done something silly: Vasyl dived straight in as soon as he arrived, forgetting he had the scooter keys in his pocket. Then, when he wanted to park it properly, he realised he didn't have them anymore. They'd fallen in the lake. So that no-one would notice, the two of them agreed that Iryna would hide in some bushes a little way away, watching the scooter, which they had to drag there. Meanwhile, Vasyl ran home to get the other set of keys. From now on, they will have to be very careful, because they've only got one ignition key.

They begin lining up to go in the water. In a neighbouring lake, a group of ducklings copy them, swimming behind their mother. The water's quite warm at the top, but below that it's freezing, so they swim slowly and silently across the paralysed water. The pondweed tangles round their legs, reminding them that this is a wild place, but its charm overcomes any fear of the unknown. Esperança is dazzled by the varied colours as she swims and she doesn't realise the men are already getting the fire ready and the women are setting the table. They spread out huge blankets on the ground and cover them with a tablecloth, leaving a frame of blanket to sit on. On it, they place three dishes, one with a salad of mashed hardboiled egg, one with balls of fish and the other with wild mushrooms. The big pot goes in the middle. It looks like an Indian mandala. The barbecue smells different to the kind she's used to in Catalonia, as the meat is covered with a sauce containing milk, beer and mayonnaise, together with mustard and pepper. Then they prick the meat with long needles. The penetrating smells of spicy food flood Esperança's senses, calling her out of the water. Bittersweet music, mixing joy and sadness, plays throughout the meal. Their laughter is contagious, even reaching their hands, which are raised in the air, leading them into a happy dance. These perfumed images will always remain in Esperança's memory whenever she thinks about what happiness means.

Then they get out the coffee and the *horilka*, as the curious passing clouds look down, leaving a shadow here and a shadow there before darting off to cover the sun. Suddenly a cold breeze blows over the plain, the rushes and grass bend and, as they bow, the rain begins. They have to pick everything up in a tremendous hurry.

Nadia's parents invite them to spend the rest of the afternoon at their home, telling stories and jokes. Esperança flicks through books written in Cyrillic and sees a photograph of a very beautiful woman on a shelf in the living room.

"Is that you, Nadiya?" asks Esperança.

"No, it's Mum when she was young. Everyone gets us mixed up."

"Here in the Ukraine lots of people have thyroid problems because of the radiation. Most of them are women who develop some kind of hypothyroidism during pregnancy. They get a lump in the throat which means they've got it. They suddenly start suffering from a slowdown in the body's functions, anxiety and even distress, difficulty in concentrating, a feeling of tiredness, mood swings and bad circulation. Their hands and legs swell up... What makes it worse is that they haven't got the right medicines. My mother needs a thyroxine pill every day. If she ever can't buy them she'll die because it's the hormone that drives the heart. Do you think she's fat? It's not because she eats a lot! You've all seen... She hasn't touched the bread, the butter or the potatoes. But, in winter it's so cold that... well, who can survive without eating butter or bacon?"

They don't know what to say to this medical lecture. Without a sound, Iryna takes the scooter and goes to the restaurant. She's not late, but he's been waiting for her for a while:

"Where have you been today?" Willy asks her.

"We've been for a picnic," she tells him, dragging the scooter into the courtyard.

"You know what? Today the director needed a pretty girl and I came to look for you. If you'd been at home you might have been in the film."

"Really? And what would my part have been?"

"You'd have been a zombie!"

"What?"

"Yes, there are zombies in the film. Dead people revived by the radioactivity. Horror, exoticism, sensuality, glamour, romanticism, action and humour – we've got it all!"

"You're having me on!"

"No, I'm serious. They need a pretty, blonde girl like you for the part of Molly. She's going to be the girl who saves the world."

"And what would I have to do?"

"Walk around in period costume pushing a barrow full of fish. You'd be made up very pale with lots of blue eyeshadow."

"And what would you do?"

"Fall madly in love with you..."

The trees planted in the courtyard are so tall they are higher than the walls of the building. The sky, which was blue at midday, is now stretching out pink and magenta layers. The clothesline with the sheets, table-cloths and napkins reflects the light of the last rays of the sun and, as they walk in front of it, the washing acts as a screen, projecting the image of a couple hand in hand. It's an image no bleach can remove. A sweet voice comes to Iryna's ear:

"In Dublin's fair city,

Where the girls are so pretty,

I first set my eyes on sweet Molly Malone..."

***

IRYNA PICKS UP EVERYTHING, wolfs down some food and is ready to go. What she doesn't have time to swallow she keeps in her rucksack, together with a bottle of milk wrapped in newspaper to keep the heat in. There's no need to take risks. What would be the price of a few minutes more warmth? She knows perfectly well what goes on in prisons. In her town, unofficial sources say that in the Girnyitsky and Kirovsky sections some police officers took a man and tortured him in custody for five days. They broke his ribs and smashed in his face, body, arms and feet. Then they put a mask on him made from a plastic bag full of poison gas, and insulted him while they hit him in the head. They let him go in front of his home and then took him away again without his family noticing. Now no-one knows where he is. None of his family know why he's been arrested. They all imagine he'll be tortured again.

The shopkeeper's words bring her back to the present.

"I've checked the scooter and it's working perfectly. It started first time. I've filled the tank for you too. The best thing is for you to head for Rivno... you've got just enough petrol to get there. Ask for the municipal library. The librarian even opens on Sundays. She knows it's the only day many people can come in to pick up a book. She's a very good woman and knows all about your case. She'll help you."

As he speaks, the man writes her name and address on a piece of paper. Iryna memorises it and throws it on the smoking stove. This year they probably won't have any gas. Relations with Russia are not good... But by then she'll be out of this accursed country which she loves so much.

Chapter 5

If they'd got up earlier, the men might have gone fishing.

"You have to go before the sun comes up," they say, having breakfast on a tablecloth embroidered with cross-stitch.

Esperança looks at it:

"What lovely roses! And what a lot of work!"

"Granny Rus did it. Would you like to go and see her then?" This time it's Olena who's asking, looking at Esperança's face.

"Of course I would! Is it a long time since you've seen her?"

"Yes, I haven't seen my parents since the winter and I'd really like to. They're getting old and... last time my father wasn't at all well."

"Is it very far?"

"If we leave now, we'll be there by lunchtime."

"Come on then, let's go!"

"Come on Iryna, get up! We're going to see your grandparents! I'll ring their neighbours so they can tell them we're going."

"We're going now? To Belarus?" says Iryna, half asleep.

"Yes! Get up! Don't be lazy! Weren't you saying yesterday that you wanted to go? Come on, pick up those medicines Esperança brought you: the antibiotics, the paracetamol, the aspirins. You know they've got nothing at all there and sometimes Granny can't get out of bed because her legs hurt so much."

Iryna doesn't answer, but reluctantly gets dressed.

"What time will we get back?" she says, complaining. "You know I have to work."

"Haven't you got a friend who can stand in for you when Marina finishes?"

"If I keep changing things around, I'll lose the job in the end."

She's right that the restaurant won't stand any nonsense, but Olena phones them and they find a way to sort it out.

"That's it! Marina's mother says that if it's just today she'll let her work the whole shift."

Iryna's not really bothered about that, though. What she really wants is to be able to see Willy again. She also doesn't feel at all well and doesn't relish the journey. She feels a little sick. She picks up the paracetamol intended for her grandparents and takes one. With the box open, she hesitates a few seconds. Finally, she puts some of the pills away at the back of the wardrobe. As she does so, she feels mean and selfish, but when she doesn't feel well, one of those pills does miracles. As she gets a lot of colds, she needs them... She remembers that when they had end-of-year exams she did them with a high temperature. What a good thing they still had half a paracetamol from Rouralba left! Without that, she wouldn't have passed. At least, that's what she tells herself by way of justification as she applies a little blusher to her pale cheeks.

Nadiya cleans the outside of her car. Especially the windows, which are covered in squashed mosquitos.

Seeing them, Esperança starts scratching the bites she has all over her body and silently curses the insects. She is beginning to understand why the children don't need insect repellent when they're in Catalonia. They must already be immune, she says to herself, looking at the map and the area where they are planning to go.

"Goodbye!" says Vasyl from the scooter.

"Where's he going now? Isn't he coming to see his grandparents?" she asks Nadiya.

"No, only the women are coming. It's a very long way to go with the car so full."

"My goodness! It's a good thing you're going to guide me!" thinks Esperança, who knows she can't get out of driving.

To the north, the road is just as straight as it is to the south, and the landscape is just as flat. The car's got new brakes, wheels and spark plugs. They've checked the accelerator, and the service it's had should, God willing, ensure it doesn't leave them in the lurch. Birches and more birches; endless meadows; fields and fields of hops; sky and land blending on the horizon. The dampness on the tarmac evaporates in the heat and shines from some angles, reflecting the green. The car is doing about 80 kilometres an hour. There's no need to go faster, even if they could. Everything is going well until suddenly the car flies into the air and...bang! They go on lurching forward, in the middle of a road covered in gravel. They've shot down a ramp about a foot high. The asphalt has clearly been taken up, but there wasn't a roadworks sign anywhere to warn them.

"What's wrong with these people?" splutters Esperança, whose heart has tightened to a fist.

"Here in Ukraine you never know what you're going to run into," says Nadiya, her eyes wide open.

"You know something? I'm still shaking. You'd better drive."

They stop for a minute and switch over. Iryna takes the opportunity to get rid of the nasty taste that had suddenly risen into her mouth with the bump.

They carry on along the road, which has become a bumpy forest track. They have to go slowly, but it's drivable.

"Do you think we'll be there by lunchtime? How far is it?"

"How should I know? And what's that?"

A large machine is blocking their path, occupying the entire width of the road. With its claws it is ripping up the old tarmac and throwing it on to the verge, but it hasn't left enough space for anyone to get on to the stretch in front of it that hasn't been dug up yet. The car stops as if it were an ant at the feet of an elephant. Olena gets out and talks to the digger driver. Over a tremendous noise, he tells her they've got to go back.

"And how do get up that great big ramp we came down?"

"No, not that far. Over there behind that big pile of gravel there's an entrance leading on to the track across the meadow. Don't miss it. It'll take you directly to that village. Go through it and you'll come back to this road the other way."

They often skid or find traps where the wheels sink and slip. Nadiya has to put her foot right down to get out of them and mud shoots out in all directions. If they can't see, they have to reach out the windows and use their arms as cloths to clean the windscreen. It's a humid day and the flies coming in the window stick to their skin. The August sun and the buzzing insects form a kind of crown above them. When they come to a puddle they stop. Olena gets out of the car and puts a stick into it so they know where they need to put the wheels.

As they approach the village, the track becomes easier to negotiate. The cow dung indicates that cattle go that way every day. Some of them, grazing in the meadow, turn to the women with a look that says "No need to make such a fuss". And they're right! Now they're back on the road and they've only been in the car three hours! They carry on at the same pace: woods, meadows, cows... Now they can see some roofs sticking up above the trees. Perhaps they're approaching Iryna's grandparents' village... But it's not a village, it's the regional capital near Belarus. They're half way and their stomachs are starting to rumble. The women want to stop and buy some food: fruit, drinks and some stuffed triangles of dough which they say are really good even though they are fried. In a corner of the shop, Esperança discovers a dusty bottle of local sparkling wine and buys it as a present. They only eat a little because Granny Rus is waiting for them and she's bound to be upset if they can't do her meal justice when they arrive. Two boys and a girl are playing in front of the shop. The boys are pretending to be firemen putting out a blaze at a nuclear power station. The girl wants to follow them:

"What can I do?"

"Be quiet! Wait!" they order. "You've got to stay at home and cry."

The road is flat now – endless and monotonous. Esperança is driving again. She's afraid of going too fast: maybe the dazzling mirages conceal another ramp or perhaps a local peasant will decide to cross with an ox-cart loaded down with straw. A barefoot boy walks along the verge in a scruffy old jumper, striped and patterned. Further on, an older woman, with a black handkerchief on her head and green stockings, is driving a cow with a stick in her right hand and a mobile phone stuck to her ear. How incongruous! Esperança is finding it hard to imagine where it will end, when Olena warns her they need to take a shortcut.

"Hey! Turn left! It's not far now."

They're driving among meadows and half-closed timbered houses.

When they arrive, Grandad Volodymyr is standing in front of the fence waiting impassively for them. You'd say he was as strong as an oak, but you can see there's something going on inside. The world he's been called on to live in leaves no room for those who suffer. If you don't look healthy, the wild beasts will devour you. He looks as tall, strong and fresh as if they'd told him "We're here!" only five minutes ago. In fact, nothing could be further from the truth: he's been here for two hours because they haven't been able to phone again since the morning. He welcomes Esperança with a hug and a look of gratitude.

"Thank you! I've been so looking forward to meeting you. Where's your husband?" they translate for him.

"Something cropped up at work."

"Iryna and Vasyl have told us all about you. You're good people. If you love my grandchildren, you love me. Come in, come in! Rus, Rus, come out! They're here!"

In the middle of the courtyard an enormous chicken, with golden feathers and a ruby crown, runs off to hide. There's no point in shouting, but last time there were guests here, the bird's partner went into the pot and today it's lost its son, who weighing almost seven kilos. They can still smell the burned feathers. The chicken doesn't like the newcomers' jokes, watching them suspiciously as they move towards the house.

Square windows with sky blue frames cover the porch. An enormous old lady with a sweet smile almost has to turn sideways to fit through the small entrance as she comes out. She's wearing a top patterned with roses that's so tight you can virtually make out her well-formed, round nipples. There are probably no bras in her size. As she approaches, her heart can be heard beating like a hammer. What noisy kisses! What blue eyes! And how she looks at them!

To get into the kitchen they have to dodge strips of cellophane hanging from the ceiling which are covered in flies. There are still lots of insects flying round the door that need catching! Esperança doesn't dare go underneath them. Granny Rus scares them off with a gesture and, with her other hand, shows the guests to the table. It's small, but it's got everything they need, and Olena puts the things she's brought on it too. She gets them to sit down and invites them to eat. The old couple watch them from a corner, saying they've already eaten.

They ask them to help themselves to as much as they like and ask if they want more.

"I want another chicken!" jokes Esperança. The stew is wonderful, but she's left all the skin because she doesn't want to share her meal with the flies.

She opens the bottle of sparkling wine they have been keeping in a bucket of well water and they make a toast. You can see it's not something they drink very often because, after toasting with "Health and hryvnias!" they gulp it down in one, as if it were vodka.

After the meal, the old couple show them the house. The oven is in a tiny corner. They say that every time they bake bread they whitewash it with lime. It is like a round, closed hearth with two doors, in the shape of a chapel.

"Who would say that something so clean could be an oven?" Esperança wonders.

The only bedroom they have, with four beds, looks like a rug display. There are several hanging from the walls to match the curtains, with their pattern of big, bright flowers. They are clearly are used for decoration and to mitigate the bad weather. A television set stands on a small table, covered with a cloth and crowned with a bunch of flowers. Stuck to the screen is a postcard of the Batlló House in Barcelona, which Iryna sent them last summer from Catalonia. It goes without saying that the set doesn't work. Perhaps one day one of the Vasyls will come and try to fix it, but first he'll have to put an aerial in. Underneath it is a basket full of herbs and ointments: it smells of camphor and turpentine. Here, in front of Esperança and her mother, Iryna gives her grandmother the medicines. No-one can say she doesn't care for them or want to help them. Her grandmother receives them with blandishments.

"Krasyva. My beautiful granddaughter! You know I'm not scared and I don't worry about dying. Do the leaves cry when they fall off the trees in autumn?"

"She never complains: last summer she got a really badly infected leg. When you pressed her knee, pus came out her calf."

"How did that happen?"

"She got an ulcer and cured it by applying bandages soaked in a preparation she made herself. You could fit your whole thumb in it, it was so deep."

"And didn't she take antibiotics?"

"How? She'd got no money!"

"My God!"

As Esperança comes out, she tries to forget the poverty and consider the situation as a whole: house, farmyard and granary, all made of wood, with steeply sloping roofs integrated into their natural surroundings ready for the snow to slide off, just like fir trees.

"It looks like a toy. It reminds me of the farms they give children for Christmas!" she can't help saying.

"Yes, it's very old. My father built it up from the ashes when he came back from the war," says the old lady. "And Volo does what he can to preserve it, don't you?" she adds, talking to her husband, standing proudly beside her.

"Which war?"

"The Second World War. Mum took me and my two brothers to the forest just before the Germans came and burned down the whole village. I still remember it although I can only have been three!"

"But how did you manage to follow her?"

"She put us on the back of a cow with lots of birch branches in our hands to camouflage us."

How can that be? If she was three in 1945 when the Russians entered Berlin, now she could only be 73, Esperança calculates. She looks at them again: they both look almost 80.

Their faces are creased by wrinkles and burned by the bad weather and their bodies bear witness to a life of hard work... Olena sees the way she's looking at them and wants to remember them when they were young.

"My father was the strongest and most handsome man in the village. He could have any woman he wanted, but his Rus wouldn't look at another man. They've had lots of children. The first ones died soon after birth for lack of health care. Dad saved me. I'd been thrown in a corner as if I was dead."

"Yes, you can see they love each other. Doesn't anyone help them look after this land?"

"Who is there to help them? Only Mum's brother and his children, when they're not drunk. They're strong old people, the kind who saw the smoke from the reactor and carried on working. If the Swedes hadn't come and warned them, they'd be working still."

As they say this, two strapping but dirty looking youths of about 17 appear on a very old moped.

"Who are these boys?" asks Esperança.

"My cousins," says Iryna, with an apologetic gesture. Ignoring her, the two of them get straight to the point:

"Where's Vasyl?"

"He's at home, helping his dad," Iryna boasts with an air of "He works, not like you, you great layabouts."

But little does she know where her brother is now, although in a way she's right. Because just after the car set off for Belarus, Vasyl went for a ride on the scooter and who should he find, very close to home, but Willy. Clearly he'd come to see Iryna. Vasyl told Willy where she was and they immediately became friends.

So, he's decided to take his prospective brother-in-law on the scooter to Pripyat' to show him how he earns a little extra cash.

"Come on, all get together and I'll take a souvenir photo," suggests Esperança. And she does take it, but Iryna keeps as far away as she can from the boys, as if they had the plague.

Then their grandfather, who loves all his grandchildren the same, decides to tell a joke to relax the atmosphere.

"You know Belarus means White Russia? Well, there are a couple of old ladies talking about Chernobyl and one says to the other 'Have you heard that it's called Belarus because we've got so many white blood cells here?'." And the other replies: 'What nonsense! I cut my finger only yesterday and my blood was still red'."

"What caustic humour!"

Ira likes to tell one about when everyone wanted to emigrate for fear of radiation.

"Do you know the one about the old lady who has to have a gynaecological examination before going to work abroad? As she doesn't know what it means, she lies face-down on the bed. The doctor's a bit surprised. He asks her: 'Where are you going, madam?' and she answers: 'America'."

And they all burst out laughing because these are like innocent stories that might even really have happened.

"Poor old ladies! Thank goodness I can still whitewash the oven and put bread and salt on the table with plates and spoons so everyone who comes can have something to eat. The people from the next village haven't been so lucky. Their chickens' crests turned black instead of red and they couldn't make cheese because their milk didn't curdle. And the authorities evicted them, scaring them, and telling them 'Get out, we've got to burn your house down' while showing them a can of petrol. It was as if the Germans were coming back."

Olena helped her tell the story and Iryna started to get tired of translating...

"All those people Dad looked after during that time. He'd probably have done it secretly... Lots of people thought they were contagious or that God had punished them. If they visited their children or relatives who lived in areas away from the black cloud, they'd spend all day cleaning everything they touched. As if they were lepers. They spent the nights wandering in the forests. They didn't know where to go. After a few months the authorities gave up trying to catch them and they could go home. Now they're back with their cats and dogs which they found, thin and breathless, waiting for them. Animals never abandon you."

"And how do they manage to live now?"

"They sell apples by the roadside. They advertise them, saying 'They're from Chernobyl'."

"And they sell them like that?"

"Yes, people buy them for their mother-in-law, their boss, their husband..."

"You're kidding!"

"You might think it's a joke, but here there are lots of people who need some sort of revenge."

"Ira, have you told her we've got a history museum in the village?" her grandfather asks.

"Grandad says we could go to the museum now," she simplifies.

"That would be interesting... But it's already gone six! I don't want to be driving around these god-forsaken roads in the dark," says Esperança, looking for support others to say it's time to go.

"It's very nearby – just five minutes in the car," they reassure her.

In the museum, the most eye-catching display is in the corner of one of the rooms, representing the German invasion of Ukraine. It gives spectators the feeling they are heading towards a burning village. It's horrifying to see how, as the fire forces the Ukrainians to leave their houses, they are all machine-gunned: women, children and old people. In the other room are photographs of the soldiers who won medals. One of them is the children's great-grandfather: they are very proud that he entered Berlin.

In front of the museum is a monument to the dead, which always has fresh flowers on it. Granny tells them she prays for all of them because, thank God, she doesn't have anyone to mourn. She begins praying and the others pray and meditate with her.

Once back home, when there's no more time left to talk, from under her apron the old lady takes a tablecloth with roses embroidered in cross-stitch, just like the one Olena has in Dobrokiv, and gives it to Esperança.

"As you look after my grandchildren, you're a daughter to me!"

Then, the grandfather takes a deer's antlers out of a bag.

"I hunted this one a while ago. I don't go out hunting now. Give them to your husband for luck! Take care!"

Full of emotion, she hugs the old couple as if it were the last time she was going to see them. She's only got one day left in Ukraine.

Towards Europe, the sky starts turning the colours of sunset, slices of magenta and yellow covering the landscape like one of the presents she's taking with her, wrapped up in crepe paper...

"Goodbye, goodbye!" they say again and again.

They can hardly move because the cows, which had been wandering along the road, are now blocking it completely, coming right up to the car without any fear.

As it gets dark, it starts raining, first just a few drops that might be mistaken for bird-droppings on the windscreen. Then the rain gets heavier and even running at full speed the windscreen wipers can't cope. To avoid the roadworks, they're driving on half-made-up forest tracks and the car keeps on bouncing around. The sky is as black as the bottom of a well. Iryna is feeling rather queasy. From time to time she gets a nasty taste in her mouth and they have to stop so she can be sick. A vicious wind howls while thick white clouds sweep against the car and rob them of visibility. They don't know where they're going. Esperança asks:

"What if we have a breakdown or come off the track. Who's going to come out to look for us?"

"No-one," they tell her.

"Well I can't go on!"

She has scarcely said these words when, as if by magic, two little red lights appear in the middle of the track. They belong to a four-wheel drive vehicle that's so close to them they might have hit it.

"Thank goodness! I'm going to stick tight to it until we find the main road. Wherever it goes, I'll follow."

It takes them more than four hours to find a village. They've gone off track, but they keep following the four-wheel drive car. Or they do until they reach the main road and, like a conjuring trick, the sky suddenly fills with thousands of stars.

"Left or right?"

"Let's try right."

Just as well. They soon find a sign indicating Chernobyl.

"It's three-quarters of an hour to Dobrokiv from here," says Olena.

The way is smooth, clear and straight and now they do start to move quickly. Suddenly, screeeeeech! there's a very sharp bend and screeeeeech! screeeeeeech! they brake, skid and almost end up on the verge. A pile of flowers announces that more than a few people have lost their lives here. Esperança is scared into silence as she stares, astonished, at a giant egg in the middle of a roundabout. The Ukrainians tell her that this is where a friend of Iryna's and Nadiya's was killed – a young man who was supposed to get married the following morning. It has also accounted for many drunk drivers. They stop for a moment and stretch their legs on the grass around them.

"What does this egg mean?" asks Esperança.

This monument was put up in memory of the explosion.

"The custom of painting Easter eggs began here, in Ukraine," says

Iryna.

"At Easter, we go to church with a basket covered with a cloth like the one Granny's given you, full of food, with walnut bread and fruit sweets that Mum makes. We also decorate boiled eggs with patterns of colours. The ceremony of blessing the food lasts all night and, the next morning, we eat it all at a party. For three days, anyone who comes into the house says:

'Khrystos voskres! Christ is risen!' And the others answer:

"Voistynu voskres! He is risen indeed!'."

"These words are also said three times every time you meet someone you haven't seen before."

"There's a game consisting of banging boiled eggs together without breaking the shell. The winner is the one who bangs the same egg most times. When you've done it with your family you go out into the street to look for new opponents. Dad knows how to choose the best eggs and he always wins. And we know a lot of games. If you like, Esperança, I'll tell you about them and you can show your pupils."

"What fun!" she says, and then asks:

"Do young people also go to church?"

"Of course they do! Did you think only old ladies went? It's full of boys and girls our age. If young people don't have faith, who will? And we have fun taking part in the ceremonies. We've also got a choir where we sing lovely songs. But, at home, the two Vasyls only want to go at Easter."

"No, Ira, that's not true. Dad goes every week now too!"

***

THEY SAY GOODBYE IN FRONT OF THE SHOP with a three-way hug, Lyuba in the middle. The scooter roars and all she needs to do is open the rucksack and put the little girl in, well covered with the blanket. She's so well covered only her eyes can be seen – eyes so blue one look from them could take you to heaven.

For the first part of the route she goes carefully over the frozen stretches, but she's not worried – there's almost no traffic on the road. She talks to the landscape, promising to be strong and to keep any homesickness deep within her. She swears that nothing will pass her lips that might make Lyuba sad. They pass the birches, the oaks and the ash trees. Dropping their leaves and shaking off the first snow of winter, they seem to be saying farewell.

"Goodbye, goodbye, goodbye... See you soon!"

If it wasn't for the flock of crows cawing loudly along behind her, it would be a joyful parting. But the birds' reproach – stupid, stupid, silly brainless girl – reminds her that Lyuba's six months old and hasn't been christened yet, and that she's not entered in any register!

Chapter 6

They don't get home until gone midnight. And, as it's so late, they are surprised to find Nadiya's parents standing outside the fence. "Where are the Vasyls? Are they asleep? Why haven't they come out to see us?" they ask.

"Good evening!"

"Don't worry. It wasn't serious. It could have been worse!"

"What are you talking about? What's happened?" They don't understand.

"Nothing's happened to Vasyl, it's his friend who fell off the scooter... It was in the ford over the torrent near Pripyat'. You can walk across perfectly well, but with the scooter... It seems they were going quite fast, the boy wasn't holding on tight and he was thrown off on to the other side of the road. There was no blood but he got a bang on the head and said he couldn't see properly. Vasyl picked him up and took him to hospital and they told the police there so they could make a report," says Nadiya's mother.

"And you don't know who he is?"

"No, Ira, we've got no idea. We thought it must be someone who goes hop-picking with your brother."

"We were waiting for you all together and the police came to see your father and asked him for the scooter's documents. Your father said he didn't know where they'd put them and that he'd hand them in as soon as he could. Then he went off to the hospital. And we ran to the place you bought it and, thank goodness, they'd sorted out the papers with yesterday's date. We went to pick them up and we were going to take them to him now. Everything's fine until something happens…"

Iryna suddenly reacts.

"We'll take the papers. Come on, Nadiya! You stay here and sleep, you're exhausted," she tells Nadiya's parents, her mother and Esperança.

As it's absolutely true that they're dead tired, they give the girls a plenty of advice and let them go off. Iryna has an idea: as Vasyl isn't hurt, she'll ask Nadiya to take the papers to the hospital on her own, after dropping her outside the hotel where she works. She'd love to give Willy a surprise! She can go on to the hospital later. They get into the car and look at one another. They understand one another so well, words are hardly needed.

"Go on, Nadiya. Stop here. This will do! You go to the hospital, I won't be long." She enters to find Marina, who has finished her shift and has her bag over her shoulder ready to go home. She asks:

"How did it go with your grandparents?"

"Fine! Have you seen Willy?"

"No, he hasn't come in yet. The actors had the day off today and they've gone to Kiev. They didn't come in for lunch or dinner. I'm going now. We've finished doing the washing up and putting the things away. My father's waiting for me. Do you want to come with us?"

"No, don't worry, Nadiya's going to come and pick me up now."

"Nadiya?"

"Yes, she's had to go and off to do something. You go home. Make a note of the days I owe you, OK?"

There's no-one in the dining room or the bar, and she sneaks across to the stairs leading to the corridor and the bedrooms. She slowly opens the door of Willy's bedroom. The lamp is off, but light from the street is coming in through the open window. She puts her head round the door. He isn't there. She'll wait for him... She shuts the door and moves further into the room. She opens her basket. There's a half-empty packed of cigarettes at the bottom. She bought it a week ago. No-one smokes in her house. She likes the smell because she associates it with the sensual way her boyfriend looks at her. She smokes in secret. Every night, before going to bed, she looks for a quiet place and, breathing in the smoke, dreams that she could live with Willy. Why is she making such plans if she's only known him for ten minutes? She rests her arms on the windowsill. There's a white van on the main road with its siren blaring. Then, silence. When she searches for the cigarette, she finds all the tablets she'd given her grandmother earlier on. Why did the old lady give them back? Perhaps she realised Iryna had taken some. Did she see the cigarettes? There are also two of those cakes her grandmother makes. Iryna always says how much she loves them, but today she hasn't felt like touching them. Her grandmother knows so many things about her... She should have told her that she's in love – that she doesn't know whether this suffering is what's called happiness. She takes such a strong first drag on the cigarette that the world slides out of focus. As she blows the smoke out, a huge vacuum inside her demands another drag and... she doesn't know how but she finds herself lying on the floor. How long has she been there? She feels with one hand until she finds the sheet hanging down, pulls it and, with a great effort, she reaches the bed, managing to lie down across it. How she used to love staying with her grandmother when she was little! Her great patience! The warmth she felt near that battered body. And, as she remembers her, she recalls once again how good it seemed when the two of them slept in the same bed, protected in a restful embrace. But now it's not her grandmother who's coming; it's not her sweet grandmother she misses so much... A shiver of tenderness drives her to seek out the pillow. She presses it against her breasts, searching for the curls on his head, the mouth on his face, the sex that joined them on his body. She always told her grandmother she'd fall in love with a very nice, handsome boy. "What are you talking about?" the old lady would contradict her. "Don't you know that love is blind?" She was just a child, but she was very sure of one thing: love couldn't be blind. Her senses know very well what she needs now. Suddenly, as she places her hands on the dark stain on her skin she feels a pain in her heart and a premonition sends her leaping out of bed: Willy's not coming back to sleep here! She jumps down the steps, three by three, and runs... until she reaches the hospital breathless. As she goes into the entrance hall, the porter calls her.

"Iryna, are you looking for your father and your brother?"

"Yes, where are they?"

"They've gone off to Kiev. The young foreigner who had the accident with your brother is very serious. He's been blinded and we haven't got the resources here to diagnose him here."

"What about Nadiya? Didn't she come to bring you some papers?"

"Yes, we've got them. When she arrived, they were all leaving and she offered to take your father to the general hospital in Kiev because only one person could go in the ambulance."

On the way to Kiev, Nadiya passed by the hotel and stopped for a few minutes, but she didn't find Iryna. How could she have known she'd be in Willy's room?

As Iryna hitchhikes, dawn begins to whiten the night sky and the Dnieper is turned gold and blood red as the sun washes the sleep from its eyes. By the time she gets to the hospital, she feels crazy, desperate. And she doesn't even know the surname of the boy she's looking for. Fortunately, Willy's a distinctive name, or at least it is here. They immediately take her to the Intensive Care Unit where he's been admitted. They find the two Vasyls and Nadiya with their faces pressed to the glass. When they see her so agitated, they block her path:

"You can't go in. No-one can go in... only the doctors and nurses."

"We've got to go home. God's will be done!" says her father.

"God's will! God's will? I'm having nothing more to do with him! How can he have allowed something like this to happen to such a young boy? You go! I'm staying here."

Hearing the shouting, the duty doctor comes out and asks them to be quiet.

"He's the love of my life! Let me see him!"

"He's had a head injury. We really need to control our emotions. He's delirious. It seems he's got no relatives here. Now we're going to call the numbers we've found on his mobile."

"Look, I can help you. He's staying at the Ivanov Hotel. The phone number is 989920672. Let me in!"

"Perhaps a bit of company would do him good, but don't say anything to him. Just hold his hand. You must wash your arms, hands and face and you'll need a hat, overall and sterilised slippers."

"Wait," says her father. "You'll need hryvnias... and we've only got enough to fill up with petrol. Haven't we, Nadiya?"

"Yes. I've got nothing."

"Don't worry, if she stays here, she can eat with us," says the doctor, reassuringly.

And they say goodbye with a sad smile.

***

SHE BANISHES THE NIGHTMARE by inventing songs for Lyuba:

"Dopey old owl,

it's not night now,

sun's on the prowl..."

The little girl moves, lifting up her arms and waving her hands to the rhythm. When there are bumps, she clings on to her mother's knees and keeps her head in the middle. With the bouncing and the monotony, she goes back to sleep. Iryna brakes for a moment to tilt the rucksack so her little girl can rest better. In the morning sunshine between the sparse birch trees, she suddenly notices a vehicle parked on the right-hand side of the road, a long way off.

It's definitely there, right on the crossroads leading to Ostrong. She knows this tactic – it's the police. What if they're the ones looking for her? She stops the engine straightaway: she doesn't want them to hear her. She hesitates, observing the colour of the landscape, and thinks that she's recently passed a river and banks can cause problems. Then she decides to go into an area of black soil between rock roses that only an expert could get through without getting bogged down to the neck. The weak light guides her forward, without straying too far from the road she'd been on. It's a good thing that as she advances towards danger the grass becomes luxuriant and there are more bushes. From among the branches a deer appears. Zigzagging, it shows the way to the birch wood cut through by the main road. Less than 200 metres from the check point, the baby wakes up and opens her eyes so wide they barely fit in her face. She's probably missing the roar of the engine or perhaps she's picked up the smell of fear and anxiety from her mother. Please God don't let her cry! Iryna moistens her dummy with honey and... one, two, three... she crosses the road. This stretch is a little uphill because they're going towards the embankment of the railway line that runs alongside the road. A really long goods train appears. Iryna looks carefully, calculating the distance and speed in a few seconds. She can't wait for it to pass. And... she goes for it! With strength drawn from desperation she's never known before she lifts the scooter over the first rail. She hears the train whistle. It's coming straight at them as she slips on the damaged sleepers. Then she, the scooter and the little girl are rolling over and over on the other side. Quickly, they blend into the trees. She turns to look at the wagons, which are getting smaller as they move further away. She breathes out the fright she's had like a demon that had been possessing her, and realises that everything that's happening is a miracle. Her family must be praying for her. She kisses Lyuba, who hadn't even been scared, again and again. Then she carries on and on, pushing the scooter, giving thanks and looking left and right like a cornered animal. But her eyes stray from the path to focus on some bushes, where a woman is moaning and calling for help.

Bozhe, pomozhy! God, help me!

At that very moment the police dogs must be looking for her trail. The woman is face down and tied hand and foot so she can't turn over. She's blonde with well-cut, medium-length hair. She's smartly dressed. Near her is a designer bag that's been turned over, the contents scattered on the ground. She must be fifty-something.

"I should have covered my ears and ignored your crying!" she swears, as she turns the woman over.

Iryna thinks she looks familiar... Perhaps someone's tried to kidnap her or even raped her. Maybe she worked in a bank and was taken hostage so the robbers could get away. It must be her the police are looking for.

"I'm dead!" she shouts. "Don't touch me!"

She's delirious. She must be badly hurt or have broken bones or something.

"My God, please help Larissa!"

"They're coming to help you now," Iryna tells her, certain the police will find her soon with all these groans.

"Stay with me. My name's Larissa Brizhik. I'm a scientist. Don't you know my name?" she says, looking Iryna in the eye.

"Maybe, but I can't," she says, picking up the scarf and turning her back on the woman. "My life's at stake!"

"Why? What's going on? What's your name? Where are you going?"

"I'm escaping. If I can't get away they'll put us in the clink and you know what happens in there."

"What did you do?"

"Nothing. I tried to kill a pig."

"Well, do me one favour then. Unscrew the toe of my right shoe. It's a USB memory stick. That's what they want from me."

Iryna tries to unscrew the shoe.

"I'll always be grateful to you. If you ever need me, call."

"Look, I'll take the whole thing. And she puts it in the space under the seat."

"Good. Now unscrew the petrol tank, wet your fingers and rub them along the scooter. That will confuse the sniffer dogs. Go on!"

And she does it. Quick as a flash, she accelerates away and doesn't look for the road to Rivno or notice that the little girl is sleeping again until she's sure she's left them a long way behind.

"Look at her, what a little angel!" she says, astonished.

As they near the provincial capital, the traffic gets heavier. Luxury cars with foreign number plates flash past ramshackle vehicles, or simple ones like Iryna's. But until the first traffic jams begin on the bridge over the River Ustje, a tributary of the Dnieper, she doesn't realise that it's going to take her a good while to get to the centre. She works out that it must be 11am, but the baby hasn't asked for her feed yet. Iryna wonders what's the matter with her. She slows down, goes up the kerb and approaches the bridge railing. She takes out the little girl and, holding her with one arm, fixes the scooter with the other. She sits in the space between with the baby in her lap:

"Hey! Lyuba! Wake up, princess! Aren't you hungry, my love?"

The movement, the noise, the roar of the traffic, the din of the lorries, the smoke and the strong smells have left the baby rather dazed. She doesn't show any sign of needing anything. How can that be? So Iryna wakes her up and makes her eat a few crumbs of bread moistened with butter. As she finds them difficult to swallow, her mother gently brings the bottle of milk to her lips to wash them down. She remembers what her teacher told her: children need to follow a timetable from a very young age. The milk is still warm and, once Lyuba has had her breakfast, her mother drinks all the rest.

Afterwards, pleased to have been able to feed her, she takes her in both hands and lifts her up in the air. She looks like the image of those virgins offering the Christ child. Someone in an Audi with a letter D for Deutschland on its number plate takes a photo of them. It must be some tourist wanting a souvenir. How dare they! "If I get out of this," she thinks, "I swear by God I shall never get into this kind of mess again, where people take pictures of me for their own amusement." She gets back on the scooter and sets off.

In the city, the first people she asks about the address she's got have no idea. Lyuba starts protesting persistently. It's no wonder, she's really fed up by now. Iryna takes her from her hiding place and she stops moaning. She moves as best she can with Lyuba in her arms, now on her back, and now under her arm... The baby doesn't like to be squeezed like this and, as she's not being held properly, she feels unsafe. Now her loud, heart-rending cries lead Iryna to abandon the scooter on the ground. Without meaning to, she's passed on her insecurity and tiredness to the little girl. She rocks her, folding her knees exaggeratedly, covering her with kisses and talking to her:

"That's it, Lyuba, we're here."

The little girl trusts her but expresses her feelings with a heart-rending moan.

**

WEDNESDAY 15 AUGUST 2007

It's some time since Nadiya and the Vasyls got home from the hospital. Now they're resting. Esperança's picking up her things and packing. She's got to catch the plane this afternoon, but first she wants to call into the Kiev ICU. Olena phones them at lunchtime. Sitting at the kitchen table, young Vasyl tells them how the accident happened:

"Willy was wandering around, hoping to meet Iryna. I thought it would be better to go out and tell him you

319

weren't here. He was in no hurry and he started talking to me. He knows a few words of Ukrainian and a little Russian, and he mixed it all with English. I thought I understood that they needed extras for a zombie film. Skeletons from all over the world come to Ukraine to get their flesh back. I suggested it would be interesting to film in Pripyat', the ghost town. I suggested going there so he could tell the director about it. On the way we might be able to pick up some interesting material. There are some basements that didn't get burned and are full of things... I'm the only one who knows how to get into them. We were nosing around there for a good while. He hardly touched anything because he was afraid it might be contaminated. I asked him 'Do I look contaminated to you? The worst thing's not the radiation, it's not having anything to eat" and he understood that. He told me he was born in Ballymun, a poor suburb of Dublin and you could only get out of there if you could get a good horse. It was when we were leaving the village that we had the accident. We were fooling around... He was shouting: 'Giddyup, off we gallop! Quickly, quickly, the zombies are coming for us!' I warned him: 'Be careful and hold on tight to my waist!' He was laughing and he only held on to the seat. But by the time I realised, we were already in the ford. And... I didn't slow down, but I didn't ever lose control of the scooter. I didn't stop until I realised he wasn't on there any more. He'd been thrown off! He was crying and shouting in the middle of the water: 'What's happened to me? What's happened to me...?' I was angry and told him off: 'You've fallen off, mate. You didn't hold on properly!' 'Have I? But why has it suddenly gone dark?' 'What do you mean why is it dark?' I said. 'It's five o'clock in the afternoon. Come on, Willy, don't talk nonsense!' But he went on and, it really scared me when I saw he couldn't get up or give me his hand. As he couldn't stand up, I had to drag him out of the torrent. Then I slung him over the scooter like a moaning sack of potatoes. I still don't know how I got to the hospital."

The days of delicious, noisy meals are over. Now they just chew in silence.

The older Vasyl loads up her suitcases. It's the last touch in a stay that would have been wonderful if it hadn't been for the accident to Willy. Olena helps her with her bags and the packets. She will come with her to the hospital in Kiev when she goes to say goodbye to Iryna and she believes Esperança will convince her daughter to come home. It hurts her so much that Iryna has stayed with Willy... she can't understand that it's the right thing for her to do, and that she perhaps needs to do it. The two Vasyls stay in the doorway saying goodbye. The scooter is under the porch. Their cheeks are wet.

Nadiya has gone to pick up her mother. As she knows Kiev very well and today is her day off, she'll drive the car today. She arrives with a box full of cakes that she's fried. The smell of them reminds Esperança of Spanish *churros* mixed with vanilla.

"They're for you to eat in the plane and to take to your daughters and your relatives in Rouralba."

"Thank you! I'm sure they'll like them! Miquel and the girls are due to arrive from London and Madrid at Barcelona Airport at more or less the same time as me. I haven't had time to miss them, but I'm really looking forward to seeing them again... I've got so much to tell them!"

In the hospital at Kiev, the four women have the chance to meet Willy's adoptive father, the director of the film, who is talking to the doctor. He's been able to speak Russian for years and they hear him having a reasonable, simple, undramatic conversation with the doctor. The case is very serious and there's no need to exaggerate guilt or pain. As soon as he sees them he introduces himself:

"Hello, my name's Oscar. Willy used to talk about her all day," he says, looking into the ICU. I love him like a son. I've known him since he was small. He used to go through the rubbish to find something to eat. Depending on what he found, he'd wave his arms about or burst out laughing. He was an expressive, good-looking little lad with a lot of charm. I followed him. We negotiated: a screen test in exchange for a few sweets. He knew how to handle himself in front of the camera straightaway. His parents died of overdoses not long ago and his brother's also hooked on drugs. He comes from a selfish family. They're only going to turn up here if they think they can get a big compensation pay-out. I understand that the boy doesn't want anyone to tell them. There's no need. They just want to see him so he can drag them out of poverty. The first few years he lived with me, they used to come at Christmas, they brought him some knickknacks. In exchange, I had to give them a fortune if I didn't want them to take him away. It was easy for them to make difficulties for me. I was a man alone against the system. I had a very bad time until the adoption was confirmed. Willy's bright and he studied minority languages at Dublin University. We've always been very close. It was only when he was a teenager that he got obsessed with seeing his parents and asking them about his family history. I helped them, but all his relatives are spendthrifts. I swear to you: Willy not the same blood. There's no need... there's no need for them to come! It's better if they don't."

As she hears this, Olena feels the bottom fall out of her world, as she watches through the glass as her Iryna gently strokes her boyfriend. No-one could be better company for him than her daughter. And the specialist thinks that, in these cases, the patient should be moved as little as possible. So it's going to be a long stay.

Oscar signals to Iryna that she should come out and he'll take over from her. Iryna leaves her sweetheart for a moment to greet her mother and say goodbye to Esperança. The girl innocently embraces her Catalan mother, who immediately fires off a volley of questions:

"How is he? Are you OK? Perhaps I shouldn't have bought that scooter."

"Don't say that, Esperança. You did it to help us." The specialist interrupts:

"He's responding to the medication and he's lucky he's got such good company. We'll have to see how things develop. Injuries to the optic nerve are very delicate. Patient find it difficult to accept being blind."

"Poor Iryna! How I'd love to help you!"

"Pray for us, because I can't. He says crazy things! He says that if I give him my hand he can see everything clearly, but when I go it leaves him without light or colours. I've got to be with him. Poor thing!" she says, moving towards Esperança, taking advantage of the last chance to ask her if she has any hryvnias left.

"Yes, I've left 1,000 hryvnias under the butter dish. Your mother or your father must have found them by now."

"They'll use them for the loan. We did all the work we've done on the house with a loan from Nikolai's parents."

"The one who sold us the scooter?"

"No, that boy who was hosted in Collença."

"I've hardly got anything left... I'd still like to go shopping at the airport for a present for the family and the girls, because I haven't had time to think about anything for anyone."

As if to contradict her, her hand goes into her purse and she gives Iryna all the money she's got left.

"God will provide! We love you. We'll call you. We'll pray and... God will help you!" promises Esperança. "As soon as I save a bit of money I'll send you some."

When Iryna goes back into the room, thinking that this year she won't be able to have new shoes even though last year's are tight and the soles are worn out, she doesn't notice that Oscar is coming out with tears in his eyes.

"He says I'm his winged horse. With me he leapt the cement walls of Ballymun. He wants to ride through the air to go back to the ford and rid himself of the nightmare of black water. He says he can smell the path of flowers that takes us to the meadow where Molly is waiting for him... Do you know who he's talking about?"

And all of them, looking into the ICU, nod their heads.

The road from the hospital to the airport is chaotic and they run into a terrible traffic jam on one of the bridges over the Dnieper to the airport. It takes them three-quarters of an hour to get through. Once at the airport it's late and there's nowhere to park, so Esperança grabs the cases and doesn't have time to say goodbye to Nadiya or her mother, let alone go to the airport shop. She checks in and dashes through the corridors to catch the plane she can see behind the windows. Yes, the plane is there on the runway. The last passengers are getting on and she doesn't understand what they're saying over the loudspeakers. It's a good thing she's got the right gate. The cabin attendant calms her, speaking Spanish:

"This way, please."

She sits down, exhausted, the fear of being stuck in Ukraine still in her body. Then she bursts out laughing, while regretting what she hasn't managed to do.

At the bottom of her handbag there's still a little loose change. Should she keep it as a souvenir or perhaps send it in a packet? What about the souvenirs for her family, she wonders and laughs inside. "The cheap Chinese shop at Monjoia!" There she saw some hats exactly like the ones those peasants selling vegetables by the roadside were wearing. She'll buy a dozen of them and that will be enough for everyone. She really feels like doing some writing on her computer again. She's missed it! Next time she travels, she thinks she'll take one of those little ones she's seen on the plane during the journey.

Chapter 7

By the time Esperança lands at Barcelona Airport, her husband and daughters have been waiting for her for more than an hour. Before she can ask them how they got on in Madrid and England, Laia and Naiara throw their arms round her and start kissing her.

"Hey! Leave a bit of her for me!" says Miquel. "I've missed her too!"

"I don't believe you have! I'm sure you've been happier signing that contract than you would have been in Ukraine."

"Well, that whole platform thing isn't really decided yet."

"Isn't it? Well, I'm sure you'll tell me all about it. Look, have we got the cases and packets? What about the car? Whereabouts in the car park did you leave it?"

By the time they've loaded up the luggage and driven round the Barcelona ring road, family normality has returned and everyone begins to play their traditional role. Mother's is to ask questions: "Have you been studying? Did you eat well? What time did you go to bed?" Father is singing along to the music of Joaquín Sabina. And the girls are phoning their friends to tell them everything that Esperança won't find out until a lot later on, when it is no longer important. The mother looks at her happy daughters in the mirror and the three come to an uneasy tacit accommodation. In fact, father and daughters have spent an unforgettable week together: staying in a hotel in central London, they have visited monuments and parks, been to shows and eaten in a different ethnic restaurant every day. Have they practised their English? Of course they have! Spoken and written. An angry Miquel managed to recover the money they'd paid for the courses and the two air tickets by presenting a complaint in English written by his two furious little devils delighted by the possibility of not going back to the language school. It was also true, although they didn't make it clear, that they had taken piles of croissants back to their room for dinner and breakfast, but lots of things can be misinterpreted when you don't have a good command of the language... What he understood was that...

"Dad, we were hungry!"

Once back in Rouralba, they realised that although it was time for the main annual festival, no-one actually stays in the town in the summer. Looking at the calendar, they see they've still got some holiday time left to enjoy the house in Tamariu. In a corner of the courtyard, a tomato plant with yellowing leaves has saved some wonderful smelling tomatoes for them. After the storms of mid-August, their skin is caressed by a sun that tans without burning. The family submerge themselves in the warm water and absorb the salt they need, balancing body and soul as best they can... The days begin to get shorter and the north wind blows the cobwebs away, as they gather their strength and common sense for the coming school year.

August ends with good news: Willy is learning to move around his room and it seems he is starting to see again. Although he can only make out shadows, he is capable of recognising people and objects. Until now, Iryna has been washing him in bed. Today is the first day he's been allowed to have a shower in a little room at the end of the corridor. He counts his steps and the doors he passes and, his courage building, says he'll try to go on his own tomorrow. But he is not free. While he is rubbing himself he feels snakes stuck to his skin. Cold air is coming in through the walls of the bathroom...

He imagines there must be bricks missing and the holes they leave take the form of mocking masks with thick lips. He manages to free himself of the wretched reptiles, stepping on them anxiously, because they resist being swallowed by the drain. Iryna watches him from a corner in silence. She would just let him get on with it and enjoy seeing that he could manage on his own if it were not for the fact that he is rubbing himself so hard she can't help screaming at him:

"That's enough! What's wrong with you?"

She cannot imagine his horrible struggle or the suffering going on in his heart.

"Can you pass me the towel?"

Things are never right when a question is answered by another question. And he continues to rub himself like a manic depressive who will tear his red skin to shreds if Iryna continues with her inquiry. She passes him his robe and dries his hair. He is quiet; waiting; thinking – and not thinking the best of people. This is the problem: he has always wanted to be free and Iryna's compassion is beginning to torture him. Yesterday their hands were entwined all day; now, her hand is constantly seeking his. For Willy, the tenderness between their fingers stings him, and he can't return it. He wants to wallow in his own misery. He may be a cripple who's fallen into a dark well, but he doesn't need Iryna drowning herself to save him. He gets one of the characters who can represent him to speak in a reasonable tone:

"You've got to go back to school in September. I know you like school and not...

"And not what? Don't you love me, darling?" she asks.

He doesn't answer – and that hurts. She needs to hear him say it. She needs him to hold her. It's not enough to have an inner voice telling her that yes, Willy loves her, perhaps too much... They fell in love so quickly that she's full of doubts, continually watching him, looking for answers. A powerful force warns her of what Willy needs and might need: when she hears him moving in bed at night, she opens one eye so she can help him. Perhaps he's thirsty? She passes him a glass of water. Is he hungry? Some fruit. A tissue? Willy always thanks her with a kiss. But tonight, when it seems that he needs to urinate and she's ready to pass him the bottle, he takes it himself. Iryna feels a strange kind of shame, as if from now on what he needs is not to need her.

The girl does not want to lose her privileged position in Willy's eyes – or anyone else's. Every morning she washes carefully and puts on her make-up to look pretty. She doesn't do it out of vanity – perhaps it's because it scares her to see herself in the mirror as white as a sheet. She suspects the reason why she's been feeling sick: her period should have arrived a few days ago. This morning, she tells him she's going out to have some breakfast and instead takes the opportunity to go to the chemist and buy a pregnancy test. She uses it in a quiet hospital toilet and it comes out positive. How are they going to take the news at home? What about Willy? But no! She's not going to tell him.

All projects and filming have been postponed:

"No filming until Willy's better!" his father replies to everyone who asks him about the film.

Esperança phones the Ukrainian family often. Meanwhile, Oscar has found out that one of the top ophthalmological institutes in the world is in Barcelona – the Barraquer. Willy's been told and, as what he wants more than anything is to get better, he allows his father to make preparations for them to go to the Catalan capital – on condition that Iryna doesn't come with them. He tells Oscar he doesn't want to turn her into a slave. Olena, meanwhile, begins to get used to the idea that her daughter will follow Willy to Barcelona and she thinks she would be very happy if she could stay with him and his father or at Esperança's house. But Esperança feels she did more than enough in the summer and she's now busy with the new school year, so she isn't thinking of inviting her.

Iryna finds it difficult to have a clear view of what her mother, her father, her brother, her grandparents and, more than anyone, Willy, expect of her. Her parents want their children to have a better life than they had and, in Ukraine, that is as difficult as winning the lottery.

"In this country there are only badly paid jobs!" she is regularly told.

But what if they knew that she's pregnant? Then her mother wouldn't let her leave. Nor does Iryna want to take the risk of travelling through the world with a swollen belly. She thinks that the mark that always worried her so much will soon expand. Looking at it, she would cry like a child if it weren't for the fact that she has become cleverer and more mature overnight.

She would go with Willy to the end of the earth, but she will also pretend the best she can that the right thing to do is to stay. She doesn't want a straightforward goodbye. She wants him to ask her to go with him to Barcelona or to disappear suddenly. But that's not going to happen. They simply thank one another, hug and Willy kisses her lightly, as a friend.

"Take care; study; carry on being so lovely. When my son's better we'll come back and you'll be the star of the film," says Oscar, giving her some notes so she can get a taxi back to Dobrokiv.

"Molly, you've helped me so much! I'll always remember that!" he murmurs, and his voice cracks from a sudden pain that makes him tremble, as if an arrow had passed through him. It is only now that he realises he loves her madly, and she will always have a place in his heart.

Willy's move to a special unit costs them 57,800 dollars, 40,000 of which were intended for the film. As the news has appeared in the press and on television, Willy receives many visits in hospital from people from the world of films and crime novels. The rich son-in-law of the former Ukrainian president Leonid Kuchma visits him and expresses his admiration and respect. He wants to thank him by replacing the money that had been intended for filming. He wants to make it clear that if other countries have better expertise it is only when it comes to eyes:

"Despite the lack of resources to carry out some medical procedures, Ukraine has a very high standard of medicine in some specialities. Did you know the first kidney transplant in the world was carried out by the Ukrainian doctor Yuri Voronoi?"

A contribution of 2,000 euros also arrives from the Sitges fantasy and horror film festival. Guillermo del Toro, who is in charge of opening the festival with The Labyrinth of the Faun, offers himself to be Willy's guide to Barcelona. He tells the Press that he will use all these experiences to hone his ideas for the new film he is planning about a blind girl: Julia's Eyes. All this money is a good thing, because as well as the whole tragedy they have lost the medical insurance taken out in Kiev which they should have been given when they picked up their Ukrainian visas. There is no way of finding the company that sold it to them and, to make matters worse, their Irish insurance does not cover medical costs abroad.

"They've taken him away," Iryna says to herself as the red mark moves over the numbers in the lift taking her up. She is going to pick up a few clothes and other things that are still in the hospital room. It's on the fifth floor, with some big windows allowing her to contemplate the meanders of the Dnieper. The river wants to show her that when it can't go straight it bends to the left and the right: the important thing is to carry on. All the windows are sealed up, probably so the air conditioning isn't wasted. The window frames don't have handles to be opened, most likely to prevent patients being tempted by negative thoughts. She searches the drawers and the wardrobe. In her bag she puts the cigarette lighter Willy gave her. She hasn't used it for days. At the door she turns... she can still see him lying on the bed.

"Back in a minute!" she can't help saying, in a strangled voice.

She finds the lift with the door open. Someone signals her to enter, but she prefers to walk down so she doesn't have to go so quickly. He was admitted two weeks ago, she says to herself, with a mixture of sadness and grief. She looks down from above on the black hole offered by the spiral staircase and she wants to allow herself fall into the void, as if she were water dropping into a basin. Every landing represents a recent experience. Fleeting images slide in and out of her mind. But they penetrate her heart and are held there forever. Is it possible that she is the only one of the two of them feeling this love? A rush of terror fills her with doubt and she suddenly thinks she is the ugliest and most unworthy girlfriend Willy could ever have had. Her pulse races and her hands are sweating. She holds tight to the railing, which weakens as she slides along it. Gravity brings her down it as if she were on a slide. A metallic sound runs all the way along it from bottom to top. The bars buzz. She's about to reach the fourth floor. Her head is spinning and the world slides out of view as she hears an evil voice calling her to:

"Jump! Jump!"

***

SHE DECIDES TO GO and ask a man who looks like an intellectual and is reading a prayer book.

"Good morning, could you please tell me where the municipal library is?" asks Iryna, head down.

He looks very odd: he's got a black hat, long black jacket and long shirt, prominent beard and curly sideburns.

"Which library are you looking for? There's more than one in the city." He has a foreign accent.

"Any... I need an Irish dictionary." It's easy for her to invent this because even now she can't stop thinking of Willy.

"Follow this street and you'll come to a small square. In the middle is a monument to the 23,000 Jews the Germans shot in the Sosenki forest near the city," he tells her as he searches for something in the bottom of his pocket. Does he want to give her a sweet?

"Oh! Yes. *Spasibo, spasibo.* Thank you very much."

He's very kind. She thinks he must be a Polish Jew. She unwraps the sweet and lets Lyuba lick it, holding it in her fingers so she doesn't swallow it. This keeps the little girl entertained and Iryna manages get her back on the scooter, which she is now holding with her right hand in the middle of the handlebars. Then she sees the monument – men and women bent backwards with their children stuck to their bodies, begging heaven for help. She walks into the square and reads in passing that this barbarous act took place in 1941 and that, before the Red Army liberated the city in 1944, the Germans executed 15,000 more Jews. The library building has a poster and the door is half open. This must be the one. She chains the scooter to a tree and then goes into the room with Lyuba on her back. A woman, who is cleaning, tells her that on Sundays the library is closed to the public but if she likes she can go to the municipal one in Soborna Street.

"*Bud' laska, kudy?* Where is it please?

It seems that she works for the city council and cleans all the libraries. She tells Iryna in Russian:

"*Tri napravo, dva nalevo.* Straight on, third on the right and second on the left."

"Thank you."

She's worried about running out of petrol but she looks at the tank and sees there's still a little left.

"Come on, let's try."

But Lyuba feels sick from so many hours on the scooter and when she sees the rucksack she resolutely refuses to go back inside. She begins to have a tantrum and her pleading sounds are increasing like words:

"Carry! Carry!" she says, stretching out her arms.

So Iryna has to struggle again, carrying Lyuba with one hand and pushing the scooter with the other. It seems as if she'll never get there, and she even tries to sit the baby on the seat. Finally, they arrive. And yes, the library is open, even though it's Sunday lunchtime. She goes into the room and sees a poster saying that books can be taken out on the upper floor. She leaves the scooter under the stairs, securing it to one of the bannisters with a padlock and climbs the marble stairs leading to some glass offices. Before she reaches the landing, a woman opens the door and asks her:

"You're Iryna, aren't you? I've been waiting for you for a while. I was starting to worry."

"The thing is..." and she shows her little Lyuba with her eyes red from crying.

"I can imagine. Come in. We've got a little kitchen and I've made you some lunch."

***

AUTUMN 2007

No-one is going up or downstairs. There are only dark shadows chasing her with mocking laughter.

"What did you expect? You can't do it! You can't do it!"

Her feet shake and a terrible chill runs through her body as she rubs against a rusty stretch of railing. The scratching makes her feel horrible, like that day when she would have ripped the dark mark from her belly. Then that black face with its shining eyes and white teeth appeared. In a flash, she recalls the words of the dermatologist who looked like an artist: "The boy who falls in love with you will love you just as you are."

Sometimes, a few seconds of light are enough to stop a person going mad. And she does jump, pirouetting to the landing like a feather. Only a selfish person would kill herself by jumping from the top. She escapes the awful idea and leaves her brain wiped clean, because she really doesn't want to cause problems.

"The important thing is getting his eyes right!" she thinks, and then, a little sadly, adds: "So he can see me again!" Suddenly she's at the bottom and, as if the baby had already been born, she sees herself reflected in the hospital glass handing Willy a little girl. "God! I hope he can see her!" Because she has the strong feeling that the baby will be a beautiful little girl – a daughter of love – and that she will call her Lyuba, which means "love". "Lyuba. Lyuba," she says to herself, playing with the word.

What if love doesn't exist? What if it's just a pretty idea someone invented? Then we must be careful and never write it down, in case some heartless person wants to rub it out for good.

The people in Catalonia wouldn't understand... In fact, until recently, she herself would have advised any friend in her position to have an abortion. She's only 15. What's she going to do with a child at 16? What will happen to her plans? She'll love her... Logic is no longer in charge, she feels it in her heart: babies should come when they are wanted, not when they are planned. "Look, baby, of all the silly things I wanted you're really the last thing I need." It's crazy. In Ukraine, many mothers have delayed having babies until they're nearly old enough to be a grandmother. Her little girl will be born with the spring flowers. She won't tell anyone until it's obvious...

The days go by. Esperança has sent them photos and the reports she got from her family during the holidays. She's mixed some 50-euro notes with the loose change and *hryvnia* notes she still had left. Sending it by registered post costs quite a lot so she just pays for a normal stamp. After a month, they tell her by phone that the packet's been lost.

"Both Nadiya and I have been several times to the post office for it and they don't know anything about it," says Iryna.

Miquel doesn't believe them, but she says:

"I should have sent it registered."

Ignoring her husband's influence, she assures them it must have been lost and that it will turn up. But, deep down, after everything she's seen in Ukraine, she doesn't trust the postal workers...

Her husband goes further:

"If they hide the photographs or rip them up and keep the money, which of course they really need, they can always ask us for more..."

She keeps these opinions to herself when they call.

"Yes, yes, it must have been lost..."

They keep on asking where Willy is. He's been admitted to La Barraquer, Iryna tells her, adding that, to avoid visits, they didn't want to give her the number or the room. She explains it all as if it were nothing; as if she were no longer in love with him.

"So you don't want us to go and see him in the Bar-raquer clinic?"

"He's not there anyway. He's gone back to Dublin to complete his recovery." Esperança and Miquel do not know that this is the last conversation they will have with the Ukrainian family for a long time.

They've run out of money on the phone and suddenly problems are piling up, like the autumn leaves that won't stay on the trees or fruit in a storm: a red velvet carpet stretching on to Christmas. When the family in Catalonia, who are themselves up to their necks in school work and the normal end-of-term upheavals, find time to phone them – which they don't do too often because they don't want the Ukrainians to think they're made of money – they never seem to be at home. They always hear a few notes of the classical melody *Für Elise* followed by a voice in Russian saying something utterly unintelligible. Several times, Esperança asks Miquel:

"What can have happened to them?"

These conversations are always the same – a soap opera with no ending:

"Listen, no news is good news. You know they're not shy when it comes for asking for things. Iryna will have a new love, Vasyl must be looking for friends with bigger motorbikes. Can't you see what's happening to our girls? All they want to do is go to the disco!"

"Yes, look at us! I dread the weekend more every week! Tomorrow's Friday and they'll be asking to go out again. And often they don't get to bed until dawn. Yes, Miquel, it's five in the morning or later when they come in... You ought to be telling them off. I can't sleep until they're home. And there you are, peacefully snoring your head off!"

"Why do you wait up for them? If something's going to happen, it'll happen whether you're worried or not."

"How lucky you are taking it all so lightly! No-one would believe you were their father!"

"Well that's better than you. You only believe the worst. You always have to be worried about something. Relax, woman! Leave your own children and those kids in Ukraine alone!"

As time goes on, these worries are replaced by others: before the holidays, Granny Griselda from El Masnou, who's nearly 90, catches pneumonia. And the woman who looks after her also has the same symptoms:

"Madam, I've got a headache, I feel sick..."

She's an Armenian who knows little Spanish and no Catalan at all. She hasn't made any friends and it seems all her family are in her own country... She didn't have any references, but the old lady found her through an advert in some magazine.

Esperança spends 13 days and nights in Mataró hospital taking care of them both. Now, as if that weren't enough, she wants to bring them to Rouralba to complete their recovery.

"You're like Mother Teresa," says Miquel, heading for the bar for a little distraction.

The old lady, who's used to doing as she pleases, imposes her conditions: she'll go, but she's got to take everything she wants from home, including her Christmas crib figures.

More work for Esperança after she's finished her teaching day! The first thing she has to do when she arrives is to empty the wardrobes in the rooms where the new arrivals are going to sleep so they can fit their things in. Then she changes the sheets and makes the beds, so they can move in properly. Meanwhile, the old lady, who used to be a teacher herself, tells the Armenian woman to take away a bunch of flowers from the dining room table because she wants to set up her crib.

"Esperança, you know your mother's always put up a crib. Do you remember when you were a little girl and you used to help me build it and paint the sky? You'll let me make a little one, won't you?"

And she says it in the kind of sweet little voice that means she can get away with anything. When her son-in-law comes in for lunch, she hugs him and asks him:

"Please Miquel, be a dear and bring me some moss as soon as you can."

They might have imagined all the extra work they would have. As the dining room has been taken over by the little crib – which has a river with running water, tree stumps from the courtyard and even a star and a fire that light up! – they have to set up two trestle tables in the corridor for all the festive meals. It's a good thing it's so wide. The two sisters, who used to have a room each, now have to share, squeezing their clothes into the same wardrobe. The problems can be measured by the mutual insults, as they steal each other's dresses, shoes and a lot else besides. But at least if there is any shouting Granny Griselda acts as the peace-making angel:

"Love one another girls, please!"

She is so skillful and firm she can get them to hug one another even if they don't want to. Then, as a reward, she tells them:

"Come close, please, because my voice is failing, and I'll recite you one of Grandad's poems:

'Now we're all here united in joy...'

How about learning it off by heart?"

"Granny, we already know it! Mum taught us when we were little!"

What a situation! Meanwhile, the carer, who has also settled in and might be expected to lend a hand with the housework, has got the idea into her head that she's just there to keep the old lady company. If she cooks one day, she does it in the style of her own country, with strange herbs and sauces... Her own tastes are refined ones and she stuffs down only the best kinds of food: cheeses, yoghurt, honey and fruit. She has two days off a week. She also has the right to have an afternoon nap and to get dressed up so she can go and make calls at the local internet cafe, where she says it's cheaper. Every time she goes she takes ages and spends about ten euros.

"Dear lady, please, could you lend me some money?" This pitiful phrase is the only thing she says that anyone can understand.

Chapter 8

WINTER 2008

Everyone gets sick of Christmas in the end and in Rouralba everyone is doing their best to get the house back to normal. Granny and the Armenian woman are busy removing the moss from the dining room table and putting away the crib figures in cardboard boxes.

Today, when Esperança gets back from school and sees them busy, she asks them:

"Well, Mum, how are you?"

"Look at this girl! She's found it difficult, but she's learning quite a lot. You know how I do it?" She calls the woman "girl" even though she's pushing 60.

"How?"

"I take a figure, for example a lamb, and I get her to pick up all the lambs from the crib. Meanwhile she repeats: 'Lamb! Lamb!' Then we put them together in a box, seal it with tape and write "Lambs" on one side. Then I let her copy it on the other side and then the other sides and then she has to do it on her own without looking. You ought to use that system with the immigrants you get at school!"

"A total of six times. That's not bad!" says Naiara, leaning round the door after hearing the conversation and winks at her sister.

Laia comes closer and says:

"Oooh! You'll have learned a lot this morning then!"

"Yes! Madam Griselda very good teacher! Very good teacher! She knows lot of teaching!" Now I know: lamb, mule, Chesus, ox, shepherd, chicken, Virchin Mary and Santy Joseph..." The woman is being exaggeratedly grateful to make please the old lady, who is happy to still be able to teach at her age.

She mixes Catalan and Spanish because of her Armenian friends, who have put it into her head that it is more important to learn Spanish, assuring her that if she speaks it she'll be able to work in any house. They don't realise that if they do that and simply turn a deaf ear to Catalan, they'll end up not learning either language. But she stubbornly only pays attention when she thinks people are speaking to her in Spanish. And in their house this only happens when it is essential that she understands something. She can make an effort after all. It's not as if she understands things in Spanish either. The other day, she put the prawns in the bin instead of in the paella.

"This paella's got no flavour," said Miquel, who's the one who likes them best. "Why are there no prawns in it?"

Naiara found them completely by chance, in their plastic bag, when she cleared the table and threw the rubbish in the bin. She's clearly not really one for recycling.

"Look at them!" said Naiara.

And the Armenian woman, holding her nose, apologised, saying they smelled bad. She's very well dressed, though, and spends hours trying to make herself look good. She wears high heels, and even stilettos, walking with short steps and wiggling her bottom. Miquel, with a mocking laugh, says it's better that she is a bit daft.

"Do you think a normal person would put up with Granny's ways all day?" he asks, while Granny Griselda makes an effort to point out to her that prawns are part of nature and can be recycled in the same way as leaves from the garden and potato peelings, and that they have to be thrown in the brown bin not the yellow one where the packaging and tin cans go.

The family are all used to Iryna and Vasyl who understood everything straightaway, or worked it out for themselves, in the month they were staying. This woman has been in Catalonia for nearly a year. She says yes to everything but only does what she feels like doing. They are so preoccupied they've got little time to talk about the Ukrainians. They're all busy and their consciences are clear: they've got quite enough to deal with the Armenian woman. So, January goes by and, when the Association calls them to see if they are thinking of hosting Iryna and Vasyl in the summer, they answer:

"We'll take a break this year. Maybe someone else will have them. If you like you can pass them our number and we'll give them a good reference."

***

THEY PASS THROUGH many corridors full of dusty yellow books. Right at the end, the librarian pushes a shelf with some books on it. Behind it is a room with a table, and sitting in front of it is a man. He gets up and shakes her hand:

"Are you OK?" he asks.

"He's a friend of mine. He's the head of the primary school at Vykoty, a little village on the border. On Sundays he comes to see me..." Iryna listens to the woman, but then interrupts:

345

"Sorry. She had stomach ache. I should change her. I've been able to smell something for a while..." she apologises, wrinkling her nose, while the librarian removes the four plates she had put ready on the table.

Lyuba's filthy all the way up her back. Seeing the situation, Iryna asks:

"Could I wash her in the basin?"

When she's all clean and oiled, Lyuba laughs at all of the silly faces they make at her. Her mother takes off the baby's yellow suit and puts a pink one on her – one of those the shopkeeper in Novograd gave her. When they go out, on top she'll put on the white furry coat which makes her look like a little rabbit. They wipe the table and set it again. Lyuba, sitting on Iryna's lap, wants to lick the tablecloth and pinch the pictures on it. Then a steaming casserole appears and Lyuba says:

"Ammm! Ammm!"

They talk and eat potatoes and croquettes.

"Ammm! Ammm!" she repeats.

"She must be hungry!"

When the plate comes near, Lyuba grabs as much food as she can. Who would have said she'd been feeling ill?

"You've been very brave bringing the baby with you. Children are the ones who suffer most from family separation. I know so many children who've grown up with their grandparents because their parents have gone to work abroad... There are so many children abandoned by their parents..." says the head teacher.

"One day, he asked me to find a poem for Mother's Day," remembers the librarian. "I liked one about the love children feel for their mothers."

"When we read it in class, all the children started crying."

"He's an idealist... he does what he can. He helps a little with the families' problems offering individual tuition in art or drama, even outside school hours."

"It's hard, but I understand parents who try their luck abroad in times like these. A few years ago I had to pay the teachers with bottles of vodka because I wasn't receiving money from the State. And you won't believe it but today we get paid 20 dollars a month at most."

"Come on, don't get carried away with that, we've got work to do. Have you got documents?"

"Here's mine," she says, taking it out of her bag. "But my daughter's not registered. Her name's just Lyuba... her father doesn't even know she exists."

"Give it to me, it'll be best if I keep it for you. As they've told us about the case, I've got things pretty well organised. From now on you're called Katyushka and you're 23. That identity belongs to a woman from my village who'll lend us her documents and has got a current passport. Some relatives of hers in Poland will help, in case you need to give details of where you're staying. Of all those who want to provide this service, she's the one who looks most like you. You'll just have to do your hair a bit differently, as she always wears a plait round her head like Yulia Tymoshenko.

"I'll find you an extension in your hair colour," says the librarian, looking in a cardboard box which looks as if it's meant for books.

"And it's really a good thing you haven't got a family record book. We'll make you one that matches and we'll even print your daughter an identity card. It's quite normal here for people to take a while to register their children and we can keep her real date of birth and name. She will appear as Katyushka's daughter. But, as it's three years since she's been to Poland, it's perfectly possible that the baby could have been born in Vykoty in that time."

"Now we can make a toast. We don't always get things sorted out that quickly," says the librarian, who has prepared the glasses and is also giving Iryna several inches of blonde hair, hair ties, clips and hair pins.

"Na zdorov'ya, Katya!"

To Iryna it doesn't seem possible. She freezes and doesn't pick up the vodka. Lyuba takes it from her and frowns, but moves it towards her mouth.

"Hey, it's not for you, you're just a little girl!" the head teacher tells her off. "Come on, my love, look at the camera."

It's a digital camera. With that and the library computer, they prepare the baby's papers.

"Katya, aren't you drinking?" She finally reacts.

"Oh, yes! But how am I ever going to repay you for all you're doing for me?"

"You don't have to give us anything, but Katyushka wants 500 dollars for the first month you're abroad with her papers. After that, you'll have to pay her 30 dollars a month. Have you got the money? Do you agree?"

"Yes, I've got 300 dollars which were supposed to be for shopping in Metro and 2,000 euros, which my brother earned in the summer working as a mechanic in Catalonia."

"It'll be a good thing carrying two currencies. Tonight you can sleep here until a quarter to three in the morning. At three o'clock sharp, the *marshrutka*, the collective taxi, will stop in front of the railway station in the street above this one. People wait for it next to the entrance archway, which you can see from a long way off. It's decorated with gold, and it's near the fir trees. I will have booked you a seat. So, to cut a long story short, you'll need to give me 1,000 euros to pay for everything. Keep the rest safely. You'll need it when you least expect it..."

"*Spasibo.*"

"No, in Ukrainian we don't say *spasibo,* we say *dyakuyu!* Above all, when you cross the border, don't even think about saying it in Russian. Nearly all the Customs officers hate the Russians ever since Vladimir Putin was heard talking in private with George Bush and saying "Ukraine? That's not even a State!" I know that near Kiev Ukrainian gets mixed with Russian, but here everyone wants to be in the EU. We only accept dependence on Russia when it comes to gas supplies and even that's under threat. We don't want anything from the Russians."

"Sorry! What about the scooter?"

"I'd forgotten about that. We'll keep it. The mechanic will come and pick it up tomorrow," he says, looking at the librarian. They can change the plates... It'll be useful for me for getting around the city. It can be a surety in case you can't make the monthly payments."

"OK, sir, OK."

"If all goes well you'll be in Poland before eight o'clock in the morning, which is a very good time for going unnoticed. On Monday's they're very busy with the people going to work. We'll come back here at dinner time. I've got to carry on doing my job as a librarian."

They promptly leave Iryna and Lyuba to rest.

In mid-afternoon, after having a nap with her mother, Lyuba is crawling on a cow-skin rug. She's reading a magazine upside down. Now she sits down and turns it round and round to look at it. It seems there are some interesting drawings in it: she rips them out, sucks them and files them in piles, perhaps according to colour. Iryna is busy putting on her hair extension and plaiting it. She's sitting on the bed they've got against the wall which is also used as a bench for the table. Hanging on the wall is a little mirror showing her the part she's brushing. Suddenly she gets up so she can see herself better. Look at those bags under her eyes! She seems to have aged in a few hours and she looks slimmer. She thinks she's so ridiculous with this hair style that she doesn't recognise herself. Since that happened in Catalonia while she was calling she hasn't done it again...

In Rouralba, every summer, a few days before going home, she used to ask Esperança to take her to the hairdresser's. The last year she wanted a shaggy cut. How she loved the highlights they put in! Last August they still shone at the ends and Willy liked to roll them in his fingers. Now her hair's more like a pan scourer. She puts it underneath the false hair and fixes the plait firmly with the hairpins. The last thing she wants is for her hair to come undone.

She hears low voices in the next-door room. She imagines it must be people asking to borrow books or reading the week's newspapers. Both the librarian and the head teacher seem like good people. But she still feels fear when she decides to take her shoes off to take the money out of the sock and put it in her purse so she's got it ready when she's asked for it. She changes sitting on the floor with her back to the door to block it firmly. When she's finished she sighs, touches her breasts and finds that they are both bone dry – not a sip of milk left. She looks at the little girl and lets her do anything she wants to. She doesn't want her to get upset and cry so they are discovered.

Her saviours appear at eight. They look at her and say:

"Perfect!" showing her how much she looks like the photograph on her papers.

"What do you think about Lyuba's?"

"It's great. It looks genuine! The photograph is just like one I've got of me when I was little."

She looks in her purse, pays and wants to show them.

"It might almost be a photocopy!"

"Mum had the picture taken to apply for State benefit. When I was little I used to get a lot of colds and she wanted to send me to Catalonia for a change of scene. We didn't get a host family in Rouralba until I was ten. Now Poland's the place for us. And who knows if we'll get there!"

"Don't worry. It's not the first time he's organised papers for people. The forgeries always come out perfect. Here's a bit of dinner for you," she says, opening a pot with some light-coloured noodles and a piece of cheese.

She also shows her a full bottle of milk and a teat to fit the neck of the bottle. At the last minute, she'll warm the milk in an aluminium pan on the little gas stove. Then she can funnel it into the bottle, put the top on and wrap it in newspaper to keep it warm during the journey.

"Oh! Noodles and cheese. Lyuba loves that. You're really looking after me!" Like a kitten smelling the food, Lyuba crawls over, squealing, until she reaches the table.

Once she's attached herself to the leg she climbs up determinedly, with the idea of uncovering the pot.

"My cleaning lady, who lives nearby, made it. If you hurry it will still will be hot. All children like pasta. But now we'll have to go. As there's no-one in the library now you can use all the space. We'll lock the door from outside. I'll give you this other key. Post it back through the door. You can open it from inside and lock it again from the street..."

"OK, OK," Iryna nods her head.

"It'll be good for you to stretch your legs. Otherwise, you'll never stand up to the journey. You can go round and round the library until nine. Then it's time to turn the lights out so as not to draw attention to yourself. If you're interested in a book, have a look at it. There are Catalan books. Take it to the room. There you can have the light on because there are no openings to give you away. When you leave, use this torch so you don't bump into the shelves, and especially to go downstairs. You'll stop in Lviv, 300 kilometres from here, for a while to pick up more people. You can change the baby there. After that there's no break until the Customs post.

"You've got Catalan books? Why's that?"

"We know that some of the population of Lviv are the result of immigration from the Ebro region in Catalonia from the period between the wars. We sometimes get these books donated. It's a very small world, you see. Here's your alarm clock. Go carefully and it will all work out fine!" she says in correct Catalan. It would take too long to explain that she herself is descended from a Catalan woman.

Iryna does everything they've advised her to: they eat all the food and then come out of their hiding place. Iryna holds Lyuba's hand and, taking small steps and with an aching back from carrying the little girl all day, she moves round the room with her. Lyuba is curious about any book with a colourful cover or gold letters. She opens her mouth all the time ready to make a letter O.

"Oooh! How lovely!" her mother helps her, pretending to be surprised too.

Meanwhile, she finds the shelf where the Catalan publications are and takes Laia, by Salvador Espriu, a slim book that has caught her eye. She thinks of Laia and Naiara. She likes the beginning: "As no-one had ever taken took much notice of her..." and she takes the book to the kitchen/bedroom, together with the story of Snow White. Half lying on the sofa-bed, she begins to read. As her mother is no longer taking any notice of her, Lyuba complains, and Iryna tells her the story from the picture book. Then she lets her amuse herself with the zips of the rucksack. Look at these! She rummages in a pocket and takes out the mobile phone.

"Ah, little rascal! Is that what you were looking for?"

But there's no sign of life from the phone – the battery's run out. She generally carries the charger in her handbag. Yes, it's there. She plugs it into the socket near the pillow and lets Lyuba have it while it's charging. Once the phone's started up again, it beeps, demanding its PIN. It's 1287, corresponding to the day, the month and the year when she made love for the first time. She keys in the number and the screen lights up. Then she realises that, after what happened, maybe she wiped him from her contacts. She searches for "Willy". She checks that his number's in the list. God, she wants to call him so much but she can't do that now. Perhaps when she's in Poland she'll dare to try. Now she settles for writing "Daddy" on the screen for Lyuba!

> *"Tato!"* It's one of the words the little girl repeats by chance. She's sure that, as there's no balance, she'll only use up the battery, so she lets her play and carries on identifying with the heroine: "In desperate struggles with stones and slings, she was the first." Like her. If one day she went home with a black eye, there was bound to be someone else who came home with two...

It keeps her distracted until her eyelids close. It's not long before the alarm rings. She packs up everything in the rucksack and slides back the door that conceals their lair. She carries the little girl in her arms, holding her legs with her left hand as well as the torch, which she points downwards. In her right, she has the key ready. She walks through the library. The high windows show the shining roofs and the delicate aureole of the moon reflected in the bright glass. What secrets of life does that light conceal? What will become of them? Where is the roof over their heads going to be from now on? She goes down the stairs. She puts the key in the lock and turns off the torch so as not to draw attention to them when they go into the street. Then she pushes the handle down, but it's as if someone were pushing back. The door doesn't open. She puts the key in the lock and tries to turn it the other way. No, that way she's locking it. She makes sure, pushing and pulling the door hard, but there's no way. She repeats it again and again until, pulling back, she hears a metallic sound. It's a chain which the little girl doesn't want to let go. She feels along it until she reaches the baby's hands and then she realises that, while she was trying to open the door, Lyuba has pushed across the bolt that she can reach. With her heart racing, she leaves the room. She's ready to close the door and throw the key in the box, as they've asked her to do. But suddenly she remembers.

Chapter 9

In Ukraine, the family was surprised not to receive a Christmas card from Catalonia.

"Iryna, didn't you send them that card with glitter on it?" her mother asks.

"Yes, Mum, I sent it. But you know they often get lost in the post,"

her daughter lies.

Because Iryna hasn't got the strength to write any card without revealing her condition to them. They're bound to find out, she thinks, but for now, as she's lost weight, she can go on without telling anyone.

"They send us money for Christmas every year," her brother recalls.

"Well, maybe they spent all their savings on the scooter. Don't bother them. I'm sure they'll help us when we need it." Their father's words make them think.

"Of course they will! When Esperança has saved up a few euros, she'll send them to us. One of these days she'll phone us at the neighbour's house, you'll see!" says Olena, who goes Of course, off to work looking at her hands, which is what she trusts most.

Iryna takes deep breaths to calm herself. She's already simulated having a period enough times. Every time it doesn't arrive, she wets a pad with red meat juice or blood from a dead animal she finds. It makes her feel sick! If she's nervous and more hysterical, it's not because of the hormones making her sick, it's because she's now repeated the procedure four times and, although it doesn't yet show, she knows Vasyl's baggy jumpers soon won't be enough to hide her tummy.

Her pregnancy may not yet be obvious, but she feels more tired every day. Today is her first school day of the New Year, but she's decided not to go. She clears her throat a few times and pretends to have a bit of a cold. It's physical education today and she can't face jumping the vaulting horse or running round the playground. When all the family are out – father and mother working and her brother out seeing his friends or his teacher – she finds her mobile phone and looks for the song *Bon Dia* by the Catalan group Els Pets which Naiara recorded for her the last time she was in Catalonia.

"Good morning! No-one asked for one but it's a good morning..."

Singing along, her legs seems less swollen and she feels like jumping on the bed: the window surrounded by icicles frames the courtyards with its apple trees and a section of street. Yesterday the snow was muffled up in metallic clouds, decorating the paths and roofs with white. Midday comes and she's seen little change during the morning. Sometimes a few light flakes, nothing more. Half asleep in the glacial silence, a few notes sometimes escape her, an air current wanting to escape like a soul to frighten the devil. But it curdles in front of her, forming white clouds. She repeats the process as if she smoked, either practising or hoping for a wish to come true. She wishes the snow would once again bombard them, slowly and persistently, until the world disappeared from view. She blinks and the dim light invites her to close her eyes. When she opens them again, a mirage appears near the fence – a tramp covered in a blanket from heat to foot is trying to get in. Who could it be? She rushes to the window and recognises him. Yes, it is! It's Grandad!

"Grandad! Grandad!" she shouts, running towards the white sheet of the courtyard.

She opens the door and lets him in. He's barely got the strength.

"My little Ira! You've become a real woman!"

"Why are you here? Has something happened? How's Granny?"

"Granny's fine. It's my stomach. It was hurting me and I thought that in Kiev they'd know if it was from eating too much cabbage or potatoes," he jokes, touching the swollen area around his liver. "But those doctors in the capital don't know anything. They kept on looking at my head and in my ears. I left the village yesterday morning and they've had me in hospital all night doing tests. What a nuisance they are!"

"What did they tell you?"

"They told me to take these pills and stick these stickers on and, when I run out, to buy some more," he tells her, showing her the little morphine gauze on his back. "What nonsense! Do you think something so small on this hard skin can help me with any pain?"

"And you have to pay for them yourself? But you've got no hryvnias to pay for medicines!"

"I don't need them. Now they've seen me, I feel better. Look what I'm going to do with these damn pills!"

He opens the door to the yard and throws them to the birds which, because they're red, eat them up like tomatoes in no time. Then he adds:

"What about you? Why aren't you at school with your brother?"

"I just didn't fancy it because of the weather so I said I'd got a cough and a temperature."

"What a shocking little liar you are! Come on, get out the vodka because the least I can do is celebrate having the prettiest granddaughter in the world!"

When Olena arrives ready to go into the kitchen and cook, she finds them both drunk. Meanwhile, the chickens, instead of demanding corn, are asleep.

"Hello Dad! To what do we owe the honour?" she hugs him, surprised.

"I've made the most of a journey. Do you remember that neighbour who was after you when you were little and who now lives in Kiev? Well, he often comes to the village to see his parents and he always asks if we need anything. This time, your mother asked him to bring me because it hurt me here," he says, pointing to his stomach. "It was bothering me but in hospital they told me it was nothing. So instead of going straight back to Belarus, I thought I'd give you a surprise. And now I've seen you I feel 100 per cent," he assures her, glass in hand.

"What a pair! And what a way to convalesce! Come on, eat your soup. That will help your digestion!"

They've barely finished eating when Grandad wants to go and catch the bus. He's sorry he hasn't seen Vasyl, who has lunch at school, or his son-in-law, who's working away. And he says goodbye:

"Let me go! I've got to help Granny Rus, who's getting old because she's praying for you so much!"

Iryna, who knows how much he's drunk, stops him, whispering in his ear:

"OK, Grandad, wait a bit and have a nap. Come on, when Mum goes to work and isn't looking, I'll come with you."

The bus doesn't leave until four o'clock and Olena can't allow herself the luxury of being late for work. Anyway, because he's under the effects of the painkiller, he's sitting there without complaining, so it looks as if the stomach complaint can't be anything serious.

"Lots of kisses for Mum. When I get a few days off, I'll come and help you." Grandfather and granddaughter remain in front of the television, holding hands.

Before three o'clock, Grandad gets uneasy again. He gets up and repeats to Iryna:

"I'm off."

"But Grandad, the bus doesn't come for another hour! And it's only ten minutes' walk to the stop!"

As if he hasn't heard, she sees him putting on all his extra clothes, covered with the blanket, and going out into the courtyard.

"Wait for me!" she begs him. But he carries on towards the street.

In no time, she packs a suitcase with the most vital things. She doesn't forget the paracetamol and the aspirins and the antibiotics the Catalans gave them. She puts on her coat and goes with Grandad. From far away, she can see that he is leaning on every apple tree along the path. She helps him, but they go so slowly that the bus overtakes them before they reach the stop.

"Grandad, we're going home! You're not well!"

"Birds like to fly. This business of crawling along the ground is for snakes. If I can spread my wings, you'll see who gets there first!"

It's a good thing his granddaughter starts running, taking risks and making signals to the bus to warn the driver to stop right there.

"Idit' syudy!"

She goes with him. She knows that however much she insists he won't want to stay in Dobrokiv.

With a great effort to get up the steps, Grandad gets into the bus, among women who offer him sweets and home-made sandwiches. When he manages to sit down, he stretches out his arm and whispers in Iryna's ear:

"Don't tell Granny I get so tired. If she knows, she won't let me smoke my cigarette after eating."

"What will you do in exchange?"

How she would love to go back to those times when she negotiated silence with her grandfather if he gave her sweets. He looks at her and goes on:

"If you keep my secret, I won't tell her you run like a goose. When you ran, Iryna, you couldn't hide the way your tummy was wobbling."

The bus passes through lots of villages to make the most of the journey. In the regional capital they get off and continue their journey by train. The strong smell of people who haven't washed for days makes Iryna feel sick. But, for Grandad, the rhythmic rocking of this iron cradle and tiredness from the journey invite him to sleep. He snores.

It's a long journey, but Iryna is alert so that they don't miss the stop.

"Come on, Grandad, we've got to get off... Get your money ready."

To get to the village they have to catch another bus and they've run out of hryvnias. They're at the stop, the passengers have got on, and, as the conductor isn't there, Iryna takes advantage, pushes Grandad on and settles him down. As soon as the conductor gets on, he asks them for their tickets and, at the same time, he searches among their things because he knows they haven't paid and he wants to take anything he fancies from what they're carrying. Iryna holds on tight, shouting:

"Don't you dare! Where were you when we got on?"

"We'll report you. You got off specially so you could steal the little we poor people have got," adds Grandad.

They reach the village at six in the morning. They're lucky: a neighbour with a car has come to pick up a relative and, when he sees the state Grandad's in, he takes them home.

"Hello there girl!" says Grandad from his seat, talking to Granny, who's come out to greet them.

She's had the door open for two days, with the bed prepared with the best sheets and the softest pillows. She gives him her hand and pulls him up. But, no, he can't manage to stand. The two of them help as best they can and he puts his arm round them. He needs all available hands and arms to get him into bed. After a rest, he strokes their hands, thanking them all the time:

"Dyakuyu, duzhe dyakuyu."

And closing his eyes, the angels show him the blue heavens and he begins to fly so high that he sleeps and never wakes up.

Granny Rus, who has sat up all night, knows the precise moment – the convulsion of the last second when the strength and warmth goes out of the hand she is stroking. She, who has always been so brave, has been crying ever since her husband told her he wanted to go to hospital in Kiev.

"You see, he never believed in doctors and yet he wanted to go for a check-up!"

With this she began to realise that her husband's decline was not a temporary condition. Now, Granny holds back her weeping and consoles Iryna.

"Look, Iryna, it's as if he were sleeping. Look after him for a moment!"

And she goes four fields up, to her son's house – the one who's got a car he can't maintain and is now a drunk with three children and a prostitute wife. As he's got a telephone, she'll be able to tell the whole family what's happened.

Olena, who has to cope with the sadness of not having known how sick her father was and not having looked after him as he deserved because of work, asks for a bank loan, not just to buy his coffin but also for the first tailored suit her father will ever wear, although cut at the back because when it arrives he's so stiff it's the only way of making use of it

. She also needs money to follow the tradition of inviting all the neighbours, friends and family to a meal of the deceased's favourite food. She doesn't care that she will be in debt for a long time – her father will have the ritual so he can rest in peace with good food.

First they eat *borsch* – a soup made from beetroot, with cabbage, onion and potato, which is very tasty. Then they have *kholodets'* – savoury meat jelly, accompanied by *olivye* – lettuce with vegetables, mayonnaise and eggs, and *kompot* – a fruit syrup. While they eat, they mourn him: Grandad was so young! Before the explosion strong people like him didn't die at that age; he was the one who reaped more grass in less time; he was a good, noble and generous person; he always put others before himself... And they say all this to his face, because he's right there as the ritual unfolds.

Iryna also looks at him and her memories go back to her childhood. Suddenly, in her mind, Grandad gets up and they all push the chairs back to the wall to leave a space in the middle so they can dance. A well-known tune can be heard: Lara's theme from the Doctor Zhivago film: "Somewhere, my love, there will be songs to sing..." Heads begin nodding and mouths singing. Grandad comes close to his granddaughter and says:

"Will you allow me this dance, young lady?"

Iryna gets up and puts her arms around Grandad's neck. She wraps her legs around his waist and they start to move, following the violins and the balalaika: big nose stuck to little nose, little hand behind grandfather's neck and the other held like a treasure in his strong hand.

"Round and round again, until we get dizzy!"

Until cheek falls on comfortable shoulder and rests there for ever and ever and never again!

"Who's going to dance with me now, Grandad? Who's going to tell me I'm the prettiest girl at the party?" she can't help saying aloud.

"Come on, Ira, don't ask those questions. You know you'll always be my queen!" her father's low voice consoles her.

But, angry with the mask of life, she swears to herself: "As soon as I can I'll go to another country with more resources, far away from the country and from animals, where they care for their people when they get sick."

"It looks as if he's smiling," some of them say.

They don't know that, when Granny Rus went to tell Olena about the death, Iryna, who's afraid of nothing, and certainly not her grandfather, kissed his forehead and put a piece of cotton between his teeth to separate his lips, which were pressed tight together. And, once they'd washed him, she stayed with him and made his cheeks up with a little blusher.

His funeral is in the pretty Orthodox church in the village. Friends and relatives carry the coffin on their shoulders. Grandad's other son – Olena's other brother who's a priest – celebrates the funeral. Iryna's and young Vasyl's uncle who baptised them in Dobrokiv is now married, and has had five daughters until he finally managed a son. The son speaks about his virtues, all the grandchildren cry and the grandfather, whose body is present, watches them, listens to them and maintains his smile. Under the arms crossed over his chest, he is holding a treasure: the poem Iryna has written which is now folded in his jacket pocket.

"Grandad, you were lucky enough to have a loving mother, a proper wife, an honourable daughter and a granddaughter who will tell her daughter about you."

During the funeral and while they are singing, the grandmother's eyes go to the ark where they keep the gold-framed mirror that the couple use for their ritual on the day they get married. They hold it while they go around the altar holding hands. Rus can't help the tears rolling down her face. She was young; she had many more expectations than have come true. Where did all that confidence and energy go? Her guardian angel has flown away. The good things trapped in the mirror define her: they are just dreams of their wedding day.

In Catalonia, few would understand that, in a country with such great poverty, people are willing to spend more than they have to combine mourning with the joy of passing over into eternity. But the mourning song sung during the Byzantine burial service would chill many a heart.

***

WHAT'S SHE DOING? SHE'S LEFT THE SHOE on the scooter. She turns and looks under the stairs to see that it's still there. She shines the torch on it, sees it and touches the seat, lifts it and takes the shoe out. She puts it in her rucksack and rushes off. Now she does lock the door and leaves the key in the mailbox.

She's a bit later setting off for the bus station than she'd planned. She has the plaits on her head, the rucksack on her back and the little girl, well wrapped up in white, in her arms. On her shoulders is the grey blanket – the mist camouflaging them. She rushes through an area of houses surrounded by trees, follows the railway line and, when she reaches the station, she sees they're already getting into the taxi. The vehicle is as big as a minibus, with four rows of seats. The taxi driver charges for each place and you have to negotiate the price with him. Iryna shows him the ticket and tells him it's already paid for. The man smiles and asks her for a tip. She opens her purse and takes out a five euro note.

"This one's better."

And he takes a ten euro one. It's a good job she hid the others.

"Sit down, please!"

He gets her to sit down in the front passenger seat with the baby on her lap. Then he takes the rucksack to put it up on the shelf, but she stops him. She refuses, saying she's got the baby's bottle and things in there. All she needs is for it to be stolen or not secured properly.

Lyuba's sweet smile, with her two little teeth, fills the *marshrutka* as it moves forward along the bumpy Ukrainian street and leaves Rivno behind in the fog and the lights.

The hedge formed by the trunks of the trees protecting the edge of the road extends into the distance. Looking through the window, the girl now known as Katya tries remain remote from the chatting of other travellers. She'd like to let her sadness out the window and smash it against a roadside tree. But a woman taps her on the shoulder:

"This is the first time you've made this journey, isn't it?"

"*Tak!*"

She introduces herself. She's called Maxa. She first asks Iryna's daughter's name and then her own.

"Lyuba."

"And you?"

"Katya."

"I've got a friend in Vykoty who's also called Katya and she looks a lot like you."

Before she asks her surname, Iryna passes her hand between the seat and the door, without anyone seeing, and passes her the five euros left in her purse. And the conversation continues, as naturally as possible:

"Yes, I've often been told that. We must look very similar. I used to live there until not long ago, in a little house on the outskirts."

As she explains, the lie grows: "My family's from Kiev. I fell in love with a Pole and my parents let me live with some relatives in Vykoty so we could see each other more often. Now Lyuba's father's parents want to see her and I'm going to visit them. Maybe I'll get lucky and find a job...

So, I look like her then, do I?"

Maxa reacts immediately. She no longer asks her what her relatives are called, or where she's going, or anything else. For the moment she considers herself paid off, saying:

"Yes, but she's a bit tubbier and she's shorter. You could pass for a film star. How lucky good-looking women are in this country!"

And she looks at another passenger, who also gives his opinion:

"Most men end up in the Czech Republic or Portugal to work in construction. Women go to Italy, though, where they go into domestic service or look after old people. We'll settle for that, even knowing that we earn six euros an hour less than the normal wages in those countries. As that's enough to maintain our families in the Ukraine, it'll do. The results of our work can also be seen in the new houses springing up like mushrooms near the border."

Her partner, leaning on his shoulder, adds:

"That's what we've done. First we had to save a lot, but we've been able to build our house at last. I'm over 40 now and I'm tired, but I've got the kitchen I dreamed of, with units covered in marble, and we've even installed a bidet in the bathroom. We have to tell some friends what it's used for," she says with a smile – enthusiastic and proud.

And she refers back to her husband, who justifies having left the country:

"The path Nadiya and I have had to follow to get our own house hasn't been easy. At the beginning of the nineties, when Ukraine became independent from Russia, we lost all our savings because of a banking crisis. Since then, I've never trusted banks. I prefer to keep my money hidden and go and pay the mortgage in cash every month."

His eyes darken with mixed feelings as he makes his confession.

"As the economic situation was getting worse and worse, we first went to Poland in 1996. To start with, he found work picking cherries, later he worked in construction and finally he got a job in a bath factory. When the factory had to close, we started selling tobacco and alcohol and we still do that, after six years. We make three dollars on each carton of cigarettes and one on each bottle of vodka. You'll find a job, dear, you'll see! Maybe your partners' parents can look after her while you're working. If they're already retired... The most important thing is that we can go to our lovely house every weekend to see our children and grandchildren," says Nadja.

"I'm 50 now, but I'm going to stay with her. If I stay in the village, Nadja's thinking of going to Italy," he says in a sad voice.

Iryna imagines him alone and drunk, wrinkled and glassy eyed by the window waiting for his wife to come back from Italy.

"You know what, girl?" she hears from behind. "The Italians go crazy for blondes."

And he smiles, suggestively, with white teeth.

The employment exodus will not change overnight. However, a new fashion has recently arrived from the West. When they've built their houses, the emigrants replace their gold teeth with porcelain bridges. They don't want to be recognised so easily abroad. So in future in Ukraine it will be possible to identify those who have been to work in other countries from their film-star smiles.

"If I end up in Italy, I'll dye my hair black," thinks Iryna. "Italian men and some Catalans label Ukrainian women as prostitutes. And I'll never be that. Stupid people think all Ukrainian women are blonde, but a lot of them are dark. So much poetry has been written devoted to their black eyes..."

The huge plain undulates and, as the bus goes up and down, her stomach is gripped by nostalgia. She misses Vasyl, and remembers that summer day in Rouralba when she called the family from the phone box in the square because it was cheaper than from the landline phone. She sees the face of the woman who scratched her and pulled her plait, calling her "foreigner" in front of a group of idiots. Simply because her ladyship was in a hurry and wanted her to hang up. Her eyes are misted with tears. She had no idea her brother was around there. How Vasyl defended her! He took his bicycle and furiously launched himself at the woman. Her brother is a true Cossack: he stood up in front of them and with three *hopak* dance movements he had them lying on the floor. It was that day when, as they were looking at how they could fix the bicycle, which had got a bit bashed, he met Morales. Although it was night-time he was going around with the motorbikes.

"Hey, boy, it looks like it's in your blood!" he told Vasyl, seeing how easily he picked up tools and fitted the spare parts.

He told Esperança and Miquel he had fallen and scratched the bicycle. He didn't want to tell anyone about these problems. Vasyl was enough of a man to solve them.

They move west, the moon sinking below the waves of an endless field of crops. It seems that the images of her mother, her father, her brother and, finally, Willy, are all melting into the sphere. Everything changes in life, she says to herself. Her luck must also revolve like the planets. It was so difficult for her to spend her first weeks without Willy. Those weeks of pregnancy when he didn't answer any of the message he received. When she saw his name on the dark screen she could still feel his warmth. Where are they hidden, all the fears and joy accumulated in her heart since Lyuba was born? No-one will answer these questions for her. All she can do is sigh. Her breasts, which a year ago were firm, childish and round, are now swinging lightly between Lyuba's head, which brushes them softly, and her flexible arms, which hold the little girl tenderly.

Through the back window, the day awakens. The rising sun shines weakly on Lviv. The dewdrops shine, Lyuba sleeps and Iryna watches her as if she were a butterfly seeking a distant flower. They are now in the city and the old part recalls the Gothic quarter of Barcelona as she saw it with Esperança: the city breathes the air of its glorious past surrounded by decadence.

The taxi stops in front of a hotel. There is a bar at the entrance. Those who do not wish to pay to go to the toilet look for a hidden place in a nearby ruined building. She offers a euro to change Lyuba on the marble and washes her bottom in the sink. Once shut inside, the takes the opportunity to get rid of the shoe. She climbs up on the toilet lid and throws it in the cistern.

When she comes out, she sees the taxi driver at the bar. She sits beside him. In the background she can hear the day's news:

"The Ukrainian scientist Larissa Brizhik has been released. Police dogs combing the Polish border found her yesterday in a deplorable state. She had many broken bones..."

Lyuba turns to look at the television like her mother, but she doesn't like the programme and complains. Iryna, who wants to hear what they're saying, takes the bottle of milk from the rucksack and unwraps it. It's still warm. She fits the teat and gives it to Lyuba to try:

"Do you like it, my love?"

She holds it in her little hands as if it were a baby's bottle and sucks it so noisily that everyone looks at her. Her mother lets her get on with it and carries on listening.

"Her research interests include the interactions of photons in electrons and the effect of electromagnetic radiation on biological systems."

"Who is she?" she pretends not to know. The waiter answers:

"Don't you know her? Here in Galicia everyone knows who she is. Larissa is a very important scientist. She's published many articles in journals and taken part in conferences all over the world. She's a member of various national and international associations, including the Shevchenko Scientific Society."

"Like the poet. You know him? When I was little, at home with my brother, we used to play at escaping like

Taras Schevchenko," she says, to get in with the taxi driver.

"Yes, I can see you're interested. Listen to what they're saying. They're going to interview her now."

"How are you, Larissa?" "Alive, thank God."

"They say you were bound and gagged."

"Yes, it was horrible."

"But when the police found you, you'd been able to get free of the ropes and the gag. Who helped you? Please explain. You seem to smell of petrol from head to toe. Did they want to burn you alive?"

Hearing this, Iryna's heart leaps and she gets up, pretending she needs something.

"Aren't you drinking anything? Come on, I'll buy you one," says the taxi driver, pulling her towards the stool.

"Yes, it was a drunk who recited poems in Ukrainian. He was carrying a bottle of petrol and he was spraying it around the forest."

"You must have been really frightened!"

"No, when I heard someone coming, I thought I was at the gates of heaven. I managed to spit out the gag they'd put in my mouth and I begged God for help. Tied up like that, it wouldn't have been long before I died of cold. You never know who to trust in this world. If they can hear me now, I want them to know that I'm grateful from the bottom of my heart and I'll do everything I can to help them with anything."

Still nervous, and as the taxi driver is insisting, she orders a coffee and a piece of cake, which seems like one her mother makes, alternating layers of pastry with hazelnuts and butter.

"They can call the Shevchenko Scientific Society and ask for me. We've also got a foundation to help people in need. What use is developing physics, law and medicine if we don't apply that knowledge to help defenceless people in a country that's so full of them? We've always had the financial support of Ukrainian business people and intellectuals. This institution is increasingly influential on both sides of the Russian and Polish borders..."

Iryna knows all these words are dedicated to her. She'll call her as soon as she can. "Of course I'll do it," she says, excited. Before getting rid of the shoe, she managed to unscrew the memory stick. The USB device looks like a leather amulet. It's small and she's hung it round her neck, fixed to a chain, next to Esperanza's virgin.

"Perhaps I'll still be in time to do a degree like Mum! If I have the chance to find someone who can look after you..." she says under her breath, looking at Lyuba.

She continues in a louder voice, talking to the taxi driver:

"Who kidnapped her, then?"

"Who knows?"

"It's the Russians, it's always the Russians. After the Second World War, they arrested many members of the Shevchenko association, sending them to the *gulags* or executing them. They're bastards," the waiter joins in again.

"Probably, probably."

"Now Ukraine is independent the society is operating again here in Lviv and, as they're doing new research that compromises the Russians, they won't leave them in peace. All Galicia is under threat.

Iryna uses her trembling fingertips to pick up some cake crumbs and she licks them, without realising that the gesture is so sensual the taxi driver might get the wrong idea.

"If you don't fill them up, you won't be able to feed her again," he says, jokingly, staring at her breasts.

"No need, thank you!" she exclaims quickly, so as not to have any more reason to be grateful.

"Take it for the little girl!" he repeats, and places another piece of cake in front of her.

Poor little Lyuba finishes it, licking, licking, just like her mother with the crumbs. "He probably gets it for a special price if he brings them customers every week," she thinks.

They've been in there half an hour by the time they get back to the *marshrutka* to follow its route westwards. Iryna imagines that the scientist must have discovered something compromising a criminal organisation. Who knows if it could be related to the people who die every day as a result of the 1986 explosion? If all this evil-doing could be proved, the Russian government would have to compensate Ukraine. As soon as she's free, she plans to call that woman.

The windscreen wipers sweep away small drops crashing against the screen. In the sky, the vapour trail left by an aeroplane evokes an idea of freedom. Anyone who could would fly again, like she did before, to Catalonia?

Anxiety grows as they get closer to the border at Medyka, in south-eastern Poland. Suddenly, the *marshrutka* climbs up the kerb on to the pavement beside the first buildings. The engine is still running but the taxi driver gets out and comes to the passenger door. He opens it and orders:

"Katya, get out please!"

"What?"

"For you, the journey's over. If you want to carry on, you can go through Customs on foot."

Iryna leans back hard into the seat and holds Lyuba tight.

"It seems this *chelnoki* doesn't want to obey," he says, using the Russian word for people who cross the border every day. "As you wish!"

He grabs her by the anorak and throws her so badly that she scratches her face on the edge of the window and ends up against the wall in front of her. The little girl slips from her arms and falls. Terrified, she cries piteously. She could have been hurt... But no-one moves; no-one gets up to help her; no-one protests. They don't want to risk getting to their destination late because of an illegal immigrant. From inside, Maxa clumsily throws her the rucksack, which gets stuck between the corner and the wheels.

"Good luck, Katya!"

Chapter 10

WINTER 2008

The days of mourning end and everyone goes back to work, but the idea of leaving Granny on her own hurts them so much that no-one argues when Iryna offers to keep her company for a while. Even her mother thinks it's a good idea for her to stay to see whether a change of scene will cure her cold once and for all.

"You can look after her for me, Mum!" she says.

They all know how exhausting a cough can be for her and they know it's because of the problem they found between her heart and lungs at the hospital in Barcelona. They realise the rest and dry climate away from the Dnieper will do her good.

"Whatever you do, make sure you phone the neighbours if anything happens," Olena asks them, and she gives them the mobile phone Vasyl had fixed, with a full payment card.

Iryna knows that by the end of January she won't be able to hide anything from her family or anyone who knows her any more. So, as she knows that she can tell Granny anything if she uses the right low, sweet voice, it's not long before she confesses her secret. She finds the moment one day at bedtime:

"Granny, I need to tell you something that will make you very happy, but I'm sorry too, because it will also make you sad..."

"Well, start with the good part and we'll see if they other bit is as bad as you say."

"You see, last summer I feel in love with an actor."

"I thought it was strange that you'd want to stay in this part of the world just because of your old Granny. So, what? Has the scoundrel left you? Is that why you don't want to go to school?"

"No, Granny, no! I'll finish telling you in bed," she lets go of her, babbling what sounds like a lament as she turns back blankets and sheets.

She sleeps with her grandmother on the side where Grandad Volodymyr used to lie. Together they can keep warmer. They repeat the stories and poems he used to recite and then Granny doesn't miss him so much.

"What's happening to me is like a half-written novel..."

"Oh my sweetheart! Life is a little story that starts every day and ends the following morning. Do you remember Iryna? Grandad Volo know lots of stories about birds."

"Yes, like the one about that boy who asked the swallows to teach him to fly, but his heart's desire was to leap above the clouds instead of being shut up in school reading and writing," recalls the girl, trying to hurry her grandmother up.

"It's a good job he forgot that nonsense the day the teacher told the class we all had a little white dove that no-one can see – a spirit which, if we're good, will fly into infinity, beyond the stars."

And she speaks, Granny Rus's hand strokes Iryna's stomach and feels its volume. She guesses the reason for it, and knows that reason already has a soul.

"Is this the secret you wanted to tell me?"

"Oh, Granny! I think it's starting to move. Maybe it's listening to us."

"Well let's sing it a lullaby!"

"Cossack Lullaby is my favourite. I like the way it sounds soft, like a whisper."

"Sleep, my sweet baby. *Bayushki-bayu.*"

"Softer, Granny, like a murmur."

"Silently, the bright moon watches you in the cradle."

Granny has always been a person who's good at carrying on and taking charge. She doesn't tell Iryna off or make bitter comments, just giving her advice and a sweet smile every time she looks at her.

Her time is organised around keeping Granny company: in the morning they're in the vegetable garden, towards midday with the poultry and, in the afternoon, they excitedly knit little jumpers and baby clothes. Iryna's belly swells to the rhythm of the snow, as it profiles the fields. At night, she often dreams she is a great bear hibernating in a cave. When she's asleep, a little furry white bear appears, locking on to her breast...

When Olena calls to find out how they are, Iryna says she's fine but that too much has happened this school year, and that she's now too late to catch up, so she'll leave it until after the spring holiday before she goes back.

Granny Rus, who has given birth several times, does not want to remind her of the children she lost because of poor care. Instead, she calms Iryna, saying she has a friend who's a midwife living near the village.

"She knows a lot! And everything's easier nowadays because of mobile phones and cars."

So they call her to try her out. In a quarter of an hour, the midwife is outside in a four-wheel-drive car which looks like a Second-World-War tank. She checks Iryna carefully, listening to the baby's heartbeat, and says:

"If you were at the hospital, they'd give you a scan and you'd know for sure if it's a girl or a boy, but I bet what you want is a girl who'll be tall and well-built like all the women in your family."

"I couldn't have put it better myself," laughs Granny. She's always right.

"Have you told the midwife that Mum doesn't know anything about me being pregnant?"

"Your mother does know, I told her the other day... Yes. The other day after she spoke to you, the mobile phone rang again. You were outside feeding the chickens and I picked it up. Poor thing, she was worried about your studies and wanted to come and take over from you for a while if I needed her. Then I had to tell her that you're pregnant, that you want to have the baby and that you're absolutely delighted. But we agreed that for the moment she won't tell your father or Vasyl. She promised me. Those two will be horrified and they'll blame Willy."

"I hope no-one tells them..."

"As you're at home all day with me, and hardly anyone comes to visit in winter, no-one will tell him. We'll wait until the baby's born. When they see her, the joy will make them forget the shame of not knowing who the father is..."

"Of course they know who it is. But I want it to be clear that no-one took advantage of me I wanted to make wild, passionate love with Willy. We loved each other. I still love him."

"And won't you want to tell him?"

"That depends on whether I can do it nicely."

SPRING 2008

By the time the baby is born it's spring. A Sunday at the end of April – just 38 weeks since she made love with Willy – at about midnight. During the birth she's assisted by her grandmother's friend, her grandmother and also her mother, who, following her own strange calculations and the neighbour's premonitions, turned up the day before it happened. She arrived laden with clothes she had kept from when her own children were born. She's also brought nappies, which she got from the hospital where she works.

Iryna screams and cries:

"Mum! Mummy! Granny! Help me!"

"Push! Push! Push!"

Iryna can't go on, and she faints at the sight of blood. Then the midwife discovers that the little girl is a breech birth.

"And it was all going so well!"

She looks in the bag she has brought, pulls out a spring of wormwood and gives it to Granny.

"Boil it, Rus, in a glass of water. We'll leave her to rest. The little girl has turned round and she can't come out like that."

"It's a girl?"

"Yes. Were you ever in any doubt?"

She hasn't heard them properly, but these words bring Iryna back to consciousness. And Granny soon appears with the drink.

"Wormwood usually improves the position of the foetus's head. Here, Iryna, drink this."

She takes a first sip, but spits out the second. It's so bitter!

"One more drink, Iryna!"

Granny says nothing, but she's terrified because the same plant is also secretly used to provoke abortions. And when her husband didn't have tobacco, and he used to chop it up fine and smoke it, he'd spend all day and all night in a world of his own.

The midwife, impervious to Rus's gestures, takes another sprig of the same plant and puts it under the pillow, telling them:

"Wormwood has many properties. In the Middle Ages it was used as a magic herb. It also works as an insect repellent. Even longer ago, it was a remedy to protect travellers against evil spirits and wild animals. Roman soldiers used to put it in their sandals so they didn't get blisters or notice how tired their feet were."

"Yes, I think Nadiya's mother uses it mixed with drinks like vermouth and beer," says Olena to kill time and calm her daughter.

The colour returns to her cheeks and they start to think the remedy is working. Then, suddenly, she lets out a piercing scream. "Mother!"

The pain in her stomach forces Iryna to bend double. Her mouth is full of saliva and there is blood – lots of blood – between her legs. Then an even stronger contraction arrives.

"Muuuuummmm!"

"Be brave, Ira!"

A tiny creature is seeking the light, desperate to get out of her belly. The baby slips and slides in the liberating blood, which is getting redder, thicker and stickier, making the pain that's on the point of breaking her more bearable.

"Keep going, she's coming out now!"

Iryna roars, holding her knees and pushing with all her strength to free that little sign of love – a hot little creature who doesn't care how much she has to expand the exit so that she can get out.

"Granny, for God's sake! You said you'd help me!"

Then the midwife grabs her from behind, lifts her up straight and shakes her, squeezing her belly downwards.

"Come on out, lazybones!" she jokes, lying Iryna back down on the bed.

She's exhausted, but just when she feels she can't go on, the baby shows its head. Six hands take her from the sticky mixture. Iryna is as white as a sheet but not just because she's lost a lot of blood. It's the emotion of having this little piece of moving, crying pink flesh in her arms.

The baby's so sweet she feels like licking her.

"You're beautiful, my little daughter! And you've got all your little fingers and toes."

"Sweet! As sweet as honey!" say the baby's grandmother and great-grandmother with their mouths and their eyes.

"What shall we call her?"

"We'll call her Lyuba – 'daughter of love'. Lyuba, you're beautiful!" says Iryna again.

"Yes. Lyuba. Lyuba!" say grandmother and great-grandmother. "Daughter of love!"

***

INSIDE THE *MARSHRUTKA* someone wipes the back window so they can see what poor unfortunate Iryna is doing. She picks up the framed rucksack and puts it on her shoulder, although she has to put Lyuba down to get it on properly. The taxi starts off and disappears into the mist. Iryna walks on breathlessly between the cars. 300 metres separate the Polish and Ukrainian Customs posts. To go through without a vehicle you have to follow a fenced path in a straight line, outside. This morning, the snow wets them and it's cold. For a few seconds she thought about hiding in the trailer of one of the lorries that's stopping and starting in front of her. They hoot at her. Lyuba is crying louder and louder. She presses her to her chest amid the noisy reprimands. The baby suddenly goes quiet. Iryna looks at her. Her mouth is open and her face is blue.

"Help! Help!" she shouts, running along the passage and pushing past hundreds of Ukrainians who are moving forwards slowly and patiently on foot.

Heels click towards her in the opposite direction. The feet of those waiting their turn move aside out of respect for a tight uniform skirt and an over-made-up face:

"What's on earth is wrong with you?" asks the police officer with the red lips.

Iryna, scared, shows her the half-choked child. The woman grabs the baby and shakes her. She pats her on the back, undoes her coat and runs her hand over her stomach... Suddenly, Lyuba, who'd lost the ability to cry, recovers it so strongly that they feel they have to carry on running. Passing the baby from one to the other, amid sobs and moans, they get to the place of the formalities ahead of anyone.

"*Dyakuyu! Dyakuyu!*" repeats Iryna in Ukrainian.

The woman sits holding the little girl so Iryna can look in her bag and take out her papers. The pages of her passport are covered with stamps. It shows that three years ago she returned to Ukraine from Polish territory. A male officer takes it and passes it to his superior officer. He repeats the operation with the family record book and the baby's identity card. They check them.

"Where are you going?"

"To show the little girl to my parents-in-law who live in" – and she names the town where Katyushka worked, where her relatives are – "Rzeszow."

Chapter 11

SPRING 2008

Iryna spends the whole night looking at her daughter, who has been put in a basket beside her. No-one would now have any idea that it had been so difficult for her to come out – she already looks a fortnight old. She is fine-featured and round, white face, a turned-up nose and a mouth all ready to suck...

A golden blonde curl decorates her forehead and the sweet smell of her mother's milk keeps her calm. From time to time, she wrinkles her nose and smiles.

"Put her here!" says Iryna, pointing to her breast.

The baby sucks down the first colostrum and the watching experts think it will be easy for her to feed the child. Mother's skin rubbing on baby's skin. Iryna feels a tremendous desire to experience this happiness and doesn't close her eyes until the early hours.

But the following morning her breasts begin to swell and become hard. The right one seems to be made of stone instead of flesh and the pain is accompanied by fever. The midwife is attending another difficult birth far away. Iryna picks up her bag, takes out a paracetamol and an antibiotic from the ones she had brought, and takes them both. She has enough medication for seven days. Both she and her mother know that's the minimum time needed for the treatment. The new great-grandmother advises her to massage her breasts. She puts hot cloths on them and gets Iryna to screw them as if she were squeezing out a cloth. It hurts a great deal but, fortunately, the nipple spits out the plug of milk blocking it, so it won't have to be opened up as they had feared it might. But as soon as this problem is solved another arrives: the milk comes out so easily that Iryna's soaked all day. And the little girl develops a rash because of the antibiotic.

"Why can't we give her cow's milk? I'm fed up with this!"

"Be patient! There's no better milk than your own! Those spots will go away," the experts advise her.

And they do.

It's a joy to see Iryna with the baby always stuck to her body. Her face is nothing like the rebellious teenager of a few months before. She has been transformed, and from her joyful expression no-one would say that the movements she's making with her foot are due to the sharp pain she feels in her cracked and bleeding nipples. But Granny Rus also knows the best remedy for this – honey.

"How would we manage without you!" Iryna repeats a thousand times to thank her.

Exactly a week after Lyuba's birth, they decide to go back to Dobrokiv to introduce her to the family. "Come with us!" say Iryna and Olena, and Granny she feels so flattered and useful that she agrees. All she asks is:

"What about the house? And the cow? And the poultry?"

"Let's sell them. Get uncle to find a buyer. Can't we, Mum?"

So they do. Olena's brother the priest lends them some money so they can hire a taxi. The five cousins come to say goodbye.

And they leave early one Sunday morning. The journey is like something out of a fairy tale: the icicles have melted now and, just like Iryna, the branches of the fruit trees are beginning to blossom. A celestial light accompanies them, the road is smooth and everything in the world is good and beautiful as it looks down on its new angel.

When they reach home, the two Vasyls are busy in the kitchen in front of the cooker, preparing a kind of omelette with lots of oil.

"Hello! Didn't you see us?" asks Great-Granny Rus, followed by her daughter and her granddaughter, carrying Lyuba.

Father and son look at them as if they were a set of Russian dolls – the *matryoskas* that you keep on opening until you uncover the mystery of the smallest one. They all understand and comprehend the game without the need for words. It consists of passing Lyuba from Vasyl to Vasyl and bringing her into the house.

Grandad Vasyl receives the baby as if she were a miracle.

"Where can such a beautiful thing have come from?" he exclaims, his eyes fixed on that little face which reminds him so much of Iryna when she was small.

"She's mine, Dad. She's my little daughter!"

"How beautiful you are!" he repeats.

And, as he raves over her, he thanks God for having been able to meet his granddaughter. And he prays quietly, asking for time to enjoy her. When he opens his mouth, the word God comes out with his breath. He never used to used to go to church, but he has recently bought a bible. Not believing in God was too easy. He wants to have faith, and time to read the book.

Time. Time... Time stretches and shrinks. There are irreplaceable seconds and whole years that go by without us noticing. Time stands still until sweet little Lyuba wakes up, angry. Then, quite naturally, Iryna sits on the sofa, lifts up her bra and brings the little girl close to what she wants. The baby, like a puppy sniffing out the milk, locks on immediately and everyone stays to look at them. A special silence surrounds them and they can hear the sucking and the breathing of the living miracle. Young Vasyl doesn't stay too long. He's a little uncomfortable with such an intimate scene and, nervous but happy, he goes to fetch Nadiya. Iryna's friend is very surprised. As well as coming to congratulate her with plenty of hugs, the next morning she goes to tell Iryna's form teacher at school. The teacher has known Iryna since she was a little girl and has always loved her for her good behaviour and hard work. Excited about the news, she tells Iryna's classmates and organises an outing so they can go and see the new arrival. Many of them bring Iryna a present or clothes in good condition handed down by little brothers and sisters. They arrive at the house happy. Granny Rus opens the door, asking them to be quiet with a finger to her lips. With the other hand, she beckons them to come in without making a sound. The baby is tired but she doesn't want to sleep. Iryna smiles a greeting but this does not distract her from her tasks as a mother: she puts Lyuba in the basket and spontaneously adapts the Cossack Lullaby:

"Sleep, sleep Lyuba. Close your little eyes. Count stars, like the angels."

The baby sleeps and the teacher admires Iryna's obvious understanding of her daughter, as well as the similarity between them.

"Sorry to have kept you waiting, she's like clockwork."

"It's a good sign that she sticks to a timetable for eating and sleeping. Oh, let me have a proper look at her! She's just like you."

"She's photocopy of Iryna when she was born," says Olena, bringing a photograph to confirm this. Great-grandmother nods her head.

The teacher picks up a folder, opens it and takes out a sheet of paper.

"I've painted a blonde doll with curly hair and I see I'm right." She is walking along a path full of flowers while the sun and moon look lovingly at one other in the sky.

Underneath she's written: "Very early in the day, sun and moon help me on my way."

"We'll frame it and, when she's a bit bigger, I'll show it to her and I'll tell her my teacher did it for her."

The teacher proudly gives Iryna the whole folder, saying:

"And this is your gift!"

"Mine?" she asks, taking out a lot of sheets with summaries and tables.

"Yes, this is everything we've been studying this year. All the teachers have given me the most important things. Study it and, if you don't understand something, call me and I'll find a way to explain it to you."

"But it's already the end of May!"

"So you've got a whole month to study and sit the June exams."

"That's crazy!"

"I'm in no doubt that you can take it all in. You've always been an excellent student. You know next year you'll graduate with a diploma, which you'll need to get any kind of job," insists the teacher, while Granny Rus listens, watching the teacher with a knowing look and waiting for the chance to clinch the argument.

"Come on, Iryna! Next year, I'll look after the little girl while you go to school. If you leave now, you'll find it difficult to get any opportunities later."

"Thank you. I'll do what I can!" she promises, thinking that September is a long way off and God knows whether she'll be able to carry on studying.

***

MAY 2008

The Pravdírivia centre usually gives notice of who has been accepted to study in Catalonia at the end of May. In fact, with everything that's been happening, they haven't gone to ask. But they receive a letter explaining that no-one has asked for them this summer.

Brother and sister argue about who's to blame:

"See! As you didn't write to them..." Vasyl blames Iryna.

"So why didn't you do it?" she defends herself.

"You know I'm really bad at those things. Anyway, I'm sure Mum didn't go along and pay the €50 they say is for registration."

"Well, it's for the best. I want to be with Lyuba now. I won't be like Natasha who, when she went off to be a helper in El Vallès, left her daughter with her mother when she was less than a month old!"

"Yes, but they paid her well. I was thinking about going to see that motorbike guy, Morales. Remember, he told me that this year we could talk about whether I could help him?"

"Do you want me to send Esperança an e-mail? Nadiya's got an internet connection. I suppose she'll still have the same address. And if they can't for any reason, maybe they could find somewhere else for you... You know she knows a lot of people."

"But what are you going to tell her?"

"I'll start off by apologising for not having written or phoned for so long. I'll tell her about Grandad dying, ask about everyone and, at the end, I'll tell her what you want. And I'll tell her I can't go because I've been lucky and I'm still working at the same restaurant as last year."

"Maybe we don't need to come across as so pathetic! I mean, one day you'll have to tell her you've had Lyuba. Do you know Serhiy? He's got a place with a host family but I've heard him say he doesn't want to go to Catalonia because it would ruin his plan to go to the Crimea for a month with a gang of friends and he's fed up with being on his best behaviour."

"Of course, as they're not short of a few dollars they can spend their holidays wherever they like. The family hosting Serhiy was from Collença. I met them at a party the first year, when I was with Pietat. They were really nice people. Maybe you could talk to them... I don't know, ask Serhiy to call them. He owes you one! You fixed his dad's laptop – that one he took to school without permission when everyone was looking at it... and I've let him copy my homework at break time more than once."

"You're right, I'll ask him to call them and tell them that this year he's got to travel with his parents and that if they take me instead they'll also be doing everyone a favour."

"So you don't want me to write to Esperança?"

"No, we won't tell her anything. If I can go to Catalonia, I'll pay her a visit."

During the first month, Iryna's friends have given her endless advice and admiration:

"Mum told me you shouldn't eat anything that causes wind or the baby'll get stomach ache."

"Milk and dairy products have got calcium: drink a lot of it!"

"In this country you need good defences from the beginning. Here's some fruit. It's from Kiev!"

"Let's see your breasts? Wow! Look at those! It looks like you've had a boob job!"

They chat, laugh and work. She asks for exercises, they help her do them and she takes the opportunity to ask them whether they think she can manage the exams. It's a good thing that when the time comes she does so well that she gets an "excellent" in everything. Everyone's pleased at home and they spend their days amazed at her intelligence and the way Lyuba is growing.

**

SITTING BEHIND THEIR DESKS, the Customs officers stamp the papers as forcefully as they can. The little girl's too. When she sees the uniform and hears the thumping of the stamps, Lyuba is paralysed and silent. She must think she has to be on her best behaviour with people who don't mess about like this. When in the end her mother picks up the papers and looks hard at her, she smiles.

"Out you go! Next!" they order her.

Once in the street, Iryna can't believe that she can breathe; that the city she sees all around is Polish and that her suffering is over. She looks in the rucksack to see if she's still got the purse and yes, she finds it next to the mobile phone.

"Hey, Lyuba! It's all over sweetheart! Do you want the phone?"

When she opens the cover she sees she has five messages and she's receiving more. And they're from Willy! He can't have changed his phone number. How has he managed to find hers? She's surprised because this phone doesn't have the number she used to use. Often her brother has to change the number to make use of cards or to release mobiles bought from people who are getting rid of them for some reason. Could her family have given him her number? No, that's impossible. They know the police are after her. Suddenly, she realises what must have happened: it was Lyuba. Well, it was probably the bang the phone got when they threw her rucksack out of the bus. It must have called the last number she'd looked at all by itself – and that number was Willy's. Like a missed call.

While he's been recovering, the boy has been studying hard on his language course. Now he's in Dublin at a conference on minority languages in Europe, defending the position of Gaelic, which, with two million speakers, has recently become an official language of the European Union. The device quivers, indicating that she's got a message. He's seen a number on the screen with a foreign prefix and decided to answer as soon as they had a break. Then, by some miracle of technology, he hears Iryna's unmistakable voice, pleading for help, with the cries of a girl he can't possibly imagine is his daughter. He tries and tries to call her, but all he hears is the tune of *Für Elise*. No-one answers.

A small Skoda drives towards Iryna and follows her.

"Good morning, madam! I know a place where you can stay comfortably for very little money. In Przemyśl, in a country house where they host recent arrivals. They'll find work for you; they'll take care of your daughter... If necessary, they'll hide you in exchange for a small donation. Please trust me. Things don't work without corruption. We need extra money!"

"No, I'd rather carry on walking. I want to go a long way from here!"

"Do you want to go to Krakow? 200 dollars."

"OK. Here you are! 150."

"175."

"OK, then."

Chapter 12

While in Dobrokiv things are falling into place, as Vasyl has managed to get Serhiy's place to go to Catalonia, in Rouralba things are getting more difficult. Granny Griselda is getting weaker, perhaps because of the pneumonia she suffered in the winter, perhaps because of her move from the coast...

Who knows? Or perhaps everything in general has soaked into her bones. Whatever the reason, where she used to be able to go for long walks around the village, now it's a tremendous effort for her to hobble a few doors down, resting and supporting herself on the fence. The nights are hard. She has massages, painkillers and anti-inflammatories, but nothing seems to work. Instead of the street, she's had to make do with the patio at home; instead of going up and down the corridor she just about gets from the bedroom to the bathroom. And now she uses a walking frame instead of her stick. As she can hardly stand up, they move her into a wheelchair. When her leg isn't hurting, it's her arm; when it's not her head it's her stomach. And when she hasn't got diarrhoeaa, she's constipated. Everything's very difficult! She complains all day because she's in pain, poor thing, and they often have to take her to casualty. They haven't got time to get involved with the Ukrainians. They can't do anything for them.

But Esperança can't help seeing their faces all over the house and in the village. If only...

So, when today a host family from Collença called to ask her what Vasyl was like she was so happy she could hardly speak to them. She hasn't got a bad word to say about him.

They told her they were the Busquets family, who used to host Serhiy, and that they'd seen her at some of the Association meetings. They said they'd soon have Vasyl to stay and they wanted references...

"For Vasyl? When's he coming?"

"In three days' time."

"Ah, he's a really good boy! Maybe he's a bit of a daredevil, but you'll love him straightaway. He's lovely, just like his sister. They're tall, strong and handsome, with an instinctive grace. No-one would say they have health problems. It's only the tests that show their defences are week..."

"Does he eat everything?"

"Well, it's not that he's fussy, but to start with he only wanted to eat macaroni, pizza, steak and chips and lots of fruit. Now he also likes paella and fish in breadcrumbs. He eats salad too. He doesn't turn his nose up at new things."

As everything she's telling them is so positive, they can't resist asking her:

"If he's such a good boy, why didn't you ask for him this year?"

"Well we're going through a bit of a difficult time. My mother's ill and the woman who looks after her has also come to live with us. We haven't got enough bedrooms and at mealtimes it's like a restaurant here. I'm at my wits' end! You know, they're elderly. They make work, and there are the costs involved..."

The conversation makes it clear that hosting is not an obligation. You just have to do what you can and only if you want to. But it's also clear that Esperança feels such affection for the children's she's sorry she can't have them this year.

"If you have any queries don't hesitate to ask me. And, above all, tell him to come and see me as soon as he can. I'm very keen to find out what he's been doing this year. Their letters don't seem to get here and they've obviously got no money for the mobile phone or the internet. I haven't heard from them at all and I'd so much love to see him...

He'll be almost a man by now!"

"Don't worry. As he's 17 now we'll let him catch the train whenever he wants to visit you."

"He loves cycling. If you show him the lane through the woods between our villages, he'll get here quite safely in no time."

"Good idea! That'll put the bike we've got hanging up in the garage to some use. No-one's touched it for years."

"Ooh! Vasyl will soon have it ready for you to use. In the place we stay in the summer we found a broken-down old bike in the woods and he didn't rest until he'd got it working with Miquel's tools and a few small parts. Then he painted it. He's brilliant with that sort of thing. I'm so pleased he can come back! Has he mentioned his sister to you?"

"Yes, but he hasn't said much about her. He's just told me he's got a sister who works in a restaurant."

"You don't know how happy your call has made me. I've got my daughters studying in England and my husband works 25 hours a day, probably so he doesn't have to see the state of things at home. And here it's all weeping and wailing. Even the dog and the cat are jealous of all the attention my mum's getting. When they hear her ring the bell to call me, the dog stands in front of the wheelchair and the cat behind. The phone's ringing non-stop: all her friends and neighbours from El Masnou where Mum used to live ask after her and come and visit her, and that's not to mention her brothers and sisters. When the Ukrainians were here my house was like a youth hostel. Now it's turned into an asylum. I really miss them."

"And haven't you got anyone to help you?" they ask, immediately regretting it in case the question makes the conversation go on too much longer.

"We've got that women I mentioned, but she makes more work than she saves, to be honest. She's really vain and fussy and she certainly doesn't want to dust or do anything strenuous. Every time my mother gets ill, she has to go to casualty too because she gets very worried. And she's allergic to animal hairs. Now she's going on holiday in her own country and to be honest I hope she doesn't come back."

"Well, we'll find out for ourselves," say the Busquets at the other end of the phone, convinced that Vasyl has left her with good memories and that she's not trying to pull the wool over their eyes.

Barely a fortnight after this call, Vasyl turns up in Esperança's house. It's late and she's watering the plants on the patio. Her mother, sitting in her wheelchair, is telling her which plants to water.

"Sage! That's useful for lots of things. It smells so good that when I'm fighting for breath it helps me breathe better.

"Yes, Mum, I'm watering it."

"The rosemary and thyme don't need so much. Keep the sprinkler away from them! And what about passion flower? Why haven't you got one of those?"

"I don't know what it is."

"It's a climber, with some mysterious flowers: they have a first layer with nine white petals, a second with a crown of half blue stamens and Christ's nails on top. It's very beautiful and beneficial. You should plant one."

"What's it useful for?"

"It cures sadness."

While Esperança is feeling sad that her mother has had to leave her own garden behind, a pair of rough hands cover her eyes.

"Who am I?"

"Oh, Vasyl! My boy! What are you doing here?"

"I've come to see you! Miquel opened the door for me..." he says, moved by how pleased she is to see him. He hugs Esperança and lifts her up in his arms so easily that she might as well be a feather. "Didn't they tell you I was staying in Collença?"

"Yes, but I thought you'd phone or they'd phone before you came. Do the Busquets know you've come to see me?"

"Yes, don't worry..."

"Really? Stay for dinner, then, and tell us everything."

Granny looks at him suspiciously, as if she's worried that if he stays she won't get looked after properly.

"Esperança, have you really got enough food for everyone?"

"Yes, Mum, don't fret. Don't you remember him? It's Vasyl."

"Sorry, I can't stay for dinner. Morales is waiting for me to clean some motorbikes. I work with him. You know who he is, don't you?"

"Of course I do! He's the guy who has that bike shop on the main road. As I hardly go out, I never find out anything."

"Not even for a bike ride?"

"Yes, but I can only go round the block, because my mother's scared I'll fall off and hurt myself."

"Don't you remember when you broke both your legs and had to stay in bed for six months?" her mother reproaches her, although Esperança must have been about 18 when that happened.

"Yes, she worries so much that she goes and stands by the fence and rushes from the front of the house to the back, pushed by the Armenian woman, to make sure I get back OK. Making signals and signs of the cross to make sure my Guardian Angel is looking after me."

"A good thing too. Without that, I'm sure you'd have fallen on your face again."

"How did you get the job?"

"Morales is the mechanic Manel Busquets, the man who's hosting me this year, goes to. As he only takes his motorbike out when the weather's good, it needed a service, so we went together. When he saw me, Morales said: 'Hey, it's Vasyl. Good to see you, mate! You're back round here again are you? Doesn't this guy trust you? You'd know how to fix the bike for him.'

And he told him that the previous year I used to go along and watch what he was doing, that I had a pretty good idea about it, and that he'd like me to give him a hand. So, he pays me 200 euros a week, he's happy and I'm even happier. I get to Rouralba at 9 in the morning and I get back to Collença at 10 at night. He's got loads of work! But today I asked him for permission to come out for a while..."

"What about Iryna? Has she got another family too?" asks Esperança.

"No, but that's fine because she's very busy helping Mum. Dad's working at the pig farm in Kiev again. He only comes home on Sundays. Grandad Volodymyr died..."

"Grandad Volo died? Why didn't you tell me?"

For a few moments he's speechless. He's about to tell her that his sister has a baby, but a kind of shame makes him keep the promise he made to her and to his parents not to say anything. In case Esperança knows Willy's address and tells him the news.

"It all happened very quickly. You couldn't have done anything. Iryna's working at that restaurant we went to last year again. The one that looked like a forest. They've given her a bit of a pay rise and they say that if she goes during the summer they also want her the rest of the year after school. Granny Rus is at home too. She wasn't feeling all that well and she was very lonely." He thinks it's best to put it like this to make the situations comparable, instead of telling her the truth.

Meanwhile, Esperança also holds back from asking him questions like: "What about Willy, is he OK?" or "Has he got his sight back yet?" She'll leave them for later, perhaps. Yes, maybe when he comes back to see her… There's no need to mention Willy now. It would be like rubbing salt into a wound.

During July, neither Esperança nor Miquel have had time to phone the Busquets and ask them how things are going with Vasyl. Vasyl's host family have tried to come to see them several times but they didn't manage to find them in. The shutters always seem to be down. Granny has been in hospital more than once. The doctors want to find out where the terrible pain she feels in her bones is coming from. Esperança stays with her all the time. Miquel visits her but spends as long as he can with his friends in the billiards club.

Every week when he gets his wages, Vasyl puts the money with the previous week's money. He spends nothing. He counts his money and imagines what he will be able to do with all those euros in Ukraine. At the end of the summer, if he behaves himself, he'll have about 2,000. It's a shame the Busquets family want to go on holiday for at least two weeks and take him God knows where. He doesn't want a holiday because if he doesn't work he doesn't earn. Maybe he could stay with Esperança. Perhaps Morales will take him in. He's the kind of guy Vasyl admires. He never has time off, not even when it's time for the big annual festival in the village. If Vasyl ever has a business one day, he'll set it up like Morales and he won't have any holidays until he's got his life properly sorted out. He counts the notes, which he keeps in a bag. One day he hides it under the mattress and another day inside a book... He doesn't trust anyone. He doesn't want the cleaning woman or anyone who hangs around his room to take the money. There are days when he gets confused. He comes to look for the bag and can't remember where he's put it. Then his heart beats like a hammer and he rummages through all his things until it looks as if thieves really have been in. When he finds the money, he lies down on the bed with the bag resting on his chest, as if it were his girlfriend. Once satisfied, he tidies up the room and throws away the cans, paper and junk that builds up so that when anyone comes in it will seem so tidy they'll go back where they've come from and not touch any of his things. He lies down on the bed ready to listen to songs he's got stored on his phone. Ukrainians like music so much they can't live without it. If he could, Vasyl would even sing in his sleep.

How he'd love to become one of the young musicians who seem to appear every day in his country!

With good behaviour and a little bit of charm, he's manipulated the situation and managed to work all summer. How did he manage that? They've left him in sole charge of the house in Collença. In the meantime, he waters the plants for them and feeds the parrot, which they didn't want to take with them. During August, the host family have been phoning Morales to find out how the boy is getting on. And he always gives them the same answer:

"Really hardworking but a little excitable. Vasyl's a bit of a dreamer. It's a good thing I don't let him try the motorbikes on his own or he would have probably come to grief. He's a bit of a speed freak."

"They think they're immortal at that age... Or don't you remember what we were like?" Busquets always asks him.

"Yes. I still like going fast, but there are no roads left where you can do it."

"Oh, you could have been a champion," says Manel Busquets.

"When I won that race, I discovered the world of racing is so unfair I wanted no part of it... nor would I advise anyone I love to get involved."

Between what he's earned and the money he's picked up in tips and presents, Vasyl is going back to Ukraine with almost 3,000 euros. And some good advice.

"It's not all about intuition, Vasyl. The world of mechanics is moving forward and it's not enough to unscrew things and bash them with a hammer. You need to study."

"Yes, I was thinking of doing one of those courses to learn to fix taps and install lights. In my town they always need people who know how to do that kind of thing, as everything is old... And my father's taught me a bit."

"Plumber and electrician? Well, it's a start... But I think what you're really interested in is engines. You need to be more ambitious. Don't waste your money, boy, and study!"

In June, Vasyl left school in the town and, if he wants to carry on studying, he'll have to go to Kiev. That will mean extra expenses, because he'll need to live in a little student flat. The Government gives grants, but the family will have to pay the rest. As Olena is now counting on the money he'll bring her, he's asked her to advance him the registration fee. Without that, they'll miss the deadline. The rest will be for hard times, when they don't get paid for months even if they carry on working.

Once again, the boy fills his suitcase with a few bits and pieces which are plentiful Catalonia but in short supply back home. When he reaches Dobrokiv and empties out his luggage, among other unexpected things there is a bag filled with little dresses, pyjamas and baby suits. What he won't confess is that he found them next to a container collecting clothes for the Third World. They were in a bag, properly folded and clean, and he put them together with some other things he bought for Lyuba in the market.

***

AUTUMN 2008

The little girl is now six months old and she's starting to crawl around the room. Now you see her, now you don't.

"Where are you, Lyuba?" her great-grandmother can be heard desperately shouting.

They put her on a blanket surrounded by chairs, but she manages to slip between the legs. She might be picking up breadcrumbs from the kitchen floor or under the bed cleaning up the dust with her tummy. Today, Granny Rus has left her for a moment to look after the poultry and Lyuba's followed her as far as the three steps in the doorway leading to the courtyard. "She's too quick for me," thinks Granny Rus. But as Iryna has to carry on studying, she looks after the baby all day while her granddaughter is at school. By the time Iryna arrives at five in the afternoon, the poor woman is exhausted. What she enjoys most is the happiness, and the cuddles she receives. She loves to hear Lyuba squeal, throwing her forwards into Iryna's arms. And there's also the grateful kisses on her cheek from her granddaughter.

"Here's your little flower! She had her baby food in mid-morning. She's eaten a good dish of mashed potato with a bit of butter at lunchtime. And now she's just finished some grated apple. Go on, pull your mother's hair!" she says before her granddaughter can ask her how the day has gone and whether Lyuba has eaten all her meals.

For the moment, since she's been with her the little girl hasn't had so much as a scratch or a bump and she's growing like a beanstalk. "Thank God," she repeats gratefully.

Olena and her husband are working. When he got back to Rouralba, Vasyl enjoyed seeing how the little girl had progressed. He ran around for a week with her on his shoulders as if she were a little monkey. But now he's in Kiev studying to be a mechanic. For her great-grandmother, Lyuba's cuteness, and being useful, help her forget the grief of being a widow and the loss of her Volo... That's why she never complains and, when they get home, everything's clean and the table's set. At weekends, the elderly childminder can rest a little because Iryna takes Lyuba out for a walk in a buggy lent by her cousin. Both dressed up, they often go as far as Nadiya's house.

"Where are you going with that thing? It looks like an old-fashioned carriage with horses."

"Rather this than carrying her in my arms all the time!"

"Lyuba, princess, if I win the lottery I promise I'll buy you a new one," promises Iryna's friend.

With these words, Iryna imagines Willy demanding the latest model for his daughter. She misses him, and when she goes home, instead of going directly, she first calls in at the restaurant where she worked that summer. She sits in the chair Willy was in the day he called her over. Because it's the first time she's been there with her baby, the owner thinks she's gone to introduce her and he calls her by her nickname.

"Hey, Molly! What a lovely little girl! What's her name?"

"She's called Lyuba."

"What can I get you?"

"Nothing, I've just come to see you."

"Come on, it's on the house so make the most of it!"

"I'll have a glass of milk for the little girl and a coffee for me, then."

"Is that all, Molly?"

Iryna doesn't respond to the nickname because it makes no sense any more. Willy's absence means she can see nothing there except scenes from the past. The little girl has drunk all her milk, but the coffee is still untouched on the table.

"Come on, it'll get cold!" the owner warns her. "Put some sugar in it! I made it strong, how you like it. Drink it and I'll hold the little girl for you."

And he takes her to the kitchen to show the staff.

Iryna gets up with the cup in her hand, as if to follow them, goes to the whirlpool of water imitating a waterfall in the middle of the forest, and slowly tips the coffee on to the ground next to it. If nothing can be like it was before, why should the grass stay green?

She picks up her daughter, sits her in the pram and heads for home. She curses her sadness and promises herself she won't feed it by going back to that place again. Chance took Willy away from her one day, but she'll fight for destiny to bring them back together again.

***

ONCE INSIDE THE CAR, she sits in the back with the little girl on her lap and takes out her phone: she sees the calls again. If she had money, she'd speak to him. The car starts up and the driver can't help looking in the mirror. Iryna has an idea:

"Listen, if you lend me your phone for a bit, I'll give you 200 euros."

The conference is still going on in Dublin and they're now talking about languages which are in danger of extinction even though they're not strictly speaking minority languages. They are saying that Ukrainian is losing ground to Russian and English because of the economy, and it's a shame, because it's perhaps the most melodic language in the world. A poem recited in Ukrainian is capable of moving you even if you don't know what it means. Willy picks up his mobile phone to call her. He feels an overwhelming need to hear her voice... He looks at the phone for a while, as if his Molly was on the screen. "Speak to me," he says softly. "It can only be you, my Molly. Say something," Miraculously, the device reacts and starts ringing. It vibrates in his hand, as if it were the heart he loves. It's another foreign number... He goes outside.

"Hi. It's Iryna!"

His words echo through the room:

"Molly! Where are you? Who was crying? Why have you changed your number?"

"Where do you think I am? What about you?"

It's enough for her to hear the voice she loves. She doesn't know where to start and she doesn't tell him her story.

"I'm in Dublin, but I've got to go back to Barcelona next week. They've got to give me another laser operation, you know. At the moment, I have to wear very thick glasses. But if it all goes well, I should be able to manage with contact lenses. What's going on?"

"I'm having problems with my phone and I've been lent this one. I'll be able to buy a new one soon."

That's what she says and that's what she'll do, because she's scared they'll track her calls. That last number of Vasyl's had been used by lots of people and the Ukrainian police could be investigating it.

At the back of the hall, now the lecture is over, a member of the audience who has been passed the microphone wants to speak in favour of language diversity in Europe. He thinks the Irish should be satisfied with their situation... and asks why Catalan, which has 9 million speakers and is the eighth most spoken language on the continent – more than Danish, Swedish and Finnish – isn't an official European Union language like they are.

The Skoda continues on its way, winding between green meadows with animals grazing. It's still snowing and the mountain peaks are already very white. Iryna touches her daughter and feels her hands are cold. If they'd had to walk all this way, they'd have ended up being found dead by the side of the road.

"Doesn't this car have heating?"

"Yes, I'll put it on. Ask me whatever you like, princess. I've got a great radio."

"Could you put a Catalan music station on, please?"

"Catalan?"

"Yes, from Barcelona. I'll find it for you if you let me."

When she's got it tuned in, she relaxes. She recognises the song that's playing...

The wheel of time turns
with the strength of the wind from the lonely souls
It turns as we follow
seeking the same answer from a star.

For a moment she wants to run from the memory, but her heart resists. She can still hear his voice and feel his lips on her neck, his fingers unbuttoning her blouse, his hands brushing her trembling skin and his eyes closing until... crossing the Carpathians she is shaken awake. They're near a ski station. The little girl is sleeping at her breast. She looks down at her and now she's sure: chance took her love from her side, but destiny will help her find him again.

My sincere thanks to the children from all the families I have hosted over various summers and visited with Toni in their village of Ivankiv, especially the Skryts. I have returned there several times to find another grandparent or father or uncle or neighbour has died of cancer. Meanwhile, their country is even more impoverished than it was and has been immersed in a struggle to defend its identity and independence...

To my friends, fellow writers and members of anti-nu-clear associations who have given me their opinions and support: Carme Arrufat, Octavi Piulats, Ramon Gasch, Esteve Pujol, Ester Homedes, Jaume Prat, Joan Pera, Pilar Basquens, Emilio Rodríguez, Júlia Garrido, Josep Jallé, Dolors Xirau, Miquel Comas, Matilde Martínez, Àn-gel Angelats, Àngel Guiu, Carme Llàcer, and everyone from the writers' workshop at the Old People's Centre in Cardedeu, Núria Montané, Carme Sala, Andreu Ca-latayud, Carme Cinca, Inés Fernández, Montserrat Tor-rents, Montserrat Jané, Salvador Coll, Josep Ontañón, Trini Viñas... and, particularly, Jordi Albertí and his team, that transformed my draft into this edition which was selected as a finalist for the Gregal Award in 2013.

Dear Svetlana Alexandrovna,

Please accept my book *Where are you going, Iryna?* as a small tribute to your literary career. All the children we have hosted at home from the Chernobyl area have come with cuttings of your interviews. All of them want to shout out loud that they love a region that is killing them. All of them bring photographs of children suffering from leukaemia and relatives born with deformities. All of them are demanding the addition of a new Right of the Child: to be born and grow up in an uncontaminated country. It is an ambitious challenge and the campaign to overcome it relies only on the generosity and bravery of a few hearts...but that won't stop us continuing to pursue it.

Rosa Maria

I would also like to thank:

MY PARENTS: Hermínia and Francesc for teaching me to enjoy life and love my brothers and sisters: Aida, Joaquim, Esteve.

MY DAUGHTERS AND GRAND-DAUGHTERS: Núria, Sergio, Fani, Josep and our grand-daughter Martina, who liked to listen to me and read the stories I made up...

ALL THE NEPHEWS, NIECES, OTHER RELATIVES AND COLLEAGUES who campaign, follow me at presentations and help me publicise the novel because they are aware of the issue: Magda, Antonio, Elvira, Cesc, Blanca, Quimi, Josep, Arnau, Imma, Pedro, Maria, Cristina, Sole, Pili, Joan Francesc, Manel, Laia, Encarna, Lluís, Mercè and others.

MY WRITER FRIENDS who have given me their opinion and support: Carme Arrufat, Octavi Piulats, Josep Mª Esd pinàs, Isabel Martí, Joan Bruna, Ester Homedes, Jaume Prat, Joan Pera, Pilar Basquens, Emilio Rodríguez, Júlia Garrido, Josep Jallé, Dolors Xirau, Miquel Comas, Matilde Martínez, Àngel Angelats, Àngel Guiu, Carme Llàcer,

Antònia Molero and others.

THE POETS who defend the rights of the child: Jordi Cots and Jordi Roig.

MY LOYAL Facebook followers: Rosamaria Trèmols, Maria Vicente and others.

MY PRESENTERS, who have followed me for no reward through various towns and villages of Catalonia: the engineer and writer Ramon Gasch with his 10 reasons for saying NO to nuclear power. To the paediatrician Carlos Casabona, who defined the novel as a tribute to motherhood. To Glòria Barbel and all my friends at the GEM, who made room for me among the group of committed writers.

ALL THE LIBRARIES, LOCAL COUNCILS AND MEDIA who, with varying degrees of fear, have lent venues for talking about such a delicate issue: the mayors, councillors responsible for culture, book clubs and interviewers: Cristina Gómez of the SAV, Jordi Xena of Sta Maria de Palautordera... Eva Bassó and Emília Illamola of Ràdio Mataró i Argentona, Oriol Casals of Ràdio Estel, Adrià Bas of the Solidaris *on Catalunya Ràdio and Assumpta Relats of the Consortium for Language Normalisation...*

REPRESENTATIVES OF ANTI-NUCLEAR AND HOSTING ASSOCATIONS: Segundo Aguado, Manel Pedraza... and particularly Rosa Martín, chair of the Éspertu Association and Josep Lluís Escriu, chair of the Collbató per la Solidaritat association, who have tirelessly devoted themselves to guiding the host parents and working to raise money to make the visas and air tickets as cheap as possible.

The TEC-CA and the MOLSA – Writing Workshop Cardedeu and Sant Antoni Vilamajor: Josep Ontañón, Salvador Coll, Josefa Forns, Núria Montané, Mercè Tre-

molosa, Carme Sala, Andreu Calatayud, Carme Cinca, Carmen Acera, Inés Fernández, Montserrat Torrents, Montserrat Jané, Mont-serrat Mestres, Joana Nevado, Merce Dutren, Trini Viñas, Anna Guardiola, Ferran, Francesc, Jaume, Otília, Pako, Paquita, Víctor, Xavier, Salustiano and others working together to present well-known writers.

THE JURY FOR THE GREGAL AWARD 2013: the writer and Catalan MP Marta Alòs; the historian Queralt Solé; the literary critic Jordi Llorach; the teacher Susanna Clarió; and the writer and publisher Jordi Albertí, who made the book a finalist.

ESPECIALLY for Susanna Anglés Querol, of the Cazarabet bookshop and EL SUEÑO IGUALITARIO, who did a lovely interview with me and introduced me to Juan Ignacio Jiménez, head of the Muñoz Moya publishing company, who is committed to cases of suffering children and has been responsible for publishing the Spanish and English versions of the novel.

AND, FINALLY, the translators who have worked on Where are you going, Iryna?: Simon Berrill for the English text and Iryna Lebedyeva for her advice on transliterating Ukrainian into English.

Rosa Maria Pascual, summer 2020